LYN COTE

Never Alone

New Man in Town

Steeple
Hill®

Published by Steeple Hill Books™

STEEPLE HILL BOOKS

Steeple
Hill®

ISBN-13: 978-0-373-65276-1
ISBN-10:   0-373-65276-3

NEVER ALONE AND NEW MAN IN TOWN

NEVER ALONE
Copyright © 1998 by Lyn Cote

NEW MAN IN TOWN
Copyright © 1999 by Lyn Cote

www.SteepleHill.com

Printed in U.S.A.

CONTENTS

Books by Lyn Cote

Love Inspired

*Sisters of the Heart

Love Inspired Suspense

LYN COTE

Lyn now lives in Wisconsin with her husband, her real-life hero, with whom she raised a son and daughter. Lyn has spent her adult life as a schoolteacher, a full-time mom and now a writer. Lyn's favorite food is watermelon. Realizing that this delicacy is available only one season out of the year, Lyn's friends keep up a constant flow of watermelon gifts—candles, wood carvings, pillows, cloth bags, candy and on and on. Lyn also enjoys crocheting and knitting, watching *Wheel of Fortune* and doing lunch with friends. By the way, Lyn's last name is pronounced "Coty."

Lyn enjoys hearing from readers, who can contact her c/o Steeple Hill, 233 Broadway, Ste. 1001, New York, NY 10279.

NEVER ALONE

It is not good for man to live alone.
—*Genesis* 2:18

For my friend Angie

Prologue

The icy January wind roared around the gray mausoleum, assaulting the group of mourners huddled several yards away, at the double graveside. Jane felt as though the piercing wind whistled right through her. Her heart had been shattered—just as Dena's and John's bodies had been shattered by a car out of control on an icy street. Only baby Angie, strapped in her car seat, had survived.

The forest green canvas canopy flapped wildly overhead. Glacial winds moaned and buffeted Jane. She shivered while tears streamed down her face.

Cash stood ramrod straight beside her at his only sister's grave. Tears blurred her sidelong view of his face, but his chin, his whole face, looked like it had been carved from stone. A sob shuddered through her. How could Cash hold in his grief? He'd adored Dena.

Standing at the head of the graves, the pastor, wrapped in a heavy black overcoat, gave her a sympathetic look. He went on, "We know John and Dena's faith was deep. We know they have claimed the promise—'To be absent in the body is to be present with the Lord.'"

But I want Dena here with me! She was my best friend. We've spent our whole lives together! She felt a touch on her sleeve as Cash handed her his handkerchief. She wept harder. She had her family. Now Cash had only Angie.

She silently endured the graveside parting to its end. The pastor said the final prayer, then walked to Cash and offered his hand. "Please accept my sincerest sympathy. Losing both of them so young is a terrible loss."

Cash shook hands. "Thank you for handling the service."

"I only wish I could do more. Grieving is a long process. If you need someone to talk to—"

"I'll handle it myself."

Knowing how much Cash hated any show of sympathy, she nodded to the minister, then slipped her hands into the crook of Cash's elbow and pulled him back a step. "Cash, Grandmother wants you to come home with us."

He looked down at her. "That's kind of her. But I have things to take care of."

Folding up the side of her collar against the wind, she knew she should insist, but her own sorrow robbed her of the strength to argue. If only they had the closeness she'd always longed for, they could comfort each other. She imagined turning to Cash, opening the front of his coat and burying her face into his starched white shirt. In wordless sympathy, he would bend and kiss her hair. She shook her head. This won't help.

"When are you going to pick up Angie?" she asked. The worrying wind swirled around her legs and flared her skirt.

"Tomorrow. After I see Tom about the will."

"Would you like me to come over and help you—"

"No."

She shivered again. She'd known he would say no, but

she'd had to offer. For Dena's sake, for her own sake. "You'll call if you need help?"

He nodded, but she knew he would never call. When had he ever called her? All those years she had dreamed he would notice what she felt for him....

He turned away from her to accept another mourner's condolences. She wanted to stay beside him, but she forced herself to walk away. Icy snow suddenly flew from the gray felt sky. Each particle stung her wet, wind-chafed cheeks like a pinprick. She joined her grief-stricken parents and grandmother, who were still standing beside the graveside.

As she followed her family into their large sedan, Tom Dawson, another old friend, stepped close. He'd pulled up the collar of his steel gray overcoat. With his face framed by these two flaps, he bent forward to keep his words more private. "Jane, I need you to stop by my law office tomorrow afternoon."

"Why? Tom, I—"

"It has to do with Dena's estate."

The bleak sky, vicious cold and her ragged sorrow twisted together and wrapped around her like a wet, raw rope—dragging her down. She couldn't bear much more. "Cash can take care of all that."

"Wills are never as simple as one anticipates, Jane. You *have* to be there."

Chapter One

"This is going to be a shock for both of you."

His lawyer's unexpected words jerked Cash's thoughts from his deadening grief. More than the words themselves, it was the way Tom said them—painstakingly—like a man connecting a detonator wire to a bomb.

What could be more of a shock than losing my only sister? Numb with sorrow, Cash glanced toward Jane, who sat beside him. Petite, dressed in a somber brown, she was looking down at her hands folded in her lap. Her chin-length red hair fell forward, concealing her face from him. "Red" and his baby sister had been best friends from the cradle. Images of Dena and Jane together as children had haunted him all morning. An impulse to smooth Red's hair behind her ear where it usually lay, touched him, but he couldn't. She wasn't a child anymore.

"I hope you'll take this calmly," Tom went on.

Tensing, Cash sat up straighter. Jane, looking delicate and vulnerable, gripped the arms of her wide leather chair. Silence welled up in the room. The mantel clock ticked a stolid counterpoint to the uncertainty, which expanded moment by moment.

"What is it?" Cash rasped at last.

Tom breathed in deeply. "Dena and her husband didn't leave guardianship of Angie to you, Cash."

Cash lunged to his feet. "I'm Dena's only remaining blood relative. Her daughter has to come to me. She's all I have left!"

Tom hesitated, then looked up into Cash's eyes. "That would be true *if* Dena and her husband hadn't specified guardianship of their daughter."

A spear of betrayal plunged through Cash's heart. *Dena, I helped raise you. How could you give Angie to someone else?* Cash took the will from Tom's hands, but couldn't focus on the print.

"Who?" Cash demanded, "Who was appointed?"

Tom averted his gaze. "Dena and her husband gave Jane full custody."

Jane gasped.

Cash struggled to mask his anguish. After losing Dena in a senseless auto accident, assuming the care of his little Angie had been his only consolation. He wanted to roar with pain and outrage.

Tom read the awful words aloud, "If we should die before our daughter, Angela Jane Johnson, is of age, we name Jane Lucinda Everett as her guardian and give her full physical custody."

"Dena left Angie to *me?*" Jane echoed in disbelief.

"You didn't know about this?" Cash picked up the document and waved it toward her.

She shook her head, tears slipping down her pale cheeks. "If I'd known, I would have insisted on taking her home with me after the accident. Not leave her in foster care for three days."

Cash watched her cry, despair surging through him. With great effort, he tightened his resolve. Control brought decision. He faced Jane. "You'll have to sign Angie over to me."

"What?" Jane stared at him. "We're talking about a *baby,* not a two-party check."

Cash tossed the document on the mahogany desk. "Jane, you don't want Angie. You're a career woman. You've never shown any interest in marriage and children."

She turned his words back on him. "What about you? You're a career man. You've never shown any interest in marriage and children, either. Does that mean you don't want Angie?"

Cash clenched his jaw. "Angie belongs to me."

"Angie doesn't *belong* to anyone."

"I'm ten years older than Dena and you. I'm better able to provide for Angie. I've already hired a nanny."

Jane leaned forward. "Obviously Dena wanted a mother for her baby, not a nanny."

He ignored her. "She's a highly experienced nanny. I have nothing against you as a person, but you've never taken care of an infant."

"That's not true. I stayed with Dena the first two weeks after she had Angie—"

"And that's the extent of your experience. Except for your visit home at Christmas, you've been in northern Wisconsin—"

"That's where I live—"

"I've visited Angie, at least once a week since her birth," he said. "Angie won't even know you."

"She's only five months old."

"Her age is unimportant. I don't know what my sister was thinking—"

"She was thinking she wanted *me* to have Angie, not you." Jane halted and colored as if with shame. "I'm sorry."

Cash looked past her. Her apology meant nothing. Anger and betrayal still churned inside him. To maintain control, he focused on the rows of legal books on well-spaced shelves lining the wall. The deep shades of burgundy, black, coffee brown, and forest green dragged his mind back to Dena's funeral. They were the colors of funeral-home carpet, casket lining, coffin finish and graveside greenery. His grief threatened to crush him. *No escape.*

He turned back to Tom. "This is legal? Jane really has been given full custody of my niece?"

"Yes. I'm sure you and Jane can come to some visitation arrangement—"

"I live in Chicago, remember? Jane lives three hundred miles northwest. I'll be a seven-hour drive away."

Tom looked at him steadily. "I am aware of the distance, and so were Dena and John."

Cash jutted his chin forward. "If Jane won't cede custody to me, I'll fight for it."

"A court challenge?" Tom questioned.

Jane stood up, knocking her purse to the floor. "You can't mean that."

Cash crossed his arms over his chest. "You leave me no other choice."

"Hold it there, both of you," Tom ordered. "Sit down."

Cash said, "Angie belongs with me. I—"

"Sit down." Tom's tone left no room for argument.

Jane took her seat. Cash didn't want to stop until he'd convinced them Angie must be with him. But after struggling with himself briefly, his respect for Tom made him follow suit.

"We've all been friends since we were kids. Otherwise, I'd let you two fight this out in court. But Dena was my friend, too. I feel obligated to protect her little girl."

"*Protect* her child?" Cash asked. "You're not making sense."

"Yes, I am. Just listen. Later today the Department of Children and Family Services will turn Angie over to Jane—"

"No!"

Tom continued, "Cash, stop interrupting. This is too crucial to ignore. They'll turn Angie over to Jane as the specified guardian—unless you contest it. If you contest Jane's guardianship, they'll likely keep Angie."

"Oh, no," Jane breathed.

"Keep Angie? I don't understand what you're saying." Cash's disgruntled gaze pierced Tom.

Tom looked at Cash grimly. "There have been a lot of spectacular custody battles lately. Social workers have gotten gun-shy. If this looks like it could become a case of contested custody, the state of Illinois might decide it's in Angie's best interest to keep her in foster care—until the custody battle is settled by the court. Do you know how long these battles can last?"

"Years," Jane murmured.

"*That's right. Years,*" Tom said, giving Cash a pointed look.

"It would be awful," Jane said.

"Worse than awful," Tom continued. "Angie might stay with the same family, or she could be shifted to a dozen different foster homes—"

Cash sat stonelike.

"She could be hurt emotionally." Jane pressed her fingertips to her temples.

"She could be scarred for life," Tom reiterated. "Is that what you want for Dena's child, Cash?"

"No," Jane almost moaned it.

Tom stared at Cash. "And I warn you, the DCFS already realized that a blood relative has been passed over. I got a call from them, asking me if I thought this would run smoothly."

"I can't believe this is happening," Cash said.

Jane echoed his words softly.

"The child welfare system comes with endless possibilities for delay and frustration," Tom said. "I can't let you take any chances with that little baby girl."

Cash stood up and began pacing. Dena, how could you keep Angie from me? I love her as much as I loved you. Did you doubt that? He asked Tom sharply, "Did Dena tell you why she named Jane guardian?"

"No, when I asked her and her husband, they refused to tell me."

"They must have had a reason," Jane said, her voice showing her own uncertainty. She searched Tom's face, then Cash's.

"There is none." Cash's mouth tightened into a stubborn line.

Jane sat up straighter. "No one chooses a guardian for their baby daughter without a reason."

Cash ignored her. "What if Jane just turns Angie over to me?"

Tom steepled his fingers. "I don't know—"

"I wouldn't," Jane said quietly.

"What?" Still standing, Cash leaned forward over his chair, rested both palms on its arm and pinned her with his intense gaze.

"An Everett never contests a will. My family would be very upset—"

"You wouldn't be contesting a will," Cash interrupted. "You'd be doing the right thing."

Jane cleared her throat. "Dena adored you, Cash. Giving me Angie goes against what *both* of us expected. That means Dena must have had a powerful motive. I don't know what it is yet, but I won't violate Dena's will."

"Dena couldn't have wanted this to happen," Cash countered. "Her husband and I never quite hit it off. *He* must have—"

"No." Tom cut him off. "Dena made it clear that wasn't the motivation. The only thing that has occurred to me is the fact Jane would have family to back her up, whereas you, Cash, are alone."

Cash slumped into his chair. *Alone.* The word hung over his head. He muttered, "I'm capable of providing good care for my only niece."

"That's not the question here," Tom said. "Frankly I've allowed you two to stray from the main point. It comes down to this. Do you want Angie in Jane's care while you two settle this? Or do you want your niece in the tender care of the state of Illinois?"

Cash looked up. "Those are my only choices?" His voice broke on the final word.

"For now…yes," Tom replied.

"What if I let Jane take Angie now, but later I decide to contest it in court? What happens in that case?"

"Then Angie might have a good chance to be left in Jane's care while the case is settled," Tom replied.

Cash gave his words a twist of sarcasm. "You mean it's a case of the lesser of two evils?"

"You can put it that way if you wish." Tom leaned forward, folded his hands on his desk and stared at Cash.

Cash glanced at Jane, but the sympathy in her steady

eyes made him look back to Tom. "So what do you want me to do?"

Tom took a deep breath. "I want you to go with Jane to pick up Angie."

"*I* have to go? Why?" Cash didn't think he could bear watching someone else claim Angie. The walls of the room pressed closer than they had at the beginning of the meeting.

"I don't want any delay. If you show up with Jane to pick up Angie and appear to favor it, there shouldn't be a hitch."

"I'm not an actor, Tom." Cash found it difficult to speak. A knot clogged his throat.

"You're a businessman. A successful businessman knows how to start negotiations. Always start in a position of strength."

"Giving *in* is a position of strength?" Cash asked.

"In this case, yes. If you let guardianship go as the will dictates, you and Jane will stay in the driver's seat. If you quarrel at this point, the state of Illinois will take the steering wheel. In that case, none of you will ever be the same."

A tense silence mushroomed until it dominated the room.

Like a man slowly freezing to death, Cash felt himself slipping into numbness. His gaze fastened on Jane's bright hair. While everything else in the room had dulled, it still gleamed like a lamp through a thickening haze.

"Cash?" Tom prompted.

"Angie can go with Jane." Even to himself his voice sounded rough with emotion.

Jane closed her eyes.

Cash felt one last surge of energy. "For now."

* * *

Jane stepped into Cash's black Lincoln and felt the whoosh of cold air as Cash closed the door beside her. He entered the driver's side, started the car and pulled out of the parking lot of Tom's office.

This morning, because Jane hadn't trusted her emotions enough to drive herself to Tom's Chicago office, she had ridden in on the commuter train. So now Cash and she sat in his sleek car on their way to a Department of Child and Family Services office to take custody of Dena's five-month-old daughter.

I will be taking Angie home with me. The words held no reality for her. Suddenly images of diapers, bottles, formula crowded her mind. *Thank You, Lord, for Mother and Grandmother. What would I do without them?* Being named Angie's guardian had never crossed her mind. *Dena, why did you do this?*

Flashes of the cold, dreary city passed by the car window, red brick apartment buildings and offices, city snow in shades of dirty white to black, people bundled in down jackets with hoods in winter colors: navy, gray, brown.

She glanced at Cash's profile. He drove smoothly as though this were any drive, but his calm outward appearance didn't deceive her. Riding alone with him was like sitting in a lion's cage.

Deep below his unruffled surface, even the overwhelming shock and sorrow he suffered hadn't blunted his dominating presence. No matter how she fought it, no matter what the circumstances, Cash Langley could always touch her heart, make her long to press her hand against his hard, chiseled jaw.

She was suffering, too. Six days ago Dena had called her full of news about Angie sitting up by herself for the first time. *If I'd only known it was our last call,* Jane thought. Pain gripped her heart, nearly forcing a gasp from her.

Her own anguish made her yearn to comfort the solemn man so near but so distant. He was a handsome man with fine, straight features, steel blue eyes and black hair combed back from his face like folded wings. His profile always put her in mind of a medieval king. Today he was a brooding king, dark emotion making the determined line of his jaw even more grim than usual.

She ached to pull him close, to murmur words of solace. But it was impossible, had always been, would always be. Cash didn't want comfort, now or ever.

"Here it is," Cash ground out the three words. He parked on the street. Shivering in the mid-January wind, she preceded him to the door. He opened it and held it for her. They walked side by side to the desk.

Jane cleared her dry throat. "I'm Jane Everett. I'm here to pick up Angie Johnson." She and Cash were asked to take seats. They sat silent, miserable, separated by an invisible wall of Cash's making. Jane tried to pray, but the overheated room and the grieving man beside her sapped her energy. She could only pray within. *Dear God, Dear God.*

Several minutes later a woman in a dark suit asked them into her office. She said, "Good day," without the slightest touch of warmth.

A chill shivered through Jane. All of Tom's warnings played through her head once more. She forced herself not to give Cash a sideways glance and tried to behave as though picking up a baby were an everyday occurrence in her life.

"May I see a picture ID, Ms. Everett?"

Jane fumbled in her purse, dropping tissues and her lipstick, but she managed to bring out her wallet.

While Jane retrieved the items she had dropped, the woman read her driver's license thoroughly.

"You live in Wisconsin, Ms. Everett?"

"Yes," Jane croaked, then moistened her dry lips.

"Mmm," the social worker said. "That might not be advisable—"

"Why?" Cash snapped.

The woman widened her eyes and stared at him. "And you are, sir?"

"Cash Langley, the child's uncle."

"I see." She pursed her lips. "I would feel better if the child weren't going to be moved such a great distance so quickly."

Jane cleared her throat. "I'll be staying with my parents in Lake Forest for a while."

"Lake Forest?"

"Yes," Jane said, holding tightly to her budding panic.

The woman eyed Cash momentarily, then changed subjects. "I have some papers for you to sign."

The woman explained each document as she placed it before Jane on the desk. The small printing on the documents wavered in front of Jane's tired eyes. She could barely focus on where to sign her name. Document followed document. Jane lost count.

Finally the woman gathered up all the papers, tapped them neatly into one stack and slid them into a pocket folder. "I'll see if the child has arrived yet."

Jane and Cash waited silently in the small, crowded office. Though she kept her attention forward, she noted the tenseness of his face. She couldn't let him suspect she yearned to kiss away the crease etched across his forehead and the small tight lines around his mouth. He would never return her feelings.

"Here she is, Ms. Everett." The social worker held the squirming baby like a sack of potatoes across one arm.

Jane jumped up to take Angie from her. The baby whined and rubbed her eyes fretfully. "Are you tired, sweetheart?" Jane murmured. Love for this child and sorrow nearly choked her with their force, but she held on to her self-control grimly. Then she recognized the white snowsuit with a bunny tail and ears Angie wore.

Tears rushed up in Jane's eyes and a sob caught in her throat. Helplessly she felt her composure give way within. "Cash," she gasped.

Before she finished speaking, he was next to her, lifting the baby from her trembling arms and leading her back to a chair.

"Is there some problem?" the social worker asked.

"I gave Dena…this snowsuit…as a shower gift for Angie," Jane gasped between sobs.

"Ms. Everett, are you sure you are able to take custody of the child today? Perhaps you aren't up to—"

"Jane will be fine," Cash insisted. Angie fussed louder.

Jane fought down her sorrow. She subdued the sobs, but was unable to staunch her tears. "My…my mother and grandmother are waiting at home."

"I'm driving," Cash added. "Are there any more formalities?"

"No, but do you have a legal car seat in your vehicle? It is against state—"

"A brand-new one from Marshall Field's is waiting for Angie in my back seat." Cash didn't bother to look at the woman.

Angie began howling in earnest, and the social worker quickly ushered them out of her office.

Jane, tears still washing down her face, stinging her skin in the biting cold, stood outside the car while Cash placed a screaming Angie into the new car seat. Feeling over-whelmed once more by the reality of Dena's death, Jane slipped by Cash into the passenger seat. Then Cash, behind the wheel, glanced at the city traffic and pulled out at his first opportunity.

Angie screeched with frustration from the back seat. Jane wept. With each passing vehicle, gray slush splattered the windshield. Though the car's heater blew full blast into her face, Jane still trembled, feeling like a frozen maple leaf fluttering on a bare tree.

At last they left the congested Chicago streets behind. After a few minutes of smoother highway driving, the baby shuddered with several more loud sobs, then dropped off to sleep slumped to the side in her car seat.

Jane laid her head back against the headrest and took a calming breath. "I'm sorry I fell apart like that. Somehow seeing the snowsuit—"

"I understand," he cut her off.

Jane bit her lower lip. Guilt clutched her. "I'm sorry about this, Cash. I didn't know—"

"Are you willing to give Angie to me now?"

Jane looked down, avoiding eye contact. "It's not that easy."

"Why not? I'm Dena's brother."

"And I was Dena's best friend. I need time to think—"

"Think about what? Angie's mine!"

"Cash, there must be more to this."

Cash made a sound filled with irritation.

"In my whole life, I never told one secret of Dena's or broke one promise to her. She has given me Angie. I will not betray her trust."

Jane watched the self-sufficient mask Cash had lowered for just a few moments snap back into place. Jane felt him withdraw from her. The distance between them grew until she felt cramped by its presence.

The man beside her drove expertly down the interstate toward Lake Forest. He finally pulled into her parents' driveway. Jane looked at the house next door where he and Dena had grown up. Though Jane couldn't have stopped herself from looking toward the house if she tried, Cash never glanced in its direction.

He lifted Angie out of the car seat, handed her to Jane, then unhooked the car seat and set it on the recently shoveled sidewalk to the house. "You might need it." He turned back to the car.

"Cash." Jane grabbed for his arm. Angie woke up and began to squall. "Come in with me. My parents—"

"I need to go." He walked around the rear of the car.

"Where? Come in. I don't want you to leave this way."

"Then give me Angie." Over the top of the car between them, he stared at her.

"Come in. You'll be better among friends."

"No." He shook his head and got into the car.

"Cash, please come in. I don't want you to be alone."

Jane barely heard his response over Angie's wails.

He said, "I'll be better off alone."

"When will I see you again?" she called after him.

Holding a squirming, whining Angie, Jane watched as he drove away. Then her parents, their coats thrown over their shoulders, helped her into the house, where Jane struggled and won the battle against more tears. Cash might not need her, but Angie did.

Cash stared at the deep blue door of Jane's parents' house. It had taken him over a week to gather the strength to face once more Dena's giving Angie to someone other than himself. If Angie weren't on the other side of this door, he wouldn't be here. But Angie was. Pressing all his anger into a tight ball of resistance, he knocked firmly.

"I was just thinking of you." Jane's grandmother, Lucy, peered around the door.

"Am I that popular here?" Cash asked gruffly and stepped inside.

"Well, why haven't you listened to your answering machine?" Petite, frail with age, Lucy stood on tiptoe to kiss his cheek.

Momentarily he stood still, then leaned down and returned the kiss. "How are you, Lucy?"

"Heartbroken. The same as you." Lucy pulled him into the foyer. "You arrived just in time to say goodbye. Phil is in the garage loading my suitcases into the car."

Cash wanted to thank her for flying home from wintering in Florida for his sister's funeral, but he couldn't bring the words to his lips. How could he put into words his gratitude for her years of putting Band-Aids on his scrapes, her gentle way of brushing his childhood bangs out of his eyes before she bent to kiss his forehead? Past images of the loving matriarch of this house threatened to drown him in sorrow over all he'd lost. First his mother, then his father, now Dena...and Angie. Instead he cleared his throat. "Headed for O'Hare?"

She nodded and led him into the living room, urging him down beside her on the beige sofa. She took his hand in hers and searched his eyes. "I won't waste words on sympathy. You and I know each other too well. If you need me for anything, you have my Florida phone number."

"There's only one person I need—Angie."

"I know, but Dena must have had her reasons."

"Of course you think I should leave Angie with Jane."

"Don't say 'of course' like that. You know if I thought Jane were wrong to keep Angie, I wouldn't mince words."

Her militant tone brought a slight smile to his lips. "I know," he murmured. "I just don't agree."

"How could you?" she asked. "If I were you, I'd do anything to be near my niece."

"But?" He lifted one eyebrow.

"But it's an Everett family law. We never contest wills. It's disrespectful to the departed and only makes lawyers rich and a family poor."

"Don't you think this is—"

Cash was interrupted by the appearance of Lucy's daughter-in-law, Marge. He stood and let her embrace him.

Marge murmured, "Lucy, we must leave now." Cash helped Lucy into her vintage tweed coat, and the two women hurried toward the kitchen.

Lucy turned back briefly. "Jane is upstairs with Angie." She motioned him to go up, then called over her shoulder, "God bless you, Cash. He would, you know, if you'd only let Him."

In the stillness of Lucy's wake, Cash stood at the bottom of the familiar staircase. He knew this house as well as he knew the one next door. Looking up, he pictured Jane and Dena, as young girls in matching white terry cloth robes, standing at the top of the stairs. *Good night, Cash,* they called down to him.

Gathering his strength against these memories, which might weaken his resolve to reclaim Angie, he walked up the steps and followed the sound of a baby's sudden wail. He stopped in the doorway of Jane's childhood room. She was lifting Angie, dressed in fuzzy pink pj's, out of a crib.

Jane turned and gave him a startled, then a questioning look.

Cash's chest tightened. Jane had never looked so femi-

nine. With a child in her arms, she no longer struck him
as his kid sister's pal. But Angie belonged within his arms.
He stretched himself to his full height. "I've come for
Angie."

Chapter Two

❧

"**O**h?" Jane's tone was calm, but her heart pounded so loudly in her ears its drumming drowned out the baby's crying. Cash's unflinching power washed through her senses, calling her as always to draw near him. But panic, so like what she'd experienced that awful day in the social worker's office, snaked through her and threatened to immobilize her.

"Is she hungry?" Cash asked.

"She just finished ten ounces of formula after a bowl of rice cereal." Outwardly calm, but reeling inside, Jane fell back on the routine she had devised to deal with Angie's frantic crying every time she needed sleep. Feeling like a windup toy, she carried Angie to the white-flounced changing table.

"What's making her cry?"

"I'm checking her diaper." Jane slid a finger between two pj buttons. "She's dry." Fighting for control with each measured motion, she reached back and pulled a pink baby blanket off the side of the crib. "Where have you been for eight days, Cash?"

"To the ends of the earth and back again. You don't look too happy to see me tonight." He still stood propped against the doorjamb.

"My grandmother was worried." *I was worried.*

"I want Angie."

Her stomach twisted, but without showing the effect of his words on her, she finished tightly bundling up the crying baby and sat in the rocker.

"What's wrong with her?" he asked sharply, peering through the shadows at Angie.

Jane felt like shouting the question back at him, What's wrong with her? But she forced herself to reply mildly, "My grandmother says that's what Angie's asking us. This is the only way we've found to get her to sleep, day or night." With that, Jane began rocking vigorously, firmly patting the baby's rump through the wrapping of the blanket. Under Cash's scrutiny, Angie's wails and Jane's fear mounted in intensity.

"Cash, this is hard enough without you glaring at me," she said with bravado.

"I'm not leaving. I want my niece."

As Jane met the challenge of caring for Angie in spite of the stress, she gained more control. She held her index finger up to her lips, motioning him to speak more softly. "Why did Dena give your niece to me, then?"

"I can't explain it." He stopped, then lowered his voice. "People make decisions. They change their minds." He held up his palms in a gesture of not knowing. "Maybe my sister made this decision after we disagreed about something."

Angie hiccuped between her sobs. Jane rocked and patted, not missing a beat, though inwardly the urge to flee the small room and Cash's moody regard still tempted her.

"That doesn't seem to be working."

"It takes time." Jane warned him away with a shake of her head. *Am I afraid of Cash?*

"Why aren't you back in Wisconsin? How long can you leave your dress shop closed?"

"My shop isn't closed. I have two trusted employees taking care of things." Still pushing down tremors of alarm, she made herself continue to concentrate on her physical movements.

"How are you going to take the stress of this when you have to get up the next morning and go to work?"

"The same way you would," she spoke in time to her rocking.

"I would have help—"

"I'll have help. I've got friends and my Uncle Henry, Aunt Claire and their daughter, Tish. I'll arrange day care just like you would."

"Family help won't last. People say they'll help—"

"Everetts help Everetts," Jane said tightly. She noticed she had forgotten one of the elements needed to calm Angie. She nodded toward the wall next to him. "See that mobile of lambs? Wind its knob, will you?"

After he complied, the tinny, music-box melody of "Rock-a-bye Baby" competed with Angie's shrieks.

"Don't you see that single parenthood is going to be too much for you?" he insisted.

"I only see that this baby needs me." Her rocking now kept time with the tune.

"I don't understand why you can't see reason. Angie is not your responsibility—"

"Dena made her my responsibility." She held on to Angie like a lifeline. Cash's shadowed eyes spoke volumes about the sorrow he'd suffered over the past week.

Over the past decade, he had isolated himself from everyone but Dena and Angie. Now there was only Angie, and Angie belonged to her. Jane bowed her head. If only he would let her show him some kindness, show him the love which abounded in her life.

Cash raked his fingers through his already-tousled hair. He pushed away from the doorjamb and strode forward, his arms out to take the baby. "This isn't working—"

Angie gave one loud gasp. With a shudder, the baby's last sob broke and her tension released.

Gently Jane reduced the tempo of her rocking, then slipped a pink pacifier into Angie's quivering lips. When the music box ran down, Jane hummed, still uneasy under Cash's gaze. At last, she stood up and laid the sleeping baby on her side in the crib.

Cash moved closer. Together they looked down at the now-peaceful child. Despite the conflict between them and her new-sprung fear, Jane still felt drawn to everything about him, the scents of his soap and his leather jacket, the quickness of his breathing and the force of the man, which nothing diminished. When Jane couldn't bear his nearness and the anxiety anymore, she tugged at his sleeve. They stepped out into the dimly lit upstairs hall.

Jane, concealing her roiling emotions, looked up into Cash's face. "So?"

The stubborn anger in his eyes troubled Jane. She shivered in the warm hallway.

"Angie is mine. Why won't you be reasonable?"

Jane folded her arms. "Dena had a reason for giving me Angie. I don't know what it was, but until I can understand her motivations, I see no room to alter her wishes."

He flung himself away from her and hustled down the stairs.

Hugging herself, she leaned over the rail of the landing. "What are you going to do?"

"I'm going to do what Lucy said she'd do!"

"What's that?"

"Whatever it takes to be near Angie." He slammed the front door behind him.

Jane held her breath, listening for Angie to stir, but the baby slept on.

Feeling suddenly drained, Jane sat down on the highest step and propped her elbows on her knees. Dena must have had a reason. *Lord, help me understand. Am I doing Your will by following Dena's wishes? All I know for sure is Angie needs me and for the first time Cash frightens me. Would he really take Angie from me? I can't believe that.* But recalling Cash's parting words sent a stark shiver through her.

"Hi, Jane!" Rona Vitelli blew into Jane's Dress Shop on a gust of a glacial, late-February wind. "I heard you were back!"

Jane grinned. It was Monday morning. After driving Jane home on Friday, her parents had spent the past weekend helping Jane settle Angie into her house. They had just left a half hour ago to drive home.

Of course, Rona, the town's "ears" would appear bright and early on Jane's first day back at her shop. Rona liked her news served up fresh. "Hi, Rona, you're just in time to help me."

"Is this little Angie?" Rona bent over the new playpen Jane had just set up near the shop's front window.

Jane nodded, her arms full of skirts on hangers.

"She's a little doll! Such dark hair! She'd fit right in with the Vitelli clan!"

"Help me, Rona." Jane's arms sagged with the weight of her burden.

Rona swung around and reached out to lift the clothing

in Jane's arms. "No." Jane stepped back and nodded toward the playpen. "Pick up Angie and follow me."

"Oh." Rona scooped Angie up and trailed Jane to a six-foot-long clothes rack at the back. When Rona first picked Angie up, the baby fussed, but when she realized Rona was her means to keeping Jane within sight, Angie calmed down and gurgled sociably.

"You have to be in sight all the time?" Rona guessed.

Quickly hanging the skirts by size on the bar, Jane nodded.

Rona entertained Angie by gently twirling right, then left. "Well, she's at that age. About seven to eight months they start wanting Mom or *else!* Do you think it has to do with losing her parents?"

"Yes, some. She's sleeping a lot better now." Jane hung and smoothed the last skirt in place. "But she is very demanding."

"You're just going to keep her here at the shop with you?" Rona gave the baby an Eskimo kiss and Angie giggled in appreciation.

"Now, while it's quiet, yes. When the resort season starts in May, I'll have to hire a baby-sitter and slowly wean her—wean both of us—from having only me on call twenty-four hours a day."

"Well, she looks happy now."

Jane took Angie back into her arms.

"Tell me, Jane…"

Jane grinned at her friend's conspiratorial tone. "Tell you *what?*"

"Are your only two employees really both pregnant and due June fifteenth?"

"No." Jane carried Angie back to the playpen and set her in it. "One is due June fifteenth and the other is due

June twenty-fifth. How did you find out I was losing both of them for the whole summer? They just told me!''

"My cousin works at the hospital, you know—"

"So anything you don't hear at the restaurant, she hears there?"

"Exactly. Which brings me to my point—you're going to need to hire—"

The front door swung open sharply, jangling a small bell attached to it. "Hi, Jane!" Carmella, Rona's daughter, walked in. "What did she say, Mom? Am I hired?"

The word, *hire,* shocked Jane's stomach with the instant sensation of disaster-about-to-happen.

"Carmella, I was just about to introduce that topic—"

The door opened a second time and the little bell jingled politely this time. It was Jane's Aunt Claire, followed by Tish, her daughter.

Aunt Claire greeted everyone, looking at them over her half glasses. "Jane, I couldn't wait any longer. I had to run over on my break from the library. Is this our little Angie?"

Jane stood, sandwiched between the two mother-and-teenage-daughter pairs. On her right were Rona and Carmella, both petite, curvaceous, with dark hair and nutmeg eyes. On her left were her Aunt Claire and cousin Tish, both tall, willowy, with fair skin and strawberry blond hair. They bent over the side of the playpen. Tish's thick hair cascaded artfully down the back of her short leather jacket to the belt of her tight, designer jeans.

Angie looked up and giggled at Aunt Claire.

"So you think your aunty Claire is amusing, do you?" Aunt Claire chuckled and touched the end of the baby's nose. "What do you think of this?" From her tan wool coat pocket, Claire pulled out a soft rubber duck squeeze toy. Angie grabbed it and shrilled her joy at the honking sound it made in her hand.

Jane eyed the two teenagers. "Is school off today?"

"Teacher conferences—" Rona replied.

"Well, Mom?" Carmella asked.

Rona sighed. "Jane, I was wondering if you'd consider trying Carmella out as a salesclerk this June. She says she's tired of busing tables and doesn't want to waitress."

"Not with my dad and uncle standing over me every minute," Rona's daughter muttered.

Jane's stomach twisted itself into a curly *Q*. This was one of the disadvantages of small-town life. Only one answer could be given, "Sure. Can you come after school some afternoons in May to train?"

"Great!" Carmella gave a little hop. "Just name the day."

"What about me, Jane?" Tish had lifted Angie from the playpen. Angie giggled each time Tish kissed the sensitive skin behind the little girl's ear. "I was going to ask you for a job this summer, too."

Jane's stomach dropped to her toes. Carmella Vitelli and my cousin, Tish, too? Even their grandmother, Lucy, called Tish a spoiled brat.

"This isn't at all the way one inquires about employment," Claire chided Tish. "Besides, aren't they expecting you back at DQ this summer?"

"Mom, two summers at DQ is enough. I'll be sixteen June first. Besides if I work here, I get twenty percent off on clothes instead of ice cream!"

"Oh!" Aunt Claire opened her eyes wider. "I hadn't thought of that." She stopped to kiss the hand Angie offered her.

Jane mentally swallowed the bitter pill labeled "Keeping Peace in the Family." "Well, I guess I won't have to

advertise for replacements.'' She smiled bravely while
Carmella and Tish exchanged glares. Oh, great! she
thought.

Within minutes Rona and her daughter departed. Aunt
Claire started to go, too.

"Mom, I'll stay here," Tish said. "I'll watch Angie
while Jane catches up on her work."

Claire turned to Jane with a questioning look.

The offer surprised Jane. "Thank you, Tish. That would
be a real help."

Claire touched her daughter's arm with affection. "I'll
bring lunch later and we'll celebrate Angie's first day at
Jane's Dress Shop." Claire walked to the door. "Remember,
Jane, never hesitate to call us—day or night. Your
uncle Henry, Tish or me."

Tish followed Jane as she went to the counter to start
to sort through the receipts for the past three weeks.

"I'm really sorry you lost your friend."

Jane looked up. "Thank you, Tish."

"I always envied you having a friend like her."

Jane struggled with the pall which fell like a shadow
across her mood.

"And her brother is *so* handsome." Tish jiggled the
baby in her arms. "Wouldn't it be romantic if you two
ended up getting married, sort of like in an old movie?"

Jane bent her head to hide the pain she felt contort her
face. "Cash never acts very romantic, Tish."

The echoing clap of the brass knocker on her front door
reverberated through Jane's head. As she walked into the
small entry hall, she put a hand to her pounding forehead.

Seven-month-old Angie was teething, and the nighttime
hours were… She couldn't think of a word to describe the

stress and exhaustion of endless dark hours spent rocking and pacing with a fussy, inconsolable baby.

Jane straightened her spine and looked down at Angie, who sat on her right hip. Knowing that Cash would be quick to criticize, Jane had spent the last hour bathing the baby and dressing her in a pink corduroy overall and a ruffled, candy-striped blouse.

Angie smiled, and Jane's heart melted. ''You little doll.'' She kissed Angie's forehead.

The brass knocker banged twice more. Jane's smile faded. She turned the doorknob, icy cold against her palm.

Cash stepped over her threshold, and a frigid March gust rushed in with him. Making it obvious he wanted contact only with Angie, his head bent immediately to be at eye level with the baby. ''Hi, Angie.''

''Hurry up and get this door shut. She just got out of the bath.'' Jane immediately regretted her harsh tone, but after weeks apart, Cash's presence struck Jane sharper than the winter wind against her face. Over his shoulder, she glimpsed an older blue Jeep Wrangler at the curb. ''What happened to your Lincoln?'' she asked. As she spoke, the dread that had marred his last visit to her parents' home ignited inside her.

He eyed her crossly, but closed the door behind him. He held out his arms to take Angie.

Reaction to his reluctance to look at her, and her own growing uneasiness, caused Jane to turn her back to him and say sternly, ''Come in by the fire and get that coat off. Handing this baby to you now would be like sitting her in an icebox.''

Cash gritted his teeth, but he trailed behind Jane into the cozy living room. He hung his heavy, beige camel coat on the coatrack at the room's entrance. A lively fire burned behind a brass, fan-shaped screen. The fire's warmth drew him, and with his back to the fireplace, he clasped his hands behind and surveyed the room to give himself time to get his rancor under control.

He watched as Jane settled into a wing chair covered in a green, flowered print. Momentarily her shining, light auburn hair against the dark background snagged his attention. Her pale, peach-tinged skin glowed, making him think of the coming spring. Then his eyes slid to Angie, who sat in her lap.

Jane had positioned the baby with her back to him. He watched Angie squirm onto her knees and push herself around. When she faced him, she smiled with satisfaction. His gaze lifted to meet Jane's. Her melancholy eyes arrested his attention and softened his heart. He wanted to gather her into his arms to comfort her, but he shook off this unexpected reaction. After she heard his news, their fragile truce would be shattered. Had her grandmother told her yet? He couldn't tell.

He scanned the room again, trying to get a feel for Angie's home. *Angie's home,* the words filled him with discontent. Angie belonged with him. But in Angie's best interest he'd been forced to accept the dictates of Dena's will—even though everything within had urged him not to. Tom's counsel about arranging joint custody without the meddling of social workers and judges had been wise, and he would heed it—as long as Jane cooperated fully. He knew what he wanted and he would get it.

With approval he noted Jane had installed a wooden gate at the base of the steps to the upstairs. A paperback book by a pediatrician lay open, facedown on the coffee table. He watched Jane lift the book off the table and guiltily tuck it between the sofa cushions. So Jane didn't know everything about babies, after all.

Other than the book, the room appeared nearly bare of

ornaments, out of character for an Everett. Everetts decorated their homes with style and grace. Each piece chosen
both to beautify and to recall memories.

Jane gave him a tart glance. "You didn't answer my
question. Didn't you drive up in your Lincoln?"

Vanilla-scented candles flickered on top of the mantel.
Mellowing in the cozy room, he fought being enmeshed
in the gracious presence of Jane Everett. "Sold it. Didn't
drive. Flew up with my instructor." He stepped forward
and, without asking permission, lifted Angie off her lap.

The news startled Jane so much she let the baby go
without a word. "Instructor? You're learning how to fly?"

He carried Angie to the overstuffed white sofa and sat
down. "I should be licensed before summer."

Jane felt her breast tighten, making it hard to draw a
breath. "You'll be flying up, not driving?"

He nodded. "I'll cut my travel time in half. I'll leave
the Jeep at the airport here and fly up from Midway."

"Oh." Jane's spirits plummeted, leaving her mind
whirling.

"Hi, Angel," he murmured, close to Angie's ear. The
baby girl eyed him curiously, then fingered his sparkling
tie tack.

"Why did you wear a suit today?"

"I was trying to keep up with Jane of Jane's Dress
Shop." He gestured at her baggy, gray sweats.

Jane flushed. Dressing Angie had taken all her time and
what had been left of her energy, but she wouldn't admit
that to him.

"I had a business meeting in town earlier," he said with
a touch of apology in his voice.

She bit her lower lip. His contracting firm was located
in Chicago. What business would he have up here? Her
panic thrummed to life. *Something is happening.*

Angie pulled on Cash's tie tack again. Rising abruptly, Jane felt a pain like a mallet striking her right temple. She crossed to Cash and reached for his tie.

He gripped both her hands in one of his. "What are you doing?"

"I'm going to take off that tie tack. She might put it in her mouth."

"*I'll* do it." He stopped her hands, undid the tie tack and slipped it into an inner pocket.

From a steady, pounding mallet, the ache in Jane's head switched to the surge and ebb of a crazy tide. She straightened up slowly, feeling a little woozy. Then she recalled she hadn't eaten since breakfast—a 5:00 a.m. breakfast.

From his suit pocket, Cash produced a stuffed toy—a black-and-white cocker spaniel. Angie squealed and reached for it.

The squeal zigzagged through Jane. Her headache level soared. She mumbled, "I'll make tea." She walked through the arched door into the kitchen. Once there, she pressed her head against the cool door of her small, rounded, white refrigerator.

Her pulse beat a rapid rhythm in her ears. Weeks of erratic sleep, bizarre meals like baby prunes with zwieback teething biscuits and adjusting her work schedule at her shop had taken their toll.

Why today of all days? The tension in Cash's visit had tipped the scales of her physical misery. This visit wasn't going as she had planned. She'd wanted to be cool, in charge, unruffled. Instead she felt like a ball of yarn unraveling under the batting paws of a determined cat. Somehow, some way she had to toughen herself, make her nerves impervious to both the charm and intimidating essence of Cash Langley.

Flying lessons? What next?

Turning to the stove, she picked up her blue-and-white enamel kettle and carried it to the sink. As she filled it, Jane gazed wearily at her kitchen. Dirty dishes with hard, dried scraps and smears filled both sides of the sink. Breakfast and lunch remains still littered the floor around Angie's high chair. Jane set the kettle on the burner and switched it on. The flames sputtered under the kettle, burning away the moisture on the bottom.

The phone jangled. Jane lifted the receiver off the black wall phone. The welcome voice of her grandmother instantly made her relax and smile.

"I wanted you to hear this directly from me, Jane," Lucy said without preamble. "Is Cash there yet?"

"You're all right, aren't you?" Jane asked anxiously. Her grandmother would be seventy-six on her next birthday.

"I'm fine. I just wanted you to know that I've sold the land on Lake Elizabeth."

"What?"

"I'm using the money to establish endowments for needy art students at several Christian universities."

"But…I…" Jane stammered.

"I sold it to Cash."

"Cash! But Cash builds condos in Chicago—"

"Not anymore," Cash's cool voice interrupted. He lounged in the arched doorway with Angie in his arms. The baby busily patted his nose with her small, pudgy hand.

Without thinking, Jane hung up the phone and turned. "You! Why didn't you tell me?"

"Lucy wanted to tell you."

"How did you get her to agree to this!" Jane braced her hands on her hips.

"She called me. It was *her* idea."

"I don't believe that for a minute. This is your doing, Cash Langley, and you know it. Why would you suddenly decide to move here after ten years of contracting in Chicago?"

"I didn't tell you where to sell dresses. Why should you care where I build houses, Red?"

"This has nothing to do with business. You're trying to take Angie away from me." Her words were irrational, but she couldn't help herself.

"You're the one who took Angie away from me. You thought you could keep me a *convenient* seven-hour drive away."

He went on. "Soon I can fly to Chicago, take care of business and be back in the same day—easy. Next month I'll be starting Eagle Shores, a new subdivision just five miles from here. As long as Angie is here, I'm here to stay."

Jane forced down tears. Cash had annihilated all her plans for limiting his involvement with Angie, with her.

Sensing tension, Angie whimpered.

"Give her to me. She needs me." Jane held out her arms.

Cash released the baby reluctantly.

The kettle whistle pierced the angry silence. Angie shrieked. Jane quickly removed the kettle from the stove. The baby rubbed her eyes and whimpered again.

"Angie needs her bottle and nap." Jane couldn't keep the brittle snap out of her voice.

"All right, but I'll be back tomorrow. And get this into your red head. Next month I'll be moving into my family's lake cottage permanently and you'll be seeing me—daily." He turned from her. In less than a minute, she heard her front door slam. Angie flinched and pressed her baby-soft cheek against Jane's neck.

Only then did Jane realize she'd hung up on her grandmother. The distance between Eagle Lake and Chicago had been the only protection between Cash's presence and her own peace of mind. How could her grandmother have erased the three-hundred-mile barrier?

Worse yet, Cash had made it plain he understood she hadn't wanted him near. Guilt hit her hard. What's happening inside me? Keeping Cash away from Angie is an awful thing to want. But she couldn't deny the alarm she felt. Angie rocked herself forcefully in Jane's arms and began to howl. It was Angie's way of announcing, "I need a nap now!"

While Jane performed the tricky maneuver of filling a bottle with formula and putting it to warm on the stove, she pressed the baby to her shoulder. She sang "This Little Light of Mine" to soothe Angie, but her own mind struggled with the implications of Cash's move. Caught between the blades of attraction and panic, Jane was being sliced in two.

She didn't want to feel this way, frightened and defensive. Cash was Dena's brother, after all. She was not showing him even a hint of God's love, the love that should shine through her. Surely in His wisdom, God would show her how to deal with her grief over losing Dena and the conflict over Angie. And only God knew how she would handle Cash's move to town, where he could drop in at will and break her heart every day of the year.

Chapter Three

Jane looked up as her shop bell rang. Rona started talking as the door closed behind her. "Jane, I'm so glad you're here." As usual, Rona allowed Jane no chance to greet her. "I came in to see if you were coming to the Jaycee's dinner tonight at our restaurant—"

"Mom...I told you." Carmella had followed in her mother's wake. "I already made out the name cards. She's made her donation and reservation—"

Rona stopped her daughter's words with a look that sizzled like hot grease in a skillet.

Jane closed the cash register and eyed Rona with suspicion. "Okay. I'll bite, Rona. What's his name?"

Rona pouted. "I don't know how you always know—"

"We should elect you town matchmaker and pay you a salary. Who is he?" With an unhappy premonition, Jane lowered her voice, "I hope it isn't Roger Hallawell?"

"Mom," Carmella whined. "We're going to be late for our dentist appointments. That's why I took today off, remember?"

"This was my day to work, Mel," Tish said to Carmella

as she came from the back of the store. The two girls glared at each other.

"So what, Le-ti-ci-a?" Mel demanded, emphasizing each syllable of the other girl's full name.

Tish retorted, "Car-smell-a, this is my day to work."

"Tish, go down in the basement and price those new skirts please," Jane said smoothly. Tish turned with a toss of her blond mane and Mel made a face at her back. After playing referee between these two for almost a month, Jane wanted to scream with frustration.

"Carmella, wait outside please," Rona requested in a saccharine tone. Though obviously put out, the girl obeyed without comment.

"Jane, you know what her father said, if she tries to get away with any of her tricks here, fire her. If she acts up, she deserves to bus tables another year. Anyway, you *will* be sitting next to Roger Hallawell. He's the best catch around. I won't rest till I'm throwing rice at you!"

Standing outside, Carmella tapped on the window. Rona looked down at her watch. "I've got to go!"

As she watched Rona and Mel rush down the street, Jane shook her head over her friend's unwanted meddling. Romance with Roger Hallawell was the last thing on Jane's agenda.

Bing. Bing. The sound from the activity center attached to the inside of Angie's playpen caught Jane's attention. She walked over and beamed down at the baby. "Did you wake up, sweetheart?"

Jane bent and lifted Angie out. "You're such a good girl to take your nap while all the ladies come in and gab about dresses. Do you want to go to Grandmother's?"

Angie clapped her hands. Jane kissed Angie's chubby cheeks and carried her to the rear of the store where a changing table sat. Just as Jane finished changing Angie's diaper, Tish came up from the basement. "Are the skirts done?"

"Yes, the skirts are done," Tish answered in a voice laced with ill temper.

"Tish, you may get away with your moodiness at home, but I won't tolerate it here. Your parents told me that if you weren't ready to work in a shop, not to hesitate to tell them. If I fire you, you'll be back at DQ for the summer."

Her cousin's face blushed hot pink.

Both of them knew that while Tish's parents doted on her, they insisted she work each summer to learn responsibility. And Jane knew it must be difficult for her cousin to attend high school where her own father taught, but Tish had to learn not to take her problems out on others, especially in a place of business.

"I'm going to Grandmother's for about two hours." Jane went on breezily, "Then I'll be back. If you need any help, call me. Keep the cash drawer locked. Here's the key."

Tish slipped on the wrist key chain. Angie's pudgy little arms reached for Tish, who often baby-sat her. Tish smiled and kissed Angie's forehead. "Bye-bye, Angie." Tish waved like a baby and Angie giggled at her.

Outside, Jane hooked Angie into the car seat. In Jane's red Blazer, they drove out of town onto the highway amid tall, green-leafed maples, pines and birches. Up the progressively steep rises and around the final curve, she approached Lucy's white cottage. Farther up the same steep hill on the left sat her parents' summer cottage. Their house perched on a modest cliff over Lake Tomahawk, making it necessary to park cars below to the rear of the house.

As she stepped down from the Blazer with Angie in her arms, the sighing of the wind through the high pines greeted her. Even in the shade of these statuesque pines, the heat and humidity of the summer day weighed her down, but her mood lifted, anyway. "We're here, Angie."

Angie grinned in reply. Jane climbed the long flight of steps to her parents' back door. As arranged, Lucy waited for them just inside. "Hello, sweethearts." Lucy kissed Angie behind her right ear.

Angie grinned and patty-caked.

"Jane, help me with these." Lucy turned and Jane tied the strings at the back of her grandmother's favorite paint-flecked smock. Jane smiled in appreciation of the bright yellow cotton gauze sundress under the smock. No old-lady colors for her grandmother.

Lucy led them inside. "I have everything ready here in your parents' air-conditioned living room. I can't believe we need air-conditioning! I've summered in northern Wisconsin all my life, and I've never seen anything like this year's ninety-plus temperatures every day. And the storms!" She paused dramatically for emphasis. "I'd like to paint your portrait outside or in my cottage, but we'd just be miserable."

Jane nodded. "It was already seventy-eight degrees at 6:00 a.m."

"Hot or not, we've got a busy summer ahead of us, don't we?"

Jane grinned ruefully. "My summers are always busy."

"And profitable. You deal in living art! If a woman doesn't leave your dress shop looking and feeling more lovely, more feminine, it's her own fault."

"Some people don't think that's very important."

"Nonsense! A woman who feels good about herself is a woman who is kinder to others. All art should add to the joy of living."

"Thank you, ma'am." Jane gave a mock curtsy. Praise

from her grandmother, a long successful portrait artist, felt good.

"You're welcome. But we have two August deadlines—"

"Two?"

"Yes, in addition to the portrait of you for your parents' anniversary, I've decided to paint a miniature of Angie for Cash to celebrate her first birthday."

Envy leaped into Jane's emotions. Setting Angie's diaper bag in the corner, Jane gently released the baby onto the polished oak floor. The child crawled toward a box of blocks beside a tweed chair. With a block in each chubby fist, Angie banged them against the floor, then against each other.

"You would make a very poor poker player, Jane."

"What?" Jane looked to Lucy.

"You're still upset with me for selling my land to Cash."

An avalanche of the recurring panic, which even the mention of Cash now created in her, landed in the pit of Jane's stomach. She lifted her chin and said evenly, "It was your property. I had nothing to say either way."

"That's very true, but I know you're unhappy about it. If you want to express your opinion, feel free."

"It's done. I accept it." Jane, avoiding Lucy, kept her eyes on Angie.

"But you don't accept having Cash so close, do you?"

The thread of anxiety over Cash's intentions concerning Angie made Jane wince inside. "I've adjusted."

"Do you think it's right to keep Cash away from his niece?"

"No, of course not," Jane said.

"You've been avoiding Cash a long time, you know."

Jane felt another internal jab. Why are you asking me

about this, Grandmother? "We've just not been involved in the same pursuits."

Lucy came a step closer. "Are you still in love with him?"

Thunderstruck, Jane couldn't speak. Shock undulated through her in wave after wave.

"Did you think you'd fooled everyone?" Lucy folded her arms in front of her.

"How?" Jane gasped.

"It began the night of your sweet-sixteen birthday party. After nearly everyone had left, Cash arrived. He was wearing a tux because he'd just come from some big charity 'do' downtown. The delicious way he looked I could have fallen in love with him myself. He gave you a pearl ring—which you never wear—and then he kissed you. I saw your face and I knew he'd be the one in your heart."

"It was just a schoolgirl crush," Jane stammered. Lucy's poignant description of the night Jane had lost her heart to Cash brought sights, sounds of that long-ago night cascading through her. That night, for the first time, she had experienced love, love so new, so innocent…so doomed to disappointment. To Cash, she would always be "Red," Dena's pal.

"You're telling me you don't have those feelings for him any longer?" Lucy appraised Jane with her steady gaze.

"Why didn't you ever say anything?" The now-familiar tightness in her breast when coping with Cash's new prominence in her life left Jane breathless.

"It wasn't the right time. You were still so young, it was merely a promise for the future."

Jane shook her head and turned away. "You're talking about ancient history."

"All I know is—as a family—we fall in love and stay

that way. Look at Tish's mother. Claire met Henry here the summer of her fortieth year. Never showed any serious interest in any other man. Six weeks later they eloped! Everetts never love moderately.'' Lucy smiled.

Jane took a deep breath. ''I'm not in love with Cash Langley.'' *Not if I can help it.*

''Well, I wish you were.''

''What?'' Jane turned to face Lucy. ''Haven't you always told me not to become unequally yoked?''

''I believe if Cash could break out of his icy shell by falling in love with you, a love of God would not lag far behind. He's not a bitter man, just a man with a frozen heart.''

As she went on, Lucy's voice softened. ''Cash deserves someone special. He's been through so much.''

''Cash doesn't want anyone—special or not.''

''Yes, and the one time he broke out of his reserve and he fell in love—''

''You don't have to tell me. Anyone could have told him she was a disaster looking for a victim.''

''Don't sound so hard, dear. It's not like you. You know it's hard for him to trust women after his mother abandoned his family.''

''That's just an excuse. Dena fell in love, married and was very happy.'' Talking about Cash made her angry, but talking about Dena choked Jane. She couldn't go on.

''I'm sorry, dear, I didn't mean to upset you. But we must talk about Dena as naturally as we can, for Angie's sake. Dena and John are at peace with God. Until we see them again, we must make them live on through our memories.''

Jane nodded, held back tears by forcing herself to breathe normally.

''When I have a chance, I'm going to make that point

to Cash. He must start talking to Angie about her mother. Until he moved up last week, Cash was only able to visit you and Angie on weekends. There just hasn't been time, but there are a few other things I might mention, too.''

Lucy leaned forward and returned to her original question. ''Jane, you're not still trying to avoid him, are you?''

Lost amid painful images of her lost friend, Jane asked, ''What?''

''Are you avoiding Cash?''

''No,'' Jane heard herself lie and felt guilt stain her cheeks. Grandmother, don't go on asking questions I don't want to answer!

''Well, good. I'm glad that's settled. It's nice to know everything's running so smoothly for you.''

The tinge of irony in Lucy's voice, and Jane's own conscience, made her glance quickly into her grandmother's face.

Lucy glanced at her Mickey Mouse watch. ''Let's get started.'' They checked on Angie, who rolled cheerfully onto her stomach and crawled to an oak basket near the stone fireplace. The baby girl puckered her forehead as she began to take one pinecone out of the basket at a time.

''That'll keep her busy,'' Jane murmured. Finding out Grandmother knew, had known for years, about her secret feelings for Cash made Jane feel exposed. Her deepest secret had never been a secret to her perceptive grandmother. Had anyone else guessed? Cash must never know. It would give him another weapon against her.

Lucy gestured for Jane to sit down on a white wicker chair near the picture window overlooking the lake. Switching on several recessed lights and a few pole lamps, Lucy directed them toward Jane. Back at her easel, Lucy hummed softly and took up her palette.

At Lucy's request, Jane wore her favorite pair of blue

jeans and peach, short-sleeved blouse with white collar and cuffs. She knew better than to question her grandmother's choice, but still she didn't feel right posing in faded jeans for her very feminine mother, who still preferred wearing skirts to slacks. "Did I wear what you wanted?"

Lucy halted her preparations. "Look at yourself against the background. You have an artist's eye." She stepped behind the easel.

Jane scanned herself and her surroundings. Peach and white to emphasize her redheaded coloring. Denim against the white wicker, the faded flowered-print cushions, and natural birch paneling created a casual, homey effect. Lucy held her palette in her right hand and her palette knife in her left and began to mix colors.

Still tense, Jane sat down on the chair. In the peace punctuated by the sounds of Angie's contented play, Jane concentrated on the swish of the brush in paint and the frequent clack of the palette knife striking wood. The scent of paint and turpentine, forever linked with Lucy in Jane's mind, permeated the room. The familiar, tastefully decorated, but homey living room wrapped around Jane like a comfy shawl on a cool evening. In an uneven rhythm, Angie banged wooden blocks together with gusto.

Jane relaxed. "I'm glad you thought of painting my portrait for my parents' anniversary. When I say they've been married thirty-five years, it makes them sound old, but they never seem that way to me."

Her grandmother smiled vaguely in reply.

Then Jane remembered what she wanted to ask her grandmother. "There's something else I wanted to talk to you—"

The back door opened and shut briskly. "Lucy!" Cash strode into the living room.

In her bright yellow dress, Lucy turned to him like a

daffodil following the sun. He leaned over and kissed Lucy's lined cheek. Angie dropped her blocks and crawled madly toward him. He bent and captured Angie, swinging her up slightly in the air, making her squeal with delight.

Jane stiffened. Dressed in work jeans and a light khaki shirt, Cash gazed across at Jane. With his face and neck tanned by days of working in the sun, he looked rugged. He looked glorious. Jane drank in the sight of him, while at the same time an impulse to grab Angie and run made her grip the arms of the wicker chair.

"Jane, how did Angie do with her second set of shots on Monday?" he asked.

"I told you I'd call if there was any problem."

"That means she had no reaction?"

"Just a little fussy." Jane stared up at him, daring him to go on.

Lucy patted his arm, then turned back to the easel. "I'm so glad you'll be nearby all summer. I'll be able to walk over anytime."

"Please call first to see if I'm home, because I'll usually be busy at the site. I'm doing a lot more hands-on with this development. But I'll look forward to sitting on my pier with you, watching the sun set. I wanted to ask you if you know someone reliable who could clean house for me once a week."

"Jane, could your friend Kathy work Cash into her schedule?"

"I'll give him her number." Jane cleared her throat. "What brings you here, Cash?"

"Cash volunteered to entertain Angie during our sittings, so we can make the most of our time," Lucy replied. "Isn't that nice?"

Many words, none of them nice, went through Jane's mind. Now she understood Lucy's question about whether she was avoiding Cash. Had Grandmother, always frank and without subterfuge, set her up? What is going on here? Jane struggled to keep her composure.

Cash, Angie in his arms, stared directly at Jane as though sending his message loud and clear. I'm here to stay. Get used to it.

Jane's awareness of Cash made her stomach feel full of fluttering butterflies, big ones with soft feathery wings. Trying to ignore him, she swung her feet up, letting herself lounge sideways in the chair. "Is this the pose you want?"

"We started without you, Cash," Lucy said. "What do you think?" Lucy rested her chin on the back of her hand that held the brush.

"Is that what you want her to wear?" Cash moved to Jane's father's favorite recliner and perched Angie on his lap.

"It's her favorite outfit. Don't you like the contrasts in color and texture?"

Jane stared at both of them in shock. Lucy never let anyone question her artistic judgment! It was the one thing she wouldn't stand for!

"I see what you mean," Cash mused. "But personally, for a portrait for Marge and Phil's living room, I see her in a flowered dress like the one you wore that afternoon when we went to the Chicago Historical Society Museum."

"You're right," Lucy agreed. "Marge would prefer something more feminine on her only daughter. As a matter of fact, I have the dress with me. You remember it, don't you, Jane? I bought it on my last trip to Paris with your grandfather?"

"I prefer jeans." Jane tightened her mouth.

"But don't you think your mother would prefer a dress?" Lucy coaxed.

Jane's mouth became a straight line. "I suppose. But shouldn't it be a dress of mine?"

"No, your mother would recognize the dress. She knows how special it is to me. I think it would make the portrait dearer to her."

How could she argue with that? Grimacing inwardly, Jane nodded.

Lucy smiled at Cash. "I can always count on your sense of style." She turned back to Jane. "For today, just sit as though you have a dress with a wide skirt flared out on each side of you." Lucy made spreading motions with her hands.

Cash pushed back in the recliner and played patty-cake with a grinning Angie. He had seen surprise, argument and reluctant agreement play across Red's expressive face. He glanced at Jane now sitting in her prim pose. Her shining cap of wavy copper hair caught his eye, as usual. Then he looked into her stormy eyes. The emerald fire in them captured his attention. Why hadn't he ever noticed how deep and true a green they were?

With only a fraction of his thoughts on the baby, Cash began a game of peekaboo with Angie. Using Angie as cover, he continued his observation of Jane. She sat still, but did not appear relaxed. Her hand touched her hair, next her copper-flecked nose. She squirmed in her seat. His gaze fastened on her narrow waist and the soft, round curve of her hip. His mind halted there. Why would he be thinking like that about Red?

Moments passed. Angie's noises and Lucy's painting sounds filled the large room.

Finally Jane said discontentedly, "I don't know how much longer I can sit still like this."

"Talk to me, dear. It will take your mind off posing," Lucy said.

"What about?"

"What did you want to discuss with me just before Cash arrived?" Lucy peered around the easel.

When Jane remained silent and frowned, Cash wondered if he had been the topic of discussion.

"It's a problem I'm having at the shop," Jane began grudgingly. "Maybe you can help me solve a mini-mystery?"

"I'm intrigued already. Go on." Lucy began stroking the canvas with short, exact strokes.

"When I was closing the shop two nights ago, I went through all the racks, checking sizes like I always do. When I went through the tennis outfits, one size eight was missing. You know how small the shop is and how carefully I choose my inventory—"

"It wasn't sold or hung on a different rack under a jacket or left in a dressing room?" Lucy stared at Jane with almost comical concentration.

"None of the above." With her lips still held in a half smile for the portrait, Jane's nose wrinkled. "That was Tuesday. The next day I searched discreetly for it."

"So?" Cash pushed up to a sitting position in the recliner. The problem snagged his attention in spite of himself.

Jane continued, "So this morning it was back on the correct rack."

"Ah." Lucy stepped back from the canvas, scrutinized Jane and frowned.

"Ah, what?" Jane asked, her tone rising.

"Sounds to me like someone took it, got cold feet and brought it back," Lucy said.

"My thoughts exactly." Cash kissed the tip of Angie's nose.

"But I hate to think that of either Mel or Tish." Jane sounded troubled.

"It could have been a customer who made a mistake or regretted shoplifting," Cash added.

"Could be." A narrow line appeared between Jane's eyebrows. "I don't like it—period. It gives me a funny feeling to suspect people."

"I can understand that, but it shouldn't happen again. You know some people only learn by doing," Lucy said.

"What do you mean?" Jane asked.

"I mean someone's conscience taught her honesty is the best policy." Lucy turned toward Cash. "Didn't you mention pilfering at your building site?"

It was a topic he didn't really want to discuss, but Lucy had made it unavoidable. "Yes. I thought up here I wouldn't have to hire a security guard for my site like I did in Chicago—"

"You're missing things?" Jane asked, sounding unconvinced.

"Not much, but it's odd." Cash's voice became edged with irritation. "Either the thieves are stupid or clever. I can't decide which."

"What do you mean?" Lucy selected a new brush.

"It means either the crook is too stupid to try to cover his tracks or it's the opening volley of trouble—"

"Trouble? Up here?" Jane said.

"A north woods version of turf wars. This is a limited market. Maybe some contractor doesn't want new competition."

"That's foolish," Jane began.

"Foolish is right. I play fair, but I always play to win." Cash stared into Jane's eyes. He easily read her resistance to him.

You'd better get used to my being around, Red. I'm in Eagle Lake full-time and you'll be seeing a whole lot more of me. Count on it. But he couldn't take his eyes from the afternoon sunlight glinting on Jane's burnished hair.

Chapter Four

Dreading the evening already, Jane parked her red Blazer outside Vitelli's Villa. As she walked beside her grandmother toward the restaurant, Jane stared down at reflections of streetlights on the wet asphalt. About an hour before, black rain clouds had opened for a brief, intense storm.

"Besides this dreadful humidity—what's bothering you?" Lucy asked.

Jane sighed. "Oh, sitting next to Roger Hallawell and being away from Angie all evening."

Lucy slipped her arm into Jane's. "You'll handle Mr. Hallawell. And whatever other failings she has, Tish is wonderful with Angie. In fact, it's been a revelation to me."

"Me, too. When I see her with Angie, it makes me forget what a pill she can be. Aunt Claire and Uncle Henry love her so much—"

"Don't worry. God will bring her through."

"How do you know that?"

"Because I remember myself at sixteen. The acorn never falls far from the tree."

Jane wanted to pursue this comment, but they had reached the entrance of the dimly lit restaurant. A couple coming out of Vitelli's held the door for them.

"It's back in the banquet room," Jane murmured.

"Lead the way. I hate these dark dungeon restaurants. An old lady with the start of cataracts has enough trouble as it is."

"I didn't know you had cataracts," Jane said.

"It's not a fact I tell someone whose portrait I've just started."

Jane shook her head ruefully. "Grandmother!"

Carmine Vitelli had decorated his restaurant to resemble a café in a vineyard—trellises with bunches of plastic grapes, colorful hanging lanterns, red-and-white-checked tablecloths topped with candles. Jane had never been able to decide if Carmine Vitelli thought this was the only way to decorate an Italian restaurant or if it was high camp and he was having a good laugh on everyone. Regardless of the interior, Vitelli's was known for miles around as the best in Italian food, so neither Jane nor anyone else had ever questioned the decor.

They entered the banquet room. Carmine stood behind the podium welcoming everyone to the dinner. Lucy and Jane slipped quietly into their seats at the table where Rona sat with Jane's Uncle Henry and Aunt Claire. In the chair beside Jane's sat Roger Hallawell. He had risen politely to acknowledge Lucy and Jane's arrival.

"Good evening, Jane. You're looking lovely as usual." Hallawell was a large man in his early forties.

Jane respected Roger. He had built a successful contracting firm with his own sweat. She could admire that, but what she couldn't accept was his blatant, unwelcome pursuit of her. She had no intention of becoming his second wife. Across the table, Jane saw the matchmaker's sparkle in Rona's eye. Jane promised herself a long chat with Rona very soon.

The waitresses began serving one of Carmine's specialties, a salad topped with minced black olives, Parmesan and a sweet red-wine-and-vinegar dressing. Jane's stomach rumbled in happy anticipation. Carmine sat down.

Jane bent to draw a tissue from her purse when an unexpected voice said, "Good evening, everyone." Jane looked up, and her spirits fell. Cash. Why hadn't she considered he might attend the banquet tonight?

Cash, dressed in a casual sport jacket in a flattering shade of dark gray, stood behind Lucy. He gazed across at Jane. His black hair was swept away from his face and brushed the back of his collar. Tieless, he'd left the top button of his white shirt open. An unwelcome shimmering coursed down Jane's arms and legs. His blue eyes taunted her. Sitting up straighter, she attempted to take firm control of herself.

"Hello, Langley." Carmine rose to shake hands. "I think you're over there with the Bannings and the Martins."

"Oh, the Bannings!" Lucy popped up from her seat. "Cash, let me trade places with you. I wanted to see them about getting our summer bridge group organized."

"Whatever you say, Lucy." Cash's attention remained fixed on Jane. Lucy left, and Cash sat down across from Jane.

"So you're Langley?" Roger barely concealed the challenge in his voice.

Cash glanced at the man, then ignoring him, opened his napkin and began to eat his salad.

"You garnered quite a plum securing that land on Lake

Elizabeth. Must be nice to have the right friends,'' Roger went on in a derisive tone.

Cash's buying Lucy's property still rankled in Jane's own mind. Obviously she wasn't alone.

"I am privileged to call Lucy Everett my friend,'' Cash said stiffly.

Like a shift in the wind, Jane felt the rest of the people at the table become uneasy. What was Lucy's reason in placing two competing contractors face-to-face? Did she think putting the two of them together socially would temper their competition?

"Cash, I'm so glad you were able to come on such short notice.'' Rona smiled. "We don't usually get to see you this often.''

Cash nodded toward Rona. "I'm happy to dine at Vitelli's anytime.''

Though Jane had lost interest in eating, she took a bite of a tomato wedge and tried to look like she enjoyed it.

"Where's Angie?'' Cash asked Jane pointedly.

Instantly Jane felt herself bristle, but she kept her tone nonchalant. "Oh, I had an offer to sell her to a band of passing gypsies—''

"Tish is—'' Uncle Henry began.

"Happy to sit with Angie. She is a beautiful child,'' Aunt Claire finished.

"That jumper looks good on you, Claire,'' Rona said.

Claire grinned and blushed. A rust-colored bandanna tied around her neck accented the denim jumper and blue chambray blouse. "I like it myself. I have this niece who keeps me in style.''

"Keeps us all in style,'' Rona agreed.

"Keeps us all broke,'' Carmine complained good-naturedly.

"Or employed. I—'' Henry said.

This began one of Aunt Claire's and Uncle Henry's famous verbal duets.

"Jane, we really appreciate your hiring our Leticia so young—" Claire cut in on her husband.

Henry took over, "We explained what an opportunity it was for her. Most sophomores are lucky—"

"To be serving hamburgers somewhere," Claire added.

By now everyone at the table followed the conversation like a Ping-Pong game.

"The job at your shop exposes her to so many job skills—" Henry went on.

"And she can buy such nice clothes—"

"At employee discount," Henry finished for them.

Jane glanced around the table to gauge the others' reactions to her aunt and uncle. Often during one of their "duets," Jane wondered how it would feel to be so close to someone, you could finish the other person's sentences.

In the conversational vacuum after Claire and Henry finished speaking, Carmine and Hallawell started talking sports. Jane nibbled at her salad and looked across the table. The stark beauty of Cash's blue eyes and his thick black lashes snared Jane's gaze. She couldn't take her eyes from him. Suddenly she realized he was aware she was studying his face. He arched an eyebrow, and she felt her cheeks warm. She looked away.

Rona announced, "Jane, I volunteered you yesterday."

"For what?" Jane asked.

"Art in the Park."

"Me?"

"I'm performing in the puppet show this year," Rona went on.

"I'm doing finger painting—" Claire began.

"With Jell-O," Henry finished.

"But," Jane said, slightly exasperated, "I'm not artsy—"

"We have a new tent—perfect for you," Rona said. "The Dress-Up Tent, filled with old clothes, high heels, you know!"

"I planned to take Angie this year," Jane said in desperation.

"I'll be glad to take her through the exhibits while you work," Cash said, delivering the coup de grâce.

Jane's spirits sank. For seven years, she'd avoided Art in the Park. Now, the year she planned to take Angie, she would be stuck at a workstation.

"My crew volunteered to help put up and break down the exhibits. In a small town, everyone takes part in civic activities." Roger directed his attention at Cash.

Instant silence ensued. Jane wished she could slip out and go home to Angie. Why couldn't Hallawell just leave things alone? What did he think he would gain by goading Cash? Or did the man think at all before speaking?

Cash sent the contractor a frigid glare. The waitress who placed bubbling lasagna in front of him interrupted the confrontation. The rich aroma of the lasagna wafted around the table.

With a defiant glance toward Cash, Roger leaned close to Jane's ear and said, "Did I tell you I just dropped a bundle on a new Sea Nautique?"

Jane shook her head.

"Do you still water-ski?"

"I don't have much time—"

"You've got to make time for yourself. Now why don't I pick you up tomorrow afternoon? We'll take my boat out and see what she can do."

"I don't think so."

"Oh, now come on, honey."

Cash cut in, sounding bored, "She doesn't want to go water-skiing with you. I can't blame her."

Hallawell's face turned scarlet, but he went on talking about the new speedboat to Carmine.

Cash tried to rid himself of the pique this man seemed to relish causing. Hallawell's presence had somehow intensified Cash's awareness of Jane. Cash couldn't stop resenting the way Hallawell hovered next to her. He didn't like any man who acted as though a woman should be grateful for his attention. On the contrary, Jane was a woman who could command any man's attention. She deserved only the best.

No matter which way Cash turned, Jane's warm, bright hair caught his eye. When she nodded and talked to her aunt, her copper waves bounced and caught the candlelight. He almost shifted restlessly in his seat, but realizing that this would send a signal of discomfort to the smug competitor across from him, he stilled his body.

Then he caught the last of a sentence Hallawell was saying to Jane. "Bigger contractors cut corners."

"By bigger contractors, do you mean me?" Cash asked. He didn't let the antagonism he felt touch his tone. Expressions stiffened visibly on the faces of the people within earshot. Suddenly their table became a silent island, surrounded by groups where friendly chatter, the clinking sound of ice in glasses continued.

"I was only speaking generally." Hallawell's conciliatory words didn't match his abrasive tone.

Around the table everyone waited for the immediate outbreak of verbal hostilities. But after exchanging looks rife with challenge, Cash and Hallawell both let it drop, and Carmine started telling a joke.

Just as the scoops of lemon and lime Italian ice were being served, a waitress told Cash he was wanted on the phone in the lounge. When he returned, the sociable atmosphere at the table quieted. "It was the sheriff." His tone was harsh. "Trespassers have been caught at my site. They were armed with cans of spray paint. Evidently they planned to *decorate* my model home, but were caught before they had a chance." Everyone except Hallawell voiced sympathy. Cash nodded in reply, then left, walking quickly.

In the semidarkness of the parking lot, Cash fumbled in his pocket, separating his keys from the loose change. He felt a touch on his arm. Whirling around, he caught Jane by her bare arms. "You!" The restaurant lights lit her face clearly. Surprise had widened her eyes.

"Me. Let go."

Against his calloused palms, her skin was smooth, soft. Resisting the urge to slide his hands farther up her sleek skin, he released her abruptly. "Sorry. But you shouldn't sneak up on people. Did I forget something?"

"I didn't sneak up on you. If you'd been listening, you'd have heard me. I'm going with you." She slipped her thumbs into the front belt loops of her denim skirt. The cream silk blouse she wore shimmered in the low light.

"What?" He lifted his gaze to her face.

"I came to keep you company while you inspect the damage to your site."

He filled his lungs with the hot, humid air. "I don't need your help—"

"I insist." Her pale skin glowed in the light from the restaurant. She fidgeted with her collar.

He grimaced. Her very feminine presence distracted him already. "That isn't necessary."

"If the tables were turned and it was my shop, wouldn't you insist on going along?"

"That's different."

"Because I'm a small, weak woman?" Her head tilted as her chin lifted to him in argument.

"Don't start that. Thank you for offering, but it isn't—"

"Necessary," she finished for him. "But now it is."

"Why?" He felt his ire rising. Not only because of her insistence, but because of the provocative pose she flaunted in his face.

"Because I'll look like an idiot. Everyone in town saw me follow you. I don't want to have to explain—"

He sighed in resignation. "Get in." He clicked open the lock, and she slipped in. He caught a breath of her cinnamon-scented cologne. It brought to mind the richness of her auburn hair in the candlelight at their table. If he ran his fingers through it, would it feel as silky as it looked?

He slid behind the steering wheel. The suffocating heat made him flip on the air-conditioning. "I'm going out to the site first." Smoothly he shifted into reverse, backed out of the space and shifted into first.

"Oh, I thought you'd go directly to the sheriff. There wasn't any damage done."

"That's right. But I want to see if the sheriff's deputy missed anything. Also I've found that letting a vandal sit in 'the tank' and count the minutes till someone comes to press charges can be very effective."

"You mean this has happened before?" Her soft voice sounded like velvet in the darkened Jeep. It caused a shiver to slither up his neck.

"In Chicago. A construction site irresistibly draws trespassers, thieves and vandals."

"I'd never thought about that before."

"That's not surprising. It's like your little mystery of the missing size eight. I wouldn't have thought that one up on my own." As she nodded, her fine golden loop earrings swayed in the low light. Her earlobes looked pale pink, soft....

With determination, he turned his eyes forward. This reoccurring awareness of Red as a woman was getting to be irritating. It must be all the pressure of the new project and all this Hallawell garbage. In silence, Cash drove trying to keep his eyes on the road, trying to ignore the tantalizing woman beside him.

The large sign lit up the entrance of the Eagle Shores subdivision while the remainder of the site sat in darkness. Cash drove directly to his model home. "I'll leave the air-conditioning on."

"I'm coming with you." Jane pulled on her door handle and jumped out.

He followed suit. Outside the Jeep the sultry night air wrapped around Cash like a cocoon. "Is this Louisiana or Wisconsin?" He swept his hand over the fine perspiration on his forehead.

He met Jane in front of the Jeep. Pointing skyward, he said, "There's the real culprit, the full moon."

Jane followed his glance, then turned back to his face. "The moon?"

"If it hadn't been light enough to see, our 'spray-paint commandos' wouldn't have been out tonight. I think I'll have to invest in some motion-activated floodlights and hire a watchman."

Crickets serenaded the night in endless crescendos. He snapped on his flashlight. "I'm going to check the door and window locks, then we'll head over to the sheriff." He glanced into her face and bowed slightly. "Shall we take our moonlight tour?"

She slipped her hand in the crook of his elbow. This simple act of trust hit him unexpectedly. It was dark, she was in heels, the ground was uneven. He knew it was practicality that motivated her touch, but her touch unlocked a deep sadness inside of him. How many times had he given his arm or hand to his sister, to lead her, to steady her? His younger sister no longer needed his protection. His eyes smarted with unshed tears, making him relieved they were in the shadows.

Breathing as evenly as he could, he concentrated on the routine he had performed so many times on other sites, and his sadness ebbed. He flashed the beam of light up and down the outer walls and directed the beam to the latch of every ground-floor window. He tested the back door and ended their circuit with a check of the front door.

"That does it." He turned back to his Jeep, but Jane's hand stayed on his arm. He wanted to thank her for touching him. It had stirred hurtful memories, but only at the start. Her touch had connected them in a way he hadn't realized he'd needed.

They settled themselves in the Jeep's interior. Cash flipped on the air-conditioning. He made a wide turn and headed for the county road. "How about a picnic Saturday?" he asked, surprising himself.

"A picnic?" Jane asked. "My, you're optimistic. It'll probably be ninety-eight in the shade and pour buckets two minutes after I put all the food out on the picnic table."

He loved the wry twist of her humor and he knew why. It was one of the many traits she had inherited from Lucy. He grinned to himself, but kept his tone even. "Why don't I pick you two up at eleven. We'll drive north to Sandy Lake Beach."

"Very well," she said.

The atmosphere in the Jeep had mellowed. They rode in companionable silence. He pulled into the parking space outside the local sheriff's office. He shut the car door behind Jane, and without a word they walked toward the entrance. Cash held the door for her, and she slipped past him.

"Langley?" The sheriff stood up at his desk and came to the counter.

Cash held out his hand. Momentarily the sheriff's eyes lingered on Jane as though questioning her presence. She nodded toward Cash and sat down.

"How did you manage to get the vandals before they had done any damage?" Cash asked.

"After I heard about things disappearing from your place—"

"How did you hear that?" Cash demanded.

The sheriff grinned. "Small town. Anyway, I decided to have a man patrol the site every hour. The deputy was already behind them when they turned into the entrance. He lagged behind, parked and trailed them on foot to your model home. They had just pulled the spray-paint cans out of paper bags and were aiming when he switched on his flashlight. It doesn't usually happen that neatly."

Cash nodded and folded his arms across his chest. "How old are they?"

"Eighteen. Shirt-tail relation to some of Hallawell's crew."

"Not minors?"

"They'll be charged as adults. But it will only be trespassing with intent to commit malicious mischief. If my deputy hadn't stopped them—"

"No. I'd rather not clean up a mess—or charge anyone with anything. I don't think this was their own idea."

The sheriff leaned back with his arms lapped over each other on his chest. "What did you have in mind?"

"A good scare."

The sheriff nodded slowly. "I'll bring them out of the

detention room in cuffs. That tends to drop a man's confidence."

Trying to keep a low profile, so that no action of hers would change or hinder what was happening, Jane moved farther back into the shadows and sat down on a vinyl, straight-backed chair. The scene unfolding before her was more interesting a character study than she would have predicted.

Cash, the hard-headed, success-is-everything businessman, was surprisingly willing to overlook youthful indiscretions. Why hadn't she realized the love he'd always shown Dena denoted a compassionate heart? Her memory recited, "Blessed are the merciful for they shall obtain mercy."

She heard the sheriff's voice, now strident and loud. Two teens, both with identical, "buzzed" hairstyles came into view from behind the counter. One teen already bowed his head in defeat, but the other's chin lifted in defiance.

"Mr. Langley," the sheriff announced in a gruff, combative tone, "these are the two perpetrators."

Cash, his hands still across his chest, said nothing, but eyed the two as he would have looked at a piece of chewing gum stuck to the bottom of his shoe. Jane was glad he wasn't looking at her that way. "I told you I didn't want to see them." Cash's voice was cutting, and the scorn he applied to the words was chilling.

The bowed head dropped fractionally lower. The defiant chin lifted another inch.

Cash went on, "I just wanted to press charges and leave the rest to the county prosecutor."

"You certain you want to go ahead and charge them?" The sheriff wheedled. "Isn't this case too minor—"

"Malicious mischief isn't minor," Cash said sharply.

"I doubt that if I went out to their car and spray-painted it, they would hesitate to charge me."

"They're both first-time offenders—"

"That isn't the point...."

The defiant one spoke up, looking at the sheriff, "Why are you bothering to talk to him. We didn't ask—"

"Quiet," Cash snapped. "You're in big trouble, haven't you realized that? This isn't the high school dean's office. You're eighteen, an adult. This fiasco will earn you a permanent record."

The defiant chin lifted only fractionally this time. "So?"

Cash's voice lowered and his tone became venomous. "How about this? How is it going to feel when you have to call your parents to post bail for you?"

Silence. The young man's mouth opened. His chin dropped in an uncontrolled free fall. The other offender uttered a slight moan.

"Mr. Langley," the sheriff wheedled, "won't you consider an apology and some sort of restitution? No actual damage was done."

As the rest of the scene was played out, Jane watched avidly. Both teens apologized to Cash, promised to steer clear of the Shores and agreed to perform twenty hours of community service during the remainder of the summer. As the boys were finishing up the details, Cash and Jane left.

During the drive back, both of them sat in a tired silence. Cash drove her back to her Blazer, then he followed her home. There he insisted on walking her to her door, and she was too fatigued to protest her independence. It was nearly midnight, the start of the stillest time of the night.

She stopped on her back step, turned toward him and paused. His compassion to the two young men tugged at her emotions once more. She longed to rest her hand along his hard jaw. Verses she had learned about kindness, "Be kind one to another…" "Love is kind…" ran through her mind.

Suddenly and completely, Cash felt the shift in Jane's mood. He could read the change in the way she leaned close to him, the inviting tilt of her head, the barely perceptible parting of her lips. All evening her presence had enticed him. Now she softened to him, invited him.

Her cinnamon cologne still sent out its faint fragrance. Her full bottom lip captured his senses. If he leaned down to skim it with his tongue, he wondered what it would taste of. His chin dropped closer to hers. She didn't move. He felt her breath against his cheek. His lips parted.

The call of a loon on the nearby lake made them both gasp. He froze. Standing up straighter, he took a deep breath with difficulty. His lungs felt constricted.

She touched her fingers to her lips. "Good night," she said and stepped inside.

After he heard her lock turn, he stood a few more seconds on her top step. He wanted to call her back, to thank her for going with him. And had that unexpected softening of Jane really happened? Would he have kissed her? Or was it just his imagination and the moonlight?

Chapter Five

Despite the uncomfortably hot, muggy evening wind, Jane walked languidly toward her shop. She disliked equally the heat outside and the air-conditioned isolation inside her shop. In spite of her dawdling, she finally arrived at the shop door and stepped in. Oh, well, only a little over two hours to closing for another busy Friday night.

"Jane, Lucy called." Tish said, "You're not supposed to drive out to Lucy's after work. Angie will be at your house."

Jane frowned at Tish's disrespectful use of their grandmother's given name. "That's peculiar. Grandmother doesn't drive at night anymore."

Tish shrugged. Several tourists browsed through the racks. Tish stood outside the fitting rooms, conferring with a customer through the closed door.

"May I help you or do you just want to browse?" Jane asked a woman near her.

"Just browsing," the woman replied quickly.

"Fine. Let me know if I can help. I'm Jane."

She politely canvassed the remaining strangers, then went to stand by the counter. Finally the first woman she'd spoken to asked to try on a black challis skirt. Jane led her to the available fitting room. "Let me know if you need anything else," Jane murmured as she shut the door.

Within minutes the woman peeked out around the door. "Do you have this in size eight? My pre-vacation diet worked!"

"Of course," Jane said mechanically.

But as she shuffled through the rack of skirts, a cold weight dropped to the pit of her stomach. Though she knew she had another black challis skirt in size eight in her inventory, none hung where it should. Is one hanging in the dressing rooms? Tish had just cleaned out the dressing rooms and returned everything left in them to the correct racks. Jane drew the dreadful conclusion that another piece of merchandise was missing. *The size-eight culprit is still with me.*

She felt like stamping her foot in frustration, but she went ahead and chose an alternate skirt she thought would be equally flattering to the customer. Along the way she added a complementary blouse, cardigan and scarf.

"I'm sorry," she told the woman. "I didn't have that exact skirt in size eight. As long as you are in the dressing room, would you care to try these on?"

The woman glanced unhappily at the clothing Jane offered her. "I suppose so."

Jane handed her the hangers. This was her usual initiation to a new client, a hand-picked ensemble suited to a woman's coloring and style.

Within minutes Jane watched another woman step out of the dressing room like an emerging butterfly from a cocoon. The customer timidly walked over to view herself in the three-way mirror. "This is lovely," she said in awed surprise. Jane smiled. The ritual of helping another woman discover how good she could look in clothes meant for her usually exhilarated Jane, but the disappearance of the size-eight had blunted her pleasure.

The customer smiled shyly at her attractive reflection. She ran her hand down the lapel of the sweater's collar. "I've never seen a sweater quite like this."

"It was hand knitted in Italy."

"For a shop way up here?"

Jane smiled at the ingenuous question. "Many of my customers find it convenient to shop here on their vacation. They make it a part of their yearly routine. I've just brought out more fall items. Is there anything else I could show you?"

The customer gave Jane a shrewd look. "I can see that you know what you're doing. I'd like a few everyday out-fits for the fall. I do quite a bit of volunteering, and I work in my husband's law office part-time...."

After listening intently to the woman's information about herself, Jane went through the racks expertly pulling together skirts, slacks, blouses, sweaters and blazers. At the mirror, Jane held them in front of the woman, dem-onstrating all the flattering combinations they created. An hour later Tish helped the woman carry out a myriad of Jane's signature gold-and-teal bags and boxes to her car.

"How did you do it?" Tish declared as she walked back into the quiet shop. "She bought everything you showed her!"

Jane smiled. "I will share my secret with you in hopes you'll learn how to do it. Most women want to dress well, but they don't know how to do it for themselves. This customer was a woman in search of quality and individ-uality. Until now, she's been afraid some pushy sales-woman—with only a commission in mind—would intimidate her into buying something expensive that she doesn't like. So she shops at very large, impersonal department stores, instead of a small shop like mine. When she realized I knew how to help her dress the way she had always longed to, she ceased to be afraid.''

"Wow!"

"When the former owner decided to retire and sell this shop, I was able to buy it because after working for six summers here, I had already established a strong clientele. That's why my parents backed me and helped me buy it.''

"Gee, I didn't know that. How did you learn how to match customers to the right clothes?''

"Well, that's a longer story, and we don't have time for it now, but in the future—if you really want to learn—I'll take time to teach you.''

"Okay!"

Jane smiled broadly. Helping a woman find her distinctive style was always a heady experience for her. Tish's unexpected, uncharacteristic enthusiasm and approval also pleased her. But recalling the disappearance of the size eight skirt still took some of the glow off the evening.

Jane sighed. "It's time to close. Let's shut her down." The two of them went through the nightly routine and parted for home.

When Jane finally walked into her house, it was dark, after 10:00 p.m. Inside, she heard Angie's muffled crying. As she hurried upstairs, the back of her neck tensed. She had hoped Angie's teething pain would take a break. She didn't want to wear Lucy out. The crying stopped, and Jane held back the greeting she had been just about to voice.

She topped the staircase, then halted at the sight of Cash's broad shoulders and dark head held high. Her stomach fluttered wildly. *Cash.* She strained to bring his name to her lips. He turned. Angie lay propped with her face against his shoulder. At the sight of Angie in his arms, a second shock wave vibrated through her, changing quickly into temper. What is he doing here with Angie?

While Cash patted Angie's back, he stared at her, then he began bouncing the baby slightly by taking exaggerated steps. He turned his back and walked away from Jane.

She pursued him. Tapping Cash on his shoulder, she whispered, "Give her to me."

She held out her arms.

He began humming, blotting out the sound of Jane's whisper. He shook his head and turned away from her again.

Breathing fast, she trailed behind him. She whispered again. "Why are you here?"

He shook his head at her. "Not now," he mouthed. "She's almost asleep. Leave me alone."

Jane flushed with anger. Cash had no right, appropriating Angie here in her house. But she didn't dare upset the infant, who was now so close to settling down for the night.

She tapped Cash's shoulder again. She mouthed to him, "Did she take her last bottle?"

He nodded.

"Does she have a night diaper on?"

He nodded curtly, then waved the back of his hand motioning her to go away.

Seething, Jane left him in the hallway, went into her room and shut the door firmly but soundlessly. There she vented her agitation by shedding her white linen suit, pitching it piece by piece into the heaping basket of clothing in her closet. She jerked on a yellow cotton knit T-shirt and matching shorts. Standing before the mirror, she raked her comb through her mussed hair.

Without any effort, she could put together the explanation for Cash's appropriation of her home, of Angie: he'd stopped by Lucy's cottage and suggested he take Angie home, so Jane wouldn't have to drive out to Lucy's after work. Jane slapped the comb down on her vanity. How could Lucy resist him? Cash Langley, the good neighbor.

A faint tap sounded on her door. She opened it.

Cash whispered, "Downstairs."

She led him down to the kitchen, the point in the house farthest from Angie's room. Standing with the kitchen table between them, Jane crossed her arms and opened her mouth.

Cash cut her off. "First thing in the morning, I'm buying an air conditioner for Angie's room."

"Air conditioner?" The word took her by surprise.

"Why haven't you realized that Angie would sleep better if she weren't so uncomfortable in this heat?"

"I...I don't like air-conditioning," she stammered.

"You have it in your shop."

"That's for the customers."

"Does Angie rate less than your customers?"

"Of course not, but I've never needed air-conditioning before." Jane felt as though she were being buffeted by wave after wave of disapproval. "Cash, why—"

"I don't care about what you've needed in the past. Angie can't sleep well in that small upstairs room without air-conditioning."

"Stop!" Jane held up both hands. "This isn't about air-conditioning! What are you doing here?"

"Didn't you get my message? Lucy looked tired to me, so I told her I would take care of Angie and let her get to bed early."

"Lucy looked tired?" Jane asked, feeling a tug of guilt.

"Yes, she hasn't been sleeping well in this heat."

"She never said anything about that to me."

"I had to worm it out of her." Cash crossed his arms in front of his chest.

"You did?"

"Yes, I did. I persuaded her to start sleeping over at your parents' air-conditioned cottage till this heat breaks. I walked her there, then brought Angie here."

Jane felt deflated, guilty. But she wouldn't let him divert her. "I'm glad you did that for Lucy, but I still want you to understand you can't just walk in and take over Angie and my house."

Cash drew himself up straighter. "Taking good care of Angie—"

"Angie is *my* responsibility. Maybe you're right. Air-conditioning might be a good idea. This has been such an unusual summer. But I'll be the one to decide—"

"How do you think it makes me feel, knowing Angie needs something and I have to argue *with you* about whether she gets it or not? I won't be pushed aside!"

"I'm not pushing you aside...."

"Yes, you are. You do it every time I try to get close to Angie."

"That's not so." Jane spoke, then realized Cash's words were true.

"Yes, it is."

Jane blushed. *Dear Lord, I didn't mean to lie. I know I'm handling this badly. Help me.*

Cash leaned forward and put his hands flat on the kitchen table. "I've had it with your possessive attitude. In the past six months, I've been busy moving here and getting the Shores off the ground, so I've let matters over Angie float. But I haven't folded. You may be in possession of my niece, but she still belongs with me—whether you're in the picture or not."

Jane's throat tightened.

"Tomorrow is our Saturday picnic. I will come early and install an air conditioner in Angie's room, then we'll talk about joint custody." He left her.

Jane slumped into the nearest chair and rested her head on her hand. She sat there a long while until she was able to think clearly again.

What is wrong with me? I started fighting with Cash—without waiting for the facts. He hadn't done anything I wouldn't have done myself. Why had she been tempted to snatch Angie out of his arms and run? She was attracted to Cash, but terrified by what he might do next. Her heart twisted painfully.

For a split second she saw Dena's face in her mind. She folded her arms on the tabletop and buried her face in them. "Oh, Dena," she whispered to the empty room, "I thought we had years and years ahead of us. Now all I have left of you is Angie." A moan worked its way up from deep inside her. Would the pain of Dena's loss ever lessen? Would the panic she felt whenever Cash held Angie in his arms ever cease?

"That should hold it in place." Cash turned the screwdriver one more time, then stepped back to look at the new air conditioner, perched in Jane's east window.

"Are you sure you want it in my room?" Jane asked guardedly.

"Yes, having Angie sleep in here, I'll be sure you can hear her. If I left her in her own room with the door closed, you might not hear her over the air conditioner."

Jane wanted to tell him, in no uncertain terms, that she would hear Angie's cry through ten doors, but she still reeled from his threat of last night. What exactly about joint custody *did* he plan for discussion today? Her heart froze. She couldn't even begin a prayer.

While she watched him rearrange the antique furniture in her room to fit in Angie's crib and changing table, she bounced Angie on her hip and worried.

The phone rang. Without a word, Cash lifted Angie from Jane's arms. When he closed the door behind him, Jane sat down and picked up the receiver of her bedside phone.

"Jane," Lucy said, "are you angry with me about last night?"

"No, Grandmother. I'm so sorry. Why didn't you tell me you were too tired to watch Angie?"

"Because I wasn't, until about 7:00 p.m. Then all my energy just drained away. If I could have persuaded Angie to settle down, it wouldn't have mattered, but she didn't have that in mind."

"I feel terrible. I won't let it happen again."

"Don't fuss, dearest. I feel much better this morning. Did Cash tell you he bullied me into sleeping at your parents' last night?"

"Yes, and this morning he's bullied me into letting him put in a window air conditioner in my room." She couldn't keep the ire from her voice.

"This morning!" Lucy chuckled. "He certainly didn't waste time, did he?"

"Oh, Grandmother, he said he still wants Angie." A quaver shook Jane's voice.

"Did that surprise you?"

"Yes! He hasn't said anything—"

"Jane, Cash isn't easily turned away from a goal. Of course he still wants Angie."

Jane bit her lower lip. "How can I stop him?"

"My only advice is not to let him roll over you like a tank. You're an Everett. Stand up to him."

"How?"

"God will provide the answer when you need it. Just ask Him. Now, your parents called. They're due in tonight."

"Tonight? Already?"

"Yes, dear, it's the end of June. They're driving up to spend Fourth of July at the lake."

"Oh, yes."

"I'll see you tomorrow morning—when you aren't so distracted." Lucy hung up.

Jane sat holding the phone. Closing her eyes, she tried to still her anxiety and draw on God's strength. But God seemed too far from her. Fear had walled her in. She put down the phone and went downstairs.

Cash was waiting for her. "Ready?" he asked.

She nodded and picked up the diaper bag on the bottom step. As she walked through the house, shutting off lights and locking doors, she reminded herself that she was an Everett. She could handle any situation.

They stowed the picnic gear behind the rear seat of Cash's blue Jeep, then took off. Cash set out down the highway till he turned down an old county road.

Jane sat back, trying to relax.

"Well, do you want to make a bet on whether or not we'll be all alone at the park?" he asked.

"I'd say yes, we'll be on our own, and I wouldn't want to take your money." Jane glanced back at Angie.

"Did Lucy ever ask the county board why there's this big beautiful park here that only we seem to use?"

"No, she was afraid that they'd put up bigger signs and soon we'd—"

"Be overrun with tourists." He nodded.

Jane smiled as Angie slapped her hands on the padded bar of her car seat.

"Having fun, Angel?" Cash asked over his shoulder.

Angie cooed.

Jane frowned.

Cash glanced at Jane. "Tom called me yesterday. You haven't drawn out any money from Angie's trust."

"I haven't really needed anything."

"The fund is ample. You're supposed to use it for Angie's expenses."

"I don't want to. I'm able to support Angie on my own."

"So am I." Cash's tone became gritty. "But the fund—"

"I want that to be a large part of her inheritance."

"She will receive an ample inheritance from me."

"But when you marry, Cash, that inheritance would have to be spread thinner."

"I'm not going to marry—"

"I think that's unlikely." Jane turned to look at him.

"I'm not going to marry," Cash insisted, leaving no room for argument. The topic of marrying hit him unexpectedly. What if Jane married? The thought of Jane marrying a stranger appalled him. Why hadn't he considered this possibility before? Why hadn't Dena? An unknown man taking part in Angie's life? *No!*

A small, weathered sign announced, "Sandy Lake Beach—Two Miles." He drove on, feeling grim.

As they turned a tree-lined corner, the park appeared before them. A small, but beautiful space with a well-groomed lawn, pristine dark green picnic tables and a wide sandy beach, all completely unpeopled, waited for their use.

"Six and a half miles south the beaches are packed," Jane said. "Every time I come here I expect to find—"

"A horde of tourists. So do I." He turned to Angie. "We're here, Angel."

Before Jane could undo her seat belt, Cash had unhooked his and Angie's and had swept the baby out of the Jeep. He swung her high, seating her behind his head, across his shoulders, with his hands gripping the baby's pale, chubby ones. Carrying the diaper bag, Jane hurried ahead of him.

Cash frowned as he watched her. In spite of himself, he was fascinated by the motion of her hips under her pale yellow sundress. The dress hung straight from the sleeveless shoulders down to the hips where it was gathered beneath the swell of her bottom. He clenched his teeth momentarily. Red had walked in front of him a thousand times. Why was he noticing the seductive sway of her hips now?

In the shade of the two large oaks, Jane shook out the quilt and laid it over the green grass and pine needles. Out of direct sunlight and cooled by the lake breeze, the temperature was warm yet comfortable. Jane reached for Angie, but Cash ignored her and swung the child down onto the quilt.

Angie crawled swiftly to Jane. Lifting the child's hands, she helped the baby to stand up. Angie giggled. Then Jane coaxed Angie down onto the soft, cotton quilt and proceeded to change the baby's wet diaper. Jane looked up and found Cash frowning down on her.

"I thought you were going to take her to the doctor about her diaper rash."

"I haven't had time," she replied defensively. "I'll make the appointment Monday."

''You know I'd take her anytime she needs to go. Just call me.''

''I'm quite capable of—''

''Let's not argue. I can take a baby to the doctor, too. And next time I won't wait for you. I'll take her myself.''

''You can't.'' Looking up at him defiantly, Jane let Angie roll onto her knees. ''Only a parent or guardian can seek medical services for a minor.'' Jane scattered a few toys from the diaper bag in front of Angie.

Frustration laced with anger zigzagged through Cash. He felt close to his breaking point. He breathed deeply, trying to rein in his anger.

Cash swung Angie up into his arms and walked toward the baby swings. Jane hurried to keep up with him. He slipped Angie into the black rubber seat, hooked the safety belt around her middle and gave her a gentle push from behind. Angie squealed.

All the months of pushing down his own feelings and making changes in his life to suit Jane rose in his throat and choked him. She'd had her way for the past six months. Now he'd have his. Jane stood in front of Angie, just beyond the range of the swing. He looked into her face. ''I want Angie.''

Jane fidgeted with her gold loop earrings and then smoothed her hair back over her ear. ''You've made that clear before today. Do you intend to sue for custody?'' She faced him directly, though her chin trembled.

He read the storm of fear in the green depths of her eyes. ''I have a right to claim my only family—''

''Dena and I were like sisters.'' Jane felt a pinching around her heart. ''Do you think I would have loved her more if we had been born in the same family?''

''It's not the same. Angie is my blood,'' Cash insisted.

''Dena was my sister, too. Blood or not.''

"You have your whole family. All I have is Angie! How can you be so selfish—"

"I'm not being selfish. I'm following Dena's wishes. Haven't you spent any time thinking about *why* Dena chose me as guardian?" Again she winced inwardly.

"It was obviously just a foolish decision that Dena would have changed if she'd had time to think it over."

"That's emotionally and intellectually dishonest and you know it."

Cash frowned.

"Has it ever occurred to you that maybe my family is one of the reasons Dena wanted Angie with me?" What had begun as a pang each time she said Dena's name, now became a full-scale tightness in her chest which made it hard for her to breathe.

"What?" He gave the baby girl another gentle push.

"Don't you realize how Dena hated being so alone?"

"She wasn't alone. She had our father and me."

"Your father traveled constantly while Dena was growing up. And you were ten years older than we were. Didn't you ever notice how she was always next door at my house or with Lucy?"

"What are you saying? Are we going to have a contest over who loved Dena more?"

"No! You're not listening to me!" Her heart pounded while the heaviness in her breast increased.

"What am I missing?"

"When you were growing up, your parents were still together—"

"I don't want to go into that."

"Just listen. After your mother left, you no longer were a complete family. Your father traveled. You were busy at school, busy with a different stage of life than Dena. You weren't a kid when she was."

"Are you making this up or did Dena really feel this way—that she didn't have a family?"

Jane nodded, controlling her reactions to her inner distress. "We talked about it a lot when we were teens together. You were away at school, and then you went to Chicago to start your business."

"If Dena resented this, why didn't she say something?"

"She didn't resent it. It wasn't your fault! She wasn't crippled by it. She was just glad she had me and Lucy and my parents." Though filled with her own suffering, Jane watched Cash. She had to make him understand the part of Dena's reasoning she had surmised. Dena hadn't given her Angie in order to wound her brother.

Cash shoved his hands into the pockets of his jeans and stared at the ground.

"Don't you see? Dena wanted to share my family with Angie. Dena loved you, but she turned to my family for what she lacked." Jane longed to add, *Dena wanted Angie to love God, too, Cash,* but she knew too well this would shatter the tentative link she was trying to forge. Cash had never understood Dena's love for the Lord.

"I never knew she felt that way," he muttered.

"Cash, you've decided to live your life solo, but I think Dena preferred Angie to be part of a choir."

"What you've said really changes nothing."

"Changes nothing?" Jane's voice shrilled, "What do you mean?"

"I mean, why do I always have to share *my* time with Angie, with you? I'd like to have her to myself."

Though she had never feared that Cash would steal Angie, her panic accelerated.

"Why do you cling so tightly to Angie? Every time I come near it's as though you're pushing me away."

"I don't push you away," Jane denied weakly.

"Yes, you do. I want to know why, and I want you to stop it."

"But Angie is so little yet." Jane quivered.

"What has that got to do with anything?"

"She still needs me to be with her."

He shrugged his shoulders in a show of irritation. "You leave her with baby-sitters on and off every week."

"Just my aunt, uncle, Tish and Lucy." She felt herself crumbling inside.

"Why not me, then?"

"It's not the same." She looked down at the open toes of her sandals.

"Yes, it is. Why won't you let me take charge of Angie some evenings?"

Her head snapped back up to face him. "Because that's what you'd do—*take charge of Angie,* just like you did last night."

"What do you mean by that?" His deep voice began to rise in volume. "Am I supposed to be in the wrong, because Angie and Lucy needed air-conditioning?"

"No, but don't you see, you didn't talk the matter over with me." Her voice and body shook. "You just came in and took over. 'You need this, so I'll do that.' No discussion. Just issuing orders." She hugged herself, trying to mask her trembling.

"Why do you have to be so touchy?"

"Why do you have to be so bossy?"

"Bossy. Touchy. It comes down to this, Red. I've turned my life upside down to accommodate my sister's twisted will and your lifestyle. I reorganized my business. I learned to fly. I moved north and started a whole new branch of my firm. Now I'm going to have Angie by myself one day a week or *else.*"

Jane felt her self-control disintegrate, just as it had that

January day in the social worker's office. Just the way it had over the past six months during private moments whenever she thought of Dena. To hide her tears, she rushed a few yards away into the forest of fir trees.

Casting a glance at the peacefully swinging baby, Cash pursued Jane. "Come back here," he called through tightly clenched teeth.

He caught up with Jane easily and spun her around to face him. "Why are you crying like this? Do you think I'll let you have your way if you cry hard enough?" He gripped her by the shoulders. "I won't be manipulated by tears."

"I can't help it," she spoke between sobs. She pressed her hands over her face. "I miss Dena so much."

"We weren't talking about Dena. Why did you bring her up? Is this some kind of emotional blackmail? Do you think if you can upset me, I'll let this drop?"

"No, but whenever I think about being away from Angie, my grief over losing Dena bubbles up and I can't stop it."

"I can't help that. I lost Dena, too."

"I know, but in some way inside me, Angie and Dena are linked. Losing Angie feels like losing Dena."

"Of course they're linked. Why else would I want Angie? If you don't let me have Angie one day a week, you'll force me to take you to court."

"No." Tears rolled down her cheeks. Cash's grip braced her, keeping her standing straight, bolstering her with his strength. A glance up into his pained face slowed her tears. She brushed away her tears with her fingertips. "I'm sorry. I didn't mean to hurt you." She looked up at him, her eyes pleading for understanding. "Truly, Cash."

"I miss Dena, too," he said gruffly, tugging her back to where Angie still swung.

"I know." She wiped away her tears. "It's still so hard to accept. I keep telling myself Dena is with God, beyond pain and sorrow. But that doesn't ease away the hurt of loss." For a moment Jane let herself imagine the comfort of resting her head on Cash's broad shoulder.

They were silent awhile. Then Cash raised his chin. "When can I have Angie to myself?"

Jane made herself think. She had lost Dena, but in spite of her grief, she was bound by her faith to do what was right for Angie and Cash. Though she didn't feel it right now, she knew God would provide the extra strength she would need to overcome her fears. "All right." Saying the words turned her insides to quivering jelly again, but she looked up into Cash's face resolutely.

"When?" he demanded.

"In two months, Angie will be a year old."

"I can have her on her birthday?"

"No, I'm planning a big party on that day. You can have her on the twenty-fourth?"

"The twenty-fourth." He wanted to press her to move the date forward, but perhaps it was better to accept this hard-won concession. He'd just hold her to it. Reluctantly, he nodded.

Jane tugged at his arm and he followed her back to Angie, who was kicking her chubby legs and cooing skyward at the large white clouds overhead. At the sight of Jane, the baby gave one quick cry. "Want your bottle, sweetie?" Jane asked.

Cash carried the baby back to the quilt and laid her down. Jane rummaged through the denim bag and brought out a bottle of formula. With the bottle finally clutched between her chubby hands, Angie relaxed and sucked loudly.

"I feel like I've run a ten-mile race," Jane murmured.

"Before we have lunch, would you mind if I stretched out for a few minutes?"

"Go ahead. I'll watch Angie."

Jane lay down beside the baby and closed her eyes. When Angie's eyes also drifted shut as she sucked contentedly, Cash lay down, too. He stared up into the blue sky for a long time, then glanced at Jane beside him. The lake breeze played with wisps of red hair around her tranquil face. One of her arms was extended and curved around Angie. The tiny freckles, flecks of gold, on Jane's arm fascinated him. The blue-tinged shadows beneath her eyes touched his heart. Jane hadn't begrudged any of the lost sleep and worry it had cost her to care for his niece.

He stirred inside and resented it. Why had he started noticing Red as an attractive woman? This afternoon when she'd wept, he'd fought the urge to pull her into his arms. In all the years he'd known her, she had never meant more to him than his kid sister's best friend.

Now every time he saw her—even when they argued— he imagined what her lips would taste like and how soft her skin would feel.

Chapter Six

"'He hideth my life in the depths of His love, and covers me there with His hand,'" Jane sang the final phrase of the chorus, then sat down along with the rest of the congregation. The gentle words of faith, penned by Fanny Crosby nearly a century before, soothed Jane's heart like warm water bathing chilled fingers. During the showdown with Cash the day before, so many memories and so much sorrow had been stirred, she needed comfort.

On the wall to her right hung a wood panel on which the Beatitudes had been carved. "Blessed are they that mourn for they shall be comforted" caught her eye. Quieting her spirit, she opened herself, asking for God's comfort. The peace of the church settled around her like a cozy blanket.

The pastor began his sermon. The summer sunshine glowed through the stained-glass window behind him, highlighting the dove of peace flying above the jewellike blue Jordan River. The quiet of church, broken only by a few throats clearing and the turning of pages, soothed Jane.

Then Lucy patted Jane's hand. The gentle touch filled with affection nearly brought tears to Jane's eyes.

As usual, Jane, with Angie in her arms, sat in the middle of the pew between Lucy and Tish. On the other side of Tish sat Aunt Claire and Uncle Henry. Beside Lucy were Jane's parents. Never before had Jane comprehended the significance of her family's placement along the church pew. The youngest, the most frail, nestled in the midst of loved ones.

When Dena and she had been children, Jane had thought they had been placed in the midst of parents so they could be watched for misbehavior. Now she wondered what it would feel like to sit all alone. No doubt Cash would insist on sitting alone. Jane shook her head a fraction. Cash's armor had always been impenetrable. Once she had dreamed of piercing it and making him love her. Now she knew it was an impossible hope.

Restless in the quiet church, Angie left Jane and climbed onto Tish's lap. Tish leaned forward and rubbed noses with the baby. Angie squealed her pleasure. When Jane automatically shook her head at Tish, she noticed a flash of white through Angie's parted lips. She slid her index finger into the baby's mouth.

"Ouch!" Jane gasped as Angie bit down.

Instant silence. The pastor stopped speaking and turned toward the Everett family. The small congregation imitated him.

Crimson with embarrassment, Jane spoke up, "I just discovered Angie's first tooth."

Laughter, then spontaneous applause rippled through the church. The pastor grinned, cleared his throat and began again. When the service ended, a throng of grandmothers cooed and crooned over Angie.

Finally Jane joined her family, who were gathered in the

shade of an old maple. Henry and Phil discussed the possible places to have lunch. Lucy turned to Jane. "I want you to invite Cash to our Fourth of July picnic."

"Oh?" Jane tried to sound unconcerned.

"Yes, Marge or I could extend the invitation, but I think it should come from you."

"Why?" The warm wind fluttered around them, catching Jane's full white skirt.

"So he'll know he's really welcome." Lucy stared into her granddaughter's eyes significantly.

"Very well. I'll call him from the shop later today." And I'll remind myself that Dena would want me to invite her brother to spend time with Angie. She stiffened her will. Though her human feelings fought against it, she would do what was right, with God's help.

With Angie on her hip, Jane waited inside the back door of her parents' summer cottage. In the background Jane heard her mother and grandmother teasing each other in the large country kitchen where they were making a "vat" of potato salad for the annual Fourth of July picnic. From a few cottages away, firecrackers burst in rapid pops like popcorn. Angie twisted in Jane's arms, trying to see where this unusual noise came from.

"Those are firecrackers. It's Independence Day, Angie," Jane said soothingly. "We're going to have fun. Uncle Cash is coming." Jane kissed Angie's soft, downy cheek. "But look. Here comes Aunty Claire, Uncle Henry and our lovely but spoiled cousin, Tish." The baby gave serious attention to the threesome walking up the steps. Jane opened the door for them. A hot wind blew against Jane's cheeks warming her unpleasantly.

"Hello—" Uncle Henry started.

"Jane," her aunt finished. They both kissed Angie and

Jane lightly on the cheek and then went in, calling greetings to Lucy and Jane's mother.

Tish paused beside Angie. "Hello, sweety." As was her custom, Tish gave Angie an Eskimo kiss.

Angie leaned toward Tish, asking to be taken. Jane tried to hold on to Angie, but the little girl pushed and grunted till Jane gave in. Triumphantly Tish hugged the baby to herself and walked toward the kitchen door.

Jane stepped outside. The lake wind wafted around her, doing its best to stir the humidity-laden heat. Cash's Jeep swooped around the bend, making Jane's stomach flutter wildly. "Don't get edgy," she whispered to herself. "I must share Angie and not let my grief spoil everything." She tried to make herself decide how to handle Cash today. What if being with him stirred her ill-fated infatuation with him? Would she do or say something that would reveal this to Cash? The thought shook her to her toes.

Cash bounded up the steps. When he came abreast of Jane, a tantalizing excitement shivered through her. Pushing aside her reaction to him, she shaped her mouth into a welcoming smile.

"Where's Angie?" he asked.

"Hello, Jane," Jane said formally, trying to teach him manners. "Happy Independence Day."

Cash paused. "Sorry. Happy Independence Day. Where's Angie?"

Beckoning him ruefully with her hand, she turned. "Come on in. All the action's in the kitchen." The nonchalance in her tone pleased her.

She led him through the house into the large country kitchen. A sudden pride in her family filled Jane with joy. Her grandmother and mother stood side by side, tapping hard-boiled eggs against the sides of the stainless steel sink. The two women were a study in contrasts. Marge, a

brunette with an ivory complexion, was fashionably thin
and taller than fair Lucy. Marge wore a sporty pair of navy
cotton slacks and a white blouse while Lucy wore a floral
sundress in shades of peach and yellow.

Her aunt and uncle sat at the table with her father, Phil,
who with his fair coloring, looked a great deal like his
mother and daughter. For a moment Jane felt like saying
something stupid like, This is my family!

"Cash!" Phil stood up. "Great to see you. Happy Independence Day!" Henry stood, also, and shook Cash's
hand warmly.

"Come here, Cash," Marge instructed. Cash obeyed.
When he was beside her, she turned and gave his cheek
an affectionate peck. "We're so glad you've joined us today."

"We'll see if he can put up with us for a whole picnic,"
Lucy put in saucily. Cash grinned and leaned over to kiss
Lucy's cheek.

At the far end of the room near the pantry, Tish was
dancing a sort of waltz with Angie in her arms. When
Angie caught sight of Cash, she squealed.

"Cash, this is my cousin, Tish." Jane motioned toward
Tish who blushed as though embarrassed. Angie's continued squealing forced Tish to bring her to Cash. At Phil's
invitation, Cash sat down beside Henry.

"Janie," Phil ordered, "break out the new deck."

From a kitchen shelf, Jane took down an unopened pack
of ornate blue-and-white cards. She tossed it to her father.

Phil broke the seal and opened the box. "Hope you're
in the mood for Crazy Eights, Cash."

"Haven't played in a long time," Cash admitted. "Why
don't I just watch—"

"No shirkers allowed in this family," Henry said with
a cheerful flourish. "In this world of constant change, there

is one constant—on the Fourth of July, the men in this house play Crazy Eights. Now we don't play for money, but we do play for honor. And I plan to defend my championship again this year.''

Aunt Claire beamed at her husband.

"Claire," Phil chided, "I always told you, you married a card shark." Phil began to deal three hands efficiently.

Tish sat down beside Cash. "I'll help you remember the rules." With her head tilted coquettishly, she smiled.

On the other side of Tish, Jane found herself squelching the urge to shake her cousin. Jane took a deep breath and went to her mother's side. "Are all your eggs cracked?"

"Yes, all the Humpty-Dumpties have taken their great falls," Lucy replied mournfully.

"Why don't you finish the relish tray?" Marge motioned toward a large platter, piled high with fresh vegetables.

Jane nodded and brought out the cow-shaped, wooden cutting board. She began peeling carrots. Her eyes were on her task, but her ears monitored the banter of the card game.

Cash held Angie in his lap and glanced down once more at his cards. The little girl was in one of her serious moods when—either due to fatigue or a personality quirk—she became relaxed. He held his cards in both hands in front of him, and Angie, though drooling onto her terry cloth teething bib, almost looked as though she were studying his cards, too.

He heard Lucy and Marge, talking in easy tones about discarding the eggs that had green around the yolks and trying to fix blame for this blight. The sounds that Jane was making as she peeled and sliced the vegetables were rhythmic, assured, soothing.

He picked up a card and mentally recalled the suit he

was trying for with this hand. He smiled to himself. He had drawn a wild card, a joker. He only had to play one other card and he would win this hand. His next turn gave him his chance. He laid down his cards and won.

The chagrin of the other two players was loud, but good-natured. The next hand was dealt, but this time Claire and Tish changed places with Lucy and Jane. Lucy claimed Angie from Cash. Again the women watched the card play, urging on their favorites enthusiastically.

Cash glanced at the cheerful group around the table. He hadn't really thought about what it would be like spending the Fourth with Jane's family. Knowing Lucy as he did, he wondered why he had not guessed the day would be casual and lighthearted.

When it had been just his own family: Dena, Dad, and himself, there had never been much fanfare on any occasion. After their father's death, Dena had chosen to spend most of her holidays with the Everetts. Now he could see why, but at the time he had been too busy with business to make much attempt at creating holiday cheer. He himself hadn't needed other people to celebrate every special day. But Dena had loved being with the Everetts. Maybe Red had been right. Maybe Dena had wanted Angie to be part of this.

The fierce competition of Crazy Eights raged till the final hand and to Cash's surprise, Henry won again.

"Hurray!" Claire exclaimed. Grinning, Henry received his champion's kiss from her.

"Now on to phase two!" Lucy declared.

Both Phil and Henry stood up with military straightness. At their encouragement, Cash followed their example. Out of the refrigerator, Claire and Jane brought a huge platter of marinated beef back ribs. The pungent aroma of garlic, spices and tomato sauce went right to Cash's taste buds. His mouth watered. "Ribs?"

Marge chuckled. "Didn't Jane tell you we always have barbecued ribs for Independence Day?"

"No, if she had, I would have skipped breakfast," he said honestly.

"Oh, dear," Marge moaned as she wrung her hands in mock anguish, "I hope the extra ten pounds I bought will be enough!"

Laughter broke out among the Everetts. Cash looked around the kitchen. Only Tish was trying to behave nonchalantly, as if she felt embarrassed for his sake. All this dreadful year, every change of season, every holiday, even an unsentimental one like the Fourth of July, had brought bittersweet memories not only of Dena, but also their father and mother, as though the loss of Dena had reinforced all his bereavements. But he hadn't been left completely alone. He still had Angie. She was all he needed.

"Be off with you!" Lucy ordered.

Ceremoniously, Phil and Henry took charge of the platter, a long-handled pair of tongs, a pot holder mitt and a spray bottle of water.

"You don't have to go out if you don't want to," Tish said softly beside Cash.

"I wouldn't want to shirk my duty. I want to earn that extra ten pounds of ribs."

Without showing any response, Jane listened to this exchange between Cash and Tish. Was it just Tish's way of separating herself from the zany humor that her family favored? Or was her young cousin falling for Cash's potent charm?

Angie began to fuss. As the door closed behind the three men, Jane turned to the refrigerator to bring out a bottle to warm. Going through the mundane routine helped quiet her nerves.

After the ribs had been grilled to Phil and Henry's standard of perfection, Cash watched as the Everetts took their places around the long redwood picnic table on the screened-in porch. The hot ninety-two-degree wind still blew, but an inside picnic was obviously impossible for the Everetts to consider.

In pleasant amazement, Cash viewed the feast laid out on the long table. The huge platter of aromatic ribs occupied the center. American potato salad with its pale mustard color had been decorated with a ''sunrise'' of egg slices. In addition, yellow corn on the cob with melted golden butter nestled beside the greens and reds of fresh vegetables on their tray. Pink-red chunks of watermelon filled a huge, green glass bowl and next to each place setting stood a tall, amber tumbler of iced tea, each with a generous wedge of lemon on the rim.

All around him, the easy banter continued. Unexpectedly he felt a thaw around his heart. He hadn't realized he had been so frozen inside since Dena's death till this day of warmth.

At the head of the table, Phil bowed his head. Everyone else became still with anticipation. Cash waited to see what Phil would pray. ''God bless this food. God bless this family. God bless this land. Amen.'' Then, as though a switch had been thrown, the chatter began again, and the bowls started their journey from hand to hand.

When the eating was complete, Cash felt unusually full and unusually satisfied. The food had tasted as delicious as it had looked. Glancing down he saw Angie at the foot of the picnic table, seated in her high chair. She had a little bit of the whole menu on her face, hair, hands, bib and tray. She was grinning widely and cooing.

Marge also caught sight of Angie. "Look at our beautiful grandchild, Phil!" Marge sprang out of her chair. "She looks good enough to eat!" She hurried to Angie and unhooked her from the chair. As Marge hugged her and kissed her on the nose, Angie beamed. "You sweet baby, we are so lucky to have you. Yes, we are. Our first grandbaby. Can you giggle for your old Grandma?" She tickled Angie once on the belly and Angie obligingly giggled.

"Should we give Grandpa a messy kiss?" Marge asked Angie, carrying her over to Phil. Angie reached out with her chubby, gooey hands and, chuckling, Phil kissed them. When he tried to take the child from his wife, Marge pulled away. "You'll get your turn later, Grandpa!"

Aunt Claire said, "Henry, I think it's time we—"

"Gave Phil and Marge their gifts," Henry finished and went into the house, returning with a large paper bag. Grinning, he drew out two white hats. "This one's for Marge."

"And this one's for Phil."

The two baseball-style caps were white except for the red lettering embroidered on the fronts. One read "Grandma". The other read "Grandpa". Obviously delighted, Phil and Marge both immediately put them on.

"Oh, Henry, they're wonderful," Lucy declared. "Where's my camera?"

Jane went in, returning with Lucy's old 35mm. Lucy quickly posed the beaming Marge and Phil as they held Angie between them.

While all this took place in front of him, Cash sat immobile. He fought the urge to break down into tears. Except for Lucy, he had never considered how Jane's parents and family would react to Angie in their midst. That Phil and Marge would accept Angie as their first grandchild with pride and love had never entered his mind. Probably because he had never known his own grandparents. For so long there had only been just Dena and him.

He stood up abruptly and hurried outside, the screened door banging shut behind him. Shoving his hands into his pockets, he walked quickly down the wide steps to the Everetts' pier and halted at the end of the wooden dock. Then he let the tears come while the hot, bold wind lashed him, drying the tears as quickly as they fell.

"Cash?"

Turning slowly, he saw Jane tentatively approaching him. It was as though he was seeing her for the first time. Her full lips the color of summer peaches were parted slightly. She glowed with life, vibrant and generous.

"Cash?" She repeated, pausing only a step from him.

Her concerned expression caused a spasm around his heart. "You didn't need to come after me. I'm all right." His mouth felt suddenly dry, and his voice sounded hoarse to his ears.

"Mom is concerned about you. She's afraid we did something that upset—"

"I'm fine. Let's go back. This wind feels like the Santa Ana in California."

He watched Jane give him one more worried glance. Then she led him back up the steps to the house.

Later, when the hot wind that had blown all day finally stilled, and darkness tinted the high clouds the color of slate, Phil announced it was time for the sparklers.

They all trooped outside to the grassy lawn overlooking the lake. Phil sat on the back porch steps, Angie reclining royally on his lap. Nearby on an old canvas-and-wood lawn chair, armed with a butane lighter and a coffee can half-filled with water, sat Henry, the "lighter" and the "extinguisher." Marge, Lucy, Claire and Jane swirled with the sparklers, twisting and exclaiming over the variety of the sparklers' fire: some traditional red and gold, and others startling green and blue.

Cash leaned against the house, watching the ladies and Angie's captivated expression as she took in her first sight of sparklers. At the display of the dancing, sputtering sparks, the little girl's mouth and eyes opened wide in absolute wonderment.

The ladies laughed and teased each other while painting bright, but vanishing, patterns against the darkening sky. The sparklers' sizzling sound punctuated the wash of waves against the nearby sandy beach. In the distance, while boats already chugged by toward town, more firecrackers and bottle rockets popped and exploded.

Cash felt a warmth that had nothing to do with the heat of this long day. The Everett family Independence Day celebration captivated him as much as Angie was captivated by the sparklers' shining colors.

Only one person did not seem to be enjoying this part of the celebration: Tish. With her waist-length golden hair reflecting the flash of sparklers, Tish walked toward him in an obviously planned-to-be-sexy walk. She leaned back against the house and assumed a seductive pose; one knee bent, her arms back. Cash smiled to himself as the young girl practiced her feminine wiles. Obviously Tish was at the age where she would not enjoy lighting sparklers. She wanted to distance herself from childish things.

The first words from Tish's mouth proved his thought true. "This is so childish." Tish grimaced. "I don't know why they do this every year."

"Angie seems to be enchanted by the show."

"Sparklers are for kids. I mean, my family must seem really weird to you."

Cash chuckled softly. "Every family should be this weird."

Jane, from behind the dazzling light of her long, red Oriental sparkler, observed her cousin's pose and the fact that Tish and Cash were talking privately. Jane felt the unmistakable nip of jealousy. At the beginning of the evening she had experienced a touch of that unreasoning fear of losing Angie to Cash. Now was she jealous of Tish? Why wouldn't her emotions make sense? Cash was not going to take Angie, and he wasn't interested in Tish. As the sparkler burned down to Jane's fingertips, she yelped in pain.

By the time the sparklers had all been beautifully burned, Cash had allowed himself to be persuaded to go by boat to Eagle Lake's fireworks display. With Angie riding on his shoulders, he walked in the midst of the Everetts as they all trooped down to the pier and boarded a large pontoon boat. On board, they settled onto lawn chairs and Marge passed out soft drinks.

Angie snuggled deep in Cash's arms. He felt mellow for the first time since Dena's death. For a moment he pictured his sister among them, smiling. For once, thinking of Dena brought no pain.

The boat slowly moved across the lake and through the narrows toward town. The distant reflections of lights from the houses they passed flickered like candle flames on the water. He imagined Dena's joy over the beauty of the night.

Within sight of town, Phil cut the motor and dropped anchor near several other boats. Friendly greetings from boat to boat were exchanged by acquaintances and strangers alike. Phil left on only the small boat lights, red and green on the front and white on the rear. They bobbed on the gentle waves. Cash leaned back in his chair, savoring the contentedness of this day, letting it spread through him.

On a hillside behind them, Jane caught glimpses of spirals from sparklers in the darkness and enjoyed the excited shrill laughter of the children, waving and twirling them. She glanced at Angie who was sound asleep in Cash's lap. For once, no warring emotion tugged at her. Cash and Angie appeared so peaceful, she could not help but smile at them. Then her father murmured that the fireworks were about to start, and everyone focused on the sky over the city park. They all waited.

Letting herself relax to the soothing rhythm of the waves beneath them, Jane closed her eyes briefly. The day had not been strained as she had feared...except for her own short attack of jealousy over Tish's attention to Cash. The spot on her fingertips where she had burned herself still felt as though it were on fire.

Boom! Jane jerked upright in her seat. She must have dozed off for a few seconds. As the town's Fourth of July pyrotechnic show got off the ground, the sky above was sprinkled with golden sparks. She quickly looked to see if the sudden noise had wakened the baby, but obviously it would take more than fireworks exploding to disturb Angie tonight.

"Do you think she'll sleep through all of this?" Cash murmured close to her ear. The flashes from the fireworks glistened in his eyes. She tried to take her gaze from him, but couldn't. Reaching out, she lightly smoothed back Angie's dark, wispy bangs.

Wap! The second projectile shot into the air, bursting into long magenta streamers. Wap! Wap! Two more escaped gravity—a huge yellow-gold chrysanthemum formation blossomed and disintegrated above them. Inside Jane, fireworks went off, too. Cash had taken her hand in one of his. She was afraid to look at him. Her breathing became shallow.

"This is the way to see fireworks," Cash said.

"Haven't you been to Chicago's extravaganza at Buckingham Fountain?" She could barely speak. She was careful not to move her hand. Why didn't he let go?

"Sure, but that's what makes this so different. No crowds. No traffic."

The display caught Jane's attention in spite of herself. "Ooh," she heard herself and all the others in the boat voice appreciation.

Wap! Wap! Boom! Boom! BOOM! The series of thundering explosions unleashed cascading bursts of shimmering gold, red, white, and blue on the breeze. That breeze also carried the oohs and ahs from the audience in town, but the dominant factor in Jane's mind was her hand in Cash's.

A full half hour of fireworks artistry dominated their attention. Cash relaxed his hold on her hand, but didn't release her. The inner turmoil his touch caused echoed the riotous display of color and sound. Then came the grand finale. The sky was overtaken with a massive bouquet of scarlet, magenta, royal blue, gold. The booms and cracks echoed deafeningly, joined by shouts of approval and applause.

Silence. Jane looked over at Cash and smiled timidly. In the shadows cast only by the boat's two small lights, she caught him studying her intently. Their eyes met. Jane's senses zipped to an even higher level of consciousness. Then he let go of her hand. He leaned down and kissed the top of Angie's sleeping head, and Jane felt as though his lips had touched her also.

"Oh, is it over already?" Lucy's complaint broke into Jane's thoughts.

"Yes, Mother. You'll have to wait till next year," Marge said not unsympathetically. There were other similar sentiments made while Phil turned on the motor and they chugged toward home.

The rapid beating of Jane's heart quieted very gradually on the long ride back. The now-cool lake breeze fluttered over Jane's face and lifted her hair around her ears. Angie slept on beatifically in Cash's arms.

Sometime later, after Jane hadn't been able to find her car keys, she found herself being driven home by Cash. He escorted her and Angie inside, a picnic hamper and the diaper bag in his hands. All the bustle of the day had ended, and Jane felt as if they were the only people left in town.

Once inside the house, Jane went directly upstairs. A little Bo-Peep lamp on the high dresser softly illuminated the baby's room. Being alone with Cash after a day together made Jane intensely aware of her movements. Feeling Cash's eyes on her felt like the touch of his hand on hers earlier.

From the doorway Cash watched Jane's hands as they changed a soggy diaper and snapped Angie into a lightweight pink sleeper. Finally, when the baby was dressed comfortably and rolled to her back, Jane laid a thin white blanket over the sleeping child. Drawn to Jane as well as Angie, Cash quietly stepped closer to the crib.

Standing beside Jane, Cash caught the last fragrance of Jane's cinnamon cologne and Angie's baby powder. It was a compelling mix of scents: woman and child. The soft light in the room highlighted the bronze of Jane's hair. The quiet buzz of the air conditioner and Angie's contented breathing were the only sounds in the cozy room.

Cash couldn't take his eyes off Jane's profile. Her gleaming, warm copper hair, creamy skin glowing in the low light, her full lower lip. He observed her shiver and wondered if it was due to her awareness of him. Because he was certainly very aware of her.

That lower lip of hers drew his eyes down. He leaned forward...and touched his lips to hers. A breathless moment passed between them. Then as his lips played across hers, she gasped, fanning her warm breath against his mouth.

"Jane." He pressed his lips to her again. They felt like satin and tasted spicy and warm. As she stepped nearer into his embrace, he felt her hands claim his shoulders.

"Jane," he whispered again. His arms went around her. She fit against him so neatly.

The phone rang, and they fell apart as though a stranger had walked into the room. Jane hurried to answer it. Angie whimpered in her sleep. Cash stroked the child's back till she quieted.

Then he walked out into the dark hall. He heard Jane's voice and then the receiver being put back into its cradle. Still mulling over what he and Red had just experienced, he took a controlling breath.

Jane came out to meet him in the hall. "It was Mother." Her voice was just above a whisper. "They found my keys behind the bread box in the kitchen. I put my purse there when I first arrived. My car keys must have fallen out. That was why we couldn't find them."

He nodded. "I'll bring them in with me in the morning."

"That's not necessary. My parents will deliver the keys and my Blazer tomorrow."

He nodded. She moved ahead of him and paused at the top of the staircase. "I'll go down and lock up after you leave."

He followed her, trying to think of what to say to her about the kiss he hadn't meant to take. Matters over Angie had just begun to ease. He had guessed the invitation to spend the Fourth with her family had been Jane's way of reaffirming her commitment to share Angie with him. So why had he kissed her? He wasn't a kid with uncontrollable hormones. Had he upset the delicate balance between them?

At the back door he cleared his throat. "I didn't— I hope I didn't offend you. I never—"

"That's okay. It's been a long day for all of us. Good night." Jane smiled tightly and let him out. He waited for her to lock the door, then walked toward the alley where his Jeep was.

With her back pressed against the door, Jane felt herself weighted down with emotion. What she had feared had happened. After all these years, Cash had finally kissed her. And then apologized. How was she going to keep a healthy distance from him now? He was evidently feeling the pull of their situation just as she was. Otherwise why would he have kissed her?

It had been devastating to know how easily he could sweep past her defenses and make her recall those first few childish years after her sixteenth birthday, those days when she had been foolish enough to think she might find a way to win Cash. Since then, it had been hard, painful work to put up walls to guard her heart against her own vulnerability to Cash.

Now her walls would have to be higher and stronger or she ran the risk of becoming even more hurt.

Chapter Seven

Jane, seated at her desk in the shop's brightly lit basement, checked invoices and a balance sheet. From upstairs she heard the scraping of clothes hangers on racks and the steady rhythm of the manual carpet sweeper. Tish was making sure all the sizes were in the right places, and Mel was doing a once-over with the sweeper on the aisles and dressing room floors. Both girls were supposed to be keeping an eye on Angie, who was in her playpen near the cash register. Occasionally Jane heard a bell ring as Angie played with her activity center.

The shop would open in fifteen minutes. Even in the basement, Jane heard the steady gush and swish of the rain over the pavement. A sharp thunderstorm which had begun an hour after dawn still washed over them. Rain would make for a busy day. Tourists, unable to boat and swim, would come in to browse.

Though deep in her figures, Jane became gradually aware that the two reassuring sounds above had been replaced by hushed, but heated, voices. Suddenly the long day ahead of sitting for the portrait and working at the shop stretched out even longer before her. The rivals are at it again. *God, give me patience. And I need it right now.* With a labored sigh, she closed her paperwork and trudged up the steps. In one hand she carried the working cash to start the day.

"You dumb blonde," Mel said, nose to nose, with Tish. "He's just using you to make Nancy Ledbetter jealous."

"Who's jealous? You are! That's who's jealous!" Tish tossed back. "Tony says it's all over between him and Nancy—"

"Girls," Jane cut in, "we open in ten minutes." Both heads swung to her reluctantly. Each of their faces wore a mulish expression.

"Okay," Mel said grudgingly, and went back to her sweeping.

Tish maintained her defiant stance a moment longer and then, with a swish of her golden mane, turned back to the rack nearest her.

After stopping at the side of the playpen to encourage Angie at her attempt to turn the dial and ring another bell, Jane walked over to the cash register drawer and unlocked it. Methodically she counted the money from her hand into each compartment: ones, fives, tens and twenties, letting the mundane task soothe her ruffled nerves.

From behind, Jane heard a sharp tapping on the front window. All three of them turned to see Cash, wearing a khaki slicker, peering into the shop. Tish, closest to the door, started forward.

"I'll get it," Jane said. Tish halted, and in a huff went to the rear of the shop. She began shoving hangers along a rack there. Scrape! Scrape!

Jane strode to the door and opened it. "What brings you to town?"

His rain-dotted face lifted into a hesitant smile.

"Thought I'd offer you and Angie breakfast, then drive you both out to Lucy's for your sitting. I won't be able to get anything else done this morning."

He sounded ill at ease. She looked up into his eyes and saw the uncertainty there. He was testing her, seeing if she would continue to resist sharing Angie with him.

The carpet sweeper nipped Jane's heels.

"Oh! Sorry, Miss Everett," Mel said from behind her.

Jane rotated and found both girls staring at Cash. "That's all right, Mel," she said automatically. The decision to go with him suddenly became easy. *Let me out of here!* To make her escape, Jane swiftly rescued Angie from her playpen and stepped to the door. "Girls, I'll be back before I go to Grandmother's."

Cash unsnapped the front of his slicker with a jerk and held up one side like a wing.

With that, she stepped out and under the cover of Cash's arm. Like children just out of school, Jane and Cash ran the block to the Eagle Café, bumping erratically into each other. Jane smelled the clean scent of rain, but also Cash's clothing, which held a mingling of forest scents: pine and cedar and his subtle aftershave. Naturally the running made her heart speed up, but the man beside her brought her senses alive and made them intensely sensitive.

Her shoulder accidentally connected with his chest, and she felt his solid strength. As she ran under his open slicker, with Angie in her arms, she was blindsided by an elemental oneness—man, woman, child.

Entering the half-filled restaurant, Jane found herself grinning in spite of being wet up to her ankles and sprinkled all over. Cash joined in the lighthearted mood by theatrically sweeping off his dripping cloak. Raindrops flew into the air around him. He then held it outside the door and flapped it twice like a scatter rug. Finally he swung it up on one of a row of hooks where other rain-coats, swamp jackets and umbrellas already dripped along the wall.

A possessive arm under hers, he escorted her and Angie to a booth near the front. For those few moments she let herself revel in his special courtesy, and she wondered if he had been aware of the fleeting connection between the three of them. They slid in across from each other, still grinning. On Jane's lap, Angie spontaneously clapped her hands, and Jane bent to kiss her forehead.

At this gesture of love, Cash felt a clutch at his heart. Dena must have known how much Jane would love Angie. Covering this sudden rush of poignant emotion, he sig-naled to the waitress to bring them two coffees.

Cash lifted the heavy white mug. As long as he could recall, this café had used the same style cups. All this summer since he had moved north, he had savored the continuity of the past, present and future here. He felt as though he had come home at last. He had deep roots here from when he was young, and he wondered if Jane felt the same way about Eagle Lake. Was that why she had opened her business and established her life here?

Jane leaned back against the red vinyl and took her first sip, then sighed luxuriously. Dressed in a tan skirt and an ivory short-sleeved sweater, Jane fit in perfectly with the backdrop of the maroon-and-white café.

Jane Everett is a beautiful woman. The thought still had the power to startle him. She wasn't gawky and fourteen—she hadn't been for over a decade. How could he have been so blind? She ran the fingers of her right hand through her burnished hair, coaxing it into its own natural waves. Watching her brought an ache, a lack, an emptiness inside him. Then it became a name, a plea. *Jane.*

The waitress brought over two menus and a high chair,

which she placed at the end of their booth. Once Angie was in it, she playfully patted the tray and tapped her heels against its footrest. Reeling with his inner confusion over Red, Cash hid behind the plastic-covered menu.

Jane smelled a mouth-watering mix of aromas in the air, but she conquered her urge to order a second breakfast. She turned her attention to the man across from her. His longish, black hair caught the fluorescent light and shone. Raindrops glistened on the crown of his head. Her fingers longed to tousle his hair and make the raindrops dance then disappear.

Why had she been cursed with the Everett family trait of constancy? Other women fell in and out of love. Why couldn't she—once and for all—get Cash out of her system? Six years ago she had become infatuated or fascinated with him. She knew that there would never be anything but Angie between Cash and her, so why did she still react to him?

Sternly she turned her thoughts to the present. She cleared her throat. "How's your work going? Has the rain held you back much?"

"A little, but fortunately it's so hot between storms that it dries out pretty fast. Today, however, I would have been sitting around just watching the mud ooze till it was time to be at Lucy's."

Before long the waitress set a platter down in front of him and recited, "Two eggs over easy, four slices of bacon, soft, two griddle cakes plate-sized and a hill of hash browns". She grinned and placed a saucer of golden, buttered toast and a small plastic glass of apple juice in front of Angie's tray. Apologetically she eased a towering homemade cinnamon roll in front of Jane. "It's the last one. I thought you might change your mind about not wanting anything."

"Thanks." Jane pointed to Cash's overflowing platter. "You're right. I can't hold out in the face of that!" The waitress grinned and left them. Angie wiggled and babbled for her juice, so Jane held the glass to the baby's mouth and let her take a long swallow.

With a smile Cash speared a combination bite of egg-bacon-pancake. "I'll help you finish that roll."

"I don't think so." She buttered her roll with real butter and refused to think about cholesterol or calories. An Eagle Café cinnamon roll was a true indulgence and should be enjoyed as such.

"Come on. You'll never finish it," he teased between bites.

"Will to." She gave him a superior smile, then took a bite of her cinnamon roll. A spot of butter slipped off her lower lip and melted its way down her chin.

Before Cash gave it conscious thought, he caught the butter with his index finger, and the tenor of their exchange instantly altered, becoming intimate, charged. Their eyes connected and held. The richness of those moments on July Fourth flooded him, making him long to reach for her hand.

Jane couldn't take her eyes from Cash's face. As he moved his hand away, his fingers brushed the underside of her chin. The touch careened through her, lighting flash fires in her veins.

A burst of laughter from behind them shattered their connection. Cash drew back his hand completely and sat up straighter.

Without invitation, Carmine Vitelli, Mel's dad, slid into the booth beside Cash. He greeted Angie, "Hi, Toots."

Angie giggled. Crumbs from her toast dotted her face and bib, and her chin was slick with butter shine.

"Now that's a breakfast," Carmine said, ogling Cash's platter.

Cash raised his shoulder, blocking Carmine's threat to his breakfast. "Get your own, Vitelli."

"Get your own, Vitelli," Jane mimicked, protecting her cinnamon roll from Carmine. Joining in the gaiety, Angie giggled and clapped again.

"Don't mind if I do." Carmine tipped his hand up as though drinking coffee. Reading his signal, the waitress came over with a fresh mug for him and took his order. Then he turned to Cash. "So what are you going to do about Hallawell?"

Cash swallowed a long draught of his coffee. "Why should I do anything? This summer's *delightful* weather is the only thing interfering with my construction project."

Carmine teased Angie by acting as if he were going to steal her apple juice. "I've heard he's tried to strong-arm some of the suppliers to slow down your materials deliveries."

"You listen to gossip too much, Carmine." A steely confidence dominated Cash's features.

Suddenly Jane felt very sorry for Roger Hallawell.

After their breakfast Jane checked in at the shop and changed into her portrait dress downstairs in her office. Feeling slightly festive as she always did in her grandmother's peach-toned flowered dress, she slipped into Cash's Jeep, and he drove the three of them out to Lucy's cottage for another sitting.

The memory of Cash's hand against her chin this morning dominated Jane's thoughts as they walked toward Lucy's door. "It's stopped raining. That's something," he said, sounding doubtful.

"Yes, now we'll *steam* for the rest of the day." Jane blew through her mouth and fanned herself with her hand against the humidity and heat which at mid-morning already suffocated them.

Lucy was waiting at the cottage door. "Good morning, sweetheart," Lucy called and waved to Angie.

"We're here, too, you know," Jane scolded.

Ignoring Jane and Cash, Lucy lifted Angie out of Cash's arms and spun around, making the child laugh in delight.

"I feel a bit slighted myself," Cash complained broadly.

"Oh, you two are just spoiled brats. Who would want you?" Lucy laughed at them and carried Angie into the house.

After a few minutes of chatter, Lucy led Jane into the living room and began preparing to paint. Taking up her palette, she said to Jane, "Spread and smooth your skirt a bit more, Jane. And then tilt your chin down and to the right. Show us your best side."

Jane obediently tilted her head. Lucy adjusted it slightly more to the right, then stepped behind the easel and began touching her small, round brush painstakingly to the canvas.

Cash sat on the dark green wicker chair near the large window overlooking the lake. Out of the corner of her eye, Jane watched him hold a blue, circular shape sorter in front of Angie and help the baby find the right slot for each of the red and yellow blocks. Angie pushed and growled, trying to force a square block into a star-shaped opening. Cash slowly rotated the shape sorter till he found the matching square hole. Angie pushed the block in and yelled her approval at conquering the challenge. Jane smiled. Did every mother think her child was brilliant?

Cash's gaze caught Jane's eye. He smiled at her, sharing the joy of Angie's small victory. In that smile Jane read his abundant love for this beautiful child they shared. She felt her eyes misting.

"What is our topic of discussion today?" Lucy asked, invisible behind her easel.

Jane blinked rapidly, holding off tears. She spoke up to divert herself, keeping her voice light, "I'm afraid I have another chapter in the continuing saga of What's Missing at Jane's Shop?"

"The skirt returned?" Cash asked.

Jane caught herself just before she nodded. During posings, she let herself become a puppet with invisible strings connected to Lucy's hand and brush. "The skirt returned and a quilted jacket vanished—"

"And now the jacket returned?" Lucy stepped around the easel.

Jane replied, "It must have, because I think Mel bought it."

"I am having a hard time figuring out what the point of all this is," Cash said.

Jane continued. "At the very least, it means that someone is taking clothes from the store, then returning them for some bizarre reason. In the case of this jacket, it's tempting to assume that, since Mel bought the jacket, she is the one who had taken it out. But why? She could have just asked, couldn't she?"

"Not if she only decided to buy it after taking it out as she had the first two items," Cash commented. "So I can't see where her buying it makes any difference in this mystery."

"If I may," Lucy said, "I would like to offer a bizarre reason for taking and returning clothes."

"Please do, Watson," Jane directed from her seat.

"It's called How to Have a Larger Wardrobe without Spending any Money."

Jane suppressed a frown, maintaining her pose expression. "Ah, I see. I'm selling some slightly used clothing."

Peering at Jane, Lucy nodded and bit her lower lip in concentration. Then she began making very short strokes and alternately eyeing Jane and the portrait.

"This really has you tangled up," Cash said. "Does it matter so much? After all, nothing is actually being stolen...."

"I think you're only playing devil's advocate with me, Mr. Langley." In spite of herself, Jane tingled at the sound of his voice and the knowledge that his attention had turned to her. "I have a reputation for distinctive clothing here. Usually I only carry a few of each item in a very few sizes. In a small town, women count on that. They don't want to see someone at church or at a restaurant in the identical dress they are wearing. And I'm charging healthy retail prices, not thrift shop ones. I have a reputation of honesty to maintain."

"Go over the events of this weekend again," Cash said softly. "The jacket Mel bought?"

Jane watched Angie in Cash's arms. Fighting her morning nap time, Angie repeatedly fluttered open her eyes, but they drooped lower and lower each time. Finally they closed in sleep, and Cash very gently arranged Angie's neck in a more comfortable position across his arm. The baby stirred, but did not wake. Again the sight of his tender care of Angie in contrast to their separateness nearly moved Jane to tears.

"I was out of the shop the day before yesterday, the Fourth." Jane pushed away her memories of that emotionally draining day. "It could have been returned that day, and then Mel could have bought it yesterday while I was on break. She didn't mention it to me, but we were very busy, and then I didn't go through all of yesterday's receipts till this morning. I'm baffled. If some stranger were shoplifting and returning items, the clothing would not be retagged neatly as though it had never left. It must be Mel or Tish because the items are always repriced and replaced exactly where they should be.''

Lucy clucked her tongue over the problem. ''And there isn't any reason for either girl to do this. That's what's vexing to me. I'm sure Carmine and Rona are very generous with Mel, and I think Claire's whole income goes on Tish's back. So what's the point?''

''There isn't any.'' Jane forgot and momentarily pursed her lips. She quickly reshaped her mouth into a half smile.

''I'm sure you'll find out what's going on and why,'' Cash said. ''Whoever is doing it will overlook something and indict herself.''

Jane glanced at him. In contrast to his matter-of-fact tone, his eyes were on her, and their intensity made her shiver. After their showdown, she was able to see Cash and their situation more clearly, but a new danger to her peace of mind had moved her to tears twice in the past hour. They were man, woman and child—but not husband, wife and daughter...and they never would be. She must always keep this clearly in mind or she might presume to behave inappropriately to their situation and bring embarrassment down on herself. A tremor of uneasiness quivered through her.

A polite tap on her back door startled Jane from her reading.

''Jane, got a minute?'' Rona peered through the screen to where Jane sat on her back porch.

''Sure. Want some iced tea?'' Jane put down her magazine.

''Desperately.'' Rona tugged at the midriff of her thin cotton blouse as though it were stuck to her skin. She followed Jane into the kitchen and took a glass of iced tea.

"I should have worn something cooler," Rona complained.

"Cooler?" Jane looked askance at Rona's neat blouse and shorts outfit.

"It's the color." Rona took a long swallow of the tea.

"That color is called pimento and it looks great on you."

"Yeah, but every time I look down I think of hot peppers and I feel hotter."

Jane shook her head and led Rona back out onto the relative coolness of the porch. They sat down across from each other.

"So what's up?" Rona asked, giving Jane a long assessing look.

"Just trying to stay cool." Jane waited, wondering what Rona had come to find out.

"Yeah, can you believe this heat?"

Jane shook her head. "Just go ahead and ask, Rona."

"What?" Rona asked innocently.

"Rona, you've got to get better at this. Usually you just dive in and say what you want. But if romantic gossip or matchmaking is your mission, you hem and haw. I'm too hot to go the long way around with you. So just ask."

Rona colored to a light shade of pimento. "Well, I hear that Cash spent the Fourth of July with you."

Jane's pulse jerked. "Cash spent the Fourth with me and my family. How did you hear about it?"

"Del Ray Martin saw him on your family's pontoon boat before the fireworks," Rona explained.

"I see. So what? Why shouldn't my family invite Cash to our picnic?"

"Well, Cash told his foreman that *you* had invited him."

"What does it matter if *I* invited him or Lucy did?" Jane couldn't keep a peevish tone out of her voice.

"Well, the whole town has been wondering how long the two of you would keep arguing over the baby before you gave in."

"Rona, I can't believe we're having this discussion!" Jane set her glass down with a thump.

"Well, you told me to just say it. And besides I thought you would have picked up on it by now."

"What exactly are people saying about me?" Jane looked at Rona grimly.

"Don't get so touchy. No one means any harm. It's just that Cash is so good-looking. Angie's such a little doll. And it would just be perfect if you two fell in love. The three of you would make such a great family!"

Jane felt like shouting with frustration. "You mean that people are sitting around actually discussing this?"

"Why, of course."

"There's nothing to it." Folding her arms, Jane flushed warm with embarrassment.

"You two are perfect for each other."

Before Jane could say her next word, the kitchen phone rang. With an exasperated shrug toward Rona, Jane hurried inside.

"Hello, Jane?"

Leaning against the kitchen wall, Jane gripped the receiver. "Roger?"

"Yeah, I wanted to call you sooner after the Jaycee's dinner, but I've been busy. Hey, how've you been?"

"So-so." She waited, not able to quell the anxiety bubbling up in her stomach over the gossip Rona had revealed. Why would Hallawell be calling her?

"I'm going to the Aquabat Show Friday night. Want to come? I'll take you out for supper after."

Waves of nervous tension surged through her. In her mind Rona's words repeated, and she saw Cash on the night of the Fourth leaning down to kiss her, then she heard his stumbling apology. Maybe a casual date would confound the gossip and blunt her sharpened feeling for Cash as well. "Friday night? Yes, I'll go." Her stomach clenched in a quick spasm.

"Great. Got to go. Pick you up Friday at six-thirty!" In the background over the phone she heard a door slam and voices.

Jane hung up. An emotion, just one step shy of panic, whirled through her. Looking up, she saw Rona, standing in the opposite doorway.

"You didn't just do what I thought you did, did you?"

Jane glanced all around the kitchen, everywhere but Rona's face. Now this would be all over town, too!

"Why would you go out with Hallawell? Carmine is concerned about him. Things might get out of hand."

"What *things* are you talking about?"

"Cash is well liked around here. The Langleys have owned property here for over fifty years. The Shores has given a lot of men work, not only for the summer, but on into the next year." Rona frowned, causing a deep horizontal line to crease her forehead. "I would have thought you'd be on Cash's side. Your families—"

"Rona, you beat everything." Jane frowned, mirroring Rona's expression. "A month ago you were the one who came to my shop, playing matchmaker—"

"I didn't have a crystal ball! I didn't know there would be trouble with Hallawell. I really don't think you should go out with him. The whole town will see you!"

Jane's mouth was dry, and her palms were wet. Cash will see you, Jane's inner voice paraphrased. She knew why she had accepted this date, a date she would never have contemplated otherwise. It was a gesture of cutting loose from her attraction to Cash, and it would supply the meddling gossips with something unexpected to stew about.

"I hope the town will enjoy it," Jane said sarcastically. "I have to do my part and give them some fresh material to work with—"

"Jane! You can't mean that!"

"Why not? It will be an unexpected episode in my story that the whole town can enjoy for several days afterward." Jane heard her own voice becoming shrill. "I'll thrive on walking in on discussions of why the Everett girl—"

Angie's crying announced the end of her nap and cut through Jane's tirade. "Coming, Angie," Jane called, turning to Rona. "I'll be right back."

"I'll be gone. And believe me when I say that no one will hear about this fit of irrational—"

"Then I'll take out an ad in the paper. That will prepare people, so they will remember to bring their cameras—"

"I can't believe this!" Rona called as she escaped through the back door, letting it bang behind her.

Jane marched through the living room and up the stairs to Angie. Finding out that the town had linked Cash romantically with her was too close to her own fear of Cash discovering her true feelings.

Two nights later Jane opened her door and, with an inward lurch of warning, took in the sight of Roger Hallawell. He was dressed nicely in black jeans and a charcoal-and-gray-striped shirt, open at the neck. But his self-satisfied smile promptly gave Jane the urge to slam the door in his face.

Instead she opened the door wider. "Come in."

He took one step inside and then one more, bringing himself within inches of her, crowding her. Slowly his gaze slid downward. "Like your outfit."

Jane had decided to wear a high-necked, light green blouse and darker green culottes. A more chaste outfit would have been hard to imagine. "Thanks."

"And these," he continued, lightly touching one of her gold teardrop earrings.

She fought the urge to slap his hand away. She stepped back from him. "Glad you like them." Jane turned, picked up two blue rectangular boat cushions and handed them to him. "Angie and I are ready."

He opened his mouth and closed it. Then he said in a slightly strained voice, "Didn't know this would be a double date."

"Oh, I couldn't leave Angie with a sitter. She'll love the Aquabat Show." *And it will keep this from feeling like a real date.*

In the two days since she had accepted this date, Jane had felt more like a traitor every minute. But she had been trapped in a limbo of indecision and inaction. She had not been able to bring herself to the point of picking up the phone to call and cancel till late this afternoon.

"Okay." He pursed his lips in a tight smile. Hanging the cushions over his shoulder, Roger held the front door open for her as she wheeled the stroller out.

They walked the two blocks down to Lake Street and stopped at the bleachers next to Yosacks's Restaurant. The Aquabat Water Ski Show took place every Wednesday, Friday and Sunday night, June through August. At 6:45 a good-sized crowd had already gathered at the cement waterside bleachers.

Unable to resist the buttery aroma, Jane stopped for popcorn and a large soda at the concession stand. She handed them to Roger and, parking the stroller near the railing along the street, she picked up Angie. "Where do you want to sit?" she asked.

He canvassed the bleachers. A hand waved from the crowd below them. Roger waved back, but he continued looking.

With Angie in her arms, she pointed to the shore where a double row of kids sat, all dressed in orange T-shirts that were emblazoned with "Camp Tomahawk."

"See the campers, Angie. They all want to get soaked, so they are sitting right on the shore. When you get about six years older, I'll let you sit there, too. Won't that be fun?"

Two gray-haired men stood up, and Roger returned their signal by holding up Jane's Coke. Then he hurried Jane and Angie down to them. Roger shook hands vigorously with both men.

"Hey there, don't maim me," one man said jokingly, pulling his hand away.

"Hi, Jane," the other man said. She had, of course, recognized John Banning, village councilman and Lucy's bridge partner, and acknowledged him with a friendly nod. He went on, "You know my wife, but do you know Sam Koch, county board supervisor?"

"Only by name. It's a pleasure to meet you, Mr. Koch," she said with a forced smile. When the introductions were finally complete, Roger lay down the two boat cushions and they sat on them.

Both couples had tried to mask their surprise at seeing Jane with Hallawell, but Jane had noted it, anyway. Already feeling uncomfortable about being with Roger, she had the distinct suspicion that this meeting had been pre-arranged to further Hallawell's well-known campaign to enter local government. What other reason would he drag them over to sit with two couples that were twice her age?

The two women made much of the baby, and Angie obligingly grinned, giggled and patty-caked for them.

"She always loves an audience," Jane said wryly, but with pride.

"Our grandson is skiing in the show this year," Mary Banning said.

"Oh, yes, I remember now," Jane said politely.

The conversation drifted away from Jane, then, in a muddle of names and connections. She was relieved when the microphone squawked to life, welcoming them to "The Oldest Water Ski Show North of Silver Springs, Florida."

She had seen this show at least once a year since she had been an infant. It was a forty-year tradition in Eagle Lake. First, the cast of amateur skiers were introduced. Many of the teens were local, but a few were from other states: Colorado, California, Pennsylvania.

She knew the agenda by heart. Tonight's show began, as they all did, with the bathing beauties in white swimsuits with red sequins, holding American flags while perched on the shoulders of young men on skis. Slalom and ski jumping events followed.

But the clowns, one young man always dressed like a girl in a mismatched, thrift-shop ensemble, and one like a bumpkin with his pants belted up under his armpits and a battered polka-dotted hat were her favorites. The two clowns, who both tried to take over the show, did pratfalls into the water, chased each other in a little round motorboat of bright orange, took the ski jump backward, and thoroughly delighted the crowd.

Angie could not understand the byplay, but she laughed and clapped along with the crowd. Through Angie, Jane enjoyed the show as though she had never seen it before and forgot that Hallawell sat beside her.

Intermission came with its appeal for donations, since the show was free to the public and staffed by volunteers.

The junior skiers went through the audience in twos. Jane glanced idly around and caught sight of Tish's tawny head nearby. She was sitting with a handsome boy. Was he the one Tish and Mel had argued over?

"Enjoying yourself?" Roger murmured, his lips much too close to the rim of her ear.

"I always do." The bucket for donations came by then. When Jane saw that Roger let it go by, she placed a wrinkled five-dollar bill inside.

Then she saw him—Cash. At first she thought her eyes were playing tricks on her, but it *was* Cash and he was heading right toward them. "Evening, everyone," Cash said with an easy grin. "How was the first part of the show?"

"The usual," Banning answered, looking uncomfortable.

Cash settled down on the other side of Jane. Her mouth was so dry she couldn't have answered, even if she had known what to say. Angie squealed a welcome to her uncle and broke away from Jane's restraining hands. Cash put down his drink and caught the little girl as she stumbled into his arms.

"She'll be walking soon," Mary Banning said. "Such a little doll."

"Langley, I was impressed by your model home yesterday. Thanks for inviting the village council out to see it firsthand," Banning said. Koch seconded the comment.

Jane observed Hallawell's spine stiffen. Without turning her head, she caught Cash's grim smile as he thanked both men.

"I'm sure Mr. Langley's model is quite impressive. But he would have been much wiser to build his development in a different location," Hallawell said smoothly.

"Where would you suggest, Hallawell?" Cash asked.

Angie stood on his lap. As he held her under her arms, she bent and straightened her knees in a bobbing dance. Cash gazed innocently at Hallawell.

"Some location that isn't as highly developed as this one already is," Hallawell continued, his neck reddening.

"The Shores will add an area of distinctive homes and enhance the tax base for Eagle Lake," Banning said firmly.

The announcer spoke up, silencing the debate. The show went on, dominated by the whine of the high-powered ski tow motors, the voice of the announcer, the clapping and cheering of the audience. Repeatedly the tow boat wakes surged up on shore, soaking the orange-shirted campers, who shrilled their appreciation.

All these noises rolled over Jane as she suffered the tension of sitting between Roger and Cash. She was intensely sorry she had come and hoped there would not be any unpleasantness when the show ended. She would never do anything this idiotic again.

Toddling back to Jane, Angie settled down in Jane's lap and drank her evening bottle. In spite of all the commotion and noise around, Angie fell asleep.

As the evening sky evolved from true blue to rose, amethyst, then deep cobalt blue, the show ended with its grand finale. Along the shore the orange-shirted campers squealed with satisfaction at their final drenching.

Jane felt like a canary, watching the barred door of the bird cage opening. At last she could go home and forget this dreadful evening.

"Why don't we all go to Kelly's for a bite?" Hallawell asked as they stood up to file out.

"Thanks, but I'm busy," Cash replied with thick irony.

The Bannings and Kochs made polite excuses.

"Okay, then I guess it's just you and me, Jane," Hallawell said.

Jane flushed. ''I have to get Angie home—''

''I'll carry her for you,'' Cash offered. She let him roll Angie into his arms.

Hallawell's face turned an alarming red. For a few seconds Jane feared a dreadful scene was about to be served up for all the town to see. But the presence of the two older couples seemed to restrain Hallawell. He said stiffly, ''Maybe some other time then.''

They walked up the steep steps. Without a parting word, Hallawell left Jane with Cash. She whispered a prayer of gratitude and promised never to do anything so stupid again.

Jane put the boat cushions and diaper bag in the seat of the stroller and pushed it home, while Cash, carrying the sleeping Angie, walked beside her.

Around their pocket of silence, the night was full of the summer sounds she knew so well: the laughter of young men and their dates as they walked up and down Main Street, and lonely young men in cars, revving the motors trying to catch the attention of girls who strolled in groups along the sidewalk. The sounds made her feel old and sidelined as though nothing she did would ever alter the way she felt about Cash or how he felt about her.

Now she saw the reason Hallawell had invited her out tonight. He had wanted to use her connection to Cash to lend more support to his campaign against Cash's subdivision. She admitted to herself that she had accepted out of anger toward the gossips as well as a desire to cut the invisible bond that persisted in connecting her emotionally to Cash.

She wanted to thank him for extricating her from an uncomfortable situation, but could not think of a way to say it that wouldn't make her sound like an idiot. And she wondered how he had known she needed to be rescued.

Who had told him? Uneasily she waited to see what Cash would say to her when they reached home.

At her back door, he watched while she maneuvered the stroller onto the back porch and unlocked her door. Then he laid the sleeping baby into her arms.

"Jane?"

"Yes?"

"Will you drive to Wausau tomorrow with me?"

"Wausau?" The crickets keened incessantly in the warm night. Jane brushed away a gray moth that had flown toward her eyes.

"Yes, I've been meaning to look at two Frank Lloyd Wright houses there. I thought you'd like to come along."

"I…" She was grateful that he had not said anything to embarrass her more than she already was about this evening, but she couldn't understand what had prompted this invitation.

"I took the liberty of asking Lucy to watch Angie for us."

"Oh?" She still hadn't a clue what was going on.

"See you in the morning then. Early."

She watched him walk away in the glow from the alley's street lamp. Saturday was the day he usually visited Angie. Why would he want to leave Angie behind? She quelled twin rushes of exhilaration and anxiety.

As Cash walked away, he pushed down the panic, still bouncing around in his stomach. Even though he had been forewarned by Rona, the shock of seeing Jane with Angie in her arms, sitting next to another man was still with him. He wouldn't let it happen again. Years of business had taught him that taking the offense was always better than a superb defense. Tomorrow he would launch his offense.

Chapter Eight

Cash helped Jane into his blue Jeep. As he glanced back to Lucy's doorway, he watched Angie in her great-grandmother's arms, waving bye-bye to them. At this gesture of affection, Cash was swept by a fierce tenderness. He wanted to rush back and scoop up the little pink bundle of ruffles and sweetness. But he had something important to accomplish this day, something that he had to do for Angie. He shut Jane's door and took in the dismal sight of the rain streaming down the Jeep's sides, making vertical lines in its coat of mud. The elements were against him in today's campaign.

As he slid behind the steering wheel, he realized Jane had picked up the feeling of the gloomy, wet day. Her expression was closed. She had dressed in a gray blouse, worn jeans and old sneakers. Even her lustrous curls had been covered with a drab green, hooded slicker. He, on the other hand, had dressed with care in crisp, new navy slacks and a maroon shirt. If he couldn't lighten her mood, it would make everything harder for him.

"Think it will be any better in Wausau?" he asked

hopefully. Distant rumbling punctuated his words ominously.

"I don't think the sky will be any bluer in Wausau. And the tourists will be flocking to town, and Mel and Tish will be swamped." She stopped and heaved a deep sigh. "But I need a day out of town." Then she looked at him. There was uncertainty in her eyes. Was she wondering why he was taking her away for a day alone?

"I'll second that," he said cautiously. "I need a day away, too."

She nodded glumly.

"At least it's cool, instead of steaming," he pointed out.

"Until the sun burns off the clouds."

"Thank you for that cheery prediction." She was in a "mood" all right. He tried to think of a way to trigger the Everett good humor he knew was waiting only a phrase away. Today he needed to put her in the right mood for his plan to work.

A strained stiffness perched between them as he drove out onto the highway. How could he launch a sustained, friendly conversation with her? In an effort to fill up the emptiness, he switched on the radio. The local station announced that rain was expected all morning, but to look forward to clearing and warmer temperatures for the afternoon.

"Should I assume he's wrong, just because I agree with it?" she said drily.

Cash shrugged and watched her shift in her seat as though she were wearing starched underwear. The station began to play a raucous country-western tune about a cheating man. He snapped off the radio. "Oh, sorry," he said instantly contrite. "Were you listening to it?"

"What was playing?"

He snorted in amusement. "I guess I didn't need to

apologize.'' He paused. ''Jane, you've had your size-eight mystery, and I've had my troubles this summer. Can't we try to enjoy getting away for a day?''

Slowly she gave him a half smile. ''Why not?''

He smiled broadly in return, relieved he'd chosen the right words. Outside, the rain slowed to a sprinkle. They rode in comfortable quiet until they came upon a lakeside restaurant. ''I didn't have time to eat. How about breakfast?'' he invited.

At her nod, he pulled into the parking lot. Inside the rustic log cabin restaurant, they sat on a screened-in porch, overlooking a small lake. They ate lumberjack-sized pancakes with warm boysenberry and maple syrups.

''I like to watch the circles rain makes hitting the water,'' he said, spearing another sausage link with his fork. The temperature still hovered in the low seventies. The fresh-rain scent was clean in his nostrils.

''I know. I like the sound, too. Kind of a restful plunk-plunk. Great breakfast.''

He nodded. ''We'll have to remember this place.''

All night Jane had tossed and turned, trying to figure out why Cash had invited her today. Now she felt her initial apprehensions dissolving. It might be possible for Cash and her to have a pleasant day together without any negative repercussions. She would have to careful, however, to draw the invisible line between her infatuation with Cash and reality. She took a swallow of coffee.

By the time Jane got back into the Jeep, the constraint between them had almost vanished.

Cash asked, ''How much do you know about Frank Lloyd Wright?''

''Why don't you ask me how much I want to know about Frank Lloyd Wright?''

''Oh, she's in a sassy mood. I shouldn't have fed her

breakfast.'' Grinning, he slammed her door and went around to his side. ''Did you know, Miss Everett, that Frank Lloyd Wright was born in southwestern Wisconsin? Near Madison there's an organization for architects interested in Wright, called the Talisien Center.''

''I didn't realize Wisconsin was so into architecture.''

''It is. Do you enjoy touring old homes?''

She wrinkled her nose at him. ''I live in one, remember?''

''You live in a comfortable thirties' house. I'm talking old, older than yours by about fifty to seventy-five years.''

''In that case, I must say yes.''

The pause in the rainstorm ended. Sheets of water enveloped the Jeep. The windshield wiper dashed the rain back and forth frantically.

Jane watched tensely as the storm devoured all Cash's attention. He drove sitting forward, trying to see the road ahead clearly. The water pounded on the Jeep's fiberglass roof.

''Do you think it would be better if we pulled off?'' Her voice was muffled by the din overhead.

''I'm afraid if I pull off just anywhere, I'll make us a target for someone else just pulling off,'' he raised his voice to be heard. ''I can still see the center line—barely.''

As suddenly as the downpour began, it ended. Cash whistled in relief.

Jane relaxed in her seat. ''You can say that again. I thought we were going to end up swimming all the way to Wausau. So how did you get interested in Wright?''

''Your grandfather was the one who got me started—''

''My grandfather? When?''

''I got the mumps when I was twelve, and he visited me with a thick scrapbook of photos he'd taken of homes all over the Midwest. The ones I liked the best were Wrights.''

"I had forgotten Grandpa's scrapbooks. Why were Wright's the most interesting to you?''

Jane, now at ease, let Cash ramble on about his favorite subject. They sped over the remaining miles. The rain still spotted the front glass, but was no real hindrance.

They stopped at the Marathon County Historical Museum near downtown Wausau to get more information. When Cash led the way back down the steps of the museum, the rain was only lightly falling, but the lady at his side still needed protection. He popped open the large red-and-white-striped golf umbrella he had brought along. Holding the umbrella over them with one hand, he read aloud from the walking-tour brochure in the other. "The most notable architect working here between 1906-1920 was George Washington Maher—"

"Not Wright?''

He glanced at her and watched her push back her hood and shake her head, making her golden-red curls bounce. The vibrancy of the color made the gray sky look grayer. He had to force his eyes away from her brightness.

"No, we'll see his two houses later, okay?''

She grinned at him. "Okay.''

He read on, "Of the Chicago-based Prairie School, Maher expounded the 'motif-rhythm theory,' the combination of natural and geometric elements to unify a particular design.'' He lowered the brochure. "Up for it?''

"Lead on.'' They were in the heart of the old city. Traffic was light but steady on the one-way, maple-lined street.

Under the dome of the shared umbrella, he took her arm and led her to the corner. "Look across the street. The A. P. Woodson house, 1914, Maher,'' he read from the guide. "What do you think?''

With obvious deliberation, she studied the two-story, ivy-covered brick house. "The chimney…"

"Yes, quite unique. Three connected, diamond-shaped stacks."

As casually as he could, he draped his free arm around her shoulders. Out of the corner of his eye, he saw her cheeks warm to a pleasant pink. He could make her react to him. He felt a surge of power.

Afraid of reading more into his closeness than he intended, Jane averted her face. Did he consider an arm around her as merely a friendly gesture, unlike a kiss? How should she react?

"Come on." Under the umbrella, he tugged her along. "This is the Underwood-Hagge house, 1894, neoclassical revival. Look at the symmetrical peaks of the roof."

Jane liked the stately home with a full porch across its front. Three peaks dominated the house, like a castle. "It looks like a perfect place to dream away a rainy afternoon. Can we go in?" She imagined an alcove high up in the house and a little girl like Angie, only several years older, reading quietly there.

"No, sorry. All these homes are privately owned except for the museum." He turned and looked directly into her eyes. She had forgotten how devastating the blue "windows of his soul" could be. She suppressed the urge to touch his curly eyelashes but she could not turn from his penetrating gaze.

She felt his fingers ruffle through her hair. Wondering why he had touched her, she looked up at him. Without warning, he brushed his lips over hers in the gentlest of kisses. In a rush, she relived the first kiss he had given her. Once again, he enticed her with his tentativeness. The web his lips spun around her made it impossible to call a halt to his tender encroachment.

Before she could respond in any way, he straightened and nudged her toward the next house on the self-guided tour.

He proceeded to show her the Claire B. Bird, 1910 Tudor revival; the Ely Wright house, an 1881 Italianate; and the Michael Hurly house, 1899 Queen Anne. The umbrella shielded them from the cars, whooshing by on the wet street. She accompanied him slightly dazed, wondering what had triggered his kissing her today. She couldn't believe it was her ridiculous date with Hallawell, but what had changed him? The pause in front of each house was an opportunity for another touch, another kiss. Jane found her blood pulsing at an unusual cadence.

She tried to study each house. The houses truly were beautiful, but his magnetism and her inner confusion robbed her of concentration. Her emotions ran rampant. She asked herself why had he begun kissing her, and why was she letting him, without asking his reasons? Could it be possible that after all these years, he had finally noticed her as a woman? Was his heart beginning to thaw? *Sweet Lord, have my prayers been answered at last?*

"There are more," he said in a husky voice, "but maybe you'd like to see the Wright houses now?"

The red-and-white umbrella over them, the street sounds of cars whizzing by in the distance; closer cars rattling over low manholes and the old brick street; the puddle under their feet—all the calls back to reality—summoned her. "You're the tour guide," she managed to say lightly.

They walked back to the Jeep. He opened the door for her, and when she stepped in front of him, he came closer and wrapped his arms around her from behind. Her head fit just under his chin, and she could feel his breath against her cheek.

"Are all your tours this stimulating?" she asked, drawing on her humor to remind him of their purpose. By way of a reply he nudged her up onto the seat and closed the door with a playful thump.

In silence they drove slowly past the two homes designed by Wright. But since both houses were in quiet residential areas and privately occupied, they didn't stop or get out. She waited in vain for him to tell her what he was thinking and why he had kissed her.

Though Jane's response to him was all that he had hoped for, Cash refused to identify the sensations he was experiencing. In any negotiations, he had learned he must keep a clear head. Staring straight ahead, he asked, "How would you like to do something unexpected?"

"I think we already have," she replied softly.

He looked at her, then, and smiled. He loved it when she showed her resemblance to her grandmother, especially with her openness and wit. He knew she would be delighted with this side trip because he knew Lucy would have liked it, and Jane was so much like Lucy.

He drove them west of Wausau, out among the hay and cornfields. The rain had stopped, but the clouds hadn't broken yet. Before he'd left home this morning, Cash had tried to plan ahead how to say what he wanted to Jane. The first kiss he had given her had been a trial. He'd hoped she would react to him. But concentrating on what her response to him might have been had left him completely unprepared for his own new desire for Jane. It burst over and through him. Kissing Jane was sweet, unbelievably sweet.

"The hay is an interesting shade of green," she murmured.

He nodded. "The color would look good on you." He was gratified to see her cheeks become rosy at his compliment.

"The Wright houses were hard to see clearly." She looked out the window away from him.

"That fits his idea that the structure should blend with its location and its purpose. Therefore, a house shouldn't stand out from its settings."

"I see."

He made a broad turn off the state highway onto a county road, and she looked at him questioningly.

He grinned. Her warm, golden-red beauty lit up the dim interior of the Jeep. "Our next destination is out of the way."

She raised an eyebrow. "Out in the cornfields?"

He nodded. The Jeep followed the route of the county road that twisted around and rolled up and down the gentle hills left by prehistoric glaciers. At last he turned off the road into a small, mowed and fenced square of lawn. A small marker stood in the middle.

Rolling down her window, Jane read aloud:

"GEOLOGICAL MARKER

This spot in section fourteen, in the town of Rietbrock, Marathon County, is the exact center of the northern half of the Western Hemisphere. It is here that the ninetieth meridian of longitude bisects the forty-fifth parallel of latitude, meaning it is exactly half the way around the earth from Greenwich, England. Marathon County Park Commission."

She turned to him with an amused expression.

"It's not every day," he observed laconically, "that one can be at the absolute center of things."

"Shall we put our feet on the exact spot?" Her brows rose with sudden high spirits.

"Thought you'd never ask."

They scrambled out into the mist. As they hurried to the marker, the saturated sod squished underfoot. They both put a foot on the small metal circle that marked the spot, denoting the exact center of the Northwestern World.

Jane grinned at him, showing her lightened mood. He had been right about her reaction to this. Again he felt that everything he wanted from today would go well.

Two fat raindrops plopped onto his forehead. Then the onslaught of rain came down as though a faucet had been turned on. Cash lifted Jane up and ran, carrying her to the Jeep. He lunged inside, slamming the door behind them.

Still in his arms, she faced him in a convoluted posture, the steering wheel behind her and her legs over the center gearshift. A bead of rain slid down her forehead and then dripped off her nose. A second one followed the first.

As the third ran down, Cash grinned and kissed her nose. He chuckled. ''You're raining on me, Red.''

Embarrassed, she moved to the passenger seat. When she watched his face draw nearer to hers, she almost pulled back. Instead, feeling his uneven breathing on her cheek, she tilted her head back slightly, inviting him closer.

The rush of warm breath as he exhaled tipped the balance, making a chill arc through her. His lips roamed over her face, enticing but innocent. They demanded nothing from her, took nothing from her. Instead, she reaped the closeness, his regard for her. Each touch of his lips felt like a gift bestowed.

Her hands found the sides of his head, and she drew his face to hers in a renewed embrace. She pressed her lips to his skin, so warm and masculine.

She felt him kiss the tip of her nose, then her closed eyes, and finally he satisfied her longing by caressing her lips with his. Her heart sighed.

''Jane, Jane, I,'' he murmured.

A loud bawl interrupted him.

Jane drew back sharply from him. "Oh, for heaven's sake," she said, putting her forehead into her hands.

Two cows had their heads over the fence and were only inches from Cash's window. Their warm breath fogged the Jeep's glass.

Jane hung her head farther and stifled a moan. Just as her mother's phone call had, the night of the Fourth, this intrusion snatched away the intimacy of the moment. She was sure he had been about to tell her why he was kissing her.

Cash's face became a mask. He put the Jeep into reverse. Mud flew up as he backed out onto the county road again.

Jane stared out her window.

The cloudburst slowed and gushed by turns as they drove down the meandering road over the green, rolling hills. At a crossroads, the pink neon sign at Bud and Pearl's Café beckoned them. Jane touched his arm. "Want to try it?"

"Have you been in there before?" He asked with surprise.

"No, but I have found in Wisconsin that these little places always have the best food."

"It looks like a dive." The building appeared to be about fifty years old and to last have been painted the year Jane was born.

"It's not a dive. Pearl wouldn't preside over a dive. I'll grant you it isn't a croissant or quiche type of place. Are you game or not?"

He studied the old restaurant. A number of muddy trucks crowded around the small, roofed entrance.

Jane's stomach rumbled aloud, and she grinned. "Well?" she challenged him.

With a shrug Cash gave in. Under the large umbrella again, he led her inside, past the pinball machines, to a booth along the wall. The interior of Bud and Pearl's did not disappoint his preconception. Its walls were painted with gray enamel. The floor was a speckled, black-and-white, industrial-grade asphalt tile which would probably last far into the next century.

There was no decor to be seen: a few booths, counter and stools in a long, narrow room. The pinball machines near the entrance were the only splashes of color. Two ceiling fans with lights were the only illumination and ventilation. Several local patrons, who were all seated along the counter, watched the newcomers with politely veiled interest.

Jane and Cash sat down in one of the booths and silently read the day's menu, which was on a blackboard behind the counter.

After eyeing them discreetly for about three minutes, a plump woman in jeans and a gray UW sweatshirt came over. "Hi, what'll it be?"

"I'll have the hot plate special," Jane said cheerfully.

Cash pursed his lips. "I'll try the Reuben."

The woman nodded and walked through the curtained doorway that obviously led to the kitchen. Cash heard her clearly tell Pearl their order.

"You should have gotten the hot plate special," Jane said quietly.

"You may regret it." He glanced around once again.

"I don't think so. Use your nose," Jane suggested.

"What?"

"You've been so busy looking the place over that you missed the most important element. Haven't you sniffed the delicious aroma emanating from the kitchen?"

Only then did he become aware of the homey fragrance in the air. "Roast beef," he said.

She nodded, grinning. "I think we hit a good one."

The waitress came back with tableware and beverages. Then she delivered several plates to the men at the counter. After a few minutes she returned to their booth with two overflowing platters.

Cash's plate was covered by a huge pumpernickel Reuben sandwich and a mound of creamy potato salad. Jane's was heaped with a hot roast beef sandwich and mashed potatoes, liberally doused with deep brown gravy. It was obvious that nothing on either plate had come from the contents of a premeasured box.

Jane sighed with satisfaction. "Hold a piece of rhubarb pie for me."

"Make that two," Cash added quickly. The waitress grinned and made a notation on their check. She turned back to the kitchen.

"I don't know why I said that," Jane whispered. "I don't know how I'll make it through this, much less have room for dessert."

"Don't worry, Jane. I'll do everything I can to help you in this challenge."

Protectively Jane covered her plate with both hands. "Don't even try it."

The food was down-home delicious. It had been a long time since breakfast. The two of them didn't waste eating time with talk. Two pieces of rhubarb pie appeared at their elbows. Though he felt uncomfortably full, he eyed Jane's pie teasingly. When he aimed his greedy fork toward her piece of pie, she—just as she had warned him—slapped his hand away.

When all their plates were clean, Cash sat back. Now as he looked around, he noted the touches that made the long room homey. The sampler over the blue gingham curtains to the kitchen read: "Home is where you hang your heart," and some child's drawings were tacked onto the wall behind the counter. Again he was struck by Jane's ability to make the mundane things of life interesting, enjoyable. He settled the modest bill, and they walked out to the Jeep. Outside, the clouds were as thick as they had been at dawn. Cash turned on the ignition and headed for home.

Jane hummed along with the country station on the radio. While she listened to the lyrics about broken hearts, trucking men and true love, she took inventory of this unusual day. She had toured streets adorned by classic homes, then had eaten lunch at Bud and Pearl's. She had been alternately sprinkled and doused by rain and had shared kisses under a red-and-white umbrella. She had stood at the center of the Northwestern World, chaperoned by two cows. What a country-western ballad that would make!

Closing her eyes, she leaned back. The hum of the Jeep's tires lulled her to sleep.

The startling noise of pounding rain over her head woke Jane. She sat up, slightly disoriented.

"It's another cloudburst," Cash muttered.

In spite of the slashing wipers, she couldn't see through the front windshield. She sat up tensely. "Cash, I—"

"I'm going to have to pull off, but I don't want to just pull off on the shoulder, it's too dangerous."

For the next few minutes, the Jeep crawled along the highway till Cash finally glimpsed an exit ramp to their right. He followed the lane cautiously till he pulled into what appeared to be a parking lot. It was impossible to see whether it was a business or a public wayside. He stopped. Jane reached for him.

"We're okay," he said, grasping her hand.

"I don't remember a summer where I've been so frightened by the weather. It makes me worry about Angie and Lucy—"

"They'll be fine. Lucy's cottage is one of the safest places Angie could be."

"I know, but this weather still worries me. Storm after storm. What is it building up to?"

In response to her worried tone, he took her other hand and tugged her toward him.

Jane knew she should—for her own peace of mind—resist this closing of the gap she had tried to maintain between them. Cash leaned closer to her. She smelled the rain in his hair and clothing and bent to claim his mouth.

Their first kisses of the day had been hesitant. This time when their mouths met, she felt like she was being swept away by a flash fire. Once again his lips passed over her brow, eyelids and throat. She whispered his name.

"Jane." He pulled her against him fiercely. He froze.

Feeling the abrupt change in Cash, she surfaced from the sensations that had overwhelmed her. "Cash?"

His arms around her had become protective. "The rain has slowed. There are two trucks parked near us. They'll be pulling out soon, and they'll be able to see us."

Jane looked around. The rain had lessened to a steady wash over the windows. She could see that they were parked at the edge of a gas station.

Cash started the Jeep again and they drove back onto the highway in silence. *It's now or never.* Everything he could surmise from her response to him today said, "green light." It was time to put over the deal.

"Jane," Cash said.

Momentarily Jane feared he would apologize once again for kissing her. She held her breath.

"Jane, I've been thinking. We should get married."

For a few trembling moments, she doubted her ears. "Married?"

"Yes." He took a deep breath. The memory of seeing her with Hallawell last night had struck too close to what he feared. It was preposterous to believe that Jane wouldn't marry. And the thought of another man, living with Jane, acting as Angie's father, filled him with an intensity of panic he had never experienced before.

He continued smoothly, "I've decided that it would be a good idea. Angie needs a family—a mother and a father—not just a guardian and an uncle. We could marry, and I'd build us a home at The Shores. I suppose you could call it a marriage of convenience, but I believe it would work out very well. What do you think?" His confidence had grown as he had explained his plan. Surely she would agree. Her response to him today had been more positive than he would have predicted.

Jane trembled with a surge of anger stronger than any she had ever felt before. For uncounted moments, she was unable to do anything except hold out against the urge to scream her fury at Cash.

Finally she surfaced from her emotional tempest. She became aware that Cash was driving through another steady rain, going north on the state highway toward Eagle Lake. What had she expected from Cash? He'd never said one word of love. She should have realized by now that only with Angie did he allow emotion. For a few moments she had thought he'd lowered the staunch walls around his heart. *Dear God, how could I have been so wrong?*

She took a deep breath to still her lingering inner chaos. Without looking at Cash, which would only have stoked the flames of her anger all over, she said with deadly calm, "No, thank you. I don't care to be a convenience to anyone."

Chapter Nine

Inside a large tent in the city park, Jane smiled down at little twin girls with identical brown bangs. They shyly looked up. Both wore gold lamé dresses much too large for them, old fox fur boas and pillbox hats with nets askew. "How about lipstick?" Jane asked, the golden tube already poised in her hand.

They nodded and submitted with serious concentration.

"Ready to show your mother?"

Without speaking, they turned and stumbled in their too-large, high-heeled shoes out the door of the tent. Their mother waited outside with a camera. Jane's assistant, Mel, cheerfully posed the duo. When the photo opportunity was exhausted, Mel and Jane helped the girls out of their finery. With shy waves, the twins left for the puppet show, which was already in progress at the far end of Tory Park.

"They're the last." Mel sighed. "Now I have to go sell hot dogs and then help with the cleanup afterward."

"Better you than me," Jane said. "I only have to rebox the clothes for use next year."

Mel hurried away, and Jane, suddenly feeling fatigued

from a very busy morning, stretched her arms over her head and scanned the park. Under the tall oaks and ever-greens of the city park were booths, very messy booths. "Art in the Park" was never neat. Wood-block sculptures, Jell-O finger paintings, pinecone-and-peanut-butter bird feeders, necklaces of dyed macaroni, littered the tables and benches and hung from low branches. All these would be claimed by the young artists after the puppet show, the grand finale. The aroma of freshly popped popcorn had taunted her all morning and now her empty stomach growled. She hadn't had time for breakfast.

At the face-painting area across from Jane's tent, Lucy, dressed as a clown in a paint-smeared smock, finished another rainbow on a child's chubby cheek. Lucy waved to Jane over the toddler's head. Jane waved back. Then she went inside her drab green tent and began sorting the clothing into categories.

"Hi."

She turned to see Cash in the tent's entrance. Within seconds she felt her neck and face blazing with her anger. Her heart beat in a dizzy tempo. Stinging words bubbled up, but she tightened her mouth to hold them back. She finally asked brusquely, "Where's Angie?"

"With your dad at the puppet show."

"I see." She wanted to know how Angie had liked her first art fair, but she would ask her father later. She wanted nothing to pass between Cash and her—not even polite conversation.

"Like your outfit."

"Really?" she said without expression. To suit her volunteering job, she had dressed herself as a twenties flapper in a beige dress and matching cloche hat that had belonged to her great-grandmother. She had added many long strands of fake pearls, and gold-sequined garters held up her knee-high hose.

"It's you all right." His words sounded forced, and she noted the dark smudges under his eyes.

But she turned away from him and started to fold dresses into a huge cardboard box.

He persisted. "Are you busy for lunch?"

"I don't have time for lunch. I have to get back to the shop. Saturday is my busiest day."

"How about Sunday brunch, then?"

His voice grated on her nerves. Provoked, she looked up. Their eyes connected and sparred. She knew she would have to see him tomorrow because he would arrive for his visit with Angie, but she wanted to accept nothing from him and give him nothing but the barest politeness. The memory of his proposal washed through her painfully. "I'll leave Angie with my parents. Why don't you stop over there after lunch tomorrow?"

"Jane, I don't understand why a simple proposal—"

She cut him off. "That's right you don't understand, and I don't feel like explaining it to you. My mother is working at the shop for me. I have to get back to relieve her."

He left without saying a word, snapping the flap closed behind himself.

She clenched her teeth. Strong emotions coursed through her in wave after wave. Furious with him, she attacked the piles of clothes, sorting and folding, then taping and labeling the boxes.

When she finished, she walked over to the park's bath house, which was the changing area for volunteers.

Retrieving her clothes from a locker, Jane stepped into one of the curtained cubicles. Carefully she hung her strings of pearls onto the wall hook and then undid the hook and eyes down the side of her flapper dress and slid off her garters.

As she slipped into butterscotch crepe slacks, a taupe silk shell and an ivory jacket for work, she simmered with outrage. Trying to calm herself enough to face customers and her mother's perceptive eyes, she fluffed her hair and outlined her lips with coral lipstick.

Jane hurried down the block to her shop and entered from the rear. Tish was with a customer, but paused to tell Jane that Aunt Marge had driven out of town before the traffic had been unleashed after the puppet show.

Another two women walked in. Jane sighed inwardly. She wanted to get away from everyone, but she went forward to greet the customers. At their question Jane directed them to the racks of the few remaining shorts and blouses, then waited by the register. Within minutes they both picked out several blouses and shorts combinations and returned to Jane.

"My, that was quick," Jane commented as she began the process of tearing off the tags.

"We told our husbands that during vacation this year, they'd have to take a turn doing the laundry at the Laundromat," one of them said.

"Yes, and we may do this every year." The other one chuckled. "They managed to destroy one load completely, so we get to buy a new summer wardrobe!"

"We still haven't figured out how they did it!" her friend explained cheerfully.

"Jane!" Lucy called as she entered by the rear door.

Jane's spirits sank lower. *I can't face Grandmother. She'll know something is dreadfully wrong.*

Jane finished the sale, then walked reluctantly downstairs, closing the door behind her. There was no escaping the inevitable.

At the bottom of the staircase, Lucy, now transformed from a clown to a chic lady in ivory cotton slacks and a blue silk tunic, waited with a large, white paper bag in her hand. The unmistakable scent of ground beef and fries emanated from it. "I was in the mood for saturated fat today. I hope you are, too."

"I didn't expect to see you." Jane, trying to smooth the strain out of her voice, cleared one side of her desk, and Lucy brought out thick hamburgers and fries. They sat down and faced each other.

"So why did you tell Cash he could see Angie at your parents' cottage tomorrow? What's happened?"

Jane tried to deflect her grandmother's words by teasing, "I'm so glad you are capable of subtlety."

"Well?"

Stalling while she thought of her answer, Jane took a bite of her burger. She barely tasted it, and her empty, nervous stomach moved her near nausea.

Under her grandmother's thoughtful scrutiny, Jane suddenly wanted to cry. She battled herself and controlled the urge. Someone had told her once, Be careful what you pray for, you might get it. She had once prayed fervently that Cash would ask her to be his wife. Now he had, and she felt as if she were chewing a mouthful of ashes. She put down her sandwich and wiped her fingertips with a napkin. "I can't seem to get my emotions under control today."

"What happened in Wausau?"

Jane shook her head. "Please let's talk abut something else." Her love was a foolish hope, and not even to her grandmother could she reveal her emotions for Cash.

"About Angie?"

Jane wanted to shout, *No! About Cash. I love him, but he doesn't love me!* Tears did come to Jane's eyes then. They ran freely, and she wiped them away with her hands till Lucy handed her a flowered handkerchief from her pocket.

In a rush of sensation Jane remembered Cash's kisses as the final cloudburst had shielded them from the world. In that private moment she had thought she and Cash had finally come together. But in light of his subsequent proposal, his kisses had only amounted to a test drive of a wife he intended to negotiate for.

"Is there anything I can do for you, dear?"

Jane sucked in a deep breath and resolutely picked up her sandwich. "I just miss Dena so," Jane spoke her only alibi. "I'll be all right."

Lucy gave her a look of heart-rending concern. "Yes, dear, I pray so."

The final evening hours of Crazy Days, Eagle Lake's sidewalk sale came at last. Main Street had been blocked off with wooden barricades. The stores had all moved their sale merchandise out onto the sidewalk and the street itself. Though the month was July, Christmas lights had been wrapped around the city light poles. Shoppers milled around in the street and huddled around the store displays. Two clowns circulated through the crowd, amusing the children and giving away candy. Jane sat at a card table in front of her shop.

"Hi, Tish. Hi, Mel." Three teenage girls stopped to browse. Hearing *Hi, Tish. Hi, Mel* one more time made Jane's jaw muscles clamp together painfully. Recalling the agony of the tension headache she had after the trip to Wausau, she consciously tightened and relaxed her muscles from the top of her head to the end of her spine.

"Miss Everett, is there anything here that my mom would like for her birthday next week?"

Jane opened her eyes. Del Ray Martin's daughter had

unhooked herself from her two friends, who were giggling with Tish.

Jane stood up and picked out a few bright scarves that would suit Del Ray's taste. The girl chose a bright-red-and-black scarf from Jane's selection. Jane let Mel take care of the sale.

One more hour, just one more hour and I can close. Shutting her eyes once more against the garish lights and the noisy combination of carnival and lounge music, she leaned back against her display window.

"Hi, I like your jewelry."

Jane opened her eyes. "Hi, Rona. Glad you like it." Rona was referring to the fact that some shop owners were dressed up as though it were Halloween to add more color to Crazy Days. Jane had decided that costuming for the event did not fit the mystique of her or her shop.

But over the past three years, she had collected a fine assortment of junk jewelry. So on this the final day of Crazy Days, she and her two assistants sported a rainbow of gaudy, plastic bracelets, rings, necklaces and earrings. Tish wore all shades of blue and purple. Mel had chosen reds and pinks, while Jane had opted for white, silver and green.

"How do you like my specs?" Jane asked, tapping her frames.

"They really do it. Whatever *it* is." Rona grinned.

This year Jane had added the pièce de résistance, three pairs of fifties-style glasses, without lenses, that she had picked up at a flea market. The pair Jane was wearing was silver and shaped like butterfly wings and encrusted with rhinestones.

"Did you hear?" Rona asked conspiratorially.

"What?"

"The word is that after dark last night Hallawell's crew dumped off trash at the entrance of The Shores."

Jane made a face. "Isn't this getting a little childish?"

"I agree. Carmine says some of Cash's crew have had it."

Jane shook her head. "What will be, will be." Her words were casual, but a tremor of warning shivered through her. She sent up a silent prayer for a peaceful end to these hostilities.

Rona gestured toward the two circular racks and one table that Jane had moved outside. "Is there anything I should buy now, or should I wait till your Labor Day fifty-percent-off, final-summer-clearance sale?"

"Take a look at the swimsuits. There are a few left you might like." Jane pressed her fingers to her temples.

Rona nodded and began intently going through the rack nearest her daughter.

"Bye, Tish. Bye, Mel." The latest trio of teens departed.

Then two high school boys paused, obviously eyeing Tish and Mel.

I will never again hire teens to work during the summer, Jane vowed silently. "May I help you gentlemen find something?" she asked pointedly.

"Uh, no, just looking." The youngest of the two blushed. They left quickly. Tish gave their backs a look that stated they weren't in her league, anyway.

Carnival music from the nearby park floated to them. The band at the Wildcat 'n' Lace, a lounge restaurant across the street competed with the carnival's taped calliope music. Every time its door swung in or out, rock music with an overpowering bass pounded, giving a throbbing background beat to the evening's atmosphere. The painful pulsing at Jane's temples picked up the same rhythm. She observed a few of the carpenters and a plasterer who worked for Cash go into the lounge.

A sudden gust of wind tossed dust up. Jane sneezed.

"Bless you, my dear," Lucy said.

"Grandmother! Where did you come from?"

"I planned my route carefully, so I could sneak up on you." Lucy had "dressed" for Crazy Days. This annual event always sparked her wearing of an outrageous lime-green-and-white sundress from the seventies.

"How long will this dress last you?" Jane asked, shaking her head.

"I know. It's so delightfully atrocious I look forward to wearing it every year! I can't help it if I'm still crazy after all these years. And you should talk! Look at those glasses!"

Jane posed artfully. "I think I should have worn them for the portrait, don't you?"

"What portrait?" Tish asked, standing at Jane's elbow.

"Never you mind, young lady," Lucy said primly. "Jane, please have someone take a picture of you in those. My cousin Dulcy had a pair just like that in 1953. I'd love to send a photo to her of you wearing them."

Tish turned her back and walked away.

Jane rolled her eyes. "I'll try, but I won't promise."

"All right. But getting back to business, I really came in to settle some of the final arrangements for your parents' party. We only have a little over a week, you know."

"I know." The wind gusted again, and Jane winced at the escalating ache at the top of her skull.

Lucy frowned at the sky. "If I'm not mistaken, we're going to get another storm tonight."

"I'd bet money on it," Rona said, stepping close to Lucy. "Here, Jane, I'll take this one. Would you put it on my account?"

In a loud stage whisper to Jane, Lucy said, "I don't think I would let her charge anything. She looks shifty to me."

Jane smiled and took the mocha-brown-and-tan swimsuit from Rona. Sitting back down at the card table, she began writing out a receipt.

"What did you decide on for the entrée for Phil and Marge's anniversary party?" Rona asked Lucy. "Veal *picotta* or prime rib?"

"I decided on the prime rib. I really wanted crab linguini, but I decided to be traditional. My son would prefer straight steak and potatoes."

Jane handed Rona her receipt and bagged the suit.

"Jane, you'll be asking Cash to be your escort, won't you?" Rona asked.

Jane frowned. Her neck tightened another degree.

"Oh!" Rona put a hand to her mouth. "I did it again, didn't I? Stuck my nose into your business. On that note, I'll move on." Rona walked briskly away.

As Jane's gaze followed Rona walking down the street, she saw three men who worked for Hallawell push their way into the lounge across the street.

Voices from behind made her look over her shoulder. Two tall high school boys had stopped to chat with Tish. Mel, with naked envy in her eyes, glared at them. Jane turned back to her grandmother. She told Lucy in an undertone, "I don't know how much more I can stand of 'cruising' teens. There were a few earlier, but tonight since around six, it's been an endless teen parade."

"In the future I suggest you don't hire such pretty girls," Lucy murmured. "A pot of honey can't help attracting bees."

Jane nodded glumly.

"I'm glad you turned Angie over to your parents for

the evening. They are enjoying her to the hilt. I think they took her on the merry-go-round five times.''

"I'm glad they were able to come up early this weekend. It's so nice they could take a turn with Angie. I always feel like I ask you too often—''

"Tut, tut, my dear. She's an angel and you know it. But I'll be off now. I haven't had my venison burger yet this year and I never miss it. I do so love telling all my vegetarian friends about it. It drives them crazy!'' With a wave of her hand, Lucy walked briskly away.

Jane waved in return and sighed.

"Bye.'' The latest males took their farewell of Tish. Jane watched Mel's eyes crackle dangerously with jealousy and wondered when the next Mel-Tish spat would begin.

Then she looked down the street and saw Uncle Henry and Aunt Claire, heading straight for her. Jane put her head in her hands, moaning inwardly.

"Hi, Jane,'' Uncle Henry launched the duet.

"We wanted to stop by—'' Aunt Claire put in.

"And warn you that a severe weather watch—''

"Is in effect—''

"Till 10:00 p.m.,'' Uncle Henry finished triumphantly.

Jane's eyes widened. How did they do it? Did they practice at home in front of a mirror?

Jane swallowed, then replied, "The wind has changed direction, and we've been getting strong gusts, too.''

Claire and Henry asked in unison, "Where's Leticia?''

"She had to go to the bathroom,'' Mel answered. She folded her hands together and a half dozen plastic, bangle bracelets slid down her arms and clanked loudly together at her wrists.

"Your jewelry is quite striking,'' Claire said.

Jane smiled at the pun her aunt had uttered without realizing it.

"Thanks," Mel said, making the bracelets slide and clack again on her arms.

"Well, we have to be moving on—" Henry began their last comments.

"We haven't bought our Aquarama tickets yet. This might be our—"

"Year to win the boat!" The two hurried away toward the raffle booth.

After they had gone, Mel said, "Tish wanted to try for Aquarama queen this year, and her mom and dad wouldn't let her. That's why she wouldn't stay out here. She's not talking to them."

Jane shook her head.

Mel went on without encouragement. "They said she had to wait till she was a junior at least. Is she ever mad!"

"I'm sure waiting a year won't harm Tish's chances."

"Yeah, but she's still mad."

Tish came outside then. Jane told the girls to check the racks to see if any sizes had been moved into the wrong places. After her uncle's warning, Jane now noticed placards on the racks, windows and tables begin to flap ominously.

Jane scanned the twilight sky. In another half hour it would be dark, and she could close up. At 10:00 p.m. there would be the Aquarama draw, which was the yearly boat raffle, and then the crowning of the Aquarama Queen, the girl who had sold the most raffle tickets. This year, at least, Tish would not be crowned.

At the far end of the block, Jane caught sight of Hallawell, sauntering in her direction. When he turned into the entrance of a men's shop, Jane excused herself and escaped inside the shop for a few moments of peace. Her headache by now was firmly entrenched. She took two aspirin, then reluctantly forced herself back outside.

The wild wind had gotten worse. Along the gutter across the street, an aluminum pop can skittered, making quick, metallic taps against the concrete curb, giving a sound to the wind. A little boy ran after the can, but the wind pushed it faster than he could run. His mother caught up with him. With an eye to the sky, she swung him up in her arms and called to his father.

Thunder rumbled in the distance. A flicker of lightning to the west caught the corner of her eye. "We may be moving in on short notice," she said to Mel and Tish, glancing at her watch. "It's only twenty minutes to closing. We'll see if we can stay open till then."

Mel nodded. Tish sighed and leaned back against the store window.

"Jane!" Lucy walked quickly toward Jane. "That weather looks threatening. The carnival is shutting down. I heard one of the carneys say they'd had too many nights end up with them tying everything down in an electrical storm."

"Don't worry, Grandmother. It will only take us three minutes to roll this stuff inside."

Lucy waved farewell and hurried by them.

After her grandmother was out of sight, Jane turned again toward the western horizon. The sunset clouds were deep purple and gray; the final rays of the sun were losing the battle to the surging clouds of the new front.

"Jane!" Tish said sharply.

She turned to see Cash, hurrying toward the lounge across the street. Tish didn't need to say more. An uneasy acknowledgment niggled in Jane's mind, too. Construction workers from both crews and now Cash were all in the same lounge on a Friday night, and a storm was coming.

Jane looked into her cousin's eyes and saw worry there, too. Tish's concern touched Jane unexpectedly. It was the first time she could remember ever feeling close to Tish. She reached out and took Tish's hand.

Tish pointed with her free hand.

Jane followed the direction just in time to see the back of Roger Hallawell going into the Wildcat 'n' Lace. "It's as dark as the black hole of Calcutta in there. Maybe they won't even see each other." *Dear Lord, make it so.* She squeezed Tish's hand and was surprised to feel Tish return the pressure.

"Jane! I'm closing now!" the pharmacist across the street called to her. "I think this one's moving in fast!"

To save herself from shouting over the wind, she waved to him. "Girls, that does it. If conservative Tim is closing up, we are, too." She motioned Tish to roll in the first rack nearest the door.

She went over to get the cash register herself. Carrying it inside, she put it back in its usual spot on the counter. Mel came in with the second rack of clothing. Jane went back out to help Tish carry in the table of scarves and accessories. One scarf fell from the table top, but never reached the sidewalk. It flew up high and away. As the three of them moved quickly, their junk jewelry bracelets clacked together up and down their arms, but now they could barely hear the bracelets above the wind. After the tables were inside, Jane went out to check if anything had been left behind in their rush.

Loud shouts caught her attention, and she turned in time to see a man propelled out the door of the Wildcat. He stumbled backward and fell heavily onto the cement sidewalk. Jane took a few steps forward as though going to his aid.

But immediately on his heels came another two men:

one of Hallawell's and one of Cash's carpenters. They were brawling. Jane sucked in her breath.

More fighters poured out of the entrance. The music blared onto the street. The wind picked up the sound and tossed it high. Jane watched as six more men came out, slugging. Some were construction workers, but not all.

"Look! Cash!" Tish exclaimed right next to Jane's ear. Glancing to each side, Jane realized she was flanked by both girls.

"And Mister Hallawell," Mel said with satisfaction.

In horror, Jane watched Hallawell and the plasterer exchanging punches. Cash was hovering beside them yelling at them both.

Jane took another step forward, but was halted by Tish's hand, gripping her elbow. "No, you could be hurt." Again, Jane felt the tie of family to Tish. She put her hand over Tish's and nodded.

Vaguely Jane thought that Tish's and Mel's parents would prefer that their daughters not be witnesses to this brawl on Main Street. But she could think of no way to force them back inside, and she could not make herself go in, either. Her pulse pounded in her ears, making it hard to concentrate. She tried to pray, but all she could whisper was "Cash, Cash…"

The ruckus continued. More and more people streamed out of the lounge, some fighting, some just trying to get clear. Men cradled their arms around dates. Some pushed aside fighting pairs to make way for themselves. Through it all, the pounding beat of the band never faltered.

Though completely ignored, Cash continued yelling at the brawlers and moving around the fighting men, who now filled a good portion of the street in front of the lounge. He returned to the plasterer who was still mauling Hallawell. Cash shouted at his man and dodged a stray punch. "Stop right now!" The words came across to Jane on a violent gust of wind.

The strident sirens of the sheriff's cars came in blasts on the buffeting wind that was tossing up dust and paper refuse. Jane shaded her eyes from the force of the wind, but stood her ground.

The fighters did not slow down till the police cars came around a barricade and pulled up right in the midst of them. The sheriff and two deputies tumbled out of their cars and began shouting at the men. The sirens were off, but the red lights on top of both cars continued rotating, giving a peculiarly wicked cast to the darkening Main Street.

The next blast of wind was like a strong hand, pushing against the three females huddled together in front of the shop. Jane looked up and realized that the red lights were only part of the flashes around her. Lightning crackled in the nearly night sky.

Suddenly the band across the street ceased. But the thunder kept its own beat. Then, in one great wave, the rain sluiced over them. Jane heard herself and her girls shriek in surprise. They turned and ran inside the shop, dripping wet and suddenly chilled.

Once inside, though, they could not help themselves. They all turned back to watch the police cleaning up the brawl. In the end the sheriff left with Cash, Hallawell and about three other men in the two police cars.

Chapter Ten

A half hour after the brawl on Main Street, Jane pulled into the police station parking lot. Outside, the storm center had moved on, but though the wind, thunder and lightning had passed by, rain still fell steadily. Since she was already soaked to the skin, she didn't bother to hurry to the sheriff's office door.

The sheriff wasn't sitting at his desk as he'd been that night over a month ago when she and Cash had come to deal with the would-be vandals. She looked around restlessly. Being here again unsettled her stomach. When she heard Cash and the sheriff coming out, she turned to meet Cash's eyes, but instead encountered Roger Hallawell's flushed face. Jane stiffened uncomfortably.

Then she heard the sheriff's voice from the hallway. "I've had it with both of you."

Hallawell's face reddened a shade darker at these words. The sheriff stepped through the doorway. Cash followed. His disheveled clothing was out of character, and she noted that his lower lip was split and swollen. She tamped down a swell of concern for him. She was here as a friend—nothing more.

"Here to post bail, Miss Everett?" The sheriff grinned.

"Do I need to?" she asked.

"We'll see. It depends."

"On?" She leaned forward against the counter, intrigued by the sheriff's determined tone.

He pointed at Cash and Hallawell. "It's up to these two."

Hallawell interrupted, "If you're not pressing charges, I'm leaving—"

"If I charge you, you'll live to regret it." The sheriff, folding his arms over his chest, braced his back against the wall. "Now, I figured the tension between you two would build till everything came to a head. This brawl is the final episode in this little soap opera. Hallawell, you're here to stay, Langley's here to stay, and I'm out of patience."

Hallawell started to bluster, but the sheriff cut him off. "I'm going to explain how it's going to be. You two are going to shake hands and agree to disagree."

"I'm all in favor," Cash said.

"Yeah, what have you got to lose?" Hallawell asked with a sneer.

The sheriff made eye contact with Hallawell. "Let's talk about what *you've* got to lose."

"So what have I got to lose?" Hallawell demanded.

The sheriff pushed away from the wall. "My cooperation."

A tense silence gripped the quiet room. Desultory traffic sounds from the outside made no impression on the three men.

Finally Cash stepped forward and held out his hand to

Hallawell. The other man hesitated, then reluctantly shook Cash's hand. Without a word Hallawell walked out.

Cash nodded to the sheriff, then left with Jane. The night sky still drizzled. Jane unlocked her car. They got in—wet, silent and distant. Keeping her eyes straight ahead, she drove out of the lit parking lot onto the dark county road.

"Is that the end of it?" she asked at last, trying to fill the vacuum of oppressive silence.

"Hallawell would be a fool to cross the sheriff in a town this size." His voice sounded gritty, defeated.

Jane nodded stiffly.

"Why did you come?" he asked gruffly. "Did Lucy call you?"

Jane pressed her lips together, then tried to lighten the unbearable pall which filled the vehicle. "I felt like asking you those same two questions last Friday night at the Aquabat Show."

There was a distinct pause.

Cash frowned. "Rona called me that night."

"Oh. Thanks for coming that night."

"No problem. Thanks for coming tonight," Cash said in a subdued voice.

"No problem."

For a moment a hint of humor trembled in the air. Then it fizzled in the ensuing silence.

Jane sighed. Cash's proposal had erected an even thicker and icier wall between them. She would come if he needed her, but that was all. That day, on their drive home from Wausau, for a few minutes, there had been a chance for them, just a chance.

As she turned a corner to the right, she glanced over at him. In the reflected light from her dashboard, she could make out his grim profile. She couldn't make another effort to relieve their gloom. Finally they pulled up beside Cash's Jeep.

"Thanks again for coming for me." He stared at her for several moments. She nodded but kept her face impassive. Then he got out, closing the door behind him.

Jane watched him amble over to his Jeep. It tugged at her heart to see him battered and tired. Aching with a devastating loneliness, she blinked back tears and wished she could go after him and put ice on his split lip and give him aspirin for his bruises. Instead, she resolutely turned her car toward home.

The next day Jane took Angie over to Lucy's house. She found her grandmother in the backyard reclining on a lawn chair.

When Lucy spotted them she said, "At last a sunny day that isn't in the nineties!"

Jane joined her grandmother under the tall birches. She glanced over the bluff and for a few seconds she lost herself in the dazzling beauty of the scene below. The rippling lake shimmered, making her think of diamonds dancing on sapphire satin.

"It's such a beautiful day I hate to go inside. Is there anything wrong, Jane?"

"Wrong? What made you ask that?" For the first time she could recall, Jane felt ill at ease in her grandmother's company. Slowly she made eye contact with Lucy.

"Something in your eyes. It doesn't matter I suppose. Let's go in, my dears. I'm all ready to work on that miniature for Cash."

Jane followed her grandmother's instructions on posing the baby. Because of Angie's active age, the miniature of her would be much less ambitious than Jane's portrait. This posing and one more would do it. Which was just as well. Angie wanted to crawl, climb the couch and play with her blocks. Concentrating on keeping the little girl entertained during the sitting took all of Jane's energy.

Lucy asked, "So everything's settled between Hallawell and Cash?"

"Seems to be."

"I'm so glad your parents and I had gotten home with Angie before the brawling last night."

"I've see a few fights before, but nothing like that," Jane said.

"And you've never seen Cash in one."

Jane made no answer. She almost broke down and told her grandmother about Cash's proposal. But some emotion—maybe pride—kept her from revealing it. Cash had shown her how little he respected her, how lightly he regarded the commitment of holy matrimony.

"I just wish this summer would come to an end. Everything's been so—" Dreading Cash's first full-day visit with Angie, that wouldn't include her, was making her miserable. She hated feeling selfish, small. Her prayers seemed to be soap bubbles floating away on an aimless breeze. She needed desperately to feel an assurance that by the time this ordeal arrived, she would have received the grace she needed to accept it. She knew God was able, but how she longed to be rid of this hard lump of dread.

"I understand, my dear. This has been a stressful year for you. Becoming a mother would have been a challenge enough for anyone. But I have faith in Cash to do what is right, not only for Angie, but you, too."

"Your faith in Cash is misplaced." The harsh words flew out of Jane's mouth before she could stop herself. Saying them made her feel sick.

Lucy stepped around her easel and stared at Jane. "What brought that on?"

Jane pressed her lips together, frantically trying to think of ways to deflect her grandmother's curiosity.

"Does this have anything to do with your trip to Wausau last weekend?" Lucy asked shrewdly.

Jane's mouth opened momentarily, then shut.

Lucy, holding her palette and brush, stared at Jane. "You might as well tell me now. I'll find out eventually."

Angie began fretting in Jane's arms. "It's time for her bottle and nap."

"All right. But while you're doing that there's no reason you can't tell me what Cash has done now."

Jane stood up and carried Angie to the kitchen. While she went through the routine of preparing a bottle, she let Angie down to crawl on the floor by her feet.

"Well?" Lucy said, leaning in the kitchen doorway.

Jane felt an echo of her initial fury at Cash bubble up. "Cash proposed to me," she said tersely.

Lucy stood up straight. "Cash proposed? In Wausau? But why haven't you two said anything?"

"It wasn't a real marriage proposal." Jane lifted Angie from the floor and carried her back to the living room. On the way Angie grabbed the bottle, and Jane stuck its nipple in her mouth. Jane sat down in the corner of the sofa and let Angie lie back in her arms.

Lucy followed her and sat in the chair opposite. "How can a man propose marriage without it being a real proposal?"

"He said he thought Angie needed a father and a mother, not an uncle and a guardian."

"Oh," Lucy said quietly. "I suppose he said it just like that?"

"Yes, he did. I was never so insulted in my life. He called it a marriage of convenience. I told him I wasn't interested in being a convenience to anyone. After knowing the kind of marriage my parents have, the one you had, I can't believe he could show so little understanding of how Everetts view marriage.''

"You turned him down.''

"Of course I turned him down. He insulted the sanctity of marriage. He insulted me and my whole family!''

Lucy sat with her hands folded in her lap. "You still love him.''

"Love him! I'd like to strangle him!''

Lucy sighed. "That's a sure sign you still love him.''

Her grandmother's words left Jane struggling with a new rush of anger.

"If you didn't love him, you wouldn't be this angry.'' Lucy glanced toward Jane.

"Grandmother, I told you. I had a schoolgirl crush on him. He never even knew.''

Lucy didn't take her eyes off her granddaughter's face. "I know. You fell in love with Cash on your sixteenth birthday and nothing's changed. Unfortunately.''

"Unfortunately?'' Angie's sucking slowed as she began to fall asleep. Looking down at the angelic face surrounded by the wispy, dark hair, Jane brushed back the little girl's bangs.

"Yes, unfortunately you still love him the way you did when you were sixteen.''

"Grandmother—''

"Don't go on denying you love Cash. I know it's the truth.''

Jane fell silent. She didn't want to admit it, but she couldn't lie, either.

Lucy said sternly, "It's time your love grew up.''

"I don't know what you mean.''

"You're still loving Cash, but with an immature love. You've never been allowed to show it, so it's stunted.''

"I'm going to stop loving Cash," Jane insisted.

"Oh, how do you propose to do that?" Lucy put one hand on her hip.

Again Jane had no answer.

"It's time you began to love Cash with a love that is patient, kind, keeps no record of wrongs. A love that hopes all things, believes all things. A love that will never fail."

Jane recognized the verses Lucy quoted from First Corinthians 13. Lucy herself had taught them to Jane when she was very young. "But Cash doesn't want my love."

"That has nothing to do with how to love him. Christian love only demands things from the one who loves, never from the one who is loved. You love Cash, so you should love him with the best that's within you!"

"I do. I mean, I did."

Lucy shook her head ruefully. "No, if you did, his cold proposal wouldn't have made you angry, it would have made you sad."

"Why sad?"

"Because it's sad when a grown man knows so little about love."

Jane avoided her grandmother's piercing gaze. Angie slept soundly in her lap now. Tears tried to form in Jane's eyes, but she forced them back. "There isn't any future in loving Cash."

"Then let your heart give up."

"I thought you just said that wasn't possible."

"You have to make a choice. Either love Cash with all that's within you and wait and pray he'll someday return your love, or give up on him. Close the book on loving him. Look for another chance. Start fresh with someone else. It's not that you stop loving Cash. You just stop hoping he'll love you in return."

Jane kept her gaze on Angie. *Close the book.* A sensation like a rock-hard hand pressed down on her, crushing her breast.

Poised over the sweater display, Jane experienced a now-familiar flash of helpless dismay. The sweater, which had been missing at the beginning of the week, was back. Today was Friday afternoon. Yesterday Mel had shared the day with Tish, so either girl could have surreptitiously slipped the sweater back among the others. The cotton sweater was an ivory pullover with a delicate design of leaves and flowers around the neck and wrist. As she examined the band around its neck closely, she stopped. A trace of pink lipstick lingered on the inside.

She turned to Mel who was standing nearby. Keeping her voice casual, she said, ''A customer has gotten lipstick on this sweater. Would you take it down to the cleaner?''

''Now?''

''Yes, I can handle things till you get back. Tell Doreen to put it on my account. Let her decide whether it should be dry-cleaned or hand washed and blocked.''

''Sure. Be right back.'' The brunette teen took the folded sweater and walked out.

Jane had detected no alarm or guilt in the girl's eyes. Mel's lipstick was a pink similar to the trace, but so what? It proved nothing. Tish usually didn't wear lipstick at the shop, but she might elsewhere. Jane sighed loudly. Enough was enough. When would she solve this mystery? Or would she ever find the culprit? That thought was too vexing to be tolerated.

The bell jingled. She turned to greet the customer.

''I haven't seen you all summer,'' Del Ray Martin complained as a greeting.

''I've been awfully busy with Angie,'' Jane replied, neatening a scarf display on one of her glass cases.

"Are your parents going to be able to spend August up here like usual?"

"They arrive this afternoon."

"Good. Anyway, I'm looking for another new skirt to coordinate with that black sweater I bought here last fall."

Jane was relieved to get down to business. She led Del Ray over to one of the fall skirt racks. "The black sweater with the shawl collar?"

"Yes, my husband told me to get something that will show off my legs." Del Ray giggled like a teenager.

Jane didn't approve of Del Ray's desire to dress younger and flashier than her two teenage daughters. But Jane went carefully through the skirts, trying to find one that would please Del Ray while still flattering her. A size-eight, black gauze skirt almost leaped off its hanger at her. It was the one that had been missing for over a week!

Before Jane could collect her thoughts, Del Ray, who was standing at her elbow, spoke up, "Oh, that's just like the one I saw your cousin, Tish, wear. It's a little longer than I like, but do you have it in my size?"

Your cousin, Tish! Jane wanted to scream it out and hear it echo off the ceiling. Tish! Her heart pounded. At last one knot of this perplexing summer slid apart like satin against satin.

"No, I only have this one left," she heard her own voice, saying calmly. "How about something more seasonal for fall like this one?" Her arm held out a nubby knit in gray and black that would be knee length on Del Ray.

"I'll try it," the customer said reluctantly.

"Good." Jane turned, and through the front window, she saw Tish's long, blond mane. Until that moment Jane had forgotten Tish was due to come in later today for her check. The bell rang as the girl opened the front door.

"Hello, Tish, what are you doing here early?" Was that really her own voice so smooth as though another person were saying the words?

"Is it ready?"

"Of course. I have it at my desk. Come down. We'll get it together." She turned to Mel, who was back and busy rearranging a small display of turquoise-and-silver jewelry done by a local Indian artist. "Would you help Mrs. Martin?"

She ignored Mel's agreement and Del Ray's objection. Without a backward glance, Jane marched to the rear of the store and down the basement steps.

At the bottom she turned and watched Tish descend elegantly. The girl stopped on the bottom step and looked at Jane, tilting her head as though asking a question.

"You've been taking clothing, wearing it and bringing it back," Jane said flatly.

Tish's eyes widened for a fraction of a second. Then she tossed her head. "So?"

The girl's brazenness fanned Jane's indignation. "It is sneaky. It is dishonest. Don't you have any idea what a reputation is? If I told this—in a town this size—no one would ever hire you again."

"You won't tell anyone," Tish answered in a cool voice, and crossed her arms over her breast.

"What makes you so sure?"

"My parents. If you talk about me, they'll be humiliated." Tish stared narrowly into Jane's face, seeming to dare her.

The girl's audacity momentarily robbed Jane of speech.

"You won't hurt my parents," Tish explained in a sickly sweet tone. "So you won't tell them. I didn't steal anything, anyway. It was just a little borrowing."

Jane found her voice. "You're fired."

This time Tish's face did register surprise, but she regained control quickly. "I quit."

"I said you're fired."

"I'm going to tell my parents that I needed to do more reading before the school year, so I decided to quit. May I have my last check please?" Tish held out her hand.

Jane reached back without looking, picked up the lone envelope and threw it at Tish.

Tish smirked, picked it up off the basement floor and exited elegantly up the steps.

When the girl was gone, Jane sank onto the edge of her desk. Several minutes passed while the confrontation played over and over in her mind: "You won't hurt my parents." How could she tell Uncle Henry and Aunt Claire the kind of emotional extortion their daughter was guilty of? Tish had attended church faithfully all her life. Hadn't anything sunk in?

Jane had wanted the size-eight mystery solved. But where could she go from here?

Chapter Eleven

Jane carefully wiped all inner frustration from her features and lifted her face into position for Lucy. She was still angry with Cash, and Lucy's scolding still stung.

Just a few feet away to Jane's right, Cash played with Angie. Her only success at distancing Cash had been that instead of letting him pick Angie and her up as usual, Jane had arranged to drive to Lucy's on her own. All the progress she had made in sharing Angie with Cash had been reversed. The thought of seeing Cash take Angie away for a day on their own made Jane ill.

Cash's playful teasing made Angie giggle. Jane's neck tightened. She cleared her throat. "I can't believe this is the last sitting and I'm still having a hard time posing."

Lucy nodded, but it was obvious that she was fully involved in finishing the portrait.

"This little girl is unstoppable." Shuffling behind Angie, Cash came into view. He was holding the child's hands above her head, helping her walk.

"She'll be walking by herself soon," Lucy murmured, then paused and stood, gazing at Jane.

Cash said, "One of my carpenters said his little girl walked at nine months—"

"That was *his* little girl," Jane snapped.

Cash looked up at her, showing his surprise. "I didn't mean anything against you—"

"Of course not," Lucy said soothingly. "Jane, let that frown go. I need your face... Yes, that's it."

While Lucy worked intensely on the portrait, Jane could hear her grandmother muttering to herself. Out of the corner of her eye, Jane kept tabs on Cash and Angie as they made their circuit around the room. Angie was endlessly intrigued by all the small sculptures and fine china on the low maple tables and shelves. Jane tried to keep her focus on the toddler.

Cash could feel Jane's attention on him...not on Angie's halting progress. He was also gripped, dominated by an awareness of her. Ever since that day they drove home from Wausau, every time he detected her cinnamon fragrance or saw sunlight touch her hair, he thought of the feel of her skin against his cheek, on his lips.

He knew that her response to him that day had been more warm and enticing than he'd ever imagined. But after his proposal, she had turned into a sharp, abrasive ice maiden. Now every time he encountered her he felt waves of frigid animosity flowing from her, warning him away.

Earlier in the year she had initially sparred with him over joint custody. After their June showdown, he thought she had gradually begun to come around. But this iciness was much worse than either previous phase. What had been so awful about his proposal? Their marrying for Angie's sake only made sense.

"It's done," Lucy announced simply.

Jane felt an unexpected shiver of excitement go through her. "May I see it?"

Lucy nodded, and Jane rose to stand beside her. Warily she looked at the canvas. There she was, in her grandmother's peach dress, sitting on the white wicker. But her expression in the portrait was what snagged her attention. Lucy had, of course, painted her granddaughter in a flattering way—Jane had expected that. But Jane's expression was at once winsome, wry and somehow wistful.

She touched her grandmother's shoulder affectionately, feeling Lucy's soft, worn cotton blouse under her fingertips. "Is that how you see me, Grandmother?"

Lucy put her hand over Jane's and whispered into Jane's ear, "Now if only Cash would be smart enough to see it."

Jane experienced a sudden desire to cry. Resolutely she pushed it away. "Mom and Dad will be pleased with it."

"Great job," Cash said, arriving beside Lucy. Angie clapped her hands and leaned forward to Jane. Jane took her into her arms.

"It's only four days away," Jane murmured, keeping her eyes on her grandmother.

"Yes, we cut it a little close," Lucy said. "Jane, why don't you wear the dress to the party? It will make the presentation of the portrait more striking."

Jane pursed her lips. "If you think I should."

"Your parents' party is only four days away, and that means Angie's first birthday is only seven days away," Cash pointed out.

Ice closed around Jane's heart. Twelve days till Angie would leave her for a day.

Jane smiled as cheerfully as she could at Angie, who sat in her car seat in the Blazer. What's wrong with me tonight? I am delighted that my parents are celebrating thirty-five years together. Angie looks adorable in her new pink dress with ruffles and lace. I know Mom and Dad will love the portrait. It would, all in all, be a festive, joyous evening with family and old friends. What had caused her emotions to snag together into a tangle of knots?

She knew the answer without voicing it. Cash Langley. Of course he would not dream of staying away tonight. Their two families had been friends for generations. But having Cash near, while she celebrated her parents' long-lasting love, would rub her like salt in an open wound.

She pulled up near her parents' summer home and parked in the crowd of cars at the base of the hill. With Angie in her arms, Jane, wearing heels, walked up carefully. Ahead in the doorway her grandmother waited. In honor of the occasion, Lucy wore one of her vintage Paris originals, a simple bell-shaped dress in pale green.

At the door Lucy greeted Angie. "I'm so happy you could come, little Miss Angie," she cooed to the baby, kissing her cheek. "Hello, my darling." She kissed Jane, also, and gave her a glance filled with love and concern. Jane could only nod in response because she was already forcing back tears.

Next in the informal receiving line were Jane's parents. Her father kissed her and teased Angie. Marge smiled in delight and claimed Angie for a quick hug. Another couple came up the steps behind Jane, so she tried to retrieve Angie from her mother, but the baby refused to leave her grandmother. Immensely pleased, Marge leaned forward to murmur to Jane, "I'll keep her. Cash has your corsage. You look wonderful in Mother's dress."

Jane nodded and entered the hall, then the living room. Her own feeling of tentativeness in these familiar surroundings unnerved her further. Her arms felt empty without Angie's reassuring company. Soft, taped music played in the background. Musicians would come later for the dancing. The large L-shaped dining-living room was already full of cheerful people, talking and eating hors d'oeuvres. Jane tried to shake off her melancholy and behave naturally.

Cash saw Jane enter. Holding the corsage box in front of him like a peace offering, he moved through the crowd to her. She turned and caught sight of him. He froze. For a few seconds he could only stare. Surely he should have gotten used to seeing her in the dress she had posed in. His mouth became dry and his hands trembled slightly like a schoolboy, picking up his date to his first dance. Jane was the most beautiful woman in the room.

As she walked gracefully to him, she moved as effortlessly as an angel hovering near the earth, creating in him a surge of anticipation. In spite of himself, he longed to pull her to him. He would kiss—

"My corsage please?" she asked coolly.

The cold tone of her voice killed his thoughts. A dangerous fire burned in her emerald eyes. He almost retreated a step. She was still angry over his proposal, and he still could not understand her reaction to a perfectly honest suggestion. Weren't flowery declarations of undying affection passé now? Had she expected him to go down on one knee and declare undying love?

She took the white box from him. As though his skin were repulsive to her, she made certain she touched only the box. Irritation bubbled up inside him. But as she walked away, he still couldn't make himself draw his gaze from the sway of her hips.

Jane clutched the box in one hand and went down the hall to her parents' first-floor bedroom. Closing the door behind her, Jane felt the room, decorated in restful blues, was a welcome haven.

But there, in front of the wall mirror was Rona, putting

on lipstick. Rona was wearing the informal uniform that she wore to catering jobs, a black tunic over black slacks. But Rona being Rona, she had added color with a russet and gold scarf at her neck.

Inwardly Jane sighed, but made herself walk forward. She hoped Rona wouldn't be in a prying mood. "Could you help me pin this on?" She held the box out to Rona.

Rona took the delicate confection out of the box and then looked at Jane's dress. "New dress?"

"It's my grandmother's."

Rona carefully pinned the flowers onto the right shoulder of the dress, high above its scooped neckline. "One of her originals?"

"No, but it was purchased in Paris."

"That explains it. I don't know how your grandmother does it. Half the time she dresses wacky, but when she wants to be beautiful, she succeeds every time."

"Grandfather said it was the artist in her. The desire to surprise and delight."

Rona stepped back and looked Jane over critically. "You look lovely, of course, but you're very pale. Aren't you feeling well?"

"I'm fine, thanks. It's just all the getting ready. Angie does make it a challenge." Jane, stepping around Rona, looked into the large mirror and fluffed her hair with her fingers, then smoothed the full skirt of her dress. "You did a good job of pinning the corsage. It feels secure and isn't sideways."

"Vitelli's offers a *full* service catering. Well, I can't hide in here all night. I have work to do. Carmine will be yelling his head off for me any moment now."

They went back to the noise of the party. Cash, holding Angie, was waiting at the entrance of the living room for her. Jane took a firm grip on her emotions.

"Good luck," Rona whispered and left her side.

Jane walked up to Cash. Wordlessly he led her to the kitchen snack bar. Perched on a high stool next to Cash's, she accepted a goblet of sparkling white grape juice and looked around.

Lucy had considered Mylar balloons as too gauche for this formal occasion. Instead small, artful arrangements of late-summer blossoms: pink asters, dusky gold mums, bright yellow snapdragons graced the end tables and mantel. And a bounty of gladiolus. There were huge floor vases of these tall, regal flowers in bold white, peach and yellow. They filled the spacious room. The abundance of flowers set the festive mood, and Jane focused on the smiles and friendly voices around her. Angie also appeared to be fascinated by her surroundings. As Angie's attention roamed the room, she sat unnaturally still on Cash's lap.

Pivoting in her seat, Jane noted the other party preparations. In Lucy's mind a formal party still meant crystal, silver and bone china for a sit-down dinner. The guests now milled around the long L-shaped living room and dinette. But outside, the large screened-in porch, which encompassed the length of the lake side of her parents' home and then curved around the far end of the house, was prepared for dinner. The porch had been adorned with a rainbow of lanterns and candles. The tables there were ready to seat thirty-eight people. And, of course, Lucy had somehow magically influenced the weather to cooperate this evening, and the summer's storms and heat were blessedly absent.

Cash cleared his throat. Reluctantly she looked up. He touched his glass to hers and leaned forward so she could hear him. "To you."

Automatically she tried to read his mood from the expression on his face and tone of his voice. He seemed merely polite. Why do I continue to look for something in him that had never been there and would never be there? Keeping the occasion in mind, she smiled politely in return and introduced a neutral topic. "I'm happy your conflict with Roger is over."

He lifted his glass in salute. He leaned forward again. "How's your size-eight mystery going?"

Her spine stiffened. She tilted her face nearer him, so he could hear her over the buzz of voices and tinkling of ice in glasses. "It's ended."

"Which was it? Mel or your cousin?"

"Tish quit and the size eights have stopped vanishing and returning, I'm leaving it at that."

"I see. If it *was* Mel, she would now be forced to stop simply because there is no longer anyone else to muddy the issue."

"Exactly." Knowing the culprit was her own unrepentant cousin made her grit her teeth, but she managed to smile.

"Jane?" an unexpected voice came from behind her.

She turned around. Tom, whom she hadn't seen since the reading of Dena's will at his Chicago office, stood before her. "Tom! I didn't know you were coming up for my parents' party." She jumped down from her stool and gave the lawyer an affectionate hug.

"Well, Lucy called me last week and invited me to come up and stay with her. I decided I could use a week away from court."

"You can forget all about briefs and judges now." She tucked her arm in Tom's, glad of his presence, which would provide a welcome distraction to the tension of being with Cash.

"Angie has really grown." Tom took Angie's small hand and shook it. "She looks so much like Dena."

"Yes," Cash answered woodenly. When would any reference to his sister stop slicing through him like a sharp razor?

"She's a doll. She has your hair, Cash."

Angie unexpectedly stretched out her arms to Tom. He lifted her gingerly as though the little girl were made of cotton candy. "She's so light!"

"Thank goodness," Jane said wryly. "She isn't walking yet."

Tom held Angie close to him and began reciting nursery rhymes. Angie listened to the chanting cadence with obvious fascination.

Cash felt a whiplash of jealously slice through him. When Jane had arrived, her beauty had rocked him from head to toe. As he had sat next to her, talking about nothing, her icy anger had washed over him in progressive, freezing waves. Then at Tom's innocent mention of Dena he had been stabbed with pain, and now jealousy ricocheted through him like live ammo. Why was everything hitting him so hard tonight? The party had just begun.

Tom nuzzled Angie's cheek and then handed her back to Cash.

Tish appeared at Cash's side. He stood up politely and nodded to her. "Hi, Cash," she said. He noted that her soft tone warred with the barbed glance she gave Jane.

Jane quelled the urge to say something back to her cousin. Tish was wearing a black cotton sheath which, instead of draining her light complexion as it should have, enhanced her pale ivory skin. That style was much too sophisticated for a sixteen-year-old. Why didn't Aunt Claire stand up to her daughter more? "You didn't buy that at my shop," Jane said pointedly.

"No," Tish said airily. "Mother and I drove to Wausau yesterday. Your shop is nice enough, Jane, but it's too small to offer much variety.'' The girl slipped her arm through Cash's and rubbed noses with Angie in their accustomed greeting.

Jane bit her tongue before she said something she'd regret. Instead of reacting with anger, maybe it was time to start praying over her relationship with her cousin.

''We're going to go again,'' Tish continued. ''To Wausau, I mean, before school starts. I saw some lovely clothes, but I just didn't have to time to try everything on. That's one thing I owe your shop, Jane. Working there gave me such a desire to wear a variety of styles. I hate wearing the same thing over and over, don't you?'' Tish turned innocent eyes to her cousin.

Jane flushed. So far she had been unable to tell her aunt and uncle about their daughter's ''borrowing'' clothing from her shop. It made her angry to think that Tish considered herself the winner in this situation. But Jane still intended to settle Tish's ''hash.'' She would put the problem before Lucy, and she was confident that their grandmother would know just what to do to teach Tish the lesson she so richly deserved.

At this thought Jane smiled. ''No, frankly, Tish, I think I take after Lucy about clothes. What I like, I like, and I don't mind wearing my favorites. I love fashion and its trends, but I hope that you will find and retain your own style. That's the mark of a truly well-dressed woman.''

''I must say that I like what you are wearing tonight,'' Tom said appreciatively.

''It's Lucy's.'' Jane swayed slightly, letting her full skirt ripple.

Tish sniffed. ''It looks like one of those weird square dancing dresses old women wear.''

''Not even a little.'' Lucy's voice came out cold and clear. She stood right beside the suddenly flushed Tish.

Over the hubbub, Lucy announced that dinner was ready and please would they all find their places out on the porch.

Tom steered Jane out onto the porch and located their name cards. Reading the other name cards at the main table, Jane found that Aunt Claire, Uncle Henry, Tish, her parents and Lucy were to be joined by Cash and Angie.

Lucy had said nothing to her about inviting Tom north for a week. Is Grandmother trying to take my mind off Cash? She told me I could choose to find someone else. Jane glanced at Tom. He had always seemed a little overly serious, but she had no doubt he would make an excellent husband and father.

"Let's sit down." Tom gently guided her into her chair. "I'm happy your grandmother seated me next to you," he whispered into her ear. "I think I am going to enjoy this week off. I had forgotten how lovely the Everett women are." His compliment was balm to her shredded pride. She smiled up at him.

As Cash watched Jane smile at Tom, he numbly put Angie in her high chair. Jane's dad's best man from thirty-five years ago rose and led them all in a toast to many more happy years for Marge and Phil. The glasses clinked. There was applause and the salads were brought out efficiently. The tables hummed with happy conversation.

Cash watched Jane's parents touch glasses again and exchange a look charged with love. He looked away as though he had come upon them kissing. His eyes touched Tish, and she smiled at him. He smiled briefly in reply, then turned to the task of helping Angie with her meal. He was glad feeding Angie gave him something to do. In spite of having to keep up with Angie's demands and his trying to eat enough of the delicious food in front of him to be polite, he still found his attention being drawn in two directions: to Jane's face and to her parents.

All through the meal, Tom kept murmuring into Jane's ear, making her smile, nod, laugh. Cash was possessed by an urge to bump Tom off the chair next to Jane and take it for himself. Why? Tom was a nice guy. In the past, he'd dated both Jane and Dena. So why did Cash want to suddenly do him bodily harm?

The other irresistible draw was Marge and Phil. At every possible opportunity their hands touched; their eyes sought out the other. There seemed to be a warm glow around them, unseen, but still evident. He had always liked the Everetts, but never had Marge looked lovelier and Phil more content, fulfilled.

The meal finally came to a close with a flaming dessert. Another toast was observed for the Everetts.

Then Lucy rose majestically. "Friends and family, tonight is a very happy evening for me. Watching my son live happily with this wonderful woman for the last thirty-five years has been an untold blessing to me.

"I know personally that it has been a happy and successful time for both Marge and Phil. So Jane and I, with Cash's assistance, planned a special gift to honor them. Will you all come into the living room to view its presentation?" She motioned everyone to rise, then led them back into the long room.

In front of the vaulted stone fireplace, an easel, draped in white, had been set up in their absence. Without another word, Lucy marched directly to it and swept the cloth aside.

Cash stared at Jane's likeness. The peach dress, her copper hair and the white wicker were harmonious, sunlit and lovely. Glorious. Spontaneous applause swept the room, and he watched Jane blush at its sound. People came forward, shaking Jane's hand, patting her shoulder and hugging her. Cash's attention alternated between Jane's portrait and Jane herself.

Cash watched Lucy, Marge, Phil and Jane being pushed forward to stand beside the portrait and accept more congratulations. When Tom came up and kissed Jane's cheek, Cash felt a charge of heat flood his face. Electronic flashes from many cameras went off in bursts. Angie, in Cash's arms, cried for Jane, and he had to give the baby to her. Awkwardly he stepped out of camera range.

"If I may have your attention please," Phil raised his voice and the gathered friends became quiet. Jane, holding Angie, stood beside Lucy. "I won't talk a long time, but this is one of those rare opportunities when a man can speak about what really matters in life.

"It goes almost without saying that I am a fortunate man. You all know my mother and so you will believe me when I tell you that she was not surprised in the least when I came home from the first day of ninth grade and told her I had met the girl I was going to marry. Her name was Marjorie. When I think of all the men who waste years vainly trying to find their true love, I am very grateful. God said, 'It is not good for man to be alone' and He has blessed me with a true helpmeet." He smiled broadly and tightened his arm around Marge.

"This portrait is a lovely gift, but Marge and I received another gift this year. Our first grandchild. Jane, bring Angie here please."

Jane walked the few feet to her parents. Her father lifted Angie into his arms. "Of all the gifts we could have received this year, having this little girl become part of our family has been the best. Don't you agree, Marge?"

"Yes, losing dear Dena was sad," Marge spoke softly. "But Angie is a precious trust from Dena. We will do our best to live up to Dena's faith in us—along with Jane and Cash, of course.''

''Thank you all for coming to celebrate this occasion tonight.'' Phil motioned to the musicians, and they began to play a slow dance.

Cash was shaking inside. Phil Everett's simple words of gratitude to God for his wife's love had shaken Cash to his core. As the music began again, the guests moved back to make room for the dancers. Cash looked around and realized that Tish was standing beside him. She had a discontented expression on her face.

Jane approached them, carrying Angie. ''Cash, would you hold Angie. Tom has asked me to dance.'' Without saying a word, Cash took Angie. The little girl yawned.

Cash said, ''Tish, would you get Angie's bottle and warm it? It's nearly her bedtime.''

''Sure,'' Tish said.

Cash watched Tom lead Jane out onto the patio, then take her into his arms for a slow dance. Cash's jaw clenched. He turned away and walked down the back hall to the master bedroom. There, a folding crib stood in the corner next to a cushioned, platform rocker.

Cash laid Angie down in the crib, which held diapers and clothing in Angie's size. He murmured softly as he took her out of her fancy dress, changed her diaper and snapped her into her lightweight summer pajamas.

''Here's her bottle,'' Tish said, still sounding disgruntled.

Cash sat down in the rocker, positioned Angie across his lap, tucked his arm under her and took her bottle from Tish. With a contented sigh, Angie stopped fretting and relaxed in her uncle's arms.

Tish flopped down on the end of the bed. Cash looked up. ''You don't need to stay here. You'll miss all the fun.''

"Fun!" Tish scowled at him. "A bunch of old people! Mother said if I didn't come tonight, she wouldn't take me shopping to Wausau. I couldn't make her change her mind—"

"Of course you had to come tonight. It's a family event," he said mildly. "You're fortunate to have such a wonderful family—"

"Wonderful!"

"Yes, wonderful. Did you ask your parents if you could bring an escort—"

"No way! I wouldn't bring anyone from school. I have the weirdest family—"

"I don't think they're weird," Cash insisted. "They're just highly individual—"

"Weird! My grandmother's wearing a forty-year-old dress—"

"It's a Balenciaga original—"

"It's forty years old, for crying out loud! And Jane is wearing a thirty-year-old dress—just because it was the dress…" Tish's voice became dramatic as she imitated her mother's voice. "'The dress Mother bought on her last trip to Paris with Father.'" Her tone hardened abruptly. "Who cares?"

"I do." Lucy's voice startled both of them.

Tish and Cash swiveled to watch Lucy enter. "You are talking nonsense—"

Tish stood up combatively, her chin thrust forward. "I don't care. What do I care about Grandfather? He was dead five years before I was born!"

"He was your mother's father," Lucy said in deadly calm. "You are a part of him. He lives through you. And will live on through your children."

Tish made a sound of disgust.

Lucy's face became scarlet.

Cash suddenly was worried about her. "Lucy, sit down. You're flushed—"

Lucy ignored him, her attention riveted on Tish's face. Her voice came out low and outraged, "I never thought I would hear anything so devoid of true feeling come from a relation of mine."

Tish's face now matched Lucy's shade of red. "You've always hated me! It's always Jane, Jane—"

"I have never hated you," Lucy went on relentlessly. "I've only hated the way your parents have overindulged you. The minute you were born, they let you take over their family—"

"No, that's not true. My parents never let me do anything I want. They didn't let me be Aquarama Queen!"

"You know yourself that only junior and senior girls are expected—"

"I don't care!" Tish stomped her foot. "If you can wear forty-year-old dresses, why can't I be Aquarama Queen a year early?"

"The two situations are completely different. A Paris original is a work of art. Can a true work of art go out of style? I don't wear my originals to be different. I wear them, so that others can see them and enjoy them."

"I don't care why you wear them. It's stupid!"

Tish glared at Lucy. Lucy stared back, not giving an inch to Tish's defiance.

"Granddaughter, I have only one thing more to say to you. Pride goeth before a fall." Majestically raising her hand, Lucy prevented Tish's retort. "Go wash the tears off your face and go back to the party."

Tish made a face at her grandmother and stomped out.

Lucy shook her head. "How did Angie fall asleep through all that?"

Cash looked down at the sleeping child. "I don't know.

I think her ears were effectively muffled by my arm and chest.''

"I'll take over now.'' Lucy held out her arms.

"No, that's all right. You go back. You're the hostess—''

"I am an exhausted hostess. Cash, I'm in my seventies—''

Cash stood up and transferred Angie to Lucy's arms. He didn't want to go back out to the party, but what choice did he have? He couldn't leave the party so early without calling attention to himself.

He stood outside the door at the end of the porch. Against clear instructions to the contrary, his eyes insisted on picking out Jane. She was still dancing with Tom. Cash made himself turn his attention elsewhere, and his gaze caught Phil and Marge just as they kissed lightly. The people around them smiled and nodded. As Phil began talking to another couple, he tucked Marge closer to him.

The song ended. The band took its first break. Once again disobeying him, Cash's eyes roamed over the gathering and picked out Jane.

Tom stood beside her as they talked to another couple. Tom's arm rested possessively on Jane's shoulder. Cash watched Jane grin up at Tom and playfully punch his chin. Tom laughed and squeezed Jane's arm. Jane moved closer into Tom's embrace.

Cash hurried from the room without a backward glance. He ducked out a side door to the back hall and then outside. Skirting the house he sought cover in the long evening shadows of the trees.

Farther down the bank beside the Everetts' boathouse, the dock projected out into the dusky water. His footsteps thudded rapidly down its length. Waves lapped against the shore and the pontoon boat moored there. He stepped onto the pontoon, knowing the boathouse and canvas cover over the boat would shield him from the house windows above.

Leaning over the railing, he scanned the opposite shoreline automatically. But instead of seeing the scene of the lake and pine trees, he saw faces—Lucy, Dena, Phil, Marge, Jane. Then all the faces faded and one stood out alone—Jane's.

"Cash." His name was murmured from behind.

He turned to face Jane. She took one more step forward. He was instantly aware of her intense concentration on him.

He struggled with himself, but he could not stir himself to speak. He turned sideways from her, keeping his taut face out of the light, not wanting to let her read his confusion. He watched Jane, silhouetted in the ebbing sunlight, continue to stare at him as though nerving herself to say something.

The lowering sun's rays caught the brilliance of her hair, and a shimmering halo lit up her face, her reddish-gold hair, creamy skin, clear green eyes. He allowed his gaze to be drawn down the line of her perfect chin. He wanted to draw her into his arms, press his face into her neck and inhale the cinnamon scent that whispered, "Jane," enticingly.

He reached for her, pulled her close. He let his eyes close in anticipation as he bent to kiss her. But his lips met her hand, not her lips.

His eyes opened.

"No," Jane said firmly. "No more empty kisses."

"What?" His voice was low and thick with emotion.

"Cash, I have loved you since you kissed me on my sixteenth birthday, but you never even noticed." She repeated, "You never even noticed. No more. Tonight I declare my independence from your hold over me. You don't love me. You never will. I accept this tonight, and I won't let it cripple the rest of my life. No more empty proposals from you. No more foolish hopes from me. You don't love me. And now my heart is closed to you.''

With that she turned and walked away slowly and deliberately. He listened numbly to her high heels tap evenly on the wooden pier. Then she was out of sight, the boathouse blocking his view.

He felt as though someone had plunged a needle into his chest and was using it to draw his heart out of him. He winced with the pain.

''I love you, Jane,'' he gasped. Unspoken, more painful realizations ribboned through his mind: I've loved you for months. How could I have missed how much I need you?

Chapter Twelve

"I took your advice. I told Cash my heart was closed to him." Jane felt her jaw harden on the word, *closed*. In Lucy's sitting room, Jane sat with Angie on her lap while Angie unknowingly posed for the miniature Lucy was painting for Cash.

"Oh, dear." Lucy's brush stilled.

"I can't waste my life—"

"I know, my dear. You don't need to explain to me. It's just that I can't believe Cash can be so mutton-headed or do I mean muddle-headed?"

"Mutton-headed sounds good to me," Jane replied drily.

Angie twisted in Jane's lap, looking up at her. The little girl squirmed onto her knees and rested her head against Jane's breast.

Jane swallowed tears and hugged Angie.

"Now let's turn around for Grandmother," Jane coaxed Angie. Angie obediently slid onto her seat again.

"I'm almost done, sweetheart," Lucy cooed and began painting with careful, intricate strokes.

"Where's Tom this afternoon?" Jane asked.

"He wanted to do some shopping in town. Are you certain, Jane, that you're not—" Lucy stopped her question.

"I'm not misleading Tom," Jane said quietly. "He is a fine man. He and I have known each other almost our whole lives. Wasn't that what you were thinking when you invited him here?" Jane paused.

"Perhaps." Lucy kept her eyes on her work in progress.

"And I have decided that I don't want Angie and me to be alone for the next twenty years—"

At this Lucy stepped around the easel. "You've truly closed your heart to Cash completely?"

Jane pursed her lips. "Yes. I told you."

"I see." Lucy looked at her granddaughter.

"I want to marry. I don't want Angie to be an only child. I want more children, Grandmother."

Lucy nodded solemnly. "I wanted a houseful, but it wasn't to be. I hope you have better luck. The miniature's finished, Jane."

Jane swung Angie into her arms and stood up. On her grandmother's easel was an oval about two inches by three. In such a small oval, there was only room for Angie's round, cheerful face.

"Beautiful. Simply beautiful." Jane kissed her grandmother's cheek.

"Thank you, dear. But really it would have been impossible to make Angie look anything but darling."

The two women stood side by side. Angie clapped her hands.

"Lucy!" They heard Tom call as he came in the back door.

Lucy replied, "Come in, Tom, and see Angie's miniature. I've just finished it."

He came quickly and stood behind the three females. "How delightful. You look great, kid." He ruffled the raven curls on top of Angie's head. "How about a swim, Jane?"

Her eyes connected with his. She let a smile take over her mouth. "Angie, too?"

"Delighted to have her. Did she bring her trunks?" he teased.

"It's a gracious invitation, Tom," Lucy interposed, "but I think Angie should take a long rock on my lap and maybe sleep."

"Still game then?" Tom asked.

Jane kept her smile in place, but the tug of tears caught at the back of her throat. When would she stop teetering on the brink of tears, moment by moment? Giving up a six-year fascination with Cash wasn't going to be easy.

But in only a matter of minutes Tom and Jane were thundering down the end of Lucy's pier. As they had done thousands of times in the summers of their childhood, they both jumped off the end.

Surfacing, Jane smoothed her wet hair back from her face and looked around for Tom. She turned a complete circle and then called, "Tom—"

She squealed. Two hands jerked her ankles and pulled her back under. The two of them thrashed frantically in the water, then began alternately chasing and dunking each other.

Tom finally swam to the side of the pier. On its vertical posts hung black, oversize inner tubes. He tossed out two. Jane swam to the farthest tube, dived and surfaced in the middle of it. She rested her arms around the tube, her feet dangling. Tom paddled his over to face her.

"Jane." He looked into her eyes. The unguarded expression on his face made it impossible for her to speak. "Jane."

Hesitantly Jane let her hand glide over the wet surface till her fingertips touched his inner tube. With a quick smile, he laid his hand over hers. Once again tears caught in the back of her throat.

Quickly she slid back under the water and struck out into deeper water, liberally splashing Tom's face.

"Mister Langley, explain yourself." Lucy glared at Cash.

Moments ago when she had entered his office, he had risen hastily, causing the blueprint he had been studying to roll shut with a hushed wap. "Lucy?"

"Explain yourself." She took another step forward, closing the slender gap between her and the cluttered desk in his on-site trailer.

"What? What's wrong? Is Angie—"

"There's nothing wrong with Angie. I am asking you to explain yourself, sir."

Her imperious, irritated manner took him so much by surprise that he couldn't think of how to answer her. Finally after at least five seconds of staring, he gave up trying to figure out what to say. He lifted a mound of paperwork off a chair next to his desk. "Won't you sit down—"

"I prefer to stand. Thank you." Lucy let her large canvas purse settle on the front edge of the desk. She folded her hands on top of it.

Cash straightened his spine. "What am I explaining?"

"Your mutton-headed behavior toward my granddaughter."

"I…I…"

The door behind Lucy opened. "Boss, that load of—"

"Pardon me." Lucy turned to face the man. "I am in

conference with Mr. Langley.'' She pulled the door's knob toward herself, forcing the man to back down the steps behind him. When the door closed, she clicked the lock button and swung back to face Cash.

''What the heck is the bee in your bonnet?'' Cash demanded.

''Calling my mood a bee in the bonnet is like calling Hurricane Andrew a thunderstorm.''

''Why don't we just get down to business? What's this all about?'' His hands found his hips. The vehemence of his voice was overshadowed by the sudden pounding of rain on the metal roof above them. He groaned aloud. ''More rain!''

''The fact it's raining one more time this summer should be of no surprise to anyone. Don't try to distract me.''

''What is it, Lucy?''

''I believe I informed you that I wanted to know why you had been playing the fool with my granddaughter.''

''I don't know what you're referring to.'' But uneasiness settled in the pit of his stomach.

''Tom would understand what I am referring to—if he knew what had been going on between you and Jane this summer.''

''Tom.'' Cash's voice was hard. ''I've been asking myself why he received a special invitation to stay with you.''

''Because it was time for Jane to have someone around who appreciated her.''

''And I don't appreciate her.''

''I believe that was my first point.''

They glared at each other.

''You proposed a marriage of convenience to Jane.''

''She told you!'' Surprise shimmered through him. He hadn't thought Jane would tell her grandmother.

''Who else? Why...how could you have blundered so

completely?'' Her tone softened, and she spread her hands in a gesture of appeal.

"I thought it made sense." He shrugged helplessly.

"My granddaughter is beautiful, successful, tender-hearted. For the past six years I have waited for you to, hoped you would, wake up and see what a treasure she was—"

"How was I supposed to know she'd been in love with me? She was the best friend of my baby sister. I wasn't a cradle robber!"

"Your past blindness is no excuse. Your proposal was an insult. An insult!"

"I didn't mean it to be." He looked down. "I can see now that it was a mistake, but—"

"You regret it?"

"With all my heart."

A few seconds of silence vibrated between them. Finally Lucy sat down in the chair he had offered her before, and he let himself settle back into his chair.

"What are your feelings for my granddaughter?"

His mouth went dry. "I love her."

Lucy gave an exaggerated sigh. "I take it you realized this after you proposed?"

He nodded glumly.

Lucy went on, "So you've finally come to see what you should have known for ages, but now you can't tell her—"

"Because she'll think I'm saying it to manipulate her into marrying me *just* for Angie's sake. I don't suppose you could talk this over with her?"

"Impossible. If I did, she'd know I've talked to you about her."

"And it would only make me more suspect."

Lucy sighed loudly again. "This is a fine mess you've

gotten us into. And it makes no sense. In fact, you haven't made sense for a long, long time.''

He looked at her quizzically. "I don't know what you mean.''

"That's obvious.'' She looked into his eyes. "Cash, you've been running from life ever since your mother walked out on you and your father.''

"I don't discuss that.''

Lucy crossed her legs and folded her arms over each other. "Too bad. We're discussing it today.''

"I don't see—''

"Exactly. You've been blind. It's time you shifted your attention from what was taken from you, to what you were given. Dena did.''

"What are you talking about?'' Cash sat back and hunched to one side.

"Dena lost your mother and then your father just like you did. But she never lost hope. Very early she let me introduce her to her Heavenly Father, the author of love, joy and hope. But every time I've tried to give you the same gift you turned away.''

"You know I believe in God, Lucy. What has that got to do with—''

"All love proceeds from God. You believe in God, but it's only a cold, dead acknowledgment of His existence. Love Him. Let Him love you! Thank Him for all the love He brought into your life!''

Cash barked an imitation of a laugh. "I've lost everyone I've ever loved.''

"No you haven't! You haven't lost me or Angie.''

"I lost Dena!''

"You were given her for twenty-two precious years. Can you imagine what your life would have been like if she hadn't been born? Don't you realize your mother had already begun to stray before Dena's birth? God knew you would lose your mother, so he sent you a beautiful sister.''

The frightening thought of never having had his sister in his life chilled Cash. ''I loved Dena every day of her life. I'll miss her every day for the rest of my life.''

''And she loved you, but more important, she turned toward God and life. She lived every day without regret. She didn't give the past any power over her. We've lost her and her husband too soon, but they loved each other with a beautiful, an eternal, love. The same kind of love Jane has in her heart for you.''

Cash froze in his chair, feeling as though Lucy's words had turned him into wood.

Lucy leaned forward. ''God gave you Jane, and you never even noticed.''

''Jane says she doesn't love me anymore.''

''Jane loves you. She's loved you for years.''

''That's not what she plans to do in the future.'' The words nearly caught in his throat.

Lucy paused and bent her head in prayer. When she looked up, she said, ''Cash, I think it's time I told you the truth.''

He looked into her eyes. ''The truth?''

''Dena came to see me before she and her husband drew up their will.''

A horrible, descending feeling gripped Cash.

''Dena told me that if anything happened to her and John, she planned to give their expected child to Jane.''

''Why?'' The single word rattled through him like an earth tremor.

''She was afraid that if anything happened to her, you would retreat into your shell completely and take her child with you.''

A tear slid down Cash's cheek.

"She paid me the compliment of telling me how much my family had meant to her and how much she loved us." Lucy's voice shook and she had to pause to wipe her eyes. "She said she knew if she gave the child to Jane that it would force you to stay in contact with my family."

Cash felt brittle. Any word or glance might shatter his fragile emotions utterly.

"You're going to have to talk to Jane about this. But before you do, you need to talk to God. Settle matters with Him, then ask Him for help."

"How?" he asked through dry lips.

"Just be honest. He's never let anyone down who asked for help. I'll leave you to it." With that, Lucy stood up and left.

For several minutes, Cash sat alone, listening to the pounding rain on the metal roof overhead. Finally, he bent his head into his hands. *God, I don't know where to begin. Lucy says I've been a fool. I think she may be right. I love Jane. I need her. What do I do?*

The rain came down harder, making an angry din. Cash felt its force echo inside him, in his pulse. Tears, pent up for months and years at great cost, released, pouring from his eyes. Images flashed through his mind. His mother, his father, Dena at different ages, Lucy, Jane, finally Angie. *Help me, Lord. I'm through running things my way. I've made a mess of everything. If I have any chance to win Jane for Angie and me, help me. Please."*

The shop doorbell jingled. Jane glanced up and was shocked to see Cash walk in. She hadn't seen him since her parents' anniversary party. Her unruly heart thudded once, then settled back to its natural pace.

"Hi," Cash said, trying to look calm. He still felt drained after his encounter with Lucy two days before, but he felt free of the past. Something new, which must be hope, had resulted from his request to God. Jane still might love him. He believed it now.

Maintaining his pose of nonchalance was difficult, but Lucy had suggested an excuse for him to see Jane tonight. In spite of his fledgling faith, his palms were wet from nervousness. What if he opened his stupid mouth and said the wrong thing again?

"Hi, what can I do for you?" Jane answered, masking her displeasure at his invading her shop.

He hooked his thumbs into the waistband of his worn denim jeans, and she could tell by his dusty appearance that he'd probably been working at his site. "Lucy said you needed someone to look at your roof. You've lost some shingles. And there's another storm on the way."

The Eagle Lake Florist delivery boy, Mel's brother, breezed in. "Flowers for Jane Everett."

Chagrined at the boy's untimely arrival, Jane stepped around the counter, her eyes avoiding Cash's.

"Roses," he explained, offering her a long, white box.

She smiled stiffly, feeling Cash's attention on her. "Now that you've told me, should I bother to open them?"

Carmine's son was not embarrassed. "Why not? Roses are nothing to sneeze at—unless you're allergic to them." He grinned and left with an undaunted wave.

She forced herself to open the box on the nearest glass counter. Twelve perfect, dewy red roses and one white one rested on the moist greenery and darker green tissue paper. The prominent note read: "To a charming lady, Tom." Flushing slightly at the memory of Tom's parting kiss, she purposefully ignored Cash and tucked the card into her skirt pocket.

"Lucy told me your roof's been leaking," he prompted.

"What can you do about it now? It's late, and I'm sure it will be raining soon," she rattled off.

"I think I'll have time to take a look at it before the storm starts." Gambling on her natural courtesy and the fact that her roof did need attention, he crossed his arms in front of his chest and waited.

"I suppose you could come home with me. I might as well just close up. No one is going to come out with the sky going dark at 7:00 p.m." He nodded, and she swallowed the last traces of her irritation. She couldn't actually blame Cash for not loving her. There was no cosmic law that obliged him to do so, just because she had been foolish over him for the past six years.

Obviously Lucy had mentioned Jane's damaged roof to Cash in passing, and out of politeness he was following it up. Feeling his unwavering attention on her, she finished up her daily closing-up routine and picked up the flower box. During the few-block walk to her house, the gusting wind rocked against them and swirled dust into their eyes, keeping them from talking. Its cool edge signaled the new and powerful front which seemed only minutes away. In silence they reached her door.

With his eyes examining the roof above, Cash left Jane's side and edged around the house while she hurried inside. Within minutes she had paid an uncommunicative Tish who, though no longer working at the shop, still sat for Angie. Tish left by the back door to go to her car in the alley. As Angie always did after a separation from Jane, she begged to be held.

With a jolt Jane's stomach rumbled, demanding supper. Outside, thunder rumbled also. Realizing that she would probably be obliged to invite Cash for supper, she grimaced. But resigned to her fate, she carried Angie and the flower box into the kitchen and slid the box onto a lower shelf in the refrigerator. With Angie settled on her hip, Jane went down the steps to her freezer in the basement.

After a hasty search she lifted out a casserole she had made in one of her cooking frenzies. Upstairs she installed Angie in her high chair with miniature crackers on the tray. "Your appetizer, mademoiselle," Jane murmured and tickled Angie under her chin.

She slid the casserole into the microwave on Defrost and began making salad for two. Fortunately her freezer held a half gallon of rainbow sherbet for dessert, and she had cleaned the kitchen the night before. "My imitation of Suzy Homemaker," she said to herself, but it was a cozy feeling to be safe at home in the face of the approaching storm.

She heard Cash let himself in the front door, thud quickly up her front stairs and on up into the attic. He thumped around noisily over her head. The sounds Cash made filled the house in a way she hadn't expected, as though some part of her had been waiting for him to come. She shook her head at herself.

Then Jane heard him exit the same way he had come in. Several minutes later he let himself back in the front door. This time the door got away from him in the wind and banged the outside wall twice before he could latch it. Then without a word he entered the kitchen and sat down at her small table.

Her physical awareness of him jerked all her senses awake. She identified the faint mixing of his scents, a mix that she found compelling as always. The deep timbre of his softly spoken endearment to Angie caught her ear.

Feeling insecure near him, she turned to say something defensive, but instead she bit her lip. His expression was either weary or morose, she couldn't tell which. She took out a pitcher of iced tea and put it on the red-and-white-checked place mat in front of him. "Stay for dinner?" she invited neutrally.

He looked up then. "Thanks. If it's not too much trouble." He eyed her warily.

"Just heating up a casserole."

"Sounds good to me." He gave Angie a tired smile and stroked her head once. Jane noted that it was a much different greeting than the exuberant ones he usually gave his little niece.

Setting the wooden salad bowl at the center of the table, she sat down across from him. He looked so lost. Suddenly she longed to say, "What's wrong, Cash?" But she reminded herself of her resolve. Whatever he was thinking was none of her business and she would have to learn to isolate herself from him emotionally.

Cash was searching his mind, trying to think of what to say to Jane now that he was here with her alone. The only ideas that came to him were mundane comments about her roof. Why did he have to be so completely hopeless when talking to a woman, especially this woman?

After a long swallow of tea, he cleared his throat. "I'll send my roofer over tomorrow. You've lost quite a few shingles on the west side. I'm afraid you'll get some leakage tonight if this storm doesn't pass us by."

"I don't think there's much chance of it passing us. Let's just hope I don't lose any more shingles tonight." As if on cue, the first large raindrops splattered against the kitchen window. At the noise Angie swiveled her head to look at the panes of glass.

"I know it doesn't seem like it, but we've been lucky," Cash said. "Eastern Minnesota got hit with tornadoes the same night your roof was damaged. Two people died."

Jane opened her mouth to reply. The microwave bell rang. Rising, she rotated the glass casserole dish and reset the timer. When she turned back, Cash was again deep in thought, and Angie was staring at him as though even she had noticed her uncle's abstraction. It was unusual for him to sit beside Angie without engaging her in conversation and teasing. Realizing this caused Jane a deep disquiet.

Trying not to call attention to herself and stir Cash's concentration, she quietly finished setting the table for the two of them. The rain dashed against the windowpanes and filled the small room with an intense, relentless rhythm. The microwave bell rang for the second time, and she lifted out the dish.

The aroma of Mexican spices: cumin, chili powder and red pepper, floated over and around the table, bringing her impromptu guest out of his inner concentration. He sniffed broadly and gave her a half smile. "That smells delicious." He looked back to the gale outside the window. "This storm is going to screw up my building schedule one more time."

So that was what was on his mind. She was vaguely unhappy and couldn't put her finger on why. Of course, he wouldn't have been thinking of her. As she set the dish on the table, she motioned toward Angie, whose head already drooped. "She looks like she may fall asleep before she finishes eating."

Jane sat down and began to dish up the cheesy beef, beans and cornmeal for Cash. For Angie to eat, she put down chunks of yellow cheese and some wheat crackers while her dish cooled.

"She likes this stuff?" Cash asked.

"You know she loves people food and hates baby food."

"What's this called?"

"Enchilada bake."

He took another forkful. "It's good."

She murmured her thanks, but turned her attention to the storm again and frowned. The center of the accelerating storm was advancing on them with frightening speed. Lightning flashed outside the darkened kitchen windows, and thunder punctuated their sentences.

"Did Tom head back for Chicago?" Cash asked as innocently as possible.

"Yes." She frowned down at her plate.

"I called here several evenings, and Tish said you were out with him." As soon as the words were out of his mouth, he was irritated with himself. Why bring up the competition—especially when the man's roses were probably in the refrigerator?

"I was." She turned to a drowsy Angie, giving her another mouthful of the casserole. She reached over to the counter and lifted the baby's bottle waiting there. The little girl's eyelids were steadily drifting lower.

"I can't believe it's only three days to her first birthday," he murmured as he watched Angie sucking her bottle.

Jane stiffened visibly.

Again, he felt her cold response to his words as though shards of ice crackling around his ears. How could he have brought up his day alone with Angie? He could easily guess how much it still upset her. Why couldn't he keep his mouth in line?

The three of them finished the meal in silence. They cleared the table and filled the sink with soap and dishes. By now the storm was relentless—flashing, booming.

"This system is not moving away as fast as I thought it would," he said, lifting his voice to be heard. "Do you have a transistor radio—"

Thunder exploded overhead. Angie screamed in fright.

Jane leaped to her feet and lifted the shrieking child into her arms.

"That was close," Jane gasped. She held Angie close, trying to soothe her. The room had gone black, but outside, rapid lightning lit the room like artificial strobe lighting.

"That was a direct hit. Where's your flashlight?"

"I only have a small one, but I'll get it." Jane opened a kitchen drawer and found the solid tube of metal by the brilliance of the staccato flashes. She handed it to Cash and he turned it on.

"Let's go downstairs and check your breakers."

With one hand she felt her way around the erratically lit room. Angie had stopped screaming, but sobbed raggedly against Jane's neck. Without speaking, Cash took Jane's arm. By the thin thread of light from the flashlight, they fumbled their way to the rear of the kitchen and down the narrow, back hall steps. The thunder was now a building crescendo. Jane felt herself tensing with each wave of sound.

Cash used the flashlight to locate the circuit breakers on the basement wall. He checked them manually. All the switches had been tripped. But when he turned them all back to On, no lights from above shone in the rippling darkness.

"Double whammy," he said.

Boom! Crack! The metallic clatter of hail struck the basement windows.

"What's happened?" Jane's voice was loud and shrill.

Cash also raised his voice over the rampaging thunder and hail. "It's an outage plus your house was just struck by lightning."

"Struck! That's never happened before!"

"It's not that uncommon in a storm like—"

Angie whimpered loudly. The sound caught Cash's

heart. He put his arms completely around Jane, cuddling the baby between them. He murmured softly into Angie's ear.

Jane felt the little body pressed against her slowly relaxing. The baby's periodic sobs ebbed, then ceased. Angie shivered once more and let go of the last of her tension.

Taking two tentative steps backward, Jane encountered the edge of the daybed she stored in the basement. Cash let her go, and she sat down on its edge and, humming close to Angie's ear, rocked gently.

"Can we go upstairs?" Jane whispered.

"Let's wait. That wind sounds dangerous." He shone the flashlight up at one of the small basement windows near the laundry area. The window rattled, straining at its latch.

With the flashlight, he showed her the sheets of wind-driven rain still buffeting the basement window. The slashes of lightning continued. Jane shivered. Angie's now-sleeping body became a deadweight across Jane's tired arms, but she held the child till she was certain Angie wouldn't stir.

At Jane's softly spoken suggestion, Cash went to the nearby dryer and brought back a basket of freshly laundered diapers. The cotton diapers made a cozy mattress and blankets. In a matter of moments, Angie, slumbering deeply, was tucked comfortably into the large, oval wicker basket.

The town's tornado siren blared. Its sudden blast jolted them both. Jane jumped up and collided with Cash. He took her into his arms, tucking her tightly to him. The siren wailed on, competing with the beating rain, pinging hail and roaring thunder.

Another bolt of lightning exploded overhead. Jane clutched Cash as though she were drowning. The thunder detonated overhead again, again, again. Each blast urged Jane closer to him, to his solid strength.

Cash's awareness of her soft, slender body surged at the same pace as the storm. Her cinnamon scent was all around him, filling his head. Though afraid she might push him away, he kissed her.

His lips caressed hers. Quivers of excitement like fragments of the lightning arced through her. She swayed in his arms.

He pulled her snugly to him again. His mouth closed over hers, searching and claiming the eager sweetness there. He moved against her, unconsciously imitating the rhythm of the tumult out of doors. The incessant crashes and flashes continued outside, but they receded in her consciousness.

In a surge of almost unbelieving joy, Cash clutched her shoulders, letting go of the flashlight. It clattered to the floor. He held her close, wrapped in the flickering blackness.

The thunder and lightning blustered unnoticed. Jane let herself stand in the shelter of Cash's arms. She knew she should bring them both back to reality. But this was the only man she'd ever loved. She had intended never again to give in to the attraction of his arms, but this would be the last kiss. One last kiss.

Chapter Thirteen

Angie screeched, breaking the silence of the peaceful morning after the stormy night. Asleep on the daybed, Jane jerked awake. Like a videotape on Fast Forward, images of her kissing Cash while nestled in his arms zipped through Jane's mind. After that bittersweet kiss, she'd lain down on the old daybed while Cash had settled himself nearby on an old reclining chair to wait out the storm.

Angie screeched again. Jane scrambled up, stumbling onto the basement's cold, concrete floor. Angie wailed continuously. Jane lifted her out of the wicker basket.

"Angie, sweetie. Oh, dear," Jane fussed. "I forgot to triple-diaper you for the night. You're completely soaked." She dug down to the bottom of the basket for two dry diapers.

Angie shivered and whimpered against Jane's bare shoulder. Jane hurried up the basement steps, through the back hall into the kitchen.

The back door opened. "Jane, it's me." Cash's voice came to her from the small porch.

"In the kitchen," Jane called back. She cleared the sink of dishes and began to fill it with fresh water. While Angie leaned against her, Jane stripped the baby of her sodden yellow romper and saturated diaper. Jane swirled a little baby shampoo into Angie's bathwater, then settled the baby into the warm, sudsy water. Angie's good nature instantly restored, she gurgled and splashed at the floating bubbles.

"You bathe her in the kitchen sink?" Cash appeared at her elbow.

"She doesn't like the big tub," Jane said defensively. "She clings to me and cries."

"She looks like she enjoys this." He peered over Jane's shoulder. "Morning, Angie," he greeted the baby. "Jane, I stopped at Lucy's to tell her you and Angie were all right. Her phone lines should be up again sometime this morning."

Suddenly Jane felt Cash's long, muscled arms—one on each side of her—stretch out and surround her. His skin slid against hers. Jane felt her body become charged with an invisible current transmitted from Cash's bare skin to hers.

Grasping one of Angie's hands in each of his, he helped the little girl splash her bathwater. Soapy water sprinkled Jane's face and bare collarbone. She batted her eyelashes to rid herself of the beads of moisture around her eyes. Then she felt Cash's lips press a kiss on the back of her neck. Jane stiffened. She said quickly, "She'll want her breakfast right away. Can you make one-minute oatmeal?"

Cash, releasing Angie's fingers, straightened up. "*Hot* oatmeal?"

"It's her favorite."

"Even in summer?"

"Her stomach doesn't know it's summer. The cereal's on the shelf over the stove, just follow the directions on the box."

"Okay, boss. Oatmeal coming up." Cash turned away and then turned back. He smiled suddenly. This would be the first morning of a lifetime of mornings for Angie, Jane and him in the kitchen for breakfast together. He pressed another kiss on the back of Jane's neck. "Mmm. You taste good. Much better than oatmeal."

Out of the corner of his eye, he saw Jane flush a deep red. He felt like laughing out loud with a teasing joy, and he waited, anticipating her look toward him, either to scold him or kiss him. He didn't really care which, a scold or kiss, because his answer to both would be a thorough Good-morning-I-love-you kiss. He waited.

Instead, Jane kept her attention on Angie. Feeling sharply disappointed that she hadn't responded as he wished, he went to the appointed shelf. His fledgling faith fluttered to life. *What's happening, God? Tell me the words to say.* Taking the box in hand, he read the directions. "Is this oatmeal for two?"

"I usually make enough for two."

"Very well. I'll make it oatmeal for three." He brought the pan over to the sink to measure in the water. As he stood next to Jane, a glance at her trim figure delighted him. He grinned sideways at her. Leaning over, he bent to kiss her shoulder again.

"Don't."

Taken by surprise, he froze. "But—"

"I'll be right back." Scooping Angie out of the water, Jane folded a clean dishcloth around her, then made a wide curve around the other side of the table and out the door.

Her avoidance of him as she left the room had been

unmistakable. Cold needles of fear pierced his chest. He went through the motions of measuring the oatmeal and water into the saucepan and setting it on the burner to simmer. Then he found the coffee canister and went to work on Jane's fifties vintage percolator.

A few seconds after the timer bell rang for the oatmeal, Jane walked back into the kitchen, Angie in her arms.

Cash lifted the pan from the burner. He smiled uncertainly. Angie squirmed, and in her private language called for him. Jane ignored this and plunked the baby into her high chair.

"Oatmeal, Angie?" Jane offered.

"Where are the bowls?" Cash, waiting with the saucepan in his hand, asked soberly.

Keeping the table between them, Jane went to the cabinets over the sink and quickly collected bowls, cups and spoons. "Please get the milk." She nodded toward the refrigerator next to him and then sat down beside Angie.

Bringing the plastic jug of milk with him, Cash set the pan of oatmeal on a trivet in the middle of the small table and sat down opposite Jane. He studied her, trying to judge what was causing her agitation. Her outward armor was in place, too. She had put on a high-necked, long-sleeved, floor-length robe.

Pressing her lips tightly, she mixed brown sugar and milk into Angie's bowl of oatmeal.

Feeling a deep uncertainty, Cash went over last night's events. He took a deep breath, said a silent prayer, then forced the issue. "Okay, Jane, what's the problem?"

She flushed.

"What's the problem?" he repeated.

She wouldn't meet his eyes. She spooned up a sugary bit of oatmeal for Angie.

"Do you regret our closeness last night?" he demanded bluntly.

Jane cleared her throat. "I should have shown more restraint."

"I don't think either of us could have shown more restraint. I held you in my arms. We kissed. Nothing more happened. I want you as my wife, Jane. I've made that clear."

"You made that clear with your *convenient* proposal," she said stiffly.

"I've changed. I don't just want you as a mother to Angie. I love you."

"No! Don't say it."

"Why not? You're the woman I love—"

"Don't!" Her sharp tone startled Angie. The baby screwed up her face and began crying. "There, there, sweetheart," Jane murmured. "Angie, here is the spoon. Angie, eat with spoon." Gently she put the spoon into the little girl's chubby hand.

Then Jane looked directly into his eyes. "We both know that you don't love me."

"I've changed. I made a mistake when I made that proposal."

"You made it quite clear that you did not love—"

"A man can change his mind."

Jane snapped, "A man can change his tactics to get what he wants."

"You wanted to be in my arms last night."

"It was that awful storm. I was frightened to be alone with Angie."

"The night of your parents' anniversary you told me you loved me."

"I also told you that night I'd decided to close my heart to you. Last night I was weak. It won't happen again."

Not taking his eyes from her, he fought for control by pouring himself a cup of coffee, then he put down the mug. "I will not let you sweep last night under the rug as though it didn't matter. Your kisses showed your love—"

"I don't want to discuss last night—"

"Too bad. We're going to. Now," he insisted.

"*You're* not in charge here." She glared at him.

He took a swallow of coffee to stop another cutting retort that nearly jumped from his lips. *God, help me. What should I say?*

Before he could speak, Angie dropped her spoon. Both of them bent to retrieve it. It had fallen on his side. He picked it up, tossed it into the sink, then handed the baby a clean one.

Jane straightened up stiffly and, even though she gave him only her profile, the anger on her features was obvious.

He again swallowed the hot words that rushed to his mouth. He took a slow breath while watching Angie as she tried to spoon oatmeal into her own mouth. A glob of it quivered just below her mouth.

"Jane, I love you and I want to marry you."

He watched her lift her chin, it trembled slightly. "I wish you wouldn't insult my intelligence. We both know you don't love me."

"No, we don't both know that. I love—"

"Stop it!" She turned to him. "I don't want to hear any more!"

He clenched his jaw, holding back another futile declaration of his love. Why hadn't he realized that he needed to talk to her last night, to speak the right words while their closeness was fresh and irresistible? How could he make her believe him now? He felt as though he were sliding down into a black hole.

Angie threw down her spoon and yelled in frustration. Jane took up another spoon, caught the oatmeal blob and slipped it into the baby's mouth.

Cash took in another tasteless mouthful of coffee. "Do you think it's impossible for me to fall in love with you?"

"It's worse than that. I think you've proven it is impossible for you to fall in love with anyone."

Full-blown, complete frustration exploded within him. He wanted to bellow: I love you, Jane! Instead he closed his eyes. For several minutes he kept his eyes shut as he listened to Jane talking to and feeding Angie.

The desire to go to Jane and pull her to him became a physical ache inside him. He craved her touch more than he had ever craved anyone's touch in his whole life. He wanted Jane. Not just sexually, he wanted all of her, for better for worse, for richer for poorer, now and until her physical beauty faded and their passion was a mere glimmer in her eyes. In the past few days he'd just begun adjusting his mind to think of eternity. Now he knew he wanted to be with Jane until death, then beyond. What could he say or do to make her believe he was sincere? He murmured, "I love you, Jane."

Looking up, he stopped, shocked at the pain he saw in her eyes. In that moment he knew she loved him with a love that was so different from any he had known before: a quality of love that he could only imagine. When Jane had come to him the night of her parents' anniversary, she had told him that she loved him. But it had been like explaining sunlight to a man born blind.

From her eyes he now learned much. Jane still loved

him, even though she denied it. She loved him in a way
he had never dreamed of, in a way he hoped someday he
might be capable of returning. Before that day in Wausau
when he had opened his mouth and spoiled everything,
Jane had wanted to give him a love few people ever imagined. A one-and-only, for-a-lifetime love. She was an Everett, after all. He felt numb. I've been a blind fool.

Two hours had passed since Cash had left Jane's door.
Before he left, Jane had been confused by his change of
expressions from angry to dumbfounded. She lowered Angie into her playpen in the den. A ''Sesame Street''
videotape already played cheerfully on the nearby televi-
sion.

Jane wandered into the kitchen and opened the fridge
for some fruit juice. The white florist box confronted her.
Tom. I forgot all about the roses, she thought.

Lifting the box, she opened it. The blooms looked dry
and neglected. She carried them to the sink and set about
trimming the stems, but her thoughts couldn't be pulled
from Cash. He told her he loved her, but she couldn't
believe him. He might even think he really did, but how
could she be sure? He'd ignored her for years. And, after
his proposal that they marry only for convenience, she
couldn't overcome her doubts.

Cash wanted her as a convenient wife. But no matter
how she denied it, she still wanted him as the love of her
life. She was cursed with the concept of lifelong love and
marriage she'd learned from her parents. Her stomach
clenched and she longed to sit down and cry. Cash had
love enough for Dena, Angie and Lucy. Why couldn't he
manage to fall in love with her? She pulled a glass vase
from a cupboard and began arranging the roses in it.

So it came down to this. She still loved Cash, but she

wouldn't, couldn't settle for less than his heart. To marry him without his loving her would be a sham, an unbearable one. Perhaps with time the pain would ebb.

Somehow, some way she was going to have to push this out of her mind and memory. She must find a way to deal with her lingering feelings for Cash. Because of Angie she would be seeing Cash for the rest of her life.

She finished placing the last flower into the cut-glass vase. She fingered one velvet petal. I'm not being fair to Tom. Right now, I still care too much for Cash.

She walked to the wall phone and dialed Tom's private line in his Chicago office. When he answered, Jane nearly choked on her misery, but she went on, anyway. "Tom, I need to be honest with you."

Angie's first birthday dawned. Promptly at 4:00 p.m., Cash knocked on Phil and Marge's door. It opened quickly. He could feel the hot sun on his back and the cool rush of air-conditioning on his face.

As Lucy let him in, she offered him a silvery, cone-shaped party hat. "Here's your hat, Cash." The living room was filled with Jane's family, just like on the Fourth of July.

Over Lucy's shoulder he spotted Tish, who was giving him a look that spoke of her excruciating embarrassment over the childish party hats. Attempting to soothe her discomfort, Cash winked at Tish. Trying to be cheerful was costing him. Memories of his lost Dena had haunted him all day. His frustration over Jane had upset his sleep. But with cheerful aplomb, which was in direct opposition to his true feelings, he put the cone on his head at a jaunty angle and snapped its elastic string under his chin.

Tish handed him a metal noisemaker for one hand and

a party whistle that would unfold and squeak when he blew it.

"Feels like New Year's Eve," he murmured to Tish.

"Feels like we're at the nuthouse," Tish said to him from the side of her mouth.

"Cash," Marge hailed him from where she sat near the fireplace. "Come here and watch this beautiful child!"

Angie stood on Phil's lap. Phil held her securely under each arm. Angie was trying—with great excitement—to grab the hat from her grandfather's head. Each time she reached up for it, Phil dodged her chubby hands. Instead of squealing with frustration, Angie squealed with enjoyment of the game. Finally Phil let her jerk the hat off his head. Angie crowed and immediately shoved it into her mouth. She was applauded and cheered by one and all— even Tish.

"Now that we're all present," Lucy said formally, "we may begin the activities on this most festive of occasions." Again there was cheering and applause. "Blind Man's Bluff will now commence." Lucy quickly chose Henry as the blind man, tied a handkerchief around his eyes, spun him three times and let him loose in the large living room.

Henry came right at Cash, who jumped backward to avoid being tagged. Tish appeared at Cash's arm and tugged at him to follow her. He let her lead the way down the hall.

"We can hide here," Tish whispered as they arrived in the master bedroom.

"Why do we want to hide?" Cash whispered back.

"You can't tell me that you want to play Blind Man's Bluff. *Kids* don't even play that anymore. When I was ten, I wanted to play it at my after-school birthday party, and none of the kids even knew what it was! Now that shows you how weird—''

"It isn't weird. The Everetts are just…" He groped for the right words.

"The Everetts are just weird.'' Tish folded her arms across her breast.

"The Everetts are blessed with Lucy—''

Tish snorted derisively and tossed her head like a head-strong filly.

"Your grandmother knows what has lasting value and how to stay young or play young.''

"I hate her. I just want to grow up and get away from her and my parents—''

He wanted to shake her then. Tish—who was blessed with a warm and unique family—wanted to run away from it. "I'd give anything to be an Everett.''

Tish shook her head at him, opened the door and waved him out. He left, unable to think of what to say to convince her that she was a princess of a royal family, not an unwilling visitor at the state mental institution.

At the end of the hall Henry grabbed him and made him the next blind man. In moments Cash stood with his arms extended for balance, disoriented, reeling from his three turns. He heard muffled footsteps and laughter. He waited till the sensation of being lost left him. Then he caught a whiff of Jane's unmistakable cinnamon fragrance.

No one moved. They waited for him to begin blundering around to mask their movements. He stood still, letting Jane's scent come to him till he felt he knew exactly where she was. Angie giggled.

Cash swung around to his left. His outflung hand caught an arm. "Gotcha!'' He tugged off his blindfold. Jane, Angie in her arms, was flushed and glaring at him.

"He got the birthday girl," Lucy sang out. "He wins the medal for this game."

Phil pinned a large paper star on Cash's shirt and stole Angie from Jane's arms, leaving the two of them staring at each other.

"You can let go of me now," she ordered.

Cash dropped her arm as though it were electrified.

The two of them were swept into a rousing game of Musical Chairs. Angie clapped and squealed her pleasure. Tish's absence was obvious, and Cash caught the glances that passed between Henry and Claire. He could read their indecision over what to do about their daughter's mutiny, but in the end they remained silent.

When the last game, Pin the Tail on the Donkey, was done, they all sat in a loose circle in the living room to watch Angie open her gifts.

"Jane, here, you hold Angie and, Cash, you sit next to her and help," Marge suggested, pointing to the love seat.

"Why don't you hold Angie, Mother?" Jane countered. "I want to take some pictures." Giving the child to her mother, Jane went to the corner and lifted her camera from her purse.

Cash understood picture taking wasn't keeping Jane from sitting next to him. Did she have to be so obvious about keeping her distance from him? He cleared his throat. "That's a great idea. I'd rather watch, anyway." He hoped he had said it with just the right agreeable, unruffled tone.

So Angie sat on Marge's lap while Phil "helped" his granddaughter open her gifts: a rag baby doll from Lucy, a musical teddy bear from the proud grandparents, a pale lavender porcelain angel with a gilded number "1" on her skirt from Uncle Henry and Aunt Claire, a bright red ball from Tish, who had reappeared, and a tiger hand puppet from Jane. Everything was opened, even some uninteresting clothes which Angie pitched out of the boxes in her search for more toys.

While Angie listened to the musical bear, Cash disappeared and returned. Jane saw him first, coming down the hall. Bent over, he pushed a red tricycle ahead of him.

"Angie," Marge cooed, "look what Uncle Cash has for you."

The little girl pushed herself off her grandmother's lap. Momentarily she stood, steadying herself by touching Marge's knees.

"Angie," Cash coaxed, pushing the shiny trike forward.

She chortled and launched herself toward Cash and the trike.

"She's walking!" Tish exclaimed.

"Jane, get her picture!" Lucy shouted as she leaped up from the sofa.

Jane in throes of several conflicting emotions: joy, resentment, awe and guilt, rapidly snapped the camera's button.

Cash lurched forward, catching Angie just as her uneven steps faltered. He spun her around, laughing. "She walked! She walked! To me!"

Jane continued snapping pictures to mask her tangled emotions. Was she really so petty she would resent Angie taking her first steps toward Cash? No, that wasn't it. But why couldn't she stop feeling like an overwound clock, so tight and tense? Jane continued shooting pictures till the film in the camera ran out. Then she went to the table at the end of the room to her camera bag there. She turned and smiled falsely. "I'll have to reload for some more priceless photos."

Phil stood up. "I'm in the mood for cake." He extended his arms to Angie. "Ice cream, Angie?" he invited. She laughed and smiled in agreement, but remained in her uncle's arms.

The party moved to the festively decorated table. The ritual of lighting and blowing out the birthday candles—one for Angie's first year and one for luck—was observed in the traditional way. Jane kept herself busy, taking pictures, serving cake and scooping ice cream. Finally they were all seated around the table, even Jane.

"Marge, that was the best coconut layer cake you have ever made." Phil patted his stomach contentedly.

"Thank you, darling." Marge leaned over and kissed his cheek.

"Angie certainly seems to have enjoyed herself," Claire pointed out. Everyone looked at the little girl and chuckled. In Everett family tradition, the one-year-old had been allowed to eat her cake and ice cream all by herself. Consequently white frosting, ice cream and flakes of coconut liberally decorated Angie's face, hands and hair.

Lucy stood up and folded her hands in front of her. All eyes turned to her. "This has been a special day. And there is one more presentation."

She cleared her throat. "Cash, today is a day of joy, the celebration of the first year of life for our dear Angie. I wanted to give you something to treasure as a remembrance of this day."

Lucy bent down, opened the doors of the pecan sideboard behind her and drew out the small oval miniature of Angie that she had painted. She gave it to Cash. "Jane helped me with the posing, otherwise I couldn't have done it."

Cash could not take his eyes off the small portrait of

Angie's bright eyes and chubby smile. Tears knotted in his throat. He couldn't speak, so he took Lucy's hand and squeezed it.

Marge stood up. "We also have something for you, Cash. And you, too, Jane. We know that it will cause you both some pain, but Phil and I decided that we should make some gesture that showed our love for Dena even though she has been taken from us."

Phil rose and returned carrying two antique brass picture frames. "Marge and I were reminiscing over old photographs this summer and we came across this picture which we thought captured Dena and Jane in their childhood exactly as we remember them, so we had two enlargements made and enhanced for you." He handed one frame to Cash and one to Jane.

Jane took hers. She trembled when she saw it. The scene was one which brought back a deluge of memories. They were about eleven years old. She and Dena were fishing on Lucy's pier. They had their heads together over a fish on the end of a fishing line. The undersized fish must have swallowed the hook because the two of them were concentrating on unhooking the stubborn fish to throw it back in.

Dena's dark head and Jane's own carrot top were so close they were nearly touching. The sunny lake behind them appeared as mere flares of light, which focused all attention on the faces of the two girls. From her memory, she could hear Dena's childish voice and the loudly lapping waves behind them caused by boat wakes. Jane began to cry. Her mother pressed a hand on Jane's shoulder in sympathy. "Thank you, Mother, Father. I'll treasure it always."

"Same here." Cash's voice was thick with emotion. "Thank you. Thank you all."

Jane saw his tears and regretted her previous anger toward him. She had a loving family. He had only Angie. She had begrudged sharing Angie with him. *God, forgive me.*

She took a deep breath. *Help me, Lord.* Regardless of her own broken heart and foolish dreams about Cash, tomorrow morning when he came to take Angie for the day, she would let the baby go with him with good grace.

Chapter Fourteen

Hot wind swirled around Cash as he stepped from his Jeep the next morning. Overhead, dark clouds in shades of gray from dove to slate tumbled over and around each other as they rolled on in a swiftly changing skyline. Cash had hoped for sunshine today, his first solo visit with Angie. He had planned to spend the day playing with Angie in the sand and shallows of the lake beyond his parents' cottage. But the high wind and racing, rippling clouds above were clear harbingers of uncertain weather.

Today he would finally achieve his goal of having Angie to himself—if just for a while. But within the past weeks, his ultimate aim had altered completely. Now what he truly desired was several hours alone with Jane, so he could persuade her—somehow—that he loved her. Then he would marry her and have both Jane and Angie with him for the rest of his life.

But today would not be the day. The way to persuade Jane that he loved her still eluded him. He ached to declare the sincerity of his love for her. But as matters stood, it would only push her farther from him. Last night, after a call to Lucy for help, Cash had spent most of the evening reading a new Bible and praying for insight.

He had made a mess of everything. Building high-rise condominiums and subdivisions of beautiful homes wasn't a challenge to him. But why had he never learned how to build a relationship with a woman? Would he ever find the way to win Jane's heart? Saying one more silent prayer, he ran a hand through his hair.

As his foot touched the bottom of her front steps, Jane popped out her door with Angie holding her hand. "Good morning, Cash. Angie's all ready."

Stunned by her cheery tone, he froze, one foot on the walk, one foot on the step. He stared up at her.

Jane smiled brightly. Today she would set the tone for these weekly visitations. She would make Dena proud of her and do unto Cash as she would have him do unto her. Hand in hand, Jane and Angie walked down the steps.

Angie squealed when she reached her uncle. Jane released the little hand—such a small parting, such a wrenching at her heart. Cash lifted Angie into his arms.

"Here's her bag." Jane held out the large denim bag. "It has everything you need. When should I expect you two back?"

"Ah…is six or seven all right?" he stammered.

"That's fine. If I'm not home, just let yourself in."

"Okay. Uh, fine."

"See you later." Jane waved cheerily, turned and walked around the side of her house to where her Blazer was parked.

Her legs trembled as she heard the distinctive sound of Cash's Jeep driving away. By the time she got behind the steering wheel, gloom descended on her, a tremendous weight bearing down on her breast. She forced herself to inhale deeply.

"I am not losing Angie," she told herself sternly. "I have lost Dena, but Angie will be home tonight in her crib." Saying the words out loud helped, even though the oppressive feeling of loss hung around her neck like a thick-linked steel chain.

She started her Blazer and headed off to a nearby lake cottage where her seamstress lived. She needed to drop off some skirts and jackets for alteration. It was the first errand of the day she had planned, a day full of work, a busy day, too hectic to allow herself time to think. By the time she closed up shop at six tonight, she would only have enough energy to stagger home and put both Angie and herself to bed.

After a half hour of conversation with her seamstress, Jane rose from the table and started distancing herself from the talkative woman. Jane finally made it out onto the back step.

Outside, the wind snatched and tossed their voices away from them. Startled, both women looked skyward. Overhead, charcoal clouds blanketed the sky. Below the women, at the lakeshore, waves surged against the sandy bank and over the end of the pier.

"This really looks bad," the seamstress shouted, folding her arms over her breasts.

"Mel is all alone at the store. Got to go!" Jane hurried to her vehicle. Rain burst over her. Raindrops hit the nearby lake with such force they splashed up huge plops. She leaped into her Blazer. Taking a deep breath, she swept her dripping hair back from her face and started the ignition.

Down the highway she sped, with great waves of water shooting up from behind her wheels. Sheets of rain rolled down her windshield; the wipers batting at them furiously. Storm darkness smothered the daylight. Her impatience to reach Mel and her anxiety over not knowing where Angie and Cash were swelled inside her with each mile.

Though praying silently, she fought her panic by shouting at the elements. "There'll be another outage. And my roof will be leaking gallons! Enough is enough!" Hail pounded the Blazer roof, blotting out her voice. Marble-sized ice balls beat against her hood and window.

As the wind's velocity grew alarmingly, she fought the steering wheel to stay on the rain-slick road. At last, town loomed ahead. The dangerous sky around her lifted from black to a strange, murky yellow-green. The hail stopped. The wind slowed. She sped up, heading straight for her alley entrance. She swung her car into place behind her shop and parked.

Suddenly in the unnatural midmorning stillness, the town siren blared. She shivered at its shrill sound. The wind swooped back. It hit her Blazer from both sides. It felt like a losing boxer in his last round, punched right and left.

When she opened her door, the wind tore it from her hands. It slammed flat against the side of her vehicle. She screamed. But she couldn't hear her voice above the churning sound. The savage wind slashed her hair and clothing. She felt it sucking her out of the car. She grabbed the door handle and clung to it.

For an unreal second the image of Judy Garland in *The Wizard of Oz* fighting the Kansas wind and stomping on the door of the storm cellar paralyzed Jane. In a terror beyond words, her spirit screamed for God's help.

Mighty strength surged through her. She ripped her hand away from the car and fought the few feet to the shop's rear door. Surprisingly it opened with ease. But as the top hinge let go, she screeched in horror and threw herself inside.

There Mel stood, frozen in the center of the shop. As in a surreal dream, Jane watched through the window behind Mel as the parking meter snapped off its base. Like a javelin, it pierced Jane's plate-glass window. Shards of glass, dust and debris sailed everywhere. Jane felt herself screaming, screaming.

Fighting the pull of the howling wind, she launched herself at Mel. She dragged the girl to the basement stairwell, then pushed Mel down the first step. She fought the door shut. At last she tugged the heavy, old bolt into place. The cheated wind shrieked its anger.

Feeling around in the awful blackness, Jane found Mel at her feet, sitting hunched over on the step. Slipping down weakly, Jane wrapped her arms around the girl. With wordless prayers pouring from her trembling lips, Jane clung to Mel, who sobbed and rocked with terror. The roar above them filled their ears. The door vibrated. The screeching wind struggled to break the bolt.

Suddenly Jane heard her own sobbing clearly, then Mel's. She realized the door above her had ceased straining against the lock. Light glowed around the doorjamb. She swallowed deeply and shivered. "Mel, it's over. It's over. Thank God, it's passed us by."

Mel's grip on her didn't loosen. Jane stood up shakily, urging Mel up with her. She drew back the latch and pushed against the door. It opened a few inches, then bumped against something and stuck. She heaved against it and, with much scraping, it opened. A twisted rack of sodden clothing lay propped against the door.

For seconds, minutes, she stared, befuddled, at the crazy disarray around them. Then Mel leaned her face into Jane's shoulder and mumbled something unintelligible. Jane looked down and saw blood. Mel's head oozed crimson blood onto Jane's white blouse. Her hands where she had touched Mel felt wet and sticky, too. With a gasp, she lifted Mel's face in both her hands. She felt nauseated at the sight of blood spattered over Mel's head and shoulders.

She took a deep breath. "I've got to get you to the medical center. It must have been the glass." Even though she said the words aloud, she felt no impetus to move. A sustained moan from Mel finally cracked the ice jam of Jane's shock.

She stumbled around as though drunk, but she managed to get the two of them outside. Her Blazer waited in the back just as she had left it—except that the driver's side door had been blown off. Farther down the alley a delivery van lay on its side. At the sight of this her mind shrieked, *Angie! Cash!* Terror sliced her heart. Where had Cash taken their baby? Had the two of them been in the path of the storm? Panic clutched her breast. She fought for breath. *God, I can't think. Help me. I can't think!*

"Oh," Mel whimpered.

Pushing down her own terror, Jane half lifted, half pushed Mel into her car through the gap where her door had been. Jane climbed in after her. She fumbled around, then realized that she was instinctively searching for her purse on the seat, but it, too, had been carried away on the wind. Then she saw that her keys still dangled from the ignition. She sighed with relief and started the vehicle. Because the van blocked her usual exit, she backed down the length of the alley till she could swing around and head out onto Main Street.

She stopped at the first intersection, not because the traffic signal was red, but because the traffic light itself lay across the road. Making a wide U-turn, she backtracked to take another route to the hospital. The short trip was torture. Downed branches and crackling power lines terrified her. She had to force herself to press on toward her goal.

At every corner she wanted to turn her car toward Lucy's cottage. Was Lucy safe? Her parents? Angie? Cash?

When the medical center came into view, Jane felt like bursting into tears of relief. She swung into the lot, parked near the emergency entrance and helped Mel out, then through the automatic emergency room doors. The normally tranquil and efficient small-town hospital buzzed with urgent voices and the sound of crying. The fearful sounds hit Jane, draining her of initiative.

Fortunately a nurse saw them and stepped around the counter quickly. "Come with me." She led them into a curtained area and helped Mel up onto an examining table. Soon she was carefully bathing Mel's face and head. She occasionally contacted a sliver of glass and gently tweezed it out. Jane leaned against the inside wall. The desire to bolt taunted her. She had to find Angie and Cash. But she couldn't leave till Mel had been treated and she took her home.

Glancing up at Jane, the nurse murmured, "Please sit down. It will be a while before I can get to you—"

"I'm not hurt—"

"You are. Just not as much." She pointed to a mirror above a small sink. Leaning over, Jane peered into it and gasped. Her own face was nicked and smeared with blood. Her complexion went white. Her knees lost their strength.

The nurse dropped her basin and grabbed Jane's arms. Without ceremony, she plunked Jane down on a straight chair and shoved Jane's head between her knees. "I guess I shouldn't have told you."

"The window broke—"

"Just keep your head down till it clears."

Nodding slightly, Jane gazed dismally at the gray linoleum floor, feeling light-headed for the first time in her life. She felt so helpless. Her family might be in need of her, and here she sat sick at the sight of her own blood. She tried to pray, but only worrying images flashed in her mind. Finally she sat up and watched the nurse finish treating Mel.

Jane stood up. "Let's get you home, Mel. Thanks. We'll take care of the paperwork on our way out."

The nurse tried to dissuade her from leaving without treatment, but Jane helped Mel down from the high table. They stepped outside the curtain and into the arms of Rona.

"Carmella Stephanie Maria Vitelli! Thank God! I couldn't get you on the phone! I went to the shop. It was awful. I was so worried." Mel wilted into her mother's arms and began sobbing.

Jane longed to throw herself into her own mother's arms—and Cash's. She visualized Angie and Cash as they had looked just hours before on her front steps. A terror beyond any she had known before ripped through her, making her gasp aloud. Where were they? Had they suffered harm? Her mind balked at the possibility that they had been hurt, but she could not stop the fear that they might already be lost to her. She felt a scream welling up inside of her. Not Angie! Not Cash!

Her mind at that moment cut away all but the essential. Angie and Cash were the two most important people in her life. Why had she refused Cash's repeated proposals? Why had she let her foolish pride stand between them? So what if he didn't love her! *Oh, God, are they safe? Help me find them. Let me tell him how much I love him. Let me hold Angie and feel her soft, baby hair once more.*

"Jane! Jane, are you all right?" Rona asked loudly, taking Jane's hands in hers.

"She should stay for treatment," the nurse insisted behind them.

Ignoring the nurse, Jane squeezed Rona's hands, then she moved toward the exit. Her fingers plucked keys from her slacks pocket. As she stepped on the rubber pad that activated the automatic exit doors, an ambulance with blaring siren and flashing lights halted in front of her, blocking her path. Two men in uniform quickly unloaded a wheeled stretcher. Jane barely noticed their activity till she saw her cousin climb out of the back of the ambulance, too.

Tish threw herself at Jane, her arms closing around Jane's shoulders. "Mother's hurt!"

"Tish!" Jane scanned her cousin, noting the girl's disheveled clothing, scrapes and bruises.

"We were driving back to town," Tish explained between sobs. "The wind just pushed us off the road! We rolled down the embankment. Over and over. Mother won't ever wear her seat belt...." She gave in to her sobs, and Jane, her arm around Tish's shoulders, turned back to lead her inside. They followed the stretcher on which Claire lay, white and silent, until it disappeared into another curtained area.

A woman with a clipboard tried to ask Tish the few necessary questions to admit her mother, but Jane had to answer for Tish. Her cousin's eyes never left the curtain, which separated her from her mother.

Tish's arrival caught Jane in a dilemma. Seeing Aunt Claire made her anxiety over Cash and Angie multiply tenfold, but she could not leave Tish. As much as she loved her aunt, it took all her willpower to stay in the chair beside her cousin. She desperately needed to see Angie, her grandmother, her parents and Cash. A yearning ignited within her, a yearning to touch Cash, to see him whole and well. This longing almost swept her into tears. But Tish, sitting next to her, had begun to cry. Jane knew if she also gave in to tears, Tish might become hysterical.

Drawing on God's strength through silent prayer, Jane began talking softly, gently to Tish.

Finally she calmed Tish enough so that she could leave her side and go as far as the desk phone. She tried to call each in turn: Cash, Uncle Henry, Lucy, her parents. Downed lines prevented her from reaching any of them, except for Tish's home, but Uncle Henry was not there. She left a message on their answering machine.

Still unconscious, Aunt Claire was wheeled from the curtained area. The doctor explained that one of her lungs may have been punctured and there was a possibility of other internal injuries. Aunt Claire was being taken to X ray immediately, then probably surgery.

Tish clung to Jane. "I'm so afraid."

"I am, too, but the Lord is here. I know we don't feel like it right now, but He is here whether it feels that way to us or not. We only have to ask."

"I don't think He will help me...." Tish began crying harder.

"Of course He will," Jane whispered. "He loves us. No matter what." She swallowed her own tears, held Tish close and smoothed her cousin's long hair back from her tear-stained face over and over.

Then Jane saw Roger Hallawell hustle in. He barked orders at the lone nurse still in sight. Jane caught only the word *injured*. The nurse followed him outside. Within minutes, the woman was back frantically paging staff. Roger returned carrying a girl about ten, who lay limp in his arms.

A rush of staff with wheeled stretchers and chairs passed Jane and Tish. Before Jane could call his name aloud, Roger was back out the door, shouting information to the nurses.

Jane and Tish watched as another four children and one

woman were brought in. All five looked battered. Their clothing was ripped and embedded with mud, leaves and pebbles. Jane waited impatiently till Hallawell emerged from seeing the last of his charges receive treatment. "Roger!"

He hurried to her. "What happened to you?" His shocked expression reminded her of her own disheveled appearance.

"Just some nicks from flying glass," she said with a shrug. She didn't mention he was dirty and blood smeared just like she was. His hands were encrusted with mud as though he had been digging earth with his fingers. "What happened to you? Who were those children?"

"They were attending a woodcraft class at the park near my office. An oak took down the roof. Do you need a ride home or anything?"

"I have my Blazer, minus one door." Then she directed his attention to Tish, who sat pitifully drawn and pale, huddled on the molded plastic chair. Jane lowered her voice. "I have to stay. My aunt is in surgery. We can't locate my uncle and I can't get my family on the phone."

"What do you want me to do? I've got to get going. We're checking damaged areas with rangers and civil defense." As he spoke he looked as though he was about to leave her.

Jane gripped his sleeve, stopping him. "I need to have someone check on my parents and my grandmother."

"Okay. I'll be out that way. If they need help, I'll radio the police. If they're okay, I'll give them your news." Even as he spoke, he pulled away from her.

She nodded, biting her lower lip against tears. He waved to her and left at a jog. Jane slipped back down beside Tish and shivered.

Tish looked up. "How much longer can they keep her up there? It's been over an hour."

She put her arm around her cousin again. "The doctor will be down soon to tell us how she is."

Tish's face trembled. "I've been awful to Mother this week. Yesterday when I was with one of my friends, I even mocked the way she talks. How could I?"

Jane hugged Tish to her, feeling her cousin's tears on her own cheek.

"Just because she and Father talk so much. I love them. I really do—"

"Of course you do."

"Then why do I say and do such terrible things all the time?"

"This is the real world. Just because we love someone doesn't mean we do and say everything we should." Jane's own words stabbed her. She'd been harsh to Cash because of his proposal. "Your parents love you, and they know you love them, too."

At last the doctor, still in green surgical garb, came down the long corridor to them. "Tish, your mother is in post-op. As soon as she is able, we will move her to IC—"

Tish stood up shakily. "That means she's really bad, doesn't it?"

"I wouldn't say that," the doctor hedged. "But we will have to watch her carefully for another day or two. Have you been able to reach your father yet?" Tish, looking down, shook her head. He patted her arm. "Keep trying, then." He turned away. A nurse immediately called him into one of the curtained areas which were all now filled with new patients. Jane and Tish sat back down, side by side.

"I'm so glad you were here, Jane," Tish murmured, looking away. "I acted so awful that day you fired me—"

"Don't talk about it now."

"But I was awful. I lied—"

"Tish, we all do and say things we regret. Grandmother always told me, 'Just don't repeat the same mistake.'"

"I won't. I prom—"

Jane touched two fingers to Tish's lips to silence her. "I have faith your mother is going to be fine. I'll stay till your father comes." She pulled Tish close again.

Father, I'll let you take care of Grandmother, Mom, Dad and even Cash and Angie. But only because I must. This is the hardest day of my life, staying here when I want to go to them. But I have faith that I am where you want me to be. Tish needs me.

Jane shut her eyes, willing away the haunting pain of not knowing where those she loved best were and if they needed help. Heaven would have to take care of them. If only she had the chance to hold Angie in her arms again and tell Cash she loved him and that she would be honored to be his wife. She sighed and rubbed her hand across her forehead.

Another few hours crawled by. The phone lines were still down, and the sheriff sent out word that everyone but rescue workers were to stay off the roads while the utility companies worked to clean up broken power and telephone lines. Jane's eyes burned with fatigue and, for Tish's sake, she had to suppress tears of frustration.

She felt her faith was a rock she was clinging to in the midst of a storm. She hadn't felt that way since Dena's funeral. Soothing Tish took all her strength. She felt beaten, drained of energy.

Finally evening darkened the sky outside the double doors of the ER. The number of people seeking medical attention slowed to a trickle. Another nurse tried to take Jane into a treatment area, but Jane waved her away. Jane's face and hands stung where she had been nicked by glass, but she wasn't in the mood to be poked and prodded by a stranger.

As they waited together, she and Tish held hands. Giving in to fatigue, Jane bent her head into her free hand.

"Tish. Jane."

Jane sat up straight. Uncle Henry stood in front of them. He was mud spattered and rumpled like both of them. "The police finally tracked me down. I was helping our neighbors," he said wearily as Tish flung herself into his arms. "I thought you and your mother were safely in Wausau—"

"It's all my fault. I started a fight with her," Tish sobbed, "so we started home early."

"I'm here now, child." He hugged Tish to him.

Jane rose stiffly. "I'll get going then. Have you heard from Mom or Lucy?"

"No, but I think the twister missed them completely. It swung west of them." He pulled Jane into his embrace, hugging both of them to him.

She rested her head against his arm momentarily. Then she straightened up.

"I should take you home, Jane." He tightened his arm around her.

"Claire and Tish need you here. I'll be all right."

Henry nodded and let her go. "Send word when you can. We'll be here."

She nodded and patted Tish's arm.

Outside, twilight was spent. Jane shivered in the cool evening air. The sweltering temperatures of the morning had been swept away by the storm. She fumbled in her pocket for her keys. Her head throbbed, and she was aware of every cut on her face, neck, arms and hands. In the dim light of the parking lot, she felt totally abandoned.

A blue Jeep careened around the corner and swooped down on her. She turned her head. "Cash!"

The brakes screeched. He leaped out and he was there, in front of her. Before she could speak, he began shouting at her, "Hallawell said you were just scratched. Is this what he calls scratched! If I'd known you were this bad, I would have come right away. How could they let you leave like this? I'm taking you right back in there—"

Suddenly feeling like a fretful child, she whimpered, "No, I want to go home. I want Angie." She tried to describe all the worries of the whole long, torturous day, but her words were garbled by gasps and tears. "Angie?"

"Angie's fine. She's with Lucy at your parents' place." His strong arms went around her, and he hugged her close. He placed fervent kisses on her forehead and mussed hair. "I'm here now. Hush. God's been good. Everyone's fine." His lips and gentle words soothed her.

She rubbed her face against his dirty, wrinkled shirt-front. He was so real she was comforted at last. She heaved several deep sobs, then she released a sigh. The tension left her so suddenly that she leaned limply against him.

"I'll take you home now." He swung her up into his arms, carried her to the passenger seat of his Jeep and hooked her seat belt for her. Then he drove smoothly through almost-empty, darkened streets. Large branches, and in some place trees and light poles, lay beside the road. Fortunately the nearly full moon was out.

Jane insisted as strongly as she was able, "I want to see Angie."

"She's fine."

Jane said, "I want—"

"I had to give in to Lucy and your mother. I tried to bring Angie, but they wouldn't let me out of the door with her."

"Are you sure she doesn't need me?" Jane leaned her head into her hand.

"It's dangerous to be out. There are lines down all over, and, as if this weren't enough, more storms are heading this way tonight. Lucy said Angie was already asleep and would be better off with them, but that I was to *get you home*." He inflected the words to mimic her grandmother's emphatic way of speaking. This persuaded Jane as nothing else might have. She slumped back against her seat. Everyone was safe.

She asked, "Where were you and Angie when the storm hit?"

"At Lucy's. After the all-clear was sounded, the three of us went straight to your parents. Then I headed into town to check on you, but Hallawell flagged me down—"

"Roger did find you then?"

"He told me where you and Tish were and that you were scratched up, but okay. I was going to come for you right then, but he asked me to help him—"

"Help Roger?"

"There was a lot of territory to cover. The rangers, sheriff's deputies, civil defense, all of us were stretched pretty thin. So after I stopped back to tell your family about you and Tish, I cruised two camping areas, then met Hallawell, and we patrolled together. He's still out there, but he sent me to get you. I stopped to get Angie before coming for you. After losing the argument with your family over bringing Angie with me, I came right to the medical center for you."

"I love you. I'll marry you." Her declaration slipped out naturally.

At first the man beside her did not react to it. Moments passed. Then he stopped the Jeep. He tugged her face to his and kissed her.

Cash's kiss had an effervescent effect on Jane. Inside her, an unseen current bubbled up from her toes, lifting her, making her feel as though she floated near him, weightless. He ended the kiss, murmured, "Jane, God knows how much I love you, but I have to get you home now." He gave her a heartening embrace before he turned to the wheel.

Soon he drove down her drive. After parking, he led her to the back door. A cold rain began falling, dampening and chilling them. But when she saw by the light of the veiled moon that her snug house was unscathed, warmth filled her heart. Inside her house the floating sensation, which had carried her in, abruptly deserted her. She slumped against Cash.

"Don't fade out on me now," he whispered. He touched the light switch on the kitchen wall out of habit. When no light flashed on, he grumbled, then swung her into his arms again and cautiously made his way through the dark house to her bedroom. He left her sitting on the edge of her bed.

She heard him making rustling noises in the dark, but she did not feel compelled to make sense of them. Her family was safe, she was in her bedroom, and Cash was with her. Gratitude filled her.

Cash said quietly, "I know we may not need this, but it will give us some light and warmth."

She saw Cash starting a modest fire in her bedroom fireplace. Watching the kindling flare made her shiver in anticipation. The cool evening air, cold rain and damp clothing made the fire very welcome. She stumbled to Cash and dropped to her knees in front of the flames flickering to life.

Cash returned the screen to its place and dropped a kiss on her forehead. "You need a hot bath. Hope you have enough water stored in your hot water heater for one."

From across the hall she heard the creak of her bath faucets being turned on and the gush of water pounding the tub. Cash came back in, pulled her to her feet, snatched a white terry cloth robe off a hook on the back of the door and led her to the warm and steamy bathroom. He sat her down on the edge of the tub.

He rested his hands reassuringly on her shoulders. "I'm going to wash your face and put some antiseptic on those cuts and nicks." He opened the medicine chest over the sink.

Jane closed her eyes, letting Cash smooth saturated cotton over her face and dabbing here and there. Even the stinging of the alcohol did not rouse her completely. Dreamily she trailed her fingers in the water, making more frothy bubbles.

Cash said quietly, "I was so worried about you. We will never let things come between us again."

She smiled and nodded. She wanted to answer him and tell him again that she loved him, but a day of panic and fear had exhausted her. Cash left the room, and she undressed and slipped into the hot water.

From that moment on, her contact with reality became more and more muted. Sustained, conscious thought eluded her, but as she went through the motions of a bath, she was aware of the intense physical sensations: the cinnamon fragrance of her bath soap, the warm water, the touch of terry cloth robe as she covered her bare skin, the gurgling of the water as it drained from the tub. She walked barefoot across the hall. Cash turned back her comforter for her and she slid between cool percale sheets.

"Don't go," she murmured.

"Don't worry. Go to sleep." While the small fire crackled with the pine tar in the logs, he sat down on the bedside rocker.

In the dancing shadows he watched Jane fall asleep. The woman he loved had been spared. She had said, "I love you. I'll marry you." She was his at last. Intense gratitude consumed him. He felt so many emotions he couldn't name them all.

When she was completely asleep, he drew close to her. Her natural scent and the fragrance of her soap had cast their power over him. Just gazing at her brought him intense pleasure. As she breathed evenly, he bent and kissed her cheek. *Thank you, Lord. Please make me worthy of this precious woman.* At last he sat back down, propping his feet on the padded ottoman and fell asleep, deeply satisfied, content.

Chapter Fifteen

$\sim$

At first Jane's eyes merely registered light, filtering through her lashes, but the warm, morning sunlight gently tugged her into consciousness. Then she heard the noisy, chattering sparrows on the boughs of the maple tree outside her window. She yawned. She stretched. She sighed. Rolling over, she buried her head into her fluffy down pillow.

Cash, her mind formed the name. Cash is here with me. She sat up.

She was alone. "Cash," she called softly, then louder, "Cash!" His name drew no response. Her face felt tight, dry. She touched it gingerly.

Rising, she walked into her bathroom. A note taped on the medicine cabinet mirror read: "Jane, I had to go out to the site to assess damage." She pulled the note off and read it again. All the fear and frustration she had struggled with the day before cascaded through her like white water surging over a rocky riverbed. Cash, I want you. I need you—here.

Warm tears slid down her cheeks. "How can I go to

Angie?'' she asked aloud. The ache of loss stunned her with its force. She needed to drive with Cash to her parents' house to see Angie and the rest of her family, to see them safe and whole. She needed to feel their arms around her, smell Angie's fresh-from-the-bath, baby-powder fragrance when she hugged the chubby little body close.

As Jane wiped her fingertips over her cheeks, she felt the scratches on her face. She looked into the mirror at her reflection and drew in a sharp breath. Dried blood starkly delineated each small nick on her forehead, cheeks and chin. A few deeper cuts were perilously close to her left eye.

A vision from the day before of the parking meter piercing her display window sent a chill down her back. For less than a moment she felt the savage wind, the flying glass, heard the wind's roar. She felt weak, and rested her elbows on the sink's rim. ''Dear Lord, anything might have happened to us. Anything! Thank You. Thank You for Your protection. Dear Lord—''

Again, images of the ones she loved most came before her, tugging at her heart. Oh, Cash, why didn't you wake me?

Finally she forced herself to straighten up. Reaching into the medicine cabinet behind the mirror, she selected a tube of antibiotic cream. She applied it to her whole face, and it eased the tightness of her abraded skin.

Then, with a sigh, she walked across the hall and into her room again. Letting her clothes match her mood, she tugged on old jeans and a faded, navy T-shirt. She made herself walk downstairs to her kitchen for breakfast, just as if it were any morning.

Another note lay on the table: ''Coffee is on the stove, Cash.'' She had already smelled the coffee as she walked down the steps. Lifting the pot, she felt it was still hot. I just missed you, Cash! Why didn't you wake me?

For a few fleeting seconds she visualized herself bathing Angie in the sink on the morning after they'd slept in the basement during the storm. She remembered the sleek texture of Cash's skin as he had surrounded her with his arms while he had splashed his hands in the water with Angie. She shivered. She almost believed she could still sense his distinctive sandalwood scent in the empty kitchen.

Her longing for Cash, Angie, everyone, gripped her. But she couldn't go to them. Cash had driven off in his Jeep, and her Blazer was at the medical center. She lifted the receiver of the wall phone. It was dead.

She poured herself a cup of coffee, but after a few sips she made her decision. Clattering her cup onto the countertop, she jotted a quick note: "At my shop" and slammed out the front door.

Outside, evidence of the storm's destruction slowed her steps and brought a deep soberness to her. Downed branches and large limbs were scattered over the sidewalk and streets. Windows had been boarded up against the night's rain. Two cars on Main Street lay "beached" on their sides.

In spite of this, her arrival at the shop jolted her. Someone had boarded up the front display window. Touching her face, she thought of Mel and unlocked the front door. Inside, she propped the door open on its catch.

The bizarre wreckage inside the shop halted her. Clothing racks were down and scattered. What remained of her current inventory was sodden, twisted and already beginning to smell of mildew. Fighting tears, she took deep breaths and passed a hand over her eyes. "It's only things, Jane," she said aloud to herself. "Only things, and to quote Grandmother, 'Hard work is good for the soul,' so don't just stand there, get busy.'' She marched briskly to the rear.

To encourage a cross breeze through the shop, she propped the back entrance open with a broken chair. With a flourish, she flipped on all the switches by the back door. Electric lights and a ceiling fan whirred to life. ''Excellent,'' she said with a sigh. Ever so slightly her spirits lifted.

Stepping carefully over the littered floor, she opened the utility closet, whose latch had held against the wind. From it, she pulled trash bags, a broom, mop and bucket. She paused momentarily to survey the task before her. Then she vigorously slapped open a large, brown plastic bag and began picking up trash blown in after the window broke.

Roger Hallawell found her bent over, carefully picking up a large pieces of glass. ''Jane?''

She stood up. ''How are all the children you brought in yesterday?''

''I just came from seeing them at the medical center. They were bruised up pretty bad. A few had broken bones, but they're doing okay. Except for the girl I carried in, they'll all be going home by eleven.''

''Oh, I'm glad to hear none of them were seriously hurt.'' She smiled at him.

''I'm off to take stock of damage to my site.''

''I'm doing a similar operation here.'' She motioned around her shop and put her hands on her hips.

''I stopped here on purpose.'' He paused and scanned the littered floor. She waited, still looking up at him.

''I was in the wrong about Eagle Shores, about Langley,'' he started hesitantly. ''I was dishonest and I didn't play it very smart.'' He halted.

She remained silent, not knowing how to respond to him politely.

He started again. "Yesterday when I watched a tree take that shelter down, I suddenly realized there was more to life than beating the competition. People were counting on me. They needed me."

Before she could reply, Uncle Henry and Tish bustled in the back door. "Jane!" Henry called.

"How's Aunt Claire?" Jane asked.

"Out of intensive care," Henry answered. "We were there when she was moved this morning. She's feeling better, but so tired. I thought we should let her rest. Tish suggested that we come and give you a helping hand. Jane, you were a godsend yesterday."

With a rueful smile, Tish shyly kissed Jane's cheek, and Jane pulled her close for a quick hug.

"I'm glad you came," Jane said.

Tish nodded, then began picking up branches, leaves and unrecognizable debris.

"While I have you two men here, would you lift a few of the heavier racks and see if we can get them to stand up?" Jane pointed to a couple of racks that had clumped together in a convoluted mass.

Henry came over to help Roger. They hoisted up a long metal pole and held it while Jane unwrapped coils of skirts that were tangled around them. She said, "This reminds me of trying to unravel a twisted necklace from my jewelry case."

Cash strode in the back door and came to her. "Here let me help with that."

At the sound of his voice, Jane's pulse raced. But the presence of the others forced her to abandon her first impulse—to rush into his arms.

Cash supported the middle of the metal bar and found that part of another rack had become enmeshed in the overall tangle.

Jane's eyes kept drifting to Cash's face, looking for a lingering spark of the concern he had shown so fully the night before. But all she read was deep concentration on the task at hand. The skirts from the twisted racks were finally separated into individual lumps on the floor. The three men carried the mangled metal tubes out to the alley and stacked them near the overturned Dumpster.

Hallawell and Cash talked briefly about yesterday's search. Then Hallawell excused himself to go to his own site. Cash walked him to the back entrance. "Call if you need any more help."

Jane felt a surge of pride in the man she loved. After shaking hands with Cash, Hallawell left.

"It's amazing, isn't it, Cash," Henry said, "how two of the display cases shattered, but one remained intact? Was there much damage at your site?"

Cash shrugged. "Not much. Just a lot of limbs down in a sea of mud. Let's get this rack up."

Jane listened and waited. Still, Cash made no effort to approach her for a welcome kiss or personal comment. Had she misunderstood last night or dreamed it?

Cash hadn't realized Jane might not be alone when he came. How could he speak to her about their future with Henry and Tish hanging on every word? He gritted his teeth in frustration, but went to help Henry.

Silently unhappy, Jane again unwound each pair of slacks from around the bent circular rack. As Cash talked her through some of the worst tangles, she recalled her anxiety yesterday morning, when Cash had come to take Angie. Earlier in the year she had equated losing Angie with losing Dena. Now she saw clearly that Angie, Cash, Dena were tangled together in her heart like the twisted clothing that she held in her hands.

After last night she could not bear to go backward in

her relationship with Cash. *God, help me. Tell me what to say or do. I love him. Does he want me, too?*

Her mind ached with doubt, and she needed a few minutes of solitude. She finished unwinding the last pair of slacks. "I have to go downstairs," she said over her shoulder. "It just occurred to me that I left the place wide open last night. I have a cash box and a lot of new fall inventory downstairs."

"The sheriff had his men out patrolling all night," Henry said.

In the basement not a thing had been moved out of place. Her newest shipment of wool skirts and blazers, awaiting tags, hung against the unfinished concrete wall. Jane shook her head over the contrast above and below the top step.

She used the quiet to try to get her emotions under control. Cash had proposed twice, but she had refused him twice. What if he didn't propose again? She racked her memory of last night. After her words of love, he had kissed her, but had he in any distinct way made his proposal again?

Momentarily she pressed her fingers to her temples, willing away the headache that was trying to come. She wanted to have a time alone to talk with Cash. But in another sense, she wished to hide from him, afraid of what he might say if she hinted at marriage. She sighed in exasperation.

She still had trouble believing Cash loved her. So much had happened yesterday. And he hadn't come in and approached her like a man in love.

Standing in the middle of the basement, she pulled up her reserves of strength and cast her concerns on God's broad shoulders. Cash might not love her yet, but he had not failed her. He had come for her the night before, and he was here now working hard to restore her shop. She was determined to make him love her or at least to make him happy if he married her. In any case hiding in the basement was no good. She had to go upstairs.

She started resolutely up the flight of steps. Pausing on the top step, she touched the old-fashioned bolt lock. She didn't want to think about what would have happened to Mel and her if this bolt had not held yesterday's wild wind at bay.

As she emerged from the stairwell, she came face-to-face with Cash. She looked up in surprise, nearly blurting out her musings to him.

Cash spoke first, "Jane, I—"

"Cash," Henry called. "Help me get this parking meter out of here. How did this thing get in here, anyway?"

Cash grimaced, but stepped back to let Jane pass in front of him.

She watched her uncle and Cash hefting the pole which had pierced the window. Tish helped direct the two men as they carried it out to the alley and laid it down.

"Sweetheart!" Jane's mother called to her.

Jane looked up to see her mother hurrying in with Angie in her arms. Close behind her came Phil and Lucy.

Jane met them and scooped up the baby. "Angie, sweetheart." She spun around hugging Angie while she crooned all her love to the plump little girl. Jane's family surrounded her, capturing her in a group hug. Tish and Henry joined the cluster, and kisses began. There was a crescendo of half-asked questions, answers and endearments.

Cash watched and felt his throat tighten with emotion. Staring at the floor, he stuck his hands into the pockets of his jeans.

Lucy looked up. "Cash!" She swooped to him, gathering him to her breast. The swarm of Everetts followed

Lucy. Marge embraced Cash, and Phil thumped his back. Cash grinned, slightly abashed.

Finally Lucy exclaimed, "Everything's ruined, Jane! Your lovely shop!"

"Everything's not ruined, but it is a mess," Jane agreed. "But now that you're all here and Aunt Claire's going to be all right…everything's really okay." Jane shrugged, then kissed Angie's nose.

Cash approached Jane and put his arm around Angie, grazing Jane's arm. She shivered at his touch. Being near him without giving in to the desire to throw her arms around him tortured her. She moved away from him.

Tish answered Angie's greeting and as always gave the little girl an Eskimo kiss. Then Henry quietly brought everyone up-to-date on Claire's condition.

Marge nodded. "We'll go to see her this afternoon. We wanted to help Jane get started here."

Phil scanned the room. "Looks like we've got a lot of work."

Lucy pantomimed looking into a crystal ball. In a mysterious voice she said, "I see a sale in Jane's future. Jane's Super-Dooper, Wash and Wear Clearance Sale." Everyone chuckled.

Suddenly feeling fatigued, Jane sat down on a nearby stool with Angie in her lap.

Henry spoke up, "Only a half mile from here one twister touched down along Highway 51 for about a mile, and a second one destroyed a swath along Bass Lake's southern shore. We were so fortunate neither of the two touched down in a populated area." A sober stillness settled over them.

"Thank you, Lord," Lucy said softly.

Cash recalled yesterday's stark terror when he thought he and Angie might have lost Jane forever. He'd bungled his first proposal to Jane and hadn't done much better since. She deserved the best and he'd begin by giving her a proposal of marriage.

He stepped closer to her and, so he could see her eye to eye, knelt on one knee. "Jane?" he said, his voice sounding gruff to himself. "Will you marry me, Jane Everett? I love you. I can't stand the thought of living without you. I've tried to think of ways to convince you—"

"Cash, dear boy, just kiss her," Lucy said.

He looked into Jane's eyes. "May I kiss you?"

Jane felt a thrill go through her. "Please." Leaning forward, she let her lips meet his.

He pulled back an inch. "Will you marry me, Jane?"

She smiled almost shyly. "Yes."

They kissed again. The Everetts all beamed at the couple. Pressed snugly between Cash and Jane, Angie clapped her hands and squealed with joy.

Epilogue

Late spring, nearly two years later

The blue Jeep came up the final rise smoothly. Jane stepped out first and turned toward the back seat. Cash waved her away and came over to her side. He reached back to the rear seat and undid the hooks of the two car seats. Angie scrambled out under her own steam, but Cash swung their year-old baby, Storme, up into his arms. Storme grinned around her pacifier at him.

Angie rushed toward the crest of the gentle rise, but Jane caught the little girl's hand and slowed her to a walk. Angie and Jane mounted the slope while Cash and Storme brought up the rear. At the top they stopped to take in the view.

Held securely in her father's arms, Storme spit out her pacifier and twisted, trying to look everywhere at once. Then she patted her daddy's chin. He responded by rubbing his face in her belly. After giggling appreciatively over this, she found the pink ribbon that attached her pacifier to her powder blue blouse. With her tiny hand, she lifted the pacifier, sucked it into her mouth. Then she rested her head on her father's shoulder.

Cash swept his free arm eastward. "This will be the view from your kitchen window—east to catch the morning sun."

Jane studied the expanse of the pine and birch forest that she would look at every morning after their house was built.

Cash continued. "I'm putting the great room and screened-in porch on the lake side as we agreed—"

"Mama." Angie stretched her arms up to Jane who lifted the three-year-old and held her close.

Cash put his free arm around his wife's shoulders. They stood, side by side with their daughters facing Lake Elizabeth. Beneath them, on gentle rises up from the lake, other homes were in the process of being built.

"I can't believe we're ready to break ground," Cash murmured.

Jane smiled at him. Then, still holding Angie, she turned toward him and rested her head on her husband's chest, almost eye-to-eye with Storme. Cash and Jane continued standing silently, listening to Storme's rhythmic sucking.

Angie squirmed restlessly, and Jane set the little girl down. Cash and Jane trailed Angie as she walked forward a few feet to a patch of wild daisies. Angie began picking the yellow-and-white top off of each tall stem. Jane soaked in the sun's warmth, the buzz of the boats on the water and the steady beat of nails being hammered into wood.

Smiling with satisfaction, Cash closed his eyes. Storme reached up and touched her father's chin again. Without opening his eyes, he kissed the small, open palm. "We're so lucky. God has been so good." He sighed deeply and kissed the top of Jane's head. "I love you."

Jane nodded her head against him. "Love you, too," she whispered.

"Love you, three," he whispered in return.

* * * * *

Dear Reader,

Thanks for picking out my book! I believe being able to write fiction is a wonderful gift from God. And writing romance is a special treat for me. God so often uses our conflicts with others to change our hearts, especially as a man and woman work out their differences, marry and establish a new home. Cash didn't know he was incomplete and lost. Jane thought her love for Cash was hopeless. But as it is written, "a little child shall lead them," little Angie drew them together, and in the end a new family was born. Cash will never be alone again. His sister's last wish for him was fulfilled.

Never Alone is my first published novel and is close to my heart for that and another, deeper reason. A few years ago I lost one of my special friends, a former college roommate, to cancer. As I wrote about Jane's grieving over Dena, I was able to work through my own deep sorrow and sense of loss. I named baby Angie after my friend. I know I will see my friend Angie again. But for now, this book is a tribute to her vivacious, loving spirit and a testament to God's unfailing love in the most difficult of circumstances.

Lyn Cote

NEW MAN IN TOWN

He leads me beside the still waters.
He restores my soul.

—*Psalms* 23:2–3

To Roberta,
Thanks for believing in my writing.
I owe you so much.

Thanks, Uncle Paul, for the help on pipe organs.
Who knows them better than you?

Chapter One

Over the phone line, Mrs. Chiverton's breathless voice grated on Thea's nerves like spilled sand underfoot. "Now just look out your west window, dear, and let me know what you can see. I'm sure somebody is there now."

Picturing the frail, prissy woman who lived across the lake looking out her window with binoculars, Thea gripped the receiver. Tension spiked up her arm and she flicked her long, single braid off her shoulder.

Why did Mrs. Chiverton have to call and designate her as spy for the day? Weren't the old lady's binoculars in good working order? Thea hated the sin of gossip, but she doubted that she, "a youngster of twenty-four", could ever change the woman who'd spent twice Thea's lifetime as the eyes and ears of Lake Lowell. She dutifully looked out the window as instructed.

Parked along the border of her own property amid the towering evergreens, still-bare trees and patches of white April snow, Thea picked out a red truck. The vehicle was plainly visible to her—as it was to her elderly neighbor. That meant the old lady was really fishing for confirmation of what she'd *already* glimpsed through her trusty old "binocs."

Thea pushed down her irritation. After all, Mrs. Chiverton was just a lonely, old woman. "I see a truck," she reported blandly.

"You do? I'm so concerned. No one seems to know what kind of people the Kramers up and sold the camp to, but there are rumors already. Someone said they may have sold it to a cult or something."

"Why would you think that?" Thea controlled her tone, keeping it unconcerned. "There's been a lucrative boys' camp there for as long as I can remember. What would make you think there would be a change?"

"Why, they sold without a word to any of us. After all those years living here. Something's fishy."

"I'm sure nothing unusual is going on."

"Strange things happen every day, Althea. Ever since your grandmother moved to the retirement center, I feel I ought to look out for you. Now, you live the closest. If the new people need anything, they'll come to you. Maybe they'll need directions or something."

Thea heard a car pull up to her back door. Relief filled her. "My next piano student has arrived. I have to hang up now."

"See what you can find out, won't you, dear?"

So that's why she called me. I'm the most likely source of the fast-breaking news. "I'll see."

She hung up, then spoke to Tomcat, her striped gray tabby, who sat at her feet. "I'll see, but I won't talk." Mentally brushing away her exasperation, she walked the short distance across her sunny kitchen. Tom followed her. Thea looked down. "Tomcat, do you think people in a cult gossip about each other?"

Tomcat meowed companionably.

"I don't plan on spying, but I will keep an eye out for the new neighbors. They deserve, at least, one pleasant welcome." Fleetingly the hope that the newcomer might be male, young and unmarried glimmered and died. No one interesting ever moved to the lake. A commotion outside drew her to the back door.

Turning the knob, Thea opened the door to—chaos. Outside, her golden retriever, Molly, yelped in an unusually frantic pitch.

Nan Johnson and her daughter, Tracy, ran toward Thea. Both shouted to be heard, but Molly's furious howling drowned out their voices.

Thea tried to pick up clues on what had caused the crisis, but was at a loss. "Quiet. Sit." Silenced, Molly obeyed.

Little Tracy yelled, "Miss Glenheim, Poodles got hurt in the car! I didn't mean to!"

Thea surveyed the ten-year-old whose face was flushed. "What happened?"

"I was playing—"

Nan Johnson cut in, her voice raspy with emotion. "On the way here Tracy was hugging Poodles too tightly. The dog decided to jump out of her arms, one front claw got caught in her sweater sleeve—"

"It pulled his toe back too far! It made him cry." Tracy started to sniffle.

Thea stuttered, "But what can I—"

"The toe is dislocated. I can't wait." Nan's voice cracked. "He's in terrible pain. I have to get to the vet now. Can I leave the twins with you?"

"But—" *Leave me alone with two-year-old twins?* Thea started to panic.

"They're sound asleep. Nothing but a bomb will wake them. I can't leave them in the van while I'm at the vet's!

If you'll help me carry them in, they'll sleep through Tracy's piano lesson. *Please!*''

A muffled but frantic whine filtered from inside the van. Its painful pitch cut right through Thea's heart, disintegrating her normal reserve. ''I'll help you get them inside.''

Nan said, ''Thank you! I didn't want Tracy to miss another lesson.''

Pulling the front of her bulky off-white cardigan closed and tying the belt to keep out the chill, Thea followed the woman and warily watched her unhook the first twin boy from his car seat. She couldn't remember when she'd last held a child. She awkwardly accepted the small body and was surprised at the dead weight of a sleeping child in her arms.

Nan suggested, ''If we can just lay them down, they should still be asleep when I return.''

Poodles' whimpering crescendoed. Spurred by worry for the suffering dog and careful of her burden, Thea hurried inside and led the mother to the spare room off the kitchen. Thea pulled the quilt from the bed onto the floor and they laid the boys on it. Then Thea and Nan unzipped the boys' snowsuits, one fire-engine red, the other bright royal blue.

As Nan hustled out the door, she called back, ''Once I know Poodles is out of pain, I'll come right back.''

Thea watched her go, feeling suddenly bereft. One of the ways Thea attracted and kept students was the fact that in snow season, she gave lessons in her students' homes, saving their parents the trouble of going out in marginal weather. She recalled how often in winter Nan had invited her to stay for a cup of tea and a chat after she'd given Tracy a piano lesson. Many winter days it had been the only satisfying adult conversation she'd had.

She eyed the babies. Two soft chubby faces; golden eyelashes to match the curls at their foreheads. Precious, natural cherubs. They certainly hadn't stirred through the coming-in. But what should she do if they woke up?

Still sniffling softly, Tracy met Thea in the kitchen.

Thea paused. She usually discussed only music with her students. "You're going to have to be strong. Crying doesn't change things." That didn't sound very kind.

How could she comfort this child who obviously felt so guilty? *Give me the words, Lord, kind words.* She bent down to bring her face to Tracy's eye level and softened her voice, "Poodles knows you'd never hurt him on purpose."

"I made him cry. I never heard a dog cry before." Fresh tears oozed up and spilled down round cheeks.

Thea patted Tracy's shoulder. "Maybe you'll feel better if you go wash your hands and face in the powder room, then come out to the piano. I have some new music I'll play for you."

"Powder room?" Tracy looked puzzled.

Thea gave a rueful grin. "That's what my grandmother calls the spare bathroom off the kitchen." Being raised by a grandparent had many drawbacks. One was using words common to an older generation. In childhood, it had tripped Thea up more than once.

"Okay." Tracy headed toward the bathroom.

Thea entered her living room and sat down at her dark mahogany baby grand piano. She gazed through the triangle created by the open piano cover to the French doors beyond. The scene of wintry lake, still partially sealed with ice, stretched out before her. Regardless of the limitations of her life, she never tired of the beautiful and refreshing setting she'd been blessed with at birth. Azure, forest green, pristine white—she savored the colors.

For a moment, she imagined the sounds that would soon

revitalize the scene: the fanfare of robins, the bellow of bullfrogs. Her fingers touched the keys and magically the quiet room filled with the presence of Chopin.

She felt Tracy mount the piano bench, scoot over, then lean against her. When Thea sensed one last gasp shudder through the child, she nearly put her arm around the little girl, but she didn't want to break the soothing spell of the music.

In the background, Thea heard her golden retriever, Molly, come through the dog entry built into the kitchen door. The dog padded into the living room and lay down on the braided rug near Thea's feet. Her gray-striped Tomcat appeared from some hiding place and leaped up to sit beside the little girl.

"Kitty," Tracy murmured, then reached out one finger and touched the cat's pink nose.

Like liquid balm, the music coursed from Thea's memory, through her heart and out her fingertips. "Tracy, I'm playing Chopin's 'Raindrop Prelude.' Listen for the drops of rain in the bass."

"I hear them. They're getting faster."

"Yes, the storm is drawing closer, louder."

"Like a thunderstorm?"

"Yes, listen for the thunder." The tempo picked up, followed by quick, strong chords—booming full, sharp.

"I hear it! It's just like a big storm over the lake!"

"Now what's happening?"

The volume began to soften, the steady rhythm slowed. "The storm's moving away."

"That's right. Finally all that's left is drops falling from leaves." Thea tapped out the steady drip-drip notes, then finished on a chord vibrating with subtlety which only heightened its impact. "This is the new piece you were to start today."

Tracy's eyes widened. "Isn't it too hard for me?"

"I played the original piece I memorized long ago. I have a simplified version for you to learn." She lifted a piece of sheet music from the piano top. "Want to try it?"

Tracy nodded vigorously. "I want to memorize it."

This surprised and pleased Thea. Tracy never wanted to memorize. Moments like this when Thea connected with a student through her music eased the loneliness she lived with daily. Her mind turned again to the possibility of a new neighbor, maybe someone younger than seventy and interesting. *Please, Lord, is that too much to ask?*

Thea touched Tracy's arm. "Well, let's see if you feel that way when you've mastered it. I'd never ask you to memorize a piece of music you don't love."

"I love this one already."

Thea nodded. She never tired of its bold theme which translated the beauty of God's world into dramatic sound.

Soon she sat concentrating on Tracy who proudly displayed her progress with her finger exercises. The rest of the lesson passed smoothly.

Near the end, Molly whined and stood up, turning toward the kitchen. She woofed once.

Thea turned her head in time to see a roll of white toilet paper unravel as it passed by the kitchen doorway. "What?" She leaped from her place, dashing to the next room. "Oh, my!"

One twin, half in and half out of his puffy blue snowsuit, had settled in front of the refrigerator finger-painting it with wet cat food from the nearby cat's bowl.

Another roll of toilet paper zoomed past Thea's toes. She glanced at the powder room in time to see the other twin, with his bright red snowsuit bunched around his ankles, drop a full roll into the toilet bowl. "Stop!"

She rushed into the bathroom and grabbed up the baby

who began shrieking at her intrusion. Baby shrieks were uncommon in her single life and made shock waves reverberate through her—like the thunder chords she'd just played. "Tracy, help!"

Running into the kitchen, the little girl met Thea in front of the refrigerator. "Naughty baby!" She shook her finger at her "painting" brother. "No, no!"

Grinning at his big sister, he chortled and licked his finger.

"Oh!" Horrified, Thea tried to think. *Can a child get ill eating cat food?*

Molly barked at the door giving her signal that someone had arrived. *Thank goodness, Nan's back!* She threw the door open and shouted over the baby's shrieks, "One of the twins ate cat food! What should I do?"

Thea's breath caught in her throat.

Not Nan. A handsome man—a tall, dark, young handsome man—stood staring at her. Behind him, a crimson truck was parked. *My new neighbor! He'll think I'm insane.* She longed to disappear with the ease of a perfect grace note.

"Cat food?" He looked puzzled. "Don't they all try that? Why not just give him a drink of water to wash out his mouth?"

She took a step back. "Water. That's a good idea." She hurried to the stainless steel sink, turning on the faucet and reaching for a white paper cup from the dispenser.

The stranger stepped inside, letting the storm door close behind him. Molly whined at him. "Don't worry, girl. I'm harmless." He stooped and picked up the "finger-painting" twin from the floor.

Thea turned and put the cup to the mouth of the baby in the blue snowsuit he held.

The stranger grinned. "Twins—wow. You and your husband must have your hands full."

Words flew out of her mouth. "I'm not married."

She dropped the cup.

Deprived of his drink, the blue-suited twin howled again.

"There, there, little guy, save that screaming for something really big." The stranger stepped past her and poured another cup of water. After taking a sip, the twin in his arms quieted.

With a start, Thea realized she'd been gawking at the stranger, letting her red-suited twin wail. "There, there, little guy," she mimicked. The twin she held rocked, strained, and stretched his arms toward his brother. "What's the matter?"

"Maybe he's thirsty?" Her new neighbor smiled.

This idea brought a new worry. *Please, God, I hope the baby didn't drink any toilet water.* A glance at the powder room reassured her that the twin's short legs had kept him from that disaster. *But he might have fallen into it. Babies can drown that way.* "I always knew I wasn't cut out to be a mother," she muttered unconsciously.

She looked up to see him staring at her, dark brows raised in a questioning expression.

His incorrect assumption unnerved her further. A furious blush spread through her in hot waves. What a great first impression she was making!

She turned briskly to the sink and filled a cup with water for the red-suited twin she held. She said with her back to the man, "These aren't mine." She nodded over her shoulder toward Tracy. "I'm their sister's piano teacher."

"Then why...?" He looked down at the twins and his expression communicated that he didn't understand why baby-sitting went with piano teaching.

"Poodles got hurt," Tracy explained earnestly, looking up at the man. "Mama had to take him to the vet right away."

Thea frowned. "Tracy is one of my students, here for a music lesson," she explained. "These two are her brothers, who were *supposed* to finish their nap on my spare bedroom floor."

He laughed.

The rich bass sound flared, making Thea think of bronzed August sunshine breaking through the tall pines. He jiggled the baby in his arms playfully. "My mom always says, 'With kids, expect the unexpected.'"

"My mama says," Tracy announced, "these twins are going to turn her gray before her time. That means her hair. Not her face."

He laughed again. The deep, joyous notes brought a smile to Thea's face. She had heard of infectious laughter, but had never experienced it firsthand. She couldn't help herself. A smile tugged at the corners of her mouth.

She masked it by cocking her head and looking down into the twin's brown eyes. What an afternoon of unexpected developments and emotions. With sudden whimsy, she bumped her nose to the baby's. The baby cooed, spraying her slightly with water.

"He got you!" The man chuckled.

By the door, Molly yelped once. Nan pushed open the door. "Thea, I..."

Thea didn't have to explain.

One look told the tale of "twin" mischief. "Oh, heavens! I'm so sorry!" The mother quickly scolded the twins. "I'll help you clean up." Nan reached for the paper towels.

"No, no." Thea stopped her. "You've had enough excitement for the day. It won't take me any time to clean this.''

''But—''

''Cleaning a little mess will give me a change. I'm tired of just dusting.''

Nan chuckled. ''If you need that kind of a change, drop by my house any day! Thank you, Thea.'' Nan glanced at the stranger who nodded at her with a smile.

Thea couldn't think how to introduce someone whose name she didn't know. *What could she say? This man just walked in?* Feeling awkward, Thea remained silent.

While Tracy gathered her music, Nan gave Thea the envelope with her payment for the lesson. ''I'm so sorry,'' Nan apologized one more time as she shepherded her children outside. She cast a curious backward glance at the stranger in the kitchen. ''I'll make this up to you. I promise!'' The Johnsons' van pulled away.

Thea, standing at the door, sighed with relief. Then she looked at the stranger who still stood in her kitchen.

Without a word, he walked past her out through her storm door.

What?

Outside, he tapped on the door and waited.

Her brow wrinkled, but she opened the door.

''Let's try a fresh start.'' He offered her his hand. ''Hi, I'm your new neighbor, Peter Della.''

A reluctant smile crept over Thea's face. She touched his hand. In spite of the chill of early April, his hand was warm, inviting hers to linger. Pulling away, she stepped back to let him in. Her ingrained manners snapped into action. ''I'm Thea Glenheim. It's very nice to meet you.'' The pat phrases rolled off her tongue.

He followed suit speaking formally, but with a hint of a smile teasing the corner of his mouth. ''It's nice to make *your* acquaintance, Miss Glenheim. I was wondering if I might use your telephone. Mine should be in service by now, but…'' He shrugged, lifting his hands, palms upward, in defeat.

She gestured toward the phone. ''Certainly.''

''Thank you.'' He went to it where it hung on the kitchen wall. While he wrangled with the phone company about when his service had been ordered, Thea slipped into her regular afternoon routine by heating milk for hot cocoa. As she stirred, she realized she had been ''stirred up'' herself today. How long had it been since a man under the age of forty had stood in her kitchen? Being shy and living in a small town…

This thought made her recall Mrs. Chiverton's phone call. She chewed her lower lip. Should she warn him? She needed to find out if he was used to small-town gossip.

Peter hung up the phone.

She leaned her blue-jeaned hip against the kitchen counter. ''Would you like a cup of hot cocoa?''

He grinned. ''What a healthy suggestion.''

Thea felt herself go pink, increasing her embarrassment. She always drank hot chocolate on winter afternoons and she hadn't thought about how it might sound to a stranger. In an age of cappuccino, espresso, and latte, she'd offered him hot cocoa.

''Hey, I meant that as a joke. I love hot chocolate. Especially with a squirt of whipped cream on top?''

Still feeling uncertain, she half turned from him. ''Sorry, no whipped cream on the menu today. How about a marshmallow?''

''That sounds even better.'' He shed his red ski jacket and draped it on the back of the kitchen chair.

''Are you sure? I can make you coffee if you prefer?''

''Hot cocoa, please. With a marshmallow.''

At the note of sincerity in his deep voice, she stirred the dark powder and sugar into the steaming milk and motioned him to sit at the round maple table by the west window. She poured the fragrant cocoa into two white mugs with little black musical notes on them—a gift from a student—topped each with a marshmallow, then sat down across from him.

He inhaled and sighed. "Mom used to serve me this after school."

She gave him a slight grin. "My grandmother did that, too."

"She must have been very wise."

"She is." Thea sipped the sweet, smooth chocolate. Sitting at her table with a handsome man who had broad shoulders and an air of easy confidence was a totally new experience, an unsettling one. She glanced away at Molly as the dog lay down in front of the refrigerator's warm base. "You bought Double L Boys' Camp?"

"Yes, I've been saving and investing a long time to be able to buy a camp like this. When this one came on the market, I grabbed it."

"I hope you'll enjoy it. It's a big job."

"I won't be working it alone. My parents will be spending the summer helping me out."

"That sounds nice. Where do your parents live?"

"Milwaukee."

"You were raised in a big city?"

"Does big-city life sound so attractive?"

"There are a lot more opportunities." *Like universities with music departments.*

"Well, *I'm* really looking forward to small-town life. I can't wait to get away from noise, traffic, pollution. I want to be able to say I know all my neighbors and feel a real sense of community."

He had just the faulty impressions she'd feared. She cleared her throat. "I see what you mean, but small-town life has its drawbacks." And she knew them all. If her grandmother didn't need her, she'd have gone to live near her father and stepmother long ago. As usual, she felt guilty just thinking about it.

"Going to caution me about the local gossips?" He chuckled.

"Well—" she paused "—yes."

"You're serious." He sounded incredulous.

She looked down. "I already got a call from…someone. They saw your car parked next door and wondered if I had seen anyone."

"They wanted you to report on me?"

She thinned her smile to a firm, straight line. "I don't gossip. But small-town gossips can take the littlest thing and blow it out of proportion."

"I can't think of anything I'm doing that could cause gossip." He looked at her, studied her.

She returned his regard steadily, pressing her point. On the scale of brown, his eyes would be the darkest shade of brown before black while hers ranked at the opposite end—golden hazel. Just as his dark hair curled, her light brown hair hung stick straight. They were opposites. He exuded confidence and warmth, which only made her feel shier and more reserved than ever. So now she knew that even though a handsome man near her age moved next door, she still probably had no chance of his even noticing her.

Placing his elbow on the table, he rested his chin on his hand. "I hadn't thought of gossip so soon, but I still can't see it. Like I told your dog, I'm harmless."

"I just wanted to warn you. Things you never expect to bother anyone can start a neighborhood battle, but you're just going to run the same old boys' camp. That should calm everyone down.''

"Well," he paused, "my camp will be *essentially* the same.''

"Essentially?"

The phone jangled.

Thea answered it and handed it to him.

After a brief exchange, he hung up. "My phone service has started. It was just a glitch on the line and it's fixed.'' He lifted his jacket from the back of his chair. "Thanks for the cocoa, neighbor. And the use of your phone.''

"Anytime." Obviously the topic was closed. She didn't want to bring it up again. She might end up sounding like the gossips she'd just warned him about.

He walked to the door. "I have to fly to Milwaukee. I'll be back in a few days.''

"Fly?"

"I've got a small private plane at Lakeland Airport. I'll commute with it.''

"To Milwaukee?"

"Yes, I still have business to manage there, too.''

"I see." She smiled politely. A man with his own plane. He didn't sound like the type who'd want to run a boys' camp. *Am I missing something?*

He opened the door and gave her a quick wave. "Goodbye, Thea. Nice meeting you.''

"Bye," Thea said softly.

Without moving, she listened to his car's motor catch, then recede as he drove away. In his absence, the silence filled the room around her like thick cotton candy expanding, muffling her. The day had run along unpredictable lines and now she felt off center, restless. "What an afternoon," she murmured with a shake of her head.

Then she replayed the sound of Peter Della's laughter

in her mind. If it were music, it would be marked *basso profundo*—deep bass, *animato*—lively and *allegro*—fast.

The phone rang. She reached for it.

"Well, who is he? What did he say?" Mrs. Chiverton's voice sparked with excitement.

Instantly, the last note of Peter Della's laugh dissolved leaving Thea bleak like the leafless maples outside her window. "He wasn't here very long," Thea hedged.

"He was there long enough to tell you who he is." The old woman turned petulant.

Thea leaned back against the kitchen door jam. "His name is Peter Della." She chose her words carefully. *Telling the name of a new neighbor to another resident isn't gossip.*

"What's he like?"

"He seemed very nice." Nice. *Such a colorless, politely obscure word. So inadequate a description for him somehow.*

The old woman grumbled, "Did he say why he bought the camp?"

"He said he's wanted to run a boys' camp for a long time. This one came on the market. He bought it."

"Is that *all* you found out?"

He likes hot cocoa or is too polite to say otherwise. He's good with children and he has a wonderful laugh. "Yes, Mrs. Chiverton."

"I still say something's fishy. Keep your eyes open, Althea. You call me if you notice anything strange."

Thea thought she heard a car pull in. Her polite "out" had arrived. "My next student is here. I must go." She hung up.

The slam of a car door caught Molly's attention. The golden retriever loped to the door, giving the warning.

A sharp rap, then the door was pushed open. Old Dick

Crandon elbowed his way into her kitchen past Molly. "Where's the new owner? He isn't next door. I tell you he's not going to get away with this. No stranger is just going to move in here and ruin our property values!"

"Ruin our property values?" Thea stared at the retired real estate agent with his white hair and portly middle, bundled in a tweed jacket. "What are you talking about?"

"I'll tell you what I'm talking about! Not long ago I got a call from an old friend who heard something through the real estate grapevine. Said Double L wasn't going to stay just a regular boys' camp. What do you think about that?"

Thea felt a sinking sensation in her stomach. *Oh, no, the rumor mill had started already!* But what if it was true? It might affect her own precarious finances. At the back of her mind, what Peter Della had said came back to her. He'd said the camp would essentially be the same. Just what did he mean by "essentially"?

Chapter Two

"What are you talking about?" Thea's words stuck to her tongue like taffy—sour taffy.

"I'm talking about our new neighbor stabbing us in the back. What's his name anyway?"

"Peter Della, but…" She caught herself just before she fell into the well-laid trap. At her sides her hands found her hips. "Did Mrs. Chiverton call you?"

"Well…" Mr. Crandon paused. "What has that got to do with this?"

"She called and told you he was here, didn't she?"

"Why shouldn't she? Everyone is curious about the new owner, but that has nothing to do with that first call I got. This Peter Della isn't going to run a private boys' camp."

"What makes you think that?"

"Because he was in Madison trying to get state money. That's why!"

"State money for what?"

"I don't know exactly, but I do know there's been some

talk down there of privatizing some juvenile correction fa-
cilities. How would you like to have a boot camp of juvenile delinquents next door?''

Thea's eyebrows rose. ''A boot camp? You mean like
the army?''

''Don't you ever read the newspaper? They take juvenile offenders and put them through a rigorous training like
a military boot camp to try to teach them some discipline.''

Thea's retriever padded into the kitchen and looked to
the door. From outside the sound of a noisy car broke the
atmosphere of friction. ''That's my next student.'' She
looked at pointedly at Mr. Crandon.

He scowled. ''Fine. I'll go. But you tell that new neighbor of ours I want to talk to him.''

Refusing to acknowledge this last statement, Thea
merely opened the door. As soon as Tom Earnest and his
mother Vickie and older brother entered, Mr. Crandon left.

Tom's teen-aged brother, Thad, wearing earphones,
slouched onto a kitchen chair. When their family van
wouldn't start, Thad had to drive them in his old ''beater.''
After hanging up their coats, Vickie followed Thea to the
piano.

Vickie sat down on the nearby vintage bentwood rocker.
''Are you planning on selling your place?''

The land had been owned by Thea's family for generations. Once much larger property, the parcel they held
now was all they had left of the fortune her great-
grandfather had made in lumber.

''How could I even think of moving? My great-
grandfather bought this land. It would kill my grandmother
to sell it. Why would you ask?'' Thea prompted twelve-
year-old Tom to bring out his music.

''I'm sorry. It just seems like Dick Crandon sniffs rumors and real estate deals out of the air.'' The woman

chuckled. "A few years ago my husband and I discussed selling our home one evening and Dick appeared at my door the next day. I asked him how he knew. He said it was just part of being good in real estate."

Vickie suddenly became serious. Thea guessed that Vickie had regretted bringing up her husband. He had left the family and town and filed for divorce a year ago. The sudden divorce had taken the community by surprise.

In the awkward silence, Thea turned on the metronome. Vickie took out her knitting. Soon her needles clicked in time to the metronome's wand.

At Thea's nod, Tom began playing his finger exercises. An exceptional twelve-year-old boy, three years ago Tom had begged for lessons. He still never needed to be reminded to practice. In fact, his mother had limited him to an hour a day. This made going over a lesson with him easy. Thea's work came in preplanning his materials, rather than keeping him on track at the keyboard.

Unfortunately, today this left her mind free to roam over the sounds that echoed from this afternoon—a whimpering poodle, shrieking twins, Mrs. Chiverton's wheedling, Mr. Crandon's bluster, and Peter Della's laugh.

As she replayed its cadence in her mind, she couldn't help smiling. Could a man who laughed like that really be trouble?

She complimented Tom on his finger exercises and briefly corrected and discussed a theory assignment he'd done. Then she asked him to begin his assignment, a piece by Mozart.

Vickie Earnest's words repeated in her mind. *Dick Crandon sniffs rumors out of the air.*

Then she recalled Peter Della scooping the twin up off

the floor and laughing when the baby had sprayed her with water. She smiled.

Why am I paying attention to any of them? It's just small-town gossip.

At midmorning Thea parked and walked to The Café. The early April air still blew cold around her ears and fluttered through her unbound hair. She pulled up the collar of her blue-and-green plaid wool jacket. On Tuesday mornings when she visited her grandmother at the retirement center, she always stopped to pick up a Café caramel roll, her grandmother's favorite. This morning, though, she walked with a slight lag to her step.

She usually parked in the alley, so she didn't have to feed the meter for such a quick stop. But today she'd decided against entering by the rear entrance. To do so would mean running the gauntlet by passing the gathering of retirees who would be, as usual, drinking morning coffee at the large back table.

The group included both Mrs. Chiverton and Mr. Crandon, neither of whom Thea wanted to encounter. She knew she shouldn't let them upset her, but she didn't like being confronted by a group. She could handle these people one by one, but en masse they were to be devoutly avoided.

A few peaceful days had ensued since that "crazy day," as she now termed it. The unruffled routine of her life had resumed. But Thea's inner self, before as calm and orderly as the steady three-beat rhythm of a waltz, had deserted her. Now she was as restless and high-strung as a violin performing the frantic "Flight of the Bumble Bee." This unaccountable, uncontrollable disquiet made her want to avoid discussing Peter Della and Double L Camp.

Bracing herself, she opened the front door and slipped inside. She slid onto a stool at the counter. If she was very unobtrusive, maybe she could get in and out without being noticed. A cup of coffee appeared in front of her on the scratched counter.

"Thanks." Thea reached for the stainless steel creamer. "The usual please."

"Two caramel rolls to go?" The waitress grinned.

Thea nodded and took a cautious sip of coffee. She breathed in the delectable scents of The Café—buttered toast, sizzling bacon and rich coffee.

The Café rumbled with conversation, the clatter of china, small explosions of laughter. Everything normal, just like the faded navy and white decor. Closing her eyes, she drew in another sip of creamy coffee.

"Thea! Thea!"

Hearing Mr. Crandon's preemptive call made her cringe. She glanced around and discovered every one of the retirees gazing at her intently.

Scraping back his chair, portly Mr. Crandon stood up and motioned to her to come back to him. "Thea talked to him." The man's voice carried over the hubbub in the room. "Come here, Thea. We want to hear exactly what he said to you."

She resented being ordered about like a child, but she didn't want to be impolite to her grandmother's friends, especially Mr. Crandon. She knew he must still be grieving for his only son who had died in a snowmobile accident less than six months ago. Reluctantly she pushed herself up. "I just came in to pick up rolls for Grandmother."

"This won't take long," the man coaxed. "Just give us a few minutes. We want to get to the bottom of this."

Her hand gripped the curved chrome back of the stool as she hesitated.

"What did that stranger tell *you* that you didn't tell us?" Old Lady Magill barked. The uncomplimentary name the woman had been called behind her back by the town for years popped into Thea's mind. Thea's grandmother and blunt Mrs. Magill had crossed words many times in the past. Knowing the woman enjoyed an argument didn't take the sting from the old woman's words. *How dare they involve her in their gossip?*

Bristling, Thea stood up straighter. "I don't know what all this curiosity is for. His name is Peter Della. He bought Double L Boys' Camp. That's all I know." Then she sealed her mouth obstinately.

"Why would he be in Madison trying to get state money? There's more to this purchase than meets the eye," Crandon insisted.

"Your source could have been mistaken," Thea replied through tight lips.

"What if it's a halfway house for convicts?" Mrs. Chiverton whined as she fussed with her short blond wig. "They did that in my cousin's town north of Wausau."

Mr. Crandon ignored this. "How many Peter Dellas and Double L Camps are there?" With his pudgy knuckles, Mr. Crandon thumped the table in front of him twice.

Thea held her temper and forced herself to relax. *I will not let them get to me.* "I've told you what I know."

"And you know next to nothing," Mrs. Magill growled.

Thea heard the soft *shush* of the back door opening. She looked past the retirees' table to the corridor which led to the rest room and back entrance. Peter Della had just walked in. Thea took in a startled breath. *Oh, no, where did he come from?*

Mrs. Magill continued stridently, "I've lived on Lake Lowell my whole life. I don't want anything to ruin it."

Thea tensed. She was about to be caught in a head-on collision. Peter Della, completely oblivious to what awaited him, was walking into… The poor man deserved, at least, a fair warning.

Looking directly at Peter, Thea raised her voice, "Mrs. Magill, I don't know why you would think Peter Della is going to do something shady with Double L Camp. Why are you jumping to conclusions over nothing?"

Peter halted, still hidden by the corridor. He looked at Thea quizzically.

Mr. Crandon boomed, "We are not jumping to conclusions! There's a lot of talk in Madison about privatizing boot camps."

"Thea, we'll find out the truth with or without your help," Mrs. Magill grumbled. Several heads around the table bobbed in agreement.

Thea fixed her gaze on Peter. How could he look so vibrant and unruffled? He didn't have a clue about how cantankerous these people could be. She shrugged, saying without words, *See, what did I tell you?*

In reply, he clearly mouthed, "You warned me."

Then he walked out of the shelter of the hallway into the café. "Good morning, everyone. I'm Peter Della."

Peter wished he'd had a camera with him to capture the expressions on the faces that stared back at him—open mouths and wide, startled eyes.

He should have realized that the tall, slender woman who stood facing him had only been speaking the unvarnished truth a few days ago in her kitchen. This community seemed ripe for misunderstanding and controversy.

He gave a slight nod of apology to Thea.

Her head moved a fraction in acceptance.

Peter faced the group of older people gathered at the table next to him. "Now what seems to be the question over my buying Double L Camp?"

"What do you plan to do with the camp?" An old white-haired man glared at Peter.

Peter offered his hand politely. "And you are?"

Reluctantly the old duffer held out his hand. "Dick Crandon."

Peter nodded in acknowledgment. "I plan to run a boys' camp—a successful one, too."

"I'm Mrs. Magill," the old woman who'd been speaking when he entered added. "You mean just like the Kramer family did?" The old woman dressed in a man's frayed flannel shirt and cap looked at him, squinting.

"A pleasure, Mrs. Magill." He smiled at the woman, but was really concentrating on Thea. The bright sunlight from the front window backlit Thea's form, accentuating her willowy figure. How had he missed that the last time he'd seen her? "The only difference about my camp will be that I will receive some backing from donors, charitable sources and churches."

His mind continued to consider the problem of how he'd missed Thea's slender form. *That's right. She was wearing that bulky sweater in her kitchen, not a dress that showed her off so elegantly.*

"This is just what I was warning all of you about," Mrs. Chiverton snapped. "It's some kind of cult."

Peter's eyebrows lifted. *I mention churches and this old woman turns the word into cults?* Obviously Thea knew just how suspicious these people could be. He glanced at her. She was staring at him, probing him, he thought. Was it to see if he needed help?

Peter flashed Thea a grin, then took a step forward. "Hold up there, ma'am. I didn't say anything about a cult."

He paused, but made sure not to link eye contact with Thea. "Someone tried to warn me about how matters can be blown out of proportion if the facts aren't fully explained. Please let me tell you what you want to know."

Peter was aware of a fitful quiet settling over the whole

café. The only sounds to be heard drifted from the kitchen where the cook went on with his duties. Peter watched Thea lower herself onto a stool at the counter in the front. She no longer appeared primed to rush to his aid at any moment and he smiled inwardly. He longed to tell her he could take care of himself.

"All right," Mrs. Magill said. "Say your piece."

Peter bowed toward them. "For a long time, I've wanted to run a boys' camp. I had enough capital to buy Double L, but I need operating funds. I intend to get these through contributions, some from individuals, some from Christian churches or other charities."

Crandon interrupted, "Then why were you in Madison trying to get state funds?"

"How did you know that?" Startled, Peter stared at the man.

"I used to be a real estate agent. I have friends in Madison."

Peter frowned. *What's going on here? Are these people for real?* But he didn't want to antagonize anyone. "I've learned when a project is just starting up, I can't overlook any possible source of funds. I was willing to take state money if my program could qualify for a grant."

Even as he spoke and appeared to be concentrating on the old man, he found himself peering out the corner of his eye to see Thea leaning her chin on her hand as she watched him. A veil of light brown hair cascaded artlessly over her shoulder. *Lovely.*

"Why would the state give a private boys' camp money?" Mrs. Chiverton yipped.

"That's right." Mrs. Magill thumped her fist on the table top. "What's the government giving money to a private camp for?"

Peter grinned. "Actually the state *isn't* contributing any

money. I wasn't willing to jump through all their hoops and hog-tie myself with their red tape."

Crandon snorted. "Well, that shows you have some intelligence. You get the government in your business and you'll wish you hadn't."

While chuckles of wry amusement rippled through the retirees, Peter observed Thea gracefully swing her head making her hair flare as it fell behind one shoulder. Had she done that to conceal a nod of approval?

"Young man, what aren't you telling us?" Mrs. Chiverton folded her bony arms across her chest.

Her testy voice brought Peter back to the subject.

"Yes, why will charities be giving you money?" Crandon glared at him. "Why won't the parents be paying the camp fees themselves?"

"Each family that sends a boy to my camp will pay whatever they can afford," Peter began. "And each camper will work a few hours a day while he attends."

"Ah-*ha!*" Crandon looked as though he was about to jump in the air with satisfaction. "I see it now! You'll be bringing poor kids to Lake Lowell! City kids."

A stunned silence followed by babble swept the café.

Peter glanced to Thea. She'd edged forward on her stool. *She's afraid I'll blow this.*

Peter held up his hands like a referee at a boxing match. He asked in a reasonable tone, "What's wrong with bringing inner-city kids out of Milwaukee for a few weeks of fresh air and sunshine? These are high-risk kids. A chance to get out of their environment can make all the difference in the world to them."

"The kind of boys you'll be bringing out here are the kind who end up in those boot camps. That's what's wrong with it!" the old man exploded.

"Why do you think we live so far from a city for? We

don't want those kinds of kids around here!'' Mrs. Chiverton's face had turned the color of a ripe persimmon with age spots.

"No one will be safe!" Mrs. Magill bellowed.

"You won't get away with this," Mr. Crandon growled. "You can't go changing the land use—zoning—like that. The county board won't hear of it."

Peter lifted his hands again. When Thea had used the words, *blown out of proportion,* she'd been one hundred percent right. When he thought of how long and hard he'd worked to get to this point, he was tempted to say something sarcastic to these people about small towns and small minds, but he held back the biting words. He needed to use diplomacy and hopefully dispel their fears before this went any further. "If you'll let me, I'll give you all the details."

A huffy calm settled over the group, worrying him. Peter glanced frontward again. Thea watched him intently over the rim of her white coffee cup.

Lord, help me calm this storm. He said soothingly, "The boys who come have not been in any significant trouble with the law."

"What do you call significant, young man?" Magill, the old woman with the sour mouth, barked.

"I deem anything that threatens another person with bodily harm is significant trouble, ma'am. These boys won't be active in gangs or known to use drugs. About all they've been guilty of might be some petty sneak thievery—"

"Sneak thieves!" Mrs. Chiverton moaned.

"We'll have to start locking our doors!" Crandon shouted.

As though he had been shooting arrow after arrow which had missed the bull's-eye, Peter felt himself lose it—like his bowstring snapping. "If your doors have locks, what's the big deal about using them? You just stick the key in and turn it!" His volume climbed with each word. "Why are you so concerned about your little selves that you can't spare some understanding for kids who need a helping hand!"

The word *aghast* described the lined faces that stared back at him.

A deep, even voice commented, "A very good question."

Heads turned, swiveling toward the front entrance. Peter followed suit. In the midst of the controversy, he hadn't noticed another customer enter.

"I'm Ed Carlson, pastor of the Church Among the Cedars. I'd like to hear more about your camp."

The retiree table became a quick study in hasty nonchalance.

"Would you let me buy you a cup of coffee, Mr. Della?" Near the front, the pastor motioned toward a tattered navy booth patched with plastic tape.

At the counter, Thea heard the waitress clear her throat and murmur, "Show's over. Are you ready to pay for these rolls?" The woman grinned knowingly at Thea, making her wonder if the waitress had detected the unspoken communication between Peter and herself.

Thea accepted the white paper bag, paid, and hurried out the front door. Peter's rich voice and Mr. Crandon's strident one and all their words flew around in Thea's head. What would happen now? Would Peter stay or leave? She glanced at her watch. *I'm late. Grandmother hates that.*

She drove her aged gray-and-black four-wheel drive vehicle to the retirement complex. Her grandmother, sitting in her wheelchair, waited for her in the solarium, a small room with plants in the bay window on the south side of the center. "You're late."

Thea leaned down and kissed the pale, lined cheek turned toward her. "I'm sorry. I was delayed." She laid the bag down and went to pour their coffee. Soon they sat facing each other by one of the large bay windows. Sunshine through the window warmed them.

"What delayed you?" Because of the stroke, her grandmother's speech was still slurred.

Thea's stomach felt tight. All the turmoil of the morning seemed to have hit her right in her midsection. Her grandmother had always thrived on contention, but Thea hated it. She took a sip of coffee and tried to think of what to say and how to say it.

"Don't try to keep things from me."

Thea glanced up. "I look worried, don't I?"

"You're worried and flustered. Is one of the animals sick?"

"Oh, no. Molly and Tomcat are fine." Thea bit her lower lip, then made eye contact with the old woman sitting across from her. Knowing how her grandmother would jump into any controversy, Thea's first words were cautious. "I met our new neighbor."

Even though her grandmother had lived at the care center for over three years, Thea never felt any place but their house at the lake could be her grandmother's home.

"What's wrong with him?" Her grandmother directed her hawklike, faded blue eyes to Thea.

"Nothing. He seems very nice, but he plans on making some changes at the camp." Thea tried, but couldn't keep the concern from her voice.

"Do you mean new buildings?"

"No, at least, he hasn't mentioned that."

The old woman made a sound of irritation. "Don't diddle. What's the man changing?"

"He's not going to have the same type of camp. It sounds like a church camp—"

"Oh, heavens, not one of those cult places."

What TV news show had featured cults recently? Or was every person over sixty-five in Lake Lowell just fascinated with them? "No, no, a perfectly respectable Christian camp. That's what it sounds like."

"Well!" Her grandmother dismissed this with a wave of her good hand. "That only means having to listen to 'Kumbaya' sung like a dirge every evening."

Thea suppressed a grin, then sighed. "There's more to it than that. Mr. Della intends on using the camp for boys…" She searched her mind for the term Peter had used. "For high-risk boys from Milwaukee."

"Good gracious! *High-risk* is a new way of saying *low-class*."

"Grandmother, please." Fearing she might have over-excited her, Thea touched the older lady's hand. "He's just trying to help them—"

"At our expense! Double L Camp has always catered to a good class of boys! What will this do to our property value?"

"What can it do to change anything?" Thea was tired of hearing about property values.

Her grandmother's jaw clenched. "Thea, you're the last of the Lowells. I would think you would take more interest in what happens on the lake named for your great-grandfather. Undesirable people make undesirable land."

Thea tried to soothe her. "But they won't be living there year-round."

Her grandmother looked at her keenly. "Is this Peter Della good-looking?"

Thea blushed and embarrassment sharpened her voice. "Why would you ask that? What has it got to do with the camp?"

"You look guilty. He's good-looking and a smooth-talking salesman. He's been charming you, so you'll go along."

Thea sat up straighter. Why didn't Grandmother ever give her credit for any intelligence? "He stopped by to use the phone before his was in working order. What's wrong with that?"

"Thea, you have no experience with men, especially men out to get their own way."

"Get their own way? All he wants to do is give needy boys a chance for time at a summer camp. How could that possibly attract a man with ulterior motives?"

"A great deal of money flows through charities. A smart man could funnel some into his own pocket."

Thea stood up. *Why am I so angry? I knew she would react this way.* "I can't believe you just said that. You've never met the man and yet you will pass judgment on his motives."

"I've lived a long time, long enough to know do-gooders always take care of themselves first."

Thea struggled to hold on to her composure. Maybe it was just all the arguing and contention. Her stomach had started to burn. She didn't want to argue. Besides, arguing with Grandmother never did any good. Grandmother never admitted being wrong even if every fact proved she was.

Thea sat down, feeling defeated. "I don't think we should consider Mr. Della a crook when he's just arrived."

"Well, whoever said that? Now you must talk to Dick Crandon about this. He'll know what to do."

Thea grimaced. "Mr. Crandon already knows."

"He does? I'm not surprised. He's a bore, but I'll admit

he always was one for knowing things. And he'll know how to fight this. A zoning challenge, I'll bet. This low-class camp could affect your piano teaching and our fishing cabins.''

Thea looked up, startled. "How?''

"Child, you have no business sense at all. Parents bring their young children and drop them off at our home for their lessons. There is only a low rail fence between the camp and our property. With those kinds of boys loose just next door, parents won't feel safe to leave their children!" A red flush flared out on each of her grandmother's white cheeks.

Alarmed at this sign of agitation, Thea stood up. "Please calm yourself.''

"And the fishermen who rent our cabins each summer leave their valuables in the cabins and their cars.'' Her grandmother's voice slurred more as her agitation increased.

"Please, this will all work itself out.'' Thea turned to go to the wall intercom to call a nurse.

A nursing aide entered. "Mrs. Lowell, I'm here to take you to your weekly physical therapy.''

Grateful for the interruption, Thea kissed her grandmother a hasty goodbye. Grandmother, still looking dissatisfied, allowed herself to be wheeled away.

Then alone in the solarium, Thea threw away the two uneaten caramel rolls. She'd lost her appetite. Was this all a tempest in a teapot as she had hoped, or would it harm her ability to support herself and supplement the last of her grandmother's annuities?

Peter's dream sounded so generous and good, but her father had warned her over and over how people with good intentions could still make errors in judgment. Had her own judgment been affected by Peter's obvious charm and good looks? Could Grandmother be right?

Her stomach churned. Closing her eyes, she silently recited the beginning of the Twenty-Third Psalm, "The Lord is my Shepherd. I shall not want. He maketh me to lie down in green pastures. He leadeth me beside the still waters. He restoreth my soul."

As always, it brought the mental picture of her lakeside home. She sighed. She wouldn't take time to do the few errands in town she had planned. She'd go directly home and have a few minutes of peace before her first piano student came.

She walked outside in deep thought. The cold wind eagerly swooped down on her. She buttoned her jacket and pulled up the collar. Snatches of Mr. Crandon's, Mrs. Chiverton's and her grandmother's words swirled inside her mind. She fought against their effect on her. For once in her life, wouldn't it be wonderful just to stay out of a controversy? But she had a strong feeling she wouldn't be allowed this luxury.

She glanced down to find her keys in her purse. When she looked up, Peter stood blocking her way.

Chapter Three

Shivering slightly, Peter watched Thea round the corner of the one-story, redbrick retirement center. With her head down as if she were worried, she moved toward him seeming unconscious of her natural grace.

He waited for her to glance up. When she did, she looked startled like the doe he'd surprised along the road on his way to town.

"Hi, Thea." Unaccountably he felt thirteen again.

"Peter?" She stared at him.

He took a step forward. "I wanted to thank you for playing Paul Revere this morning."

"What?" She paused. "Oh, I see." She looked down and pushed her hands into her pockets.

He tried to read her mood. She appeared so remote today. He grinned remembering how she'd looked a few days ago with a shrieking baby in her arms. Yes, he'd seen the cool Miss Glenheim ruffled that day.

When she glanced up, her eyes narrowed. "How did you know I'd be here?"

"The waitress told me as I was leaving."

"Why would she do that?" She gave him a bewildered look.

"Maybe because I asked her?" He smiled. "I always like to keep track of where attractive women may be found."

Her eyes widened.

Oh, no, I blew it. "I'm sorry. I should have known. You're already dating someone. Probably a guy you've known since kindergarten."

"What are you talking about?" The wind wafted her long hair forward. Avoiding his eyes, she smoothed it back from her face.

How did she make a commonplace gesture elegant?

He shoved his chilled hands into his pockets. "All right. Let's start over."

She tilted her head, giving him the barest of smiles. "Do you say that often?"

He grinned. "I love a dry sense of humor." He glanced around, then reached for her arm. "Let's walk."

She must have read the exasperation in his look. She took a step back.

Leaning forward, he muttered heatedly, "Don't look now, but there are, at least, a half dozen little old women gawking at us through the glass doors of the entrance."

She closed her eyes for just a moment, then sighed with resignation. "Follow me. We'll take a walk toward the bike trail. It's the only place nearby where our conversation won't be on display."

"Lead on." He tamped down his aggravation. That the town was filled with nosy people wasn't Thea's fault.

She turned and hurried east toward the rear of the retirement center.

He followed, admiring the straightness of her spine and the swing of her long legs.

She led him to the end of the parking lot, then past a cluster of evergreens onto a narrow gravel path that crunched under their feet.

"This is the bike trail?" He looked around with interest.

"It dips into town near here." She pivoted and raised one eyebrow. "Now, what did you want?"

Feeling as though he'd turned a corner and run face-first into a spiderweb, he gave her a questioning glance. He'd come expecting a friendly chat, but this didn't sound like the start of one. "You've changed. Are you sure you're the woman who gave me the warning at the café?"

She met his gaze for a moment, then shivered. "Let's walk. It'll help us keep warm." Without waiting for his reply, she started off briskly.

A vague warning, an uneasiness slithered its way through him. He caught up with her. "What's wrong?"

Keeping her gaze forward, she replied, "I had no idea you were going to change things at the camp."

"I'm not changing much. It's still going to be a boys' camp." He kept up with the brisk pace she set.

"Don't beg the question. You *are* making a big change."

"I don't see it that way. Why do you?" Along with the cold, sharp air, he breathed in her pleasant scent—Lily of the Valley, one of his mother's favorite flowers. The light floral fragrance suited her fair complexion and delicate features.

"You need to see it. You've got to recognize what you've started."

He halted and glanced at her. "What do you mean by that?"

She paused with him, then started walking again. "Don't you understand? You're like a really big rock dropped into a tiny pond. Did you think you could come here, make changes, and create no waves at all?''

He detected a touch of irritation in her voice. Why would his camp upset her? ''But what I'm doing at the camp won't affect anyone else.'' He jammed his hands into his pockets again. ''I should have packed my gloves. Is it always this cold here in April?''

She ignored his second question. ''How can you be so certain your camp won't affect anyone?''

Her steady tone made him hold back a phrase intended to brush her question aside. *Lord, what am I missing? Is she reacting to me or the camp?* Annoyed, he took the effort to keep his tone reasonable. ''Well, you live next door and it won't affect you.''

''It won't?'' she said in a shocked voice. ''After what you heard this morning, you still think something like this won't affect me?''

''I don't get it.'' Tension crept into his voice. ''You'll be at your place. The campers and I will be at mine. What's the problem?''

''My grandmother doesn't see it that way. She says parents won't want to drop off their children at my place for piano lessons if you have a camp of high-risk boys next door.''

''Nonsense. Your grandmother is probably a lovely person, but your piano students won't be in any danger.'' He smiled at her reassuringly.

She shook her head. ''You don't even understand what you've set in motion.''

''I don't?'' In spite of his words, he felt anger flare inside him. Again he fought to keep his cool. *Is this just exaggeration or is there something here I need to know?*

''I tried to warn you at my home. In a situation like this, facts don't matter that much.''

"What?" Gently he swung her toward him by her shoulder, halting her, then planted his hands on his hips. *How could she say that?* "You're not making sense."

She was tall enough to look him straight in the eye.

He liked that. When she spoke, sincerity radiated from her. But as he watched her, she erased all emotion from her face. His irritation was riding him hard. How could she do that? Just stand there, deep inside herself?

She spoke patiently, "Some people aren't interested in facts. They're interested only in what they *think* is true."

Her words came out as puffs of white in the chilled sunshine. *The temperature must be dropping.*

Frowning and disgruntled, he studied her for a few moments, sifting through her words, grappling with them, trying not to resist their import. "You mean facts aren't important here. Perception is."

"Exactly. It doesn't matter if the boys at your camp would be a danger to my students or not. What *matters* is if the parents believe their children are in danger and stop bringing them for lessons."

"But that's foolishness." He threw his hands up in the air. "Just because of rumors, you'll go along with people who don't care? These boys need help." His words were provocative and he didn't try to soften them.

She began pacing on the path in front of a blue spruce. "This is not about you and me. People here care about kids, but their own kids come first. You don't understand how powerful gossip can be in a small community like this."

"I don't get you." He pushed his hands through his hair. "You helped me, coached me at The Café. I saw you!"

She stopped and turned toward him. "Of course. I wouldn't let anyone walk into a pack of wolves without calling out a warning. Besides, I hoped you would be able to head off the gossip.''

''I tried to, but Mr. Crandon and his crew didn't want to let me!'' Anger was getting the best of him.

''I know.'' She folded her hands tightly.

His mind ran over all the years of saving, planning and praying he'd endured to come this far. He couldn't believe he'd be opposed so close to victory. ''Can't you see that I'm right and they're wrong! If you stood with me as my closest neighbor, *we* could head this off.''

''I'm not like you. I hate wrangling.''

''They just don't understand. Help me explain this to them.''

She shook her head. ''What I think doesn't matter to people like Mr. Crandon. You're what people call a mover and shaker. You came here expecting no opposition, but there's going to be opposition. Now you'll just have to see it through or give up.''

''*I* don't give up. Not when I know this is what the Lord has led me to do. Whether the people here want it or not, God wants this camp here.'' He felt belligerent.

A strand of perfectly golden brown hair blew in front of her face. Distracted, he nearly brushed it off her cheek. She still managed to remain serene. This drew him as much as her elegance.

Calming himself, he let his gaze rove over the tall evergreens that lined the trail as though guarding them from prying eyes. *This could make me paranoid. Lord, have I taken a wrong turn or is this just a test?*

If he couldn't persuade this gentle woman, how could he begin to sway anyone else here? His frustration came through in his tone. ''Are you going to back me or not, Thea?''

She pressed her folded hands to her mouth briefly. ''If

people ask me, I'll give them honest answers. I won't go along with the gossip or irrational fears. But if you can't somehow neutralize it, it will affect everyone near you, me included.''

''Then fight it with me!''

She looked down at the path. ''We're different people. You make waves. I don't. You're a stranger. I was born here and have lived here my whole life.''

''So?''

''I support myself and my grandmother through my music and by renting out three fishing cabins on our land. I live on a tight budget and I must help keep up the center's fees for my grandmother's care. I'm not independently wealthy.''

''Neither am I.'' He thought about the cost of all the improvements for the camp, including the two buses he needed.

''I didn't say you were, but you said you have business in Milwaukee.'' Her voice grew stronger. ''Your income doesn't depend on this boys' camp, does it?''

He shook his head no. *But my income alone won't support the camp, either.*

''I live and work on the land my great-grandfather bought before the turn of the century.'' Her love of home broke through her quiet manner, raising her voice in the winterlike stillness. ''I'm part of this town. This place is my home. If this blows up and people start boycotting my property because it's next to your camp, I can't just pack up and go elsewhere. I'll be forced to weather the storm. You have to take the community into consideration.''

Her love of home touched him and drained away his anger. He already loved his camp with the same devotion. He'd dreamed of this camp over half his life. ''You can't expect me just to give up!''

"Becoming upset won't help." She studied him.

Looking away, he acknowledged the tangle of irritated emotions within himself. Though he wanted to vent his anger, he held his peace trying to think. He'd already "lost it" with the old people at The Café. He couldn't lose it with this lovely and wise woman. *Lord, I never expected anything like this.* A few moments of silence passed between them. "But—"

She held up her hand. "I think you're used to easily persuading people to go along with your ideas. That isn't going to happen here. You're going to have to work at it."

She wove her fingers together and held them toward him. "This is a small town. Our lives are intertwined. You say your camp won't affect me. Can you guarantee that?"

He stared at her, sobered. "No." He cocked his head to the side, observing how the pale sunlight glinted in her hair. Her unmistakable concern for him, in spite of her belief that his camp would cause her trouble, moved him. At least she took his plans seriously. If Alanna had, matters might have ended differently for them.

She nodded, looking sad, then murmured, "I have to get home." She turned and began walking back toward the parking lot.

Peter followed, mulling over everything he'd heard this morning. He'd been able to dismiss the dustup in The Café because of the calm good sense Pastor Carlson had spoken to him over a cup of coffee.

He had sought out Thea because he wanted to thank her and he'd wanted to pursue her acquaintance. But now all the points this self-contained woman had made so calmly spelled trouble for him, for his mission, his dream.

His vision had always been clear. This camp coming up for sale this year had seemed an answer to prayer. Had he misjudged things?

He felt drained, as though they had sprinted, not walked. "Do you have any suggestion about how I could neutralize this opposition?"

She stopped and gazed at the gravel path. "It would have been good if you could have involved the community in the decision, gotten some key people on your side. I'm sorry. I told you, in a small town, things you never thought would bother anyone can start a battle. And the results can be dreadful." She shivered. "This wouldn't be the first war in Lake Lowell."

Wearing a gray wool suit, Thea began to lay out her Sunday morning sheet music on the pipe organ at the front of the church.

"Thea?" A familiar booming voice hit her from behind.

Thea turned and faced Mrs. Magill who wore her Sunday outfit, a shapeless navy suit and clean white sneakers.

"We've got that organ meeting in the basement now."

Thea frowned. "I know Pastor Carlson wants me to attend, but I'll have to play the prelude before the service soon."

"You've got to be there. I know you always try to squirm out of committee work, but no more." The old woman pointed toward the basement staircase in the foyer of the church decorated in off-white and rich maple. "Let's get this over with." The old woman lumbered down the two steps, then up the aisle.

Thea trailed after her. Mrs. Magill was right. Thea didn't like being on committees. In fact, so far she had successfully avoided them completely. But she hadn't thought anyone had noticed this omission on her part. She just didn't like meetings. She'd hated the way her grandmother had always made certain she dominated every committee she'd ever taken part in. The cutting remarks Grandmother had made to the other members at the meetings hadn't been nearly as bad as those she made about them at home afterward.

Thea picked up her pace and marched after Mrs. Magill down the steps to the basement. A few children in their Sunday best clustered, chattering around their Sunday School teachers who were unpacking workbooks and crayons at low tables. Little Tracy, holding one of her twin brother's hands, stopped Thea. Thea stooped momentarily to greet Tracy and pat the baby's cheek. With a smile, Thea waved bye-bye to them and hurried after Mrs. Magill.

Thea and Mrs. Magill halted in the immaculate church kitchen. The other members of the committee waited around the table—Vickie Earnest, Nan Johnson with one twin on her lap, and finally Mrs. Chiverton. Thea sighed inwardly. At least she wasn't doomed to listen to the two old women wrangle all alone. After years of giving weekly piano lessons to their children, Thea felt at ease with Nan and Vickie.

Sitting down near the end of the table, as far from the others as she could without being thought impolite, Thea felt hemmed in by white kitchen cupboards and cornered by the four other committee members.

Her memory dredged up the fleeting, unpleasant impressions of all the committee meetings her grandmother had led at home and here at church. *I'll just sit here very quietly and this will be over before I know it.*

"Well, let's get started." Vickie Earnest, the local hairstylist with the plainest haircut in the room, opened a small black notebook.

"Are you the self-appointed chair of this committee?" Mrs. Chiverton inquired in that insincere sweet tone that always grated on Thea's nerves.

"No, I just want to get this started and over. We only have a few minutes before church," Vickie replied.

"That's why I suggested the meeting be held now," Mrs. Magill said in her gruff voice. "It will prevent long, wandering discussions."

"Fine, but we still need to elect a chairwoman." Mrs. Chiverton looked grim.

"That's not difficult," Nan said. "There's only one person here qualified to be chair—Thea."

Thea nearly bolted from her seat. "Me? No!"

"Your grandmother chaired this committee the last time it was formed fifteen years ago." Mrs. Chiverton smiled at Thea conspiratorially.

"B-but…" Thea sputtered trying to think of a way out.

"You're the church organist." Nan smiled encouragingly at Thea as she played patty-cake with her son. "You know more about organs than all of us put together."

"I couldn't." Thea held up her hand like a drowning woman. "I'm just here to give technical advice."

"You're the one who's going to have to play the organ, so you should be the chair," Vickie said.

"That settles it." Mrs. Magill finally lowered her bulk into the spindly kitchen chair.

Mrs. Chiverton nodded, her dangling pearl earrings jiggling just beneath her Sunday platinum blond wig. "It's time you followed in your grandmother's formidable footsteps in this church."

"But I'm not like my grandmother," Thea said desperately.

"Your grandmother always did a lovely job," Mrs. Chiverton cooed. "She was such a leader."

Thea caught the glances that passed between the two younger women. Mrs. Chiverton was about the only one in town who had enjoyed Grandmother's high-handed ways. "I really don't think—"

"All those in favor of Thea as chair raise your right hand." Mrs. Magill raised her man-size hand.

The two younger women and Mrs. Chiverton followed suit.

"Majority rules. Thea, start the meeting," Mrs. Magill ordered.

Thea sat, stunned. She'd barely adjusted to being on a committee and now she was expected to chair it?

"Thea, how would you like to start the meeting?" Vickie glanced in her direction with a smile.

"With prayer?" Nan suggested.

"Would you, please?" Thea murmured, feeling trampled and railroaded.

Folding her hands in front of her little boy, Nan started, "Dear Father."

Thea closed her eyes and folded her hands.

Nan continued, "Please be with us as this committee meets. We want to do Your will in deciding how to be good stewards of the money the church has for the organ. Thank you. Amen."

At the prayer's end, within herself Thea prayed simply, *"Help me, Lord. How do I do this?"* She looked up.

All the ladies gazed back at her expectantly.

"Thank you, Nan." Thea cleared her throat. "I hadn't anticipated chairing this committee." *Or any committee. I might as well admit my incompetence right away.* "Does anyone have a suggestion for how to begin?"

"I think someone should discover what our options are," Vickie said.

Thea nodded.

"What options?" Mrs. Chiverton whined. "We have a perfectly good pipe organ. We just need to have it refurbished again. You young women just don't remember the Depression.''

"This meeting has gone on long enough.'' Mrs. Magill stood up. "I'll look into the price of new pipe organs.''

Thea knew she should object to this abrupt ending, but if Mrs. Magill wanted to look into the prices for new pipe organs, why should she complain? And Thea was needed upstairs at the organ now.

"I'll look into the price of electronic organs.'' Nan stood up and settled her son on her hip.

Fine. Thea nodded with relief.

"Thea, why don't you look into the cost of repairs for our present organ?'' Vickie asked, gathering her purse and Bible.

"That makes sense.'' Thea nodded again.

Soon only she and Mrs. Chiverton sat in the kitchen.

"Well!'' Mrs. Chiverton stood up and pinned Thea with a withering glance. "Your grandmother would never have handled—or should I say *mishandled*—a meeting like that! She always ran a tight ship.''

Thea silently agreed with the woman who'd been her grandmother's crony for as long as she could remember. Grandmother would have been appalled.

"Everyone has a job but me!'' The old woman huffed.

Thea thought quickly. "Why don't you write up the notes of the meeting?''

"I suppose I'd have time to do that.'' Mrs. Chiverton flounced out, her high heels tapping indignantly on the linoleum.

While Thea headed upstairs to begin playing the prelude, she tried to make sense of the so-called committee meeting. Without shirking her duty to help make the right decision about repairing or replacing the organ, how could she get out of chairing the committee gracefully? Sitting down at the organ, she said a prayer for guidance, then began the strains of Bach's "Jesu, Joy of Man's Desiring."

Later, near the end of the morning worship service, Thea sat still, prim and uneasy beside the church organ. From her viewpoint, she observed the pastor's profile as he finished his sermon. After playing the church organ since she was in high school, she had become accustomed to her unobtrusive place beside the organ at the front of the church. But today she felt conspicuous.

Because Peter Della sat in the second pew on the center aisle. Dark, handsome wearing a fashionable gray herringbone suit.

Keeping her mind on her music this Sunday morning had been torture. Her eyes kept straying to the second pew, center aisle. To stop herself, she'd found herself staring at the pastor.

She knew the end of the service was near by the inflection in Pastor Carlson's voice. He was just about to turn to her and signal the closing hymn.

"And finally I want to repeat James's words, 'My brothers, what good is it for someone to say he has faith if his actions do not prove it?' That, dear friends, is my question. I know you have faith, but do you have enough to put that faith into action?"

Thea scooted forward, ready to rise at his nod.

But Pastor Carlson continued to face forward. "Today I want to introduce someone who can give you a chance to put your faith into action."

Caught in midmove between chair and organ bench, Thea froze. Her peace shattered. *Oh, no, he wouldn't.*

"Peter, will you come forward and explain your mission and its needs?"

Thea didn't have to look. She pictured Peter's handsome

face beaming at everyone and she heard him bounding forward to the pulpit.

She sank back into her chair, but her eyes seemed of their own accord to turn to Peter. It was as though he'd been waiting for her to look at him. He gave her a brilliant smile. Feeling herself blush a hot red, she pressed her palms to her burning cheeks. What would the gossips make out of this reaction?

"Thank you, Ed." The two men shook hands and the pastor sat down in his chair opposite Thea.

As though watching a train wreck about to happen, Thea looked helplessly at Peter's profile.

He gazed over the congregation, gripping the sides of the pulpit. "Friends, no doubt you've heard I've bought Double L Boys' Camp and I'm making a change. I'm going to run it as a nonprofit camp for high-risk boys from Milwaukee."

The morning worship service always left her feeling refreshed, but now Thea felt jumpy. *The mover and shaker is back at it again.*

"A few local people have already expressed some concerns about this change. They've pointed out that these kinds of boys aren't desired in your community."

Thea knotted her hands in her lap. Peter thought he was helping, but didn't he understand? People here didn't want someone from outside telling them what to do, to think.

"I'd like to direct your attention to the verses that come before the one your pastor quoted." Peter picked up the open Bible and read, "'You will be doing the right thing if you obey the law of the Kingdom, which is found in scripture: Love your neighbor as you love yourself. But if you treat people according to their outward appearance, you are guilty of sin....'" He closed the Bible.

Thea's mouth dropped open. She imagined the sounds

of a milling lynch mob like the ones in an old Western movie forming outside of the church. How did he have the courage to stand up there and dare them all? His words bordered on the foolhardy.

"God provided me with the funds to buy this camp for my mission, but I still need operating cash. For hot dogs, marshmallows, a camp nurse and much more. I want to give the residents of Lake Lowell a chance to get in at the start of this exciting opportunity to put their faith into action."

Thea's body grew tense. She felt fear—fear for Peter, fear for his dream. The opposition would use every weapon at their disposal.

He grinned. "I look forward to meeting each and every one of you and if God leads you to offer help, I'll accept it gladly. I'm ready and eager to include you in this mission for these boys—God's kids."

Thea closed her eyes. *Lord, he doesn't know what he's in for.*

Chapter Four

Later that Sunday evening, Thea parked in her garage, then lingered in the absolute stillness and near-darkness. *What a day.*

Peter Della's announcement at the end of the church service had whipped up a variety of reactions. Thea felt as though she had been dropped into a blender and "whipped." Those who opposed Peter's camp and those who favored it had made themselves heard. Insistently. Repeatedly. Vocal discord disturbed Thea as much as poorly played music. With each comment, she'd retreated from both sides.

Unfortunately she had promised to play music at the retirement center that afternoon. While she played "Let Me Call You Sweetheart" and "Don't Sit Under the Apple Tree" for the elderly residents, the buzz of opinions competed with the piano. Her grandmother had railed against Peter and his camp. Before she had left, Thea had been forced to endure a stiff lecture from Grandmother Lowell—Thea must stay away from that Peter Della, a handsome flimflam man.

Thea gave a weary sigh, then wandered through the breezeway-laundry room to the kitchen where she slipped out of her heels. She stood a moment, letting her feet luxuriate in their freedom on the cool linoleum. Reaching up, she released the clip that had held up her hair all day. As the wave of hair flowed down around her shoulders, she kneaded her scalp with her free hand. *Wouldn't it be nice to have someone here to massage my shoulders? Where did that idea come from!*

Gray-striped Tomcat, appearing suddenly, began rubbing against Thea's ankles and purring with the determination of a tiny buzz saw. "Miss me, Tom? Or just in the mood for your Sunday dinner?"

Tomcat's "motor" revved more urgently.

"So much for my attraction." Thea dropped her shoes on a kitchen chair and dutifully served Tomcat his once-a-week repast of "people" tuna in oil. "Where's Molly?"

Tom didn't flicker a whisker in response.

"I know. Dogs aren't your business, but she should be here now begging for her Sunday dinner, too."

Tom ignored her.

"What do you think? Molly's just chasing some interesting critter and she'll be home soon?" Thea glanced down at the oblivious cat. "It's so nice to have someone to share my concerns with."

Tom swished his tail as though telling Thea not to bother him. Thea picked up her shoes and padded on stocking feet to her bedroom. She undressed, carefully hanging up her Sunday outfit, then tugged on faded, navy sweats, thick socks and well-worn loafers. Home at last.

Back in the kitchen, she opened the refrigerator and stared at the neat but unappetizing contents. Strident voices like out-of-tune violins had dampened her appetite at lunch. Now, though her stomach growled with hunger, she shook her head and closed the door. She glanced down at Tom who licked his paw, then brushed the paw over his mouth. "Why didn't you thaw something for me and invite company?"

Tom eyed her benignly. The tuna had mellowed his mood.

Again she looked at the dog's dish, sitting empty next to Tom's licked-clean bowl. *Molly should be here.*

She walked to the door and leaned out. "Molly! Here, girl!"

No distant bark answered her. She locked the door. She considered going out to look for Molly, but the retriever could be almost anywhere around the lake. Thea absently fixed herself a cup of hot cocoa, hoping she'd hear Molly come through the dog door or some appetizing recipe would pop into her mind.

Sipping the warm drink and staring into the darkness outside the window, she noted the little sounds the house made—the furnace fan coming on, the refrigerator cooling, the ticking of the mantel clock. The disgruntled growly babble she'd endured all day contrasted with the silence. Thea hated angry voices. But now the empty quiet isolated her as though she'd been wrapped up in tissue paper and stored away.

A pounding on the back door exploded that peace.

Unnerved, Thea ran to the door and threw it wide. Peter rushed inside; Molly clutched in his arms.

Thea gasped.

Looking at Thea with sympathy, Peter nodded toward Molly's left front paw. "She's hurt herself. She whined and scratched outside my door. At first, I didn't get what she wanted. I thought she wanted to shake, you know, because she kept offering me her paw. But then she showed me she was having trouble walking."

While Peter explained, he let Thea draw him with Molly to the kitchen sink. She switched on the light above it. Taking the injured paw in her hands, she examined it carefully.

In sympathy, Peter leaned close. He hated to think of Molly limping painfully to the nearest house for help. Thank God, he'd been home. "Do you think the vet could meet us at his office?"

"Wait. I need to see what the problem is." Thea ran water and washed the dirt and dried blood from the paw. Molly whimpered. "Don't worry, girl," Thea murmured, as she examined the dog. "There it is. A thorn. Where'd you get that, girl?"

"That looks deep. I'll drive!" He moved to go.

Thea checked him with a hand on his sleeve. "I'll take care of it."

He studied her. "Are you sure? Won't she snap at you?"

"At me?" Thea blinked at him. "I've always taken care of her."

"You think you can get it out without numbing the area?"

"It's just a thorn."

"You're certain?" He returned Thea's direct gaze.

She nodded and held out her arms to take Molly.

He swallowed and hugged Molly to him. Did Thea think he'd just leave her to deal with this alone? "Where do you want to do it?"

"You don't have to help." She reached out again.

He took a step back. Molly whined. He still wasn't convinced, but Molly belonged to Thea. "I don't mind helping. In fact, I insist."

"Very well. Having someone hold her will help me and comfort Molly. Bring her into the spare bathroom." Thea led him there and flapped down the commode lid. "Sit down."

Holding Molly with care, he obeyed without demur. If she didn't get the thorn out soon, he'd insist on driving her to the vet.

Thea opened the medicine chest and took out tweezers, a long needle, alcohol, cotton swabs and a tube of antibiotic cream. She laid them out in a neat row on the narrow counter. Then bending close, Thea cradled Molly's chin in both her hands and gazed into the dog's eyes. "Molly," she said firmly, "Thea will take care of Molly. Okay? Thea will help Molly." She stroked the dog's ears.

Molly gave a soft "whoof."

Thea fastened her long hair back with an elastic band, then washed her hands. "Okay, girl."

Peter held the dog across his lap and watched as Thea swabbed the area around the deeply embedded thorn. He knew the alcohol must be stinging because Molly tensed. But the retriever didn't flinch. "There, girl," he whispered.

Thea lifted the paw and turned it into the light. Holding a long needle, she probed the area around the thorn. Molly let out a low plaintive howl, but did not move. Trying to distract the dog from the pain, Peter stroked her and murmured comforting phrases. The probing dragged on.

Just as Peter meant to intervene, Thea clamped her front teeth over her lower lip. She put down the needle and poised the tweezers over the paw, then dipped down and grasped the thorn down on its shaft, not at its brittle, broken point. He closed his eyes. A quick tug. Molly jerked in his arms and moaned.

"Got it," Thea breathed.

Peter looked up. Thea held the nearly inch-long thorn.

"You got it." He couldn't keep the surprise from his voice.

"I've done this before. Molly didn't doubt me. Did you, girl?" Thea tossed the thorn into the waste basket, then smoothed the antibiotic cream over the soft pad of the paw. "All done, girl. Peter, you can let her go now."

Molly strained against him. He released her and she launched to the floor. "I can't believe she let you do that without snapping or even growling."

Thea put away the medical supplies and washed her hands. "Molly trusts me. She knows I'd never hurt her without a good reason."

Molly barked from the kitchen.

Thea gave a gentle laugh. "Molly says supper's late."

Feeling the tension inside him ebb, Peter followed Thea into the kitchen. Opening a can of dog food, Thea filled Molly's dish. The golden retriever emptied the dog dish with one noisy gulp.

Peter smiled. "Well, it didn't affect her appetite."

Standing by the sink, Thea turned toward him, her face friendly, amused. "I don't think she's been traumatized."

The soft expression enhanced her natural loveliness. Even in sweats, she looked willowy, elegant. Had he ever seen a more honest expression of enjoyment? Pleasure warmed him.

With a loud satisfied sigh, Molly sprawled at the base of the refrigerator and thumped her tail twice as though saying, "At last!"

Thea laughed out loud.

The musical quality of her laughter charmed him. *Everything about her is so graceful and sure.* He felt himself grinning, a large, sappy grin, but he couldn't help himself.

As Thea's laughter melted away, she folded her hands in front of her and looked at him.

He regarded her in return. That gesture, her folding of hands, spoke so much about the lady. She eyed him expectantly. *Say something to her, stupid. Don't just stare.* ''Hungry?''

She raised her eyebrows and glanced around the spotless counter and stove. ''I didn't feel like cooking.''

''I cook.'' *I sound like an idiot.*

''You do?''

''Yes, when Molly stopped at my door, I was just going to whip up a mushroom omelet. Would you like to join me?''

His invitation floored Thea. She voiced the only clear idea in her mind, ''That sounds delicious.'' *Does he really want me to have supper with him or is he just being polite?*

''Well, would you like to go back with me?'' He shoved his hands into his pockets.

To Thea, he sounded uncertain. *I should say a polite no.* A chorus of the day's negative words jabbered inside her head. Her stomach twisted with hunger.

Peter frowned. ''Maybe it's a bad time. Were you expecting someone—''

One thought bobbed to the top of Thea's mental hubbub. *If you turn him down, you'll have to eat alone—in this empty house. He may never ask again.* A polite phrase flowed from her lips. ''I'll be happy to have supper with you.'' She eyed him uncertainly. ''Should I bring something?''

''How about jam?''

In her agitated state, she couldn't think why he'd want jam with a mushroom omelet. ''Jam?''

''I'm going to make toast, too.''

''Of course.'' Relief whistled through her. She had jam. ''How about wild strawberry? I made it myself. Or wild raspberry?''

''They both sound great!''

At his obviously genuine enthusiasm, she reached into

the cabinet and brought out two small glass jars. Within minutes, Peter had helped her over the low fence that separated their properties and they walked into his lodge, the private residence at the camp.

Thea glanced around the familiar property for any changes. She detected none until she stepped inside the lodge kitchen. The kitchen gleamed with stainless steel appliances. "All new!"

"I wanted the best for my mom." Peter helped her off with her coat. "They'll be living here full-time this summer."

Peter's words reminded Thea of all the contention over the camp again. Molly's need and Peter's presence had banished her loneliness and made her forget the controversy.

"Please sit down, Thea." Peter motioned toward a chair at the rectangular kitchen table. "I hate eating alone, don't you?"

"Yes, I do." Still she felt as though she'd strayed onto enemy territory. *But why don't I just declare neutrality?* This new idea grabbed Thea. If she remained neutral, what could a quiet supper together hurt?

"Then sit down—or don't you trust my cooking?" Peter joked as he washed his hands.

Thinking of all the economical, nutritious, boring food awaiting her at home, Thea grinned and wrinkled up her nose. "It has to be better than mine."

"I bet you cook like an angel." Peter smiled, then turned to the stove.

Thea settled onto the pine chair. This engaging man spouted compliments as easily as he breathed. A mental picture of Peter plying his charm on Grandmother Lowell amused her. "I didn't know angels cooked."

With one hand, he cracked two eggs into a glass bowl,

another two, then two more and began to whisk them. "Haven't you ever eaten angel food cake?"

"That is such a stale joke." But his warmth and friendliness brought an easy smile to her lips.

"I'm practicing my juvenile humor for this summer." Making swift *tat-tat-tat* sounds, he sliced fresh mushrooms with a French chef's knife, just like a cook on TV. "How did you think my announcement this morning went?"

Thea didn't know what to say. Why didn't he see his announcement this morning had amounted to throwing down the gauntlet? Something told her Peter wouldn't understand her dawning desire to stay neutral.

He turned, nibbling a mushroom slice. "What do you think about adding a little provolone?"

Thea glanced up at him. "What? I wasn't listening."

"You look worried. Is it about the omelet or the camp?"

She leaned forward. She'd never met anyone as confident as Peter before. "Why aren't you worried?"

He stopped munching. Opening the double-door refrigerator, he took out a round of white cheese and a carton of orange juice. "I don't worry much. Do you worry a lot?"

The question brought her up sharply. "Doesn't everyone worry?"

"What do you think? Take your time." He shredded the white cheese, then slid two plates into the oven to warm and handed her tableware and glasses for two.

While she set the table, she pondered "worry." "I don't think I worry more than the average person." Her tone sounded unsure even in her own ears. He studied her and she squirmed inwardly.

"How much does the average person worry?" He asked the question as though posing it before a college class.

Thea turned it back on him. "You said you don't worry much. How *much* do you worry?"

"Not much." He grinned provocatively at her. "I believe worry is a negative drain on a person's life."

"I never thought about it that way." His words brought an interesting picture to mind. As she played the pipe organ at church, someone sucked air from the bellows. Her music quavered, then died.

Peter melted butter in the skillet, then poured in the whisked eggs. They sizzled cheerfully. The rich aroma of melted butter made Thea's mouth water. With keen anticipation she watched him sprinkle the mushrooms over the eggs, then the cheese. He motioned to her to press down the lever on the toaster. He folded the eggs over gently, flipped the omelet once, divided it into two, then moved the pan off the burner. Within minutes, Peter set the omelet, toast, and orange juice on the table. Everything appeared so professionally done, she almost asked where the parsley garnish was.

Peter sat down across from her. After saying a brief grace, he lifted his glass to her. "A toast to good neighbors."

As Thea smiled and lifted her glass, her grandmother's final words came back to her, "You stay away from that Della. He's up to no good." *But I'm not taking sides!* The heaviness inside her lifted, then vanished.

Peter prompted, "You're supposed to touch your glass to mine, neighbor."

"Oh! Sorry." The gesture made her feel shier, but she touched her glass to his. His dark eyes smiled at her over his glass. This caused a sudden tightness around her ribs, making it hard for her to inhale.

"Now eat up. There's nothing worse than a cold omelet." He grinned and took a forkful.

His aura of assurance was having its way with her. She nodded and followed suit. Her first bite delighted her. "You're a great cook."

"Just a simple omelet." He slathered a slice of toast with her bright red strawberry jam and took a bite. "Mmm. Your jam is delicious."

In spite of herself, she felt her cheeks warm at his compliment. "Thank you. I enjoy berry picking."

"Are there many strawberry patches around here?"

She swallowed a delicious mouthful of buttery eggs. "I'll show you if you like."

"I'd like that, but I think this summer is going to be a pretty busy one for me. Now, have you come to an opinion about the negative effect of worry?"

She touched her napkin to her lips. "I see your point, but I think what I'm feeling is really caution, not worry."

"Caution?" He appeared to consider the word. He shook his head. "*No.* I wasn't born with a silver spoon in my mouth. I've fought for and earned everything I have. Caution won't get you anywhere in this world."

Instead of the controversy, why couldn't they discuss something interesting? She wanted to ask him what kind of music he enjoyed. Opera? She imagined his deep bass voice singing the opening bars of "The March of the Toreadors." He had that air about him—cocky, convinced of his own strength. Thea paused with her fork in midair and gave in. "Didn't you hear any of what was said to you today after the service?"

"I heard it all. I just didn't take it all seriously."

"Why not?" How could he just discount the uproar he'd single-handedly created?

He put his fork down and began gesturing with his hands. "Because there are always naysayers. Don't you think I should be more concerned about what God thinks?''

She resisted responding archly, *So what does God think, Peter?* Instead she spoke slowly. ''Sometimes people think they know what God wants, but they have made mistakes. How can you know this camp is what God wants?''

''Some people do make mistakes. But I've asked for God's guidance year after year. I began planning the camp when I was only fourteen. Doesn't nearly twenty years of praying and trying to follow His will count? I can't believe God would bring me this far only to let me be defeated.''

Thea picked up her fork and took a small bite. He might be right. If God had helped Peter focus on the same goal for twenty years. But... Finally she said lamely, ''I see what you mean.''

He gazed at her. ''Pastor Carlson is going to ask the church board to call for an immediate congregational vote on supporting my camp financially and in every other way.''

''So soon?'' She stared at him. This man never stopped.

''Why wait? You said I needed to get local cooperation. That was good advice. That's what I'm asking for.''

Asking for cooperation? He was asking for opposition. Why couldn't he just take time and let people get used to the idea? ''That's asking for a lot here.''

''Then God will have to help me out. Will you pray for me, Thea? For my camp? Nothing is too hard for God.''

She nodded hesitantly and lowered her eyes. She would pray, but not simply for the success of this camp which she still couldn't decide to support actively or not. Was this really God's will for Peter, or just his nonstop determination? What do you do with a man like this? She made a wry decision. She'd pray that Peter would have the strength of Samson and the wisdom of Solomon because he certainly didn't have the patience of Job!

She longed to warn him one last time, but her words would hold no weight with him. Peter was committed. He just didn't understand how determined others in this community could be.

She sighed silently. She'd decided to remain outside the dispute, knowing full well it would be a struggle to resist Peter's charm. And even so, neutrality didn't guarantee her protection. In the upcoming storm, Thea had the feeling that she'd be a leaf tossed and tumbled by powerful winds.

Four days later on Thursday evening, Thea perched in the shadows in the back of the crowded church.

"So you see my plans are quite detailed," Peter declared as he stood beside the overhead projector. Behind him, a large white screen displayed two neatly lettered columns of figures. One side in black marker showed the camp's assets. The other side in red listed its needs and their costs. Peter smiled at the rows of church members.

Thea observed the smile, but couldn't analyze how the man could put so much confidence and energy into a simple uplifting of the corners of his mouth. Maybe it was more. Maybe all of him smiled.

Near the front, Mrs. Magill moved irritably in her pew. "Looks to me like you don't need our money. You own the camp free and clear." The old woman, dressed in her usual flannel shirt and baggy slacks, grumbled, "Why don't you just borrow what you need? You don't have a mortgage to pay."

"I don't believe in a Christian mission paying interest. I think it's a waste of donors' money. As an investment counselor in Milwaukee, I know that bankers never lose money."

A small smattering of laughter greeted this. In contrast, Thea felt a tightening inside. She'd known Peter was a successful man, but an investment counselor sounded so imposing.

He grinned. "Not that I have anything against bankers or their donations." More laughter.

One person present intrigued Thea. Thad, Vickie Earnest's older son, slouched on an aisle seat near the front, his mother, then brother to one side of him. Thad was sixteen, and he only attended church when forced to on Sunday mornings. Greeting him then usually earned one a monosyllabic grumble. How and why had Vickie persuaded him to come?

Thea tried to accurately gauge the currents swirling around her. Some people responded to Peter; some passively observed. Would Peter get church support or not? Obviously everyone present knew of the brewing controversy, but so far only Mrs. Magill expressed periodic barbs. Mr. Crandon, the leading opponent, didn't attend their church, so couldn't be present. Sitting behind Thea in the last row, Mrs. Chiverton had so far remained silent. Thea hadn't been able to figure that out. Why wasn't the fidgety woman complaining?

"Now, not all the needs of the camp are monetary. I'll also need volunteers to do hands-on work with the boys." Peter clicked off the projector and motioned for the lighting to be raised.

Vickie Earnest waved her hand. "How old do the volunteers have to be?"

Peter turned toward her. "Well, the average camper will be between the ages of eight and twelve, so volunteers should be at least sixteen."

Vickie turned to Thad. "See you are, too, old enough to help."

Thad lunged to his feet and stormed up the aisle past Thea. All eyes followed him. The church doors slammed behind Thad, echoing ominously.

Thea understood the boy's pain. Why would Vickie, an otherwise sensible mother, call attention like that to her teenaged son? Didn't she realize how sensitive boys his age were?

Memories of a few occasions from her own teens briefly flashed through her mind. Whenever she'd asked her grandmother not to embarrass her by saying personal things about Thea in public, all she'd ever gotten was, "Don't be concerned about what other people think. Most of them are fools anyway."

"Althea!" Mrs. Chiverton's shrill voice shot up Thea's back like an exploding ice cube.

Thea leaped to her feet and spun to face the old woman. The sight that met Thea's eyes left her speechless. She'd thought Mrs. Chiverton had addressed her with her full name, which had been Thea's mother's and her grandmother's. But Mrs. Chiverton had not been talking to Thea, but her grandmother.

Mrs. Chiverton, with her platinum blond wig pushed slightly askew, scurried to the rear entrance and fluttered around Grandmother Lowell, who was in her wheelchair and accompanied by a male nurse from the care center. He piloted the wheelchair the few steps down the aisle to Thea.

Thea stammered, "Grandmother—I never expected... If you had told me—"

Her grandmother cut Thea off with a lift of a hand. Another imperious motion directed the nurse to park the wheelchair next to Thea's place.

The nurse muttered to Thea, "We thought she'd have another stroke if we didn't get her here."

Thea leaned down, concerned. "Grandmother, do you think it was wise to come tonight?"

"I had to. I knew I couldn't count on you to put a stop to this." Her grandmother's words sounded more slurred than usual due to her obvious agitation. Mrs. Chiverton flittered around her lifelong friend in excitement. "Stop fussing, Louella," Grandmother snapped under her breath. Mrs. Chiverton quivered to a halt. Thea hurt for the little woman. Why couldn't Grandmother be kinder?

"Here, Althea." Grandmother handed Thea a note. "Read this for me."

Thea accepted the paper, dread churning inside her. She didn't glance at the words on it, only stared into her grandmother's obstinate expression.

Thea wanted to refuse. She liked Peter. She'd decided to remain neutral in this debate. But what could she do? Refuse to read the statement? Show a lack of respect to her invalid grandmother?

Thea bowed her head for a moment in prayer, then stepped into the aisle. As always, speaking in public brought a warm blush to her face. She glanced at the front of the room, but did not look directly at Peter. She cleared her throat, then began, "My—"

A nudge from behind stopped her. Looking back, she saw that this wasn't good enough. Her grandmother was insisting she go to the front. Thea's blush burned her cheeks. She marched to the front row and turned.

In a voice devoid of emotion and avoiding any eye contact, she said, "My grandmother would like me to read this. 'Dear friends at the Church Among the Cedars, I have made the effort to come tonight because the issue of whether or not our church should formally support this new venture is such an important one. While this camp may be of God, it is an untested venture. Its future is uncertain since a zoning challenge is certain now. I would suggest, dear friends, that a decision—either way—is too early to be merited. Why not let this remain a matter of personal conscience? Thank you. Althea Lowell.''

In the ensuing silence, Thea retreated to her place beside her grandmother's wheelchair and sat down. As the words had passed between Thea's lips, all the blood, all the life, had flowed out of her. *I'm a grown woman. Why do I feel like a cowed child?*

Her grandmother's ploy was transparent to Thea. A reasonable call for a delay should disconcert Peter and keep for Grandmother the moral high ground. If Peter disagreed, he'd be branded pushy, opportunistic. And by mentioning the zoning, Grandmother had validated the rumors which asserted that Peter was changing his land use and would be faced with a county board challenge.

Finally Pastor Carlson rose and strode to the front. ''Peter, did you have anything more to say?''

Peter looked around the room as though weighing the reaction to the note, to him, to his camp. ''I'd like to say that Mrs. Lowell makes a good point.'' He paused to bow in her direction. ''I am happy you let me come and speak to you tonight, but I am quite content to let the official vote be postponed. In fact, I would prefer it.''

Thea tried to fight it, but a smile lifted one corner of her mouth. Grandmother had expected almost any response from Peter but this one. *He outmaneuvered you, Grandmother. What do you think about that?*

Chapter Five

Late in the afternoon, Thea chased Molly up the steep winding asphalt drive to their house. The tops of the leafless trees and evergreens swayed in the balmy late April wind playing a subtle accompaniment to her breathing.

Molly turned and barked as though teasing Thea.

Winded, Thea gasped, "Think you can beat me?" She shook her fist playfully. "I'll catch you!" The retriever bounded ahead, disappearing around a turn. Thea, though breathless, sprinted after her around the blind tree-lined bend. She ran straight into Peter. "Oof!"

Losing her footing, she stumbled backward. He caught her before she fell. With his strong hands, he drew her close. For a few exquisite seconds, she nestled safe against him. His clean soap scent blended with the natural pine fragrance around them. She battled the urge to snuggle closer.

He steadied her, then set her back on her feet. "Are you all right?"

She nodded, bracing her hands against her knees, trying to get her panting and her reactions to him under control.

"Sorry. I heard you and was coming down to join you for the last of your run."

She swallowed. "I ran into you."

They hadn't seen each other since the church meeting. Now they stood gazing at each other. Peter's uncharacteristic silence made it harder for Thea to speak. She tried to come up with a polite, coherent thought. But all that came to mind was *Hold me again.* Her attraction to him had grown more powerful in their days apart.

His eyes searched her face as though delving into her thoughts. Avoiding this, she pushed a few strands of wayward hair back over her ear. Finally she managed to ask, "What can I do for you then?"

He said in a husky voice, "I wanted to apologize to you."

Startled, she looked up into his face. "Apologize? Why?"

"I didn't listen to your gentle warnings about the camp controversy." The trace of a smile tipped the corners of his mouth as though appealing to her.

She struggled against her awareness of him. "I feel bad, too."

"Why?" His dark eyes widened.

"My grandmother's statement. I—"

"Don't apologize. How could you refuse? Besides, why would I hold you responsible for your grandmother's words?"

In the days since the meeting, Thea'd been too stung to face him. How could someone as fearless as Peter understand Thea's dislike of making a public scene?

Obviously frustrated with their idleness, Molly charged back. With two firm barks, she summoned each of them.

Peter chuckled. "Well, we've been told. We're holding up the parade."

Thea smiled, relieved there would be no bad feelings between them. The warm breeze wafted around her ears, blowing strands of hair from her braid into her eyes. Again she smoothed them off her face. Glancing up, she found Peter studying her.

"Ready? Let's go for it." Peter jogged up the final incline.

Thea caught up with him. Molly leaped and raced around yelping her encouragement. They jogged side by side. Thea felt wonderfully free after days of doubt.

The winter had played its finale and departed. Spring had begun its first movement—hopeful, ardent. Was it the fresh spring air, the robin hopping on the edge of the grass—spring-green again from melting snow—that lifted her heart? Reaching their goal, they both flung themselves onto the dark green bench outside Thea's back door.

When Thea breathed normally again, she glanced at Peter. He was so handsome, with his dark hair and eyes and tanned skin above the collar of his red windbreaker. Sitting side by side like this, they must look like a bright cardinal and his drab mate. She'd never be able to attract such a dynamic man. She carefully damped down his appeal and spoke in a detached tone. "From what you just said, I take it you're finally considering using some caution?"

"I wouldn't go that far." He grinned at her, a boyish teasing grin.

"Why did you back off from the congregational vote?" To talk openly freed her. Her confidence unfurled like the daffodils blossoming by her feet.

"What you mean is, how did I know *not* to press for a vote?" He draped his arm over the back of the bench, his nearness wrapping her in invisible warmth.

A kind of bubble inflated inside her windpipe making it hard to talk. She swallowed. "Got me."

''You tried to prepare me. I didn't listen. Your grandmother's statement showed me it would be wrong to force people to takes sides.'' His deep voice curled through her like a blues melody, lulling, mellowing her.

''Why?'' Thea let the harmony of the moment heal her frazzled nerves.

''Once a person takes a stand it's very hard to change that person's mind.''

Thea was impressed. ''That's very wise.''

''Wise? No one has ever called me that before.''

Thea didn't know what to say to this, so she ruffled Molly's fur at the back of her head.

Peter petted Molly, too, as though avoiding Thea's gaze. ''May I ask you a question?''

His sudden seriousness brought her up short. Would he ask her to do something she didn't want? Uncertainty tinged her voice. ''What?''

''Do you think there will be a zoning challenge?''

''Yes, they say you're changing the way the land is used because you're changing from a private to a charitable camp.''

''You mean they'll actually file a zoning challenge against me with the county board?''

Picturing a blustering Mr. Crandon, Thea nodded.

''Well,'' he paused. ''Guess I'll be spending extra time in prayer. How soon do you think it will come?''

A wave of admiration rushed through her. A full-scale fight didn't even make him flinch! ''Soon.''

''What about you, Thea? Still sitting on the fence?'' He brushed his fingertips through her hair. ''Pine needles.''

His touch beckoned her to draw closer. She resisted.

''I shouldn't have asked you that. I came to ask you something else.''

"What?" Fighting her inner confusion, she focused on the nearby robin pulling at a worm.

"I have to fly down to Milwaukee. Business." He pulled a key ring from his windbreaker pocket. "A carpenter is coming to do several repairs at the lodge. Would you hold these and give them to him when he comes?"

"Certainly." Thea accepted them.

"Thanks. You don't think it will make you seem to have taken my side?"

"I'm just being a good neighbor." Her resolve to stand apart had nothing to do with that.

"Good." He stood up, gazing down at her. "I believe you will give me your support in time, Thea. But I only want it when you will give it to me freely."

After years of being commanded what to think, what to do, how to do it, she couldn't speak because so many words crowded in her throat.

Peter had charted his course. Her grandmother had planned hers. But Peter, who possessed a strong personality, had extended respect to her. He'd left the decision to her alone. Finally she said, "When will you be back?"

"I'll be gone nearly a month."

Glancing away, she hid the downturn in her mood at his news. "It'll be warmer when you return."

He stood up and offered her his hand and gently pulled her to stand in front of him. She couldn't stop herself from studying his face. She found him studying her, too. Unspoken words hung in the warm air around them.

"Thanks." Pulling away slowly, he patted Molly's head and walked to his red van.

He drove away, but the phantom sensation of his strong hand in hers lingered. Tonight it would be difficult to look over and see the lodge dark and vacant. To know that she would not see him again for several weeks. She felt a yawning emptiness at the realization. She heard her phone ring and hurried inside.

As soon as she recognized Mrs. Chiverton's scratchy voice, Thea wished she'd let the answering machine pick up. "Althea, what was he at your place for?"

"I wish you wouldn't spy on me." The words slipped out of Thea's mouth before she could stop herself.

"I'm not spying! I'm keeping my eye on that man. Now what did he want?"

To brush pine needles from my hair. Thea shook her head. "He just stopped to tell me he's flying back to the city on business." Why not tell this? Peter flying out of the county airport would be common knowledge within the hour.

"Why?"

"He left me a key for the carpenter." No doubt the older woman would notice Thea giving something to the carpenter anyway.

"You refused to take it, didn't you?"

"Now why would I refuse such a simple favor for a neighbor?"

"You think I'm just an old nosy busybody," Mrs. Chiverton said unexpectedly. "But I just don't want you to get hurt!" Then abruptly she hung up.

Thea shook her head and also hung up. Instantly the phone rang again. Frowning, she refused to answer ring after ring. The recorded message played, then Thea heard, "It's Myra. If you're there, please pick up." Why had her stepmother called?

Thea hurried to pick up the phone. "Myra, is everything all right?"

Myra laughed. "You sound like I never call."

Thea couldn't shrug off the feeling something might be wrong. "How's Father?"

"He's fine. On the road this week."

Her father had spent her childhood on the road, marketing for a hardware chain. "You mean the usual?"

Her stepmother laughed dryly. "We just hadn't heard from you for a while so I thought I'd call."

As Thea chatted with her stepmother for a few minutes about inconsequential matters, she tried to figure out Myra's reason for calling. Myra never called just to chat like this. Maybe she needed something for Thea's stepsister. "How's Cynda? Is she looking forward to getting her driver's license soon?" Thea asked.

"Not yet. Well, I just wanted to hear your voice. Give our regards to Grandmother Lowell. Bye."

Thea hung up. *What was that all about?*

"Peter, please, I wish you hadn't asked me." As far as the cord allowed, Thea paced her kitchen.

"I had to ask, Thea. You're the first friend I made at Lake Lowell and I'd like to see one friendly face looking back at me at the meeting tonight." Peter's opponents had finally succeeded in getting onto the board meeting agenda tonight.

She tried to ignore the coaxing tone in his voice. Or the undeniable happiness she felt hearing his voice again after so many weeks and knowing he was back, only steps from her door. "You'll have many friendly faces there. Both Vickie Earnest and Pastor Carlson have called me already."

"So I'm not the first to call?"

"No."

"You're committed to staying out of this?"

"Yes, I want to stay completely neutral." *And I don't want to have to listen to hours of arguing.*

"Just coming isn't taking sides," he said.

"I just don't want to go."

He sighed with audible disappointment. "Okay. And thanks. You've really helped out while I was away."

"We're neighbors," she replied in what she hoped was a friendly, but not too familiar tone.

"You're sticking to that story?" he teased.

"It's the truth."

A moment of silence. "I won't press you then. I guess I won't see you this trip. I'm just here for the meeting."

At this news, frustration pinched Thea. She wanted to see Peter. They hadn't seen each other since that brief jog at the end of April. Now Memorial Day and the summer camp season loomed just days away. Thea knew he'd be so busy once the camp opened, she probably wouldn't see him all summer.

"Will you pray for me tonight, Thea?"

"I have been."

"Thanks," he said quietly, then hung up.

Peter's voice, so rich and vibrant, had nearly enticed her to change her mind and go. Molly gazed up from where she sat at Thea's feet. "Yes, that was your friend Peter."

Molly whoofed.

Thea patted Molly's head, then glanced upward. "God, Your will be done tonight." Thea looked down at the retriever. "That is the best prayer, Molly. I don't know all the answers and I'm tired of hearing everyone's loud, incessant arguments and emotional opinions."

Molly barked encouragingly.

Thea strolled to the open windows over the sink. She inhaled the soft late May air drifting in, scented by the lilac bush in full bloom outside the window. The bullfrogs across the lake bellowed their raucous wooing. When Molly ducked out the dog door, Thea murmured, "Have a date, Mol?"

The phone rang.

Thea turned, then leaned back against the counter. She couldn't listen to another summons. After the answering machine picked up and played its message, a brusque male voice demanded, "Thea? This is the care center. Please pick up."

Thea's heart jerked in her breast. She reached for the phone. "What's wrong?"

"Your grandmother insists you come in right away."

"Is she in pain? What happened?"

"It's just one of her whims."

Thea sighed. "You haven't been able to talk her out of it?"

"When have we ever been able to talk her out of anything?"

Thea sighed and looked down at her jeans. Grandmother hated women in denim. "All right. It will take me a few minutes to change though."

"She says there isn't time. Come as you are."

"What?"

"That's what she says."

Thea shrugged. "Very well."

After running a brush through her hair, Thea drove down the winding drive through the gathering twilight into town. Parking at the care center, she walked into her grandmother's room.

"It's about time. What took you so long?" Her grandmother's angry, though slurred demand stung.

Usually Thea would have greeted the woman in the wheelchair with a kiss, but now she stopped just inside the doorway. Stifling her own annoyance, she replied calmly, "What is it, Grandmother?"

"The county board meeting is tonight." The old woman sounded like a fretful child.

"I know."

"I want you to attend—"

What! "I—"

"Don't interrupt. I want you to represent our family."

"Represent our family? Is something to do with our family going to happen at the—"

Grandmother flung up her good hand in irritation. "The zoning challenge is tonight. You know that. Why must I still tell you to do things you should just know enough to do?"

Thea gazed at her grandmother. *Please, Lord, not another statement to read.* "What do you think I should do there tonight? You know I don't like speaking in public."

"I've long given up hope you'd take your rightful place in this community. You've never appreciated the position you were born to here. If something important is on the county board agenda, as a Lowell, you should attend."

Just thinking about listening to an evening of ill-tempered wrangling and mind-numbing parliamentary procedure made Thea seethe inside. "What do you expect me to do?"

"I want you to listen and observe what happens for me."

Was that what I raced into town for? To be her eyes and ears. Thea's irritation grew. "Why? I'm sure Mrs. Chiverton will be there. Can't she recount the meeting for you?"

Grandmother pursed her lips sourly. "Louella has been my friend since we were babies, so I can say—without hesitation— she was born a fool and will die a fool. She'll just tell me what she thinks I want to hear. I can't count on her getting anything straight. *You*—whatever your failings—can at least get the facts straight."

Thea was inured to her grandmother's slights, but she

cringed at the unkind assessment of Mrs. Chiverton. How could her grandmother say that of her lifelong friend? "Wouldn't it be better to attend yourself? You went to church—"

"Why must I explain everything to you? That was a small, private group. I'm not going to put myself on display in public, let people gloat over me now that I'm like this! No! Never!" The old woman trembled.

Watching her grandmother's agitation, Thea felt concerned. Of course, this controversy over Peter's camp loomed large in the older woman's mind. Grandmother had been intimately concerned with her family's land and social position all her life. Thea felt obligated to do as she wished.

"I'll go as long as you don't want me to speak." Just before this agitated outburst, Thea had almost declared her decision to remain neutral. But that would only upset her grandmother dangerously.

"It'll be too late for you to come back tonight to tell me what happened. Come tomorrow."

Pursing her lips, Thea drew close to the wheelchair and straightened the light afghan over the old woman's lap. She leaned over and kissed her grandmother's cheek. "Good night."

Grandmother Lowell nodded like Queen Victoria dismissing an ambassador.

Outside in her car, Thea, disgruntled, thought over what had just taken place. Grandmother had done it again. If she had played "poor little me," Thea would have known how to refuse, but Grandmother would not give in to her declining health and weakening influence—even if it threatened her health.

If Thea refused to help, who knew what Grandmother

might do. The old woman's precarious health forced Thea to give in to her. A no-win situation.

But worse than going to the meeting would be returning to be debriefed the next day. Thea cringed. Was there any way to delay or avoid that unpleasant exchange tomorrow? Thea watched the dash clock tick around. The board meeting started in twelve minutes. An idea occurred to her. *Yes!*

She drove quickly to the church. As church organist, she possessed a full set of church keys. Unlocking the side door, she hurried to the locked equipment closet, checked out one of the excellent tape recorders on the list, and a blank tape, locked everything back up, and dashed out to her car.

The clock told her she still had seven minutes to go. Five minutes later she pulled into the parking lot, then rushed into the high school. In anticipation of a large turnout, the county board meeting was to be held in the cafeteria. As she hustled along the hall of sickly beige lockers, her sandals made a shooshing sound on the polished linoleum floor.

She walked in at the back of the cafeteria, crowded to bursting. Voices, humming like angry bees, buzzed in Thea's ears. Her stomach tightened. As she surveyed the scene, she noted Peter hadn't arrive and heard Mrs. Chiverton calling her name. In response to Mrs. Chiverton, she held up her recorder and shook her head. After her grandmother's unkind comment, sitting with Mrs. Chiverton would make Thea too uncomfortable.

When she'd almost given up finding a seat, she saw some men begin to unfold another row of metal chairs at the front. Though hating to sit on display at center stage, Thea scurried forward and claimed one of the aisle seats. As discreetly as she could, she sat her tape recorder down on the floor beside her chair and prepared it to record.

Then Thea sat rigidly avoiding eye contact with everyone. She heard voices she recognized—Mrs. Chiverton's, Mr. Crandon's, Mrs. Magill's, Vickie Earnest's, even Thad's. But she was really listening for Peter's voice.

Realizing this made her stop. She tried to discount this. But she couldn't shake it. *How could I not be drawn to him? His voice would be the one that counted tonight. But he's just my neighbor. And that's all I am to him.*

Then the board walked in, led by Joe Swenson, the county board chairman. Mr. Swenson, a large man about sixty years old with a gruff voice and an abrupt manner, had never agreed on anything with Grandmother.

The board meeting began. As usual, the most mundane questions topped the agenda. The statements, questions, comments and replies from the front droned on, lulling Thea into a restless calm before the storm.

Around Thea, people fidgeted, whispered, grunted, burped, snored. A baby cried. Thea's agitation waned. The warm early summer stillness made the room stuffy. Men got up and propped open doors and windows. Finally the zoning challenge came up for discussion.

Mr. Crandon, the one making the challenge, hustled to the front. In spite of the room's uncomfortable closeness, he wore a suit and a starched white shirt and he carried a thick, official-looking black notebook.

Thea pressed down the red button on the tape recorder. The county chairman motioned Mr. Crandon to the microphone and asked him to state his case.

Mr. Crandon cleared his throat. ''Chairman, County Board Members, and fellow citizens, I am here to cite the change in the land use at the Double L Boys' Camp necessitates a change in zoning.'' He launched into a detailed explanation of the reason for zoning and several cases that had needed zoning changes which had been ignored, reaping negative land values. "Now in the case of the Oxbow Inn in Marathon County…"

Thea tried to concentrate on the convoluted reasoning Mr. Crandon had constructed, but only became embarrassed for him. Didn't he know his transparent words only showcased his bias?

"Okay," Joe Swenson barked. "We've heard enough."

Startled, Thea jerked and her foot knocked over the tape recorder with a clatter.

Joe glared at her. "And, who, young lady, gave you permission to tape-record this meeting?"

Thea blushed and couldn't think of any reply.

"Don't answer that." Joe tempered his tone, "I didn't mean to take this out on you, Thea. But you can tell Her Highness, your grandmother, that this board is quite capable of doing the work we were elected to do without her…help."

Thea blushed more hotly.

"This has nothing to do with Althea Lowell." Dick Crandon brought all eyes back to him. "It has to do with changing land use—"

"Double L has been zoned for a boys' camp for nearly thirty years, Dick." Joe motioned toward the rear of the room. "Mr. Della, stand up please."

Thea kept her focus forward, but all around her the sound of people shifting in their seats told her that everyone else must have turned to look at Peter.

"Yes, Mr. Swenson." Peter's voice came out deep and sure.

At its sound, Thea wished with all her heart the two of them could be transported magically back to the bench at her back door. Instead of wasting a beautiful May evening in this stuffy cafeteria with contentious people, they could be watching the sun set over Big Bear Bay.

"This is a small town, Pete. Just call me Joe. Now I want to know, when you bought the property from the Kramers, it was a boys' camp, right?"

"Yes, Joe, it was a boys' camp."

"And tell me—what do you intend to use the property for?"

"A boys' camp."

"Nothing else? You're not planning on subdividing or building condos or turning the camp into a landfill?"

"Of course not."

"Then you're not changing the land use?"

"Yes, he is!" Dick Crandon bellowed. "He is changing it from a private camp to a—"

"We all know what Peter is doing. It's all you and your gang have talked about since April. But a boys' camp is a boys' camp. Now if there are no other matters to discuss, will someone—"

Mr. Crandon, with cheeks inflated like a crimson hot-air balloon, shouted, "I'm not done!"

"Yes, you are," Joe said firmly. "You knew you didn't have a legal leg to stand on when you started."

Swenson adjourned the meeting. Mr. Crandon, sputtering with indignation, marched out in the company of his cronies.

Thea felt sorry for Mr. Crandon. Had he thrown himself into the battle against Peter's camp to keep his mind off losing his son, Scott? She clicked off the tape recorder, but didn't rise to leave. She didn't want to speak to anyone, especially Peter. What would he think about her coming—and with a tape recorder, no less—after she'd refused his request? When the cafeteria quieted and the custodian was locking up, Thea picked up the tape recorder and walked out to the parking lot.

In the glow of the streetlight, Peter leaned against her

vehicle. A rush of pleasure suffused her, followed by a slither of uncertainty. The now cool night air chilled her. Just a few steps from him, she paused holding the tape recorder in front of her.

Slowly he looked her over, a grin breaking over his face. "We have to stop meeting in parking lots like this, Miss Glenheim."

A tingling feeling raced through her limbs. "Yes, we do, Mr. Della."

"But I wanted to say goodbye before I flew back to Milwaukee."

He'd said on the phone earlier he'd be leaving tonight. But he'd waited to see her anyway. She couldn't help herself. A happy glow radiated through her. But she kept her tone even. "Did you need me to do something for you while you're away?"

"No. Just wanted to gloat."

"Gloat?" Her eyes widened.

"Looks like your county chairman knows the law. So much for the zoning challenge."

Thea looked away and then back up at him. Did he really think this was over? *Should I warn him again or not?*

She decided not. He still didn't comprehend where he now lived. He'd just won the first skirmish and he thought the war was won.

He stepped toward her. "I won't be seeing you for a few weeks, but my parents will be arriving soon. Can I tell them you'll help them out?"

"I am your closest neighbor," Thea said simply. She was having a hard time not letting the slump in her spirits creep into her voice.

"Here. Let me take that for you." He lifted the tape

player out of her hands. This action took her by surprise, so she reached out reflexively.

Peter caught her hand. Before she recognized his intent, he lifted her hand to his lips.

For a second, she couldn't breathe. The touch of his lips moved her beyond anything she could have imagined. Through a glorious haze, she let him help her up into her car and bid her good-night. On sheer intuition and habit, she made her way through the dark streets to the care center where she left the tape for her grandmother to listen to in the morning.

By the time she arrived home, the euphoria inspired by Peter's kiss had evaporated. As she drove up the road, her eyes lingered on the dark Double L Camp. All was normal.

Peter's optimism seemed to be endless and in the quiet darkness, she began to doubt her own fears. Perhaps the opposition would grouch and mutter but do no more. A tempest in a teapot after all.

No one had ever kissed her hand before. During the two years she had commuted an hour south to the community college, she had dated a few music students casually. But her heart had not been touched by any of the young men attracted to her. They had been as quiet and reserved as she. None of them had possessed even a fraction of the charm Peter exuded without effort.

After closing up the house for the night, Thea fell asleep easily, lulled by hopes for a peaceful summer filled with Peter Della smiles.

Thea jerked upright in bed. Frantic barking. Molly jumped and turned and jumped again on the side of Thea's bed. Molly never gave false alarms. "What's the matter, girl!"

Thea scrambled out of the bed, throwing on her robe

and slipping on her sandals. Molly raced ahead toward the kitchen. Grabbing up a flashlight, she ran out the back door behind Molly.

The sound of breaking glass shattered the silence.

Chapter Six

Shattering glass. Molly howling.

"Hush, Molly," Thea whispered urgently from where she cowered on the drive. The dog paid no attention, but clamored louder and rushed the fence.

Afraid Molly would get hurt, Thea moaned loudly. Instantly Molly ran back to her. Thea grabbed her collar and, huddling close to the ground, dragged Molly into the kitchen.

Thea slammed and locked the door and dog hatch. Trembling, she went immediately to the phone and dialed the sheriff's number. But when she heard his voice, she faltered. Weak in the knees, she sank onto a chair. "Sh-sheriff," she stammered over Molly's frantic barking. "It's Thea. Can you come?"

"What is it?"

Howling, Molly hurled herself against the back door. "Somebody's over at the camp. I hear glass breaking." Trembling, Thea hung up the phone.

Within minutes, Molly gave up barking and lay down, though she still eyed the door. Glancing often at the wall clock, Thea kept her vigil at the kitchen window. Twelve minutes later, she saw the white sheriff's car, with its siren blaring, driving through the camp entrance.

Through her binoculars, Thea watched as the sheriff got out of his car. He left the headlights on and by their light, examined the grounds around the lodge and tried the doors. Then he got back into his patrol car and drove toward her place.

The sheriff's presence reassured her, but still feeling jumpy inside, Thea folded her arms in front of her. "Molly woke me, then I heard glass shattering."

He frowned. "I'm not surprised. Crandon's heated things up pretty good."

"Mr. Crandon wouldn't—"

"Not directly, no. But he has everyone stirred up. I'll need to get inside—"

"Should I come with you? I have keys."

He studied her for a moment. "Sure." He held the door open for her. Freed at last, Molly charged outside, baying. She leaped the fence and raced onto Peter's property. The sheriff drove them down the long lane to the main road.

At the camp's entrance, his headlights lit up the large sign. Thea cried out. The sheriff halted. The headlight beams focused on the large wooden sign etched with the words: "Welcome to Double L Boys' Camp". The sign had been sprayed with neon green words, "This Isn't Over!" The violent color and ominous message screeched at Thea.

"Someone's idea of art?" the sheriff commented dryly.

Chilled despite the warm night, Thea pressed her hands together in her lap. "Would it be easier to clean off now before it dries?"

"I'll need to take pictures of this for evidence and daylight makes for better shots."

Thea shivered. "I didn't think."

The sheriff drove up to the lodge. Again the headlights showed the damage done. Jagged glass remained in the window frames; the rest lay in shattered shards beneath.

"I want you to stay in the car while I take a quick look inside."

"Fine." She had no desire to step into the menacing shadows. She offered the sheriff the ring of keys. While he stalked off, the beam from his large lantern flashlight caused dancing shadows on the two-story log lodge. He unlocked the door then entered. Thea relived the shock of being woken by the disturbance.

Waking to blackness, frantic barking, breaking glass! Gooseflesh raced up her arms.

Angry words spoken earlier at the county board meeting were one matter; vandalism in the night was quite another. She pictured the scrawled neon green letters—This Isn't Over! *Oh, Peter, you thought you'd won.*

"Thea?"

Early the next morning, hearing Peter's voice on the other side of her door shocked her. "Peter?" Her heart vibrating like a tremolo, she unlocked the door while running shaking fingers through her hair, which was still wet from the shower. "Has something else happened?"

He walked in. "All the excitement last night wasn't enough for you?" Gently he took hold of both her arms.

Brushing aside thoughts of last night's clamor, Thea drank in the steadying sight of Peter. "You flew back?"

"The sheriff woke me about 2:00 a.m."

"I didn't think you'd come." Peter's nearness warmed her, but she fought it.

"Thea, are you all right?"

More than last night's shocking events, Peter's gentle

grip compelled her attention now. She controlled her voice. "I just lost a little sleep."

"I never thought anything like this would happen. I should have been here." He released her and stalked to the window overlooking his camp.

Losing Peter's warmth, she hugged herself. "I'm glad you weren't! You might have been hurt."

He turned back sharply. "*You* might been hurt!"

"*Did*…the vandal want to hurt anyone? Just paint and broken—"

Peter's voice surged above hers, "From that first day at The Café you told me my camp would affect you and I wouldn't listen. Now this!"

She urged him toward a kitchen chair. "It's just vandalism. Some spray paint and broken windows." Her easy tone surprised herself. Where were these calm words coming from?

"It could have been worse. What if you'd been there, checking on something for me—"

She poured them each coffee and sat down across from him. "In the middle of the night? Not likely. Besides, the sheriff said the vandal may have known no one was around."

"I don't like any of this, Thea." He shook his head. "I don't know what to do."

This stopped her. "Peter, you always know what to do."

"No, I don't."

"Well, you always seem to." She couldn't help grinning.

He grimaced. "You're sure you're not worried?"

"I have been *worried* from the start—you know that—but I'm *not scared*." If she didn't want to be frightened, this wasn't lying, was it?

He sipped his coffee. "I see. Still sitting on the fence?"

She added cream to her white mug and stirred, choosing her words. "I'm worried. I'm not scared. I'm still neutral."

Peter chuckled suddenly. "I can live with that. I just can't let anything happen to you."

His words touched her, bringing a blush to her cheeks. She did her best to ignore her reaction and his tender gaze. "You're being overly dramatic. I've lived here my whole life. I've never been in danger and I'm not now."

"I don't want you to become a target, too. I'll make certain everyone knows you're staying neutral."

"I'll call it into the weekly newspaper." Teasing him gave her an unexpected lift.

Peter chuckled again, then he drained his cup. "You're sure you're okay?"

Tomcat appeared and began winding around her ankles. She gazed at Peter, wishing she could thank him for his concern. He hadn't told her it was all her own foolish fault. He hadn't ignored the whole thing and gone away on business. His concern strengthened her, made her want to bolster him, too. "Don't worry."

He lodged his elbows on the table, leaning forward over the pyramid of his hands. "I can't stay. I've got to fly back for a 1:00 p.m. meeting. I've asked the sheriff to patrol more often. I never expected anything like this." He stood. "And God will have to take care of it. He can be here when the sheriff and I aren't." He stood up. Pausing as if he didn't want to go, he leaned down and cupped her chin. "Be careful."

At his touch, her breath stilled, but she nodded.

His hand brushed her cheek, then he waved and walked out the door.

Thea closed her eyes and caught her breath. At her feet, Tomcat mewed, begging for breakfast. The sound echoed her own feeling of loss. She'd almost believed Peter's prediction that everything would go smoothly after the zoning challenge failed.

God, help me walk my own path this time. I'm tired of feeling as though I can't stand up to people or make up my own mind. But don't let me read more into Peter's friendship than there is. His outgoing personality makes me imagine things which will never come true. Please don't let me make a fool of myself over him. But she traced the skin where the memory of his touch lingered.

Two weeks later, Tom Earnest played Brahms' "Lullaby" at Thea's baby grand piano. Thea closed her eyes and savored the gentle andante melody.

Vickie's knitting needles clicked in the background. "How soon is Peter coming back?"

Thea reminded Vickie about the lesson in progress by putting her index finger to her lips.

"Sorry," Vickie whispered.

Thea closed her eyes again, concentrating on Tom's lulling performance.

The phone rang.

"I'll get it!" Vickie hopped up before Thea could stop her. Thea always let the machine pick up during lessons.

Tom played the last bars of the Brahms.

"Well done, Tom." Thea touched his shoulder

"Thanks." He gave her a dubious smile. "I practice a lot. It zones out Mom and Thad yelling at each other."

Before Thea could think of what to say to this rare revelation, Vickie interrupted from the other room. "It's your stepmother."

Apprehensive, Thea walked to the kitchen. She took the receiver from Vickie. "Myra, hello, what is it?"

"I told that woman it wasn't important, but she insisted I stay on." Myra sounded fretful.

"Is there something wrong?"

"No, no. Just wanted you to know your father will be in California for the two weeks of training."

"Oh?" He went for training once or twice a year and Myra had never called before to tell her.

"Yes, I wanted you to call me if anything comes up."

What was Myra expecting to come up? Thea tried to get up enough gumption to ask Myra why she'd called. "Myra—"

The phone went dead.

Thea hung up and slowly walked back to the piano. Were Myra and her father having problems?

"It's so nice your stepmother calls you like that." Vickie smiled up from her knitting.

Thea nodded and sat down on the chair next to the piano. *It isn't nice. It's peculiar.*

"Should I do my finger exercises, Miss Glenheim?" Tom asked.

Thea stared out the windows at the untroubled blue sky, trying to come up with a reason for her stepmother's calling twice in two months for no obvious reason.

"Don't you want to correct my theory while I play the next piece like you always do?" Tom prompted.

Thea looked at him as he offered her a music book. "Of course." *I need to call Myra and just ask her.* Thea wished she knew her stepmother better, but they'd never gone deeper than surface politeness. Tom played; she corrected. At the end of the lesson just as Tom and Vickie were leaving, an older, silver-gray station wagon pulled up.

"Who's that?" Vickie asked, stepping back down from her van.

Thea liked Vickie, but right now she would have liked Vickie to go home. Myra's peculiar phone calls occupied Thea's mind. Maybe there was something Myra wanted to tell her about her father, but couldn't get up her courage. *Is he sick? His heart?*

"Hello." A plump, gray-haired woman waved cheerfully from the car window. "Are you Thea?"

"Yes." Troubled, Thea stepped up to the side of the car. She'd already guessed who this couple was.

The woman looked Thea in the eye. "Child, you look worried to death. What's wrong?"

The woman's keen perception shocked Thea speechless. Drawing close, Vickie offered her hand to the woman in the wagon. "I'm Vickie Earnest and this is my son, Tom."

"We're the Dellas—Irene and Aldo." The woman shook Vickie's hand. "Do you know our son, Peter?"

Thea sighed silently. Peter's parents—just as she'd thought. Together Irene and Aldo looked like a couple who'd stepped out of a sixties children's film. Wearing a yellow smock printed with giant sunflowers, Irene looked as round and soft as a comfortable cushion, while Aldo was distinguished-looking with salt-and-pepper gray hair and a long lean body.

Vickie exclaimed, "He said you would be coming!"

Tom touched his mother's sleeve. "Mom, I've got to pick up my papers and get them ready to deliver."

Vickie looked disappointed, but started to move away to her van. "Well, it was nice meeting you."

The Dellas nodded and smiled. "We came to ask Thea if she'd go to town with us. We need to pick up a few things."

Thea's stomach quivered at this news. Go to town with the Dellas? They'd draw the camp's opponents like bees to honey.

Tom touched his mother's arm again. Vickie seemed to have to tear herself away from the scene of "breaking news," but finally she waved one last time and she and Tom drove away.

Pressing down her misgivings, Thea stood beside the wagon in the sudden stillness.

"Thea, are you still upset about that vandalism?" Irene asked in a soft, sympathetic voice. "Peter told us you're the one who called it in. How awful for you."

"Some coward who has to do his dirty work in the middle of the night." Aldo tamped down his full mustache. "Must have upset you."

"We're so sorry you were upset, dear." Irene patted Thea's hand, which lay on top of the rolled-down car window.

Through the window, Thea tried to read them. Their resemblance to Peter wasn't so much physical as it was in personality. They sounded and acted just like him. Warm. Exuberant. Two kind, concerned faces stared back at her. Thea pushed aside her reluctance. She was being a poor neighbor. "I'm fine. Wouldn't you like to come in first?"

"No, thank you, dear," Irene said. "We didn't drive up all in one day. I can't sit that long any more. We stayed in Wausau last night."

"We'd just like you to ride into town with us if you can spare the time today," Aldo invited in a cheerful rumble of a voice. "Show us around."

"We need some bread and milk. Some fresh fruit." Irene smiled at her brightly.

"Add a few nails and sandpaper to that," Aldo interjected.

Thea didn't want to go into town with them, but she didn't have the heart to refuse. It would be like slamming the door in Santa's face. "I have a few hours before my next student."

Thea climbed into the back seat of the station wagon

for the ride to town. They shopped at the Hanleys' grocery, and Carver Hardware. At each place, the Dellas blithely declared their identity to one and all as though the dispute over the camp didn't exist, as though they expected a welcoming committee. *They're just like Peter. Warm. Open. Personable. They don't understand.* Thea groaned inwardly.

With a stomach already tightening, Thea walked into The Café with them. She felt like she'd just entered the Temple of Doom. Though well after the lunch rush, Lake Lowell's grapevine must have been working at high speed because The Café was full. As they walked in, every eye turned to them.

"Something smells delicious," Irene exclaimed, seeming completely unconcerned about the audience.

Thea led them to a table near the front. *Why try to hide? Might as well be on full display.*

The waitress came over and handed them menus. "Hi, folks," the waitress said with her pad in hand.

Thea wondered how the woman could keep such a deadpan expression amid the avid interest all around.

"What is it that smells so delicious?" Irene asked.

"Pasties."

"Pasties?" Irene repeated.

Thea was glad to hear Irene repeat the name of the regional specialty correctly so it rhymed with "past", not "paste." She'd been raised eating the folded pastries filled with meat, gravy and vegetables, but today the heavy food didn't appeal to her.

"I haven't had a pasty for a long time. Do yours have turnips?" Irene asked.

"Some," the waitress answered, still showing a complete lack of interest.

"Sounds good to me, Irene." Aldo handed back his menu. "What about you, Thea? Our treat."

"I'll just have a cup of soup."

"Chicken with wild rice?" the waitress intoned, scribbling on her pad. Thea nodded.

After the waitress waddled away toward the kitchen, Irene beamed at Thea. "Peter said you were a pretty little thing."

Thea felt herself blush, not just over the compliment, but because of all the ears listening to it.

Aldo objected, "No, he didn't. Said she was tall and elegant."

Irene slapped his hand. "Stop it. We're embarrassing her. Now, Peter said your grandmother is at the nursing home."

"Yes, she is."

"When we get settled, I'll have to drop over and take her one of my calzones."

Oh, no. Thea felt herself break into a cold sweat. She'd read about them in books, but she'd never actually felt it. She stammered, "G-grandmother isn't usually up to visitors."

"And she isn't crazy about Peter's camp, either," Aldo said. "Irene, this isn't the neighborhood back home. Here you have to let people get used to you."

"Oh." Irene made a hushing gesture toward him. "People are people. Here or in Milwaukee. Don't you think so, dear?"

Before Thea could say something to moderate Irene's enthusiasm, the waitress delivered the pasties and soup. As Thea took her first sip of thick rice soup, she heard a "Humph" from someone standing beside her. She glanced up to see Mrs. Chiverton. *Oh, no.* Thea hoped Mrs. Chiverton would act neighborly, but the older woman quivered with emotion. "Are you really that Peter Della's parents?"

Aldo stood politely. "Yes, we are. How do you do? I'm Aldo Della."

Mrs. Chiverton bristled.

Remembering her grandmother's cutting remark about Mrs. Chiverton and her own desire for peace, Thea took a deep breath and pasted a smile into place. "This is Louella Chiverton. She lives directly across the lake from both of us. She's my grandmother's oldest and dearest friend. I depend on her so much now that Grandmother is at the care center."

At Thea's unexpected tribute, Mrs. Chiverton's expression changed from hostile to surprised, but gratified.

"Well, how nice to meet a neighbor." Irene held out her hand.

Mrs. Chiverton shook it, still looking startled.

"You must come over some time," Aldo said. "And I'm quite handy with tools if you need any small jobs done."

Looking confused, Mrs. Chiverton nodded. "Nice to meet you." Glancing back at Thea repeatedly, she nodded and walked out.

"She seemed sweet." Irene lifted a forkful of pasty. "Mmm. Yummy."

Thea sat astonished at the effect her simple tribute had had on Mrs. Chiverton. Maybe she'd been unfair to the woman who had been a part of her life as long she could remember. Mrs. Chiverton was maddening, but obviously the verse in Proverbs, "A soft word turneth away wrath" worked!

"I liked that woman." Aldo nodded agreeably. "I think *she* would like one of your calzones, Irene."

Thea now knew where Peter got his charming ways. *It must be genetic.*

"I hope, Thea, people here will begin to have a change of heart about the camp," Aldo said quietly.

Irene nodded. "Yes, it's been Peter's dream since he was about fourteen."

"He'd only been ours about a year then," Aldo said.

Startled, Thea asked, "What?"

Aldo grinned. "Didn't he tell you? We adopted Peter when he was thirteen."

"Peter's adopted?"

"All our children are adopted." Irene reached for her large bursting-full handbag.

"Please, Irene, don't start with the pictures." Aldo held up his hands good-naturedly. "Thea will start avoiding us."

"She should be right now." Mr. Crandon hurried up to them.

Thea looked up sincerely nonplussed. Would this never end?

Aldo and Irene looked to Thea.

"Aldo and Irene Della, this is Dick Crandon," Thea said with resignation. *Let the games begin.*

"Dick," Aldo greeted him and Irene smiled.

"You won't be happy to see me after I tell you I'm the one who's organizing the opposition to your son's camp."

Why did he sound so proud of all the unpleasantness he was causing? Thea wished she could ask him that.

"Sorry to hear that." Aldo gave a wry grin.

"Yes, you should really save yourself all this trouble," Irene said amicably.

"Why?" Crandon demanded, "Has your son decided to change his plans?"

Thea folded her hands in her lap. She couldn't eat with an argument exploding around her.

"Oh, no." Irene gave a bubbly giggle. "Only an act of Congress could make Peter change his plans."

Aldo chuckled. "Yeah, that's our Peter. You know, he worked his way through college on his own and stayed on the honor list the whole time, then got his first job and did his MBA at night. Nothing stops that boy when he's on his path."

"*Well,* he's never run into me before." Mr. Crandon pointed to a clipboard in his hand. "*This* is going to stop him."

"What is it?" Thea asked against her own will.

"A petition to change the zoning of Della's property. That's what." Mr. Crandon looked smug. In an acid tone, he went on, "I would ask you to sign, Thea, but we can see which side *you've* chosen."

Aldo surged to his feet. Peter's father towered over Mr. Crandon. For one breathless moment, Thea feared Aldo would lift the portly retired real estate agent right off his feet.

Aldo spoke deliberately, "Thea has made it clear to our son that she is remaining neutral in this…debate. I don't think that just because she was raised to be a good neighbor it should be held against her, *do you?*"

Mr. Crandon glowered at him. Aldo stared back not giving an inch.

Thea heard no sound in the restaurant, not even a dish rattle in the kitchen. She hated all this. Why couldn't Mr. Crandon and everyone else just wait and see what Peter's camp did or didn't bring to Lake Lowell?

Mr. Crandon looked away. "I suppose not. Sorry, Thea." Then he glared up at Aldo. "But I'm not giving up until I win."

Aldo sat down. "Well, a little vandalism and a petition isn't going to stop us."

"I had nothing to do with that," Mr. Crandon snapped.

"I thought you said you were organizing the opposition," Aldo said coolly.

"I'm using only legal means. And I'm going to win." Mr. Crandon's face had turned pink.

Aldo lifted a forkful of food to his mouth, then paused. "Who wins this will be up to God, don't you think?"

"You mean just because your son is supposedly doing a charitable work, he's doing God's will?"

"We're glad to hear you're such a quick learner," Irene put in with a sprightly grin.

Red-faced, Mr. Crandon huffed and walked out.

Thea felt like a rubber band that had been snapped one time too many.

Irene patted her arm. "Now, dear, eat your soup. All this will blow over. You'll see."

This comment made Thea recall Peter's identical resilience. "Are you *sure* Peter is adopted?"

Both Aldo and Irene chuckled warmly at this. "Peter didn't say you were witty, too. But we like it!" Aldo took a big bite of his pasty.

Thea climbed out of the back seat of the Della station wagon. "Thanks for lunch."

"You didn't eat enough to feed a cricket," Irene scolded.

Aldo asked, "You're sure you don't want me to drive you to your door?"

"No, it's so close I'll just walk back to my place. I have a few minutes before my next student." Thea waved and set off at a brisk pace. The trip to town had been as stressful as she had expected. Peter's parents were as intrepid as Peter himself.

As Thea walked over the uneven ground of the camp, she gazed longingly at the lake. A small skiff with a rainbow-colored sail wended a path eastward on the rippling blue surface. The peaceful sight eased Thea's tension. She scooted over the fence. A few minutes relaxing on her chaise on the porch overlooking the lake was just what she needed. Add to that a tall glass of iced tea with a slice of lemon. Already savoring her first cooling sip, she opened the kitchen door.

''Hi, Thea, do you always leave your door unlocked?''

Thea froze, her hand on the doorknob; shock waves lapping through her.

Chapter Seven

"Surprised you, huh?" Her petite stepsister with tousled short blond hair and china blue eyes sat at the kitchen table, sipping iced tea.

"Cynda." Thea stared; her thoughts scattered like dry leaves on the wind. "Cynda."

"That's my name. Don't wear it out—as your dad would say."

Does your mother know you're here? Had her stepsister run away? But why to here? Alarm bells clanged shrilly in Thea's mind. Thea's voice broke, "Cynda, what are you doing here?"

"Can't you even say hi before you start sounding like my mother?"

Though Cynda said the words with a cocky lilt and a grin, Thea heard anger behind them. She reeled in her own rampant reaction. "What's wrong?"

Cynda stood up. "Just needed a change of scenery. Duluth is a drag."

This time Thea detected unshed tears just behind the flippant reply. Unsure, but sensitive to the tender feelings of a sixteen-year-old, she hesitated a moment. If everything were normal, what would she ask her stepsister? "Can I get you anything?"

"I'm a little hungry."

Her mind racing with what she should do next, Thea opened the refrigerator and surveyed her usual neatly plastic-wrapped lumps of food. Nothing appetizing looked back at her. Then she recalled how she'd enjoyed the omelet Peter had made her. The scent of buttery eggs floated through her mind. "Would you like an omelet?"

"No, but a fried egg sandwich sounds good."

So much for the Della touch. I don't have it. "Fried egg sandwich coming up." The butter melted in the iron skillet; the eggs sizzled. So many questions crowded into Thea's mind. But she had never had more than a merely polite conversation with her stepsister. *I should know Cynda better. I need to change that. She's been my stepsister for nearly six years. I've never gotten close to her.*

Within minutes, Cynda wolfed down the sandwich.

"More?" Watching Cynda intently, Thea asked from beside the stove.

"Please."

Thea cracked another egg into the skillet. "How's your mom?"

"Fine," Cynda replied tartly. "How's your grandmother—as grim as I remember?"

Thea looked askance at Cynda. "Whatever Grandmother Lowell's eccentricities, she's still my grandmother."

Cynda squirmed on the kitchen chair. "Did I go too far? Sorry."

Thea said with a touch of sternness, "She's a sick old woman." She scooped the egg out of the iron skillet and made the second sandwich.

Cynda kept turning the salt and pepper shakers around and around and crossing and uncrossing her legs. She seemed edgy, as though she were an engine idling too fast.

Thea put the plate in front of Cynda and now prepared to confront whatever had prompted Cynda's arrival. "Now what—"

Outside Molly interrupted her by barking vigorously to announce a silver van pulling up.

A rap on the screen door frame and little Tracy Johnson leaned in. "Miss Glenheim, I'm here!"

"Come in." Thea smiled. In the months since the "twin disaster" day, she'd become closer to this sweet, spontaneous child.

The little girl, clutching her music books to her, stepped in, then halted. "Who's this?"

"My…sister, Cynda." Thea felt instinctively she should drop the "step" today. A brand-new protectiveness for Cynda touched Thea. After all, Cynda was the closest thing she had to a sister.

"Are we still gonna have a lesson?" Tracy twisted one of her brown pigtails around her finger.

Thea's concern over Cynda ratcheted higher, but Tracy had come for a lesson.

Cynda nodded, then wiped a yellow egg drip from her chin. "Go ahead, you two. I'll be fine."

Thea eyed her stepsister. Had she just stopped for a meal? Would she disappear while Thea was distracted?

Nan walked in, a twin holding each of her hands. The twins wore matching blue-and-white sailor short sets and white sailor hats.

"Twins. Wow!" Cynda put down her sandwich.

"I wish I had a dollar for every 'Twins. Wow!' I've heard in the past two years." Nan, also wearing a blue shorts outfit, grinned. "Isn't this sunny weather great?"

Still uneasy over Cynda's plans to stay or go, Thea introduced Nan. "Let's go, Tracy." As Thea guided the little girl toward the living room, she wanted to say, 'Cynda, stay. We need to talk,' but too many ears were listening. *God, keep her here.*

"Say, Cynda," Nan asked, "do you baby-sit?"

Tracy looked up at Thea as they reached the piano. "Nobody wants to baby-sit for us. My brothers are a handful."

"Two handfuls." Thea chuckled.

Tracy replied in a serious tone, "That's what Daddy says."

Thea laughed out loud. Soon Tracy proudly played the "Raindrop Prelude" from memory. Right in the middle of the "thunderstorm" part of the piece, Thea heard a car pull up outside and doors slamming. Who could that be? Had Myra actually left home to pursue her daughter? Maybe her earlier call had been made from a pay phone.

Cynda came to the arched living room doorway. "Thea, two fishermen are here for the weekend."

Thea stood up. *I forgot all about them!* "They're early. I haven't taken down the linens and made up their beds." The trip to town with the Dellas had put her behind in her day's schedule.

"I can do it," Cynda offered. "Where are the linens?"

"You wouldn't mind?"

"No problem."

Thea told her where to find the linens and keys, then sat down with Tracy again. Having someone to lend a hand was a new experience for Thea. Making beds would keep Cynda busy for a while. Outside enjoying the sunny day, the twins with Nan running behind them raced past the French doors on their way to the lake. Their short, chubby legs churning, they squealed with delight.

"Can I go wading, too?" Tracy asked wistfully.

The sounds of splashing and cheerful yelling called to Thea to come and go wading, too. She said with a slight smile for Tracy, "You'll have to ask your mother when we're done. Now play the prelude all the way through."

With the two fishermen—wearing cloth hats studded with colorful fishing flies—Nan, twin boys, Cynda, Molly and Tomcat breezing in, out and around the house, Thea and Tracy stayed at the piano, the eye of a cheerful, active storm.

Though anxious over Cynda, Thea kept on with the lesson. Tracy's attention wandered occasionally, but in spite of all the interruptions, Thea was pleased with her performance. "You did an excellent job on your memory work."

"Do I get a sticker?"

"Two."

"Two!" Tracy hopped up from the bench. "That was a funny day when the twins got into trouble here," the little girl said, making the connection between the "Raindrop Prelude" and the day Peter had arrived.

Remembering that peculiar day, Thea touched Tracy's nose affectionately. "Yes, that was a funny day."

Peter's arrival in Lake Lowell had been just the beginning of so many challenges and changes this spring, now this summer. Now Cynda had come. What would that lead to? What had happened to her well-ordered, predictable life?

"All done?" Windblown, Nan stood at the doorway. The twins hugged her knees.

Tracy picked up her music and skipped to her mother. "I got two stickers—a horse and a flower!"

"Good job!" Nan started to turn away, but turned back. She pointed a finger at Thea. "Remember, Thea, the next organ committee meeting I'll be calling you about it. Don't forget your report on repairs.''

Thea sighed as she followed Nan outside where Cynda joined her in waving goodbye to the Johnsons. How did Nan keep up with a daughter and twins?

Thea glanced at Cynda, wondering what the fishermen whom Thea had known for years had thought of Cynda greeting them. ''Everything okay at the fishing cabin?''

''Done. And Nan is neat. She hired me to baby-sit Saturday night.''

Thea's eyebrows rose. *And I was afraid she'd leave before Tracy's lesson ended?* ''Are you staying that long?''

''Well, I kind of thought I'd spend the summer.''

For several moments, Thea couldn't speak. ''The summer?'' she repeated lamely.

''Yes, the summer,'' Cynda said, sounding ready for a fight.

''I didn't think you liked it here. You always complain about having to come for a visit.'' Thea studied Cynda. *Were things that bad at home?*

''I told you, Duluth is a drag.'' Cynda pouted.

In order to buy time to think, Thea poured two fresh glasses of iced tea, sliced more lemon, then sat down. The citrus scent hung in the air. Cynda had been very ready to show her anger. Perhaps honesty would be the best policy. ''Cynda, sit down here at the table, please.''

Her stepsister sat down, but wouldn't look at Thea.

Saying a quick prayer, Thea sipped her chilled tea, then coaxed gently, ''Now, just tell me what's happened.''

''Nothing.'' Cynda snapped out the staccato word.

''But—''

''You don't care. You never come to visit us. You never even call.'' Cynda concentrated on the floor.

Then why come to me if I don't care? Thea put her tea

down sharply. "Have you ever considered that you never call me?"

Startled, Cynda glanced up, guilt showing in her expression. "I hadn't thought of that. I'm sorry, Thea. We don't, do we?" The teen put her hand on the table near Thea's. "I never thought about how Mom treats you. She ignores you, too! That means you'll know how I feel!"

Thea chose her words with care. "Was there anything in particular that made you leave?"

Cynda made a sound of disgust, stood, and started pacing. "Mom—she just talks and talks *at* me. And your dad just comes and goes and goes. No one listens. Sometimes I think I'm not a real person at all."

Thea nodded. Remembered sadness began to ache inside her. Though her stepsister had trouble putting her frustrations into words, Thea understood the kind of emptiness Cynda tried to describe. Often as a teen, she had felt like a mannequin that her grandmother merely enjoyed dressing to suit herself as though Thea weren't a real person. "Myra said Dad was off to California for more training."

"He's always gone! And Mom just golfs and lunches at the country club." Cynda paced more.

"What do you do, Cynda?" *Do you practice piano for hours to drown out an unkind voice?*

Cradling one arm within the other, Cynda said with exaggerated aplomb, "Oh, I'm supposed to get all *A*'s, make no trouble and be popular. What else?"

Tears jammed in Thea's throat. She'd felt just the same way— though her grandmother had substituted "be a lady" for "be popular."

Cynda stopped pacing and glanced at Thea. "What's wrong?"

"Just remembering." Thea fought the regret and pain that rippled through her.

"Did your grandmother treat you the same way?"

Thea nodded. She brushed away a tear. It was foolish to cry over the past.

"I didn't mean to make you cry."

Thea took a deep breath. Giving in to unnecessary emotions wouldn't help Cynda now. "This has been a kind of upsetting spring and summer. The camp next door..." Thea swallowed. "There's been a lot of controversy over it and people keep trying to draw me into it."

"I'm sorry. I didn't think you had any problems. Except for your grandmother, I mean. My mom says your grandmother is your main problem."

Afraid asking for clarification would only lead to more mauled feelings for her, Thea tried to think what this could mean. Did it mean that taking care of her grandmother was a chore or something else, more personal? She didn't like to think of what else her stepmother might have said behind her back.

"Can I stay, Thea?"

Thea looked at Cynda's very fair face, flushed with emotion. "I know your mother won't want you to stay here. And don't you usually spend part of the summer with your father?"

"You mean my real father, Doug?"

The tart tone Cynda had used alerted Thea to more bad news on the way. "Yes?"

"Well, I can't. He's getting married this summer. He'll have me come when his new wife, Tara, can *bear* to have me around—when the honeymoon's over." Cynda's voice dripped with sarcasm.

Thea felt awful for her. The new bride's name led Thea to wonder if Cynda's stepmother might be much younger than Myra, maybe closer to Cynda's age. What Cynda had said about Thea's father had been true in Thea's childhood, too. Cynda must feel doubly rejected. *At least, I was only disappointed by one father.*

"I'm not very well off financially, Cynda. I don't think my budget will stretch for one more person."

"I'll get a job. I'm sixteen now. I helped you today. And I've already got a baby-sitting job. I'm not a total zero."

"No one would ever call you that." Hearing *zero* stabbed Thea's heart. She knew what it felt like to be treated like a nothing.

Cynda grimaced. "Don't bet on it. You could lose."

"Your mother doesn't know you're here then?"

"She might have guessed. I told her you were the lucky one. No parents."

Curious about her stepsister's resourcefulness, Thea asked, "How did you get here? Did a friend drive you?"

"Oh, I hitchhiked," Cynda said airily.

"You didn't!" Thea nearly knocked over her glass of tea. "Cynda, that's so dangerous!"

"It's not as bad as you think. A trucker picked me up and spent the first one hundred miles lecturing me about never hitchhiking again. He drove me to the Kwikee Shop near here and I walked the rest of the way."

"Thank Heaven!" Though horrified, Thea had to admire her stepsister's pluck. *I would never have had the courage to run away.* "We'll have to call your mother."

Thea picked up her iced tea. The chilled glass had left a little puddle on the table. Another thought occurred to Thea. Today had been the second peculiar phone call from Myra. "Did you try something like this about a month ago?"

"Yeah, I stayed away for a weekend. One of my friends hid me in her room."

Well, that explains Myra's first call.

Thea walked to the phone and dialed. Just then a noisy, disreputable-looking older car drove up by her door.

"Hello?" Myra's voice came over the line sounding teary.

"Myra, this is Thea. Cynda's here."

"Why didn't you tell me before? I thought she might go to you." The close-to-tears quality switched to outrage.

"She just got here." Thea hoped Myra would show some sensitivity.

Myra barked, "Put her on the phone. I want to talk to her."

In a mute appeal, Thea held out the phone.

Cynda backed away with her hands up in the air as though touching the phone might sting. "I'm not talking to her."

Thea stepped closer to her sister and said urgently, "She's your mother. You need to talk to her."

Through the screen door, Thea saw Thad Earnest get out of his car, push his long hair behind his ears, and stride to the house. *Just what I need—more company. What's Thad doing here?*

Cynda let him in. "Hi."

Acknowledging defeat, Thea put the phone back to her ear. "Myra, I can't get her to come to the phone right now."

"That's fine!" Myra screamed into Thea's ear. "If she wants you more than me, she can stay with you!" She slammed the phone.

Both teens stared at Thea. She didn't doubt Myra's words had been audible to them. Her ear still rang from the overload of sound. Regretfully she hung up the phone. "What can I do for you, Thad?"

"Mom left her knitting, so I had to come get it for her."

He stepped farther into the kitchen looking sideways at Cynda.

Without speaking, Thea went to the living room and picked up the denim knitting bag. Back in the kitchen, she handed it to Thad. *Please go.*

He made no move to leave, but glanced significantly at her stepsister.

Thea sighed inwardly. Why postpone the inevitable? Cynda and Thad were bound to meet each other in a small town. "Thad, this is my stepsister, Cynda Chasten. Cynda, this is Thad Earnest. His brother takes lessons from me."

"Hey, Cynda." His throat colored a touch.

"Hi, Thad."

The two teens grinned at each other.

"You here long?" Thad asked.

"For the summer," Cynda replied.

"Cool."

They grinned on. Cynda fluffed her hair.

"Did you need anything else, Thad?" Thea asked.

His face lost its smile. "Guess not. Bye." Within minutes, his old car creaked and rumbled away.

"I didn't know you had any cool guys in this little berg," Cynda said appreciatively.

Thea closed her eyes. *When did I lose control of my life?*

A week later, Thea stood at the kitchen sink, scrubbing a cookie sheet. A car door slammed. She glanced out her kitchen window and saw Peter's van. Her breath caught in her throat. *He's back.* Looking like a dream come true, Peter sauntered toward her screen door, carrying a large bouquet of pink and white roses.

Thea froze with her hands in the sudsy warm water in the sink. For a few seconds, she let herself hope the roses were for her. But, of course, they were probably for his mother. She was too mousy, not the kind of girl men brought roses to. He'd probably stopped to say hi before he went next door.

This morning Irene had walked over to bring still-warm, homemade cinnamon rolls. Their delicious aroma lingered in the kitchen. The Della attraction was hard to resist.

Outside, blond Cynda, dressed in light blue sweats, jogged up the drive straight to Peter. Thea overheard her say, "Hi! I bet you're Peter."

Thea quickly rinsed the final dish left from a late lunch which had been followed by another new set of fishermen arriving for the weekend and three piano lessons. She drained the sink and dried her trembling hands on the terry towel hanging from the refrigerator door.

Peter, wearing khaki slacks and a dark blue knit shirt, followed Cynda into the kitchen.

Cynda flashed Thea a big smile and said in a wicked tone, "I finally met your mystery man."

Thea wished her sister hadn't used the word, *your*. But she had found out this week that Cynda spoke first and thought whenever.

Peter grinned at her. "Hi, Thea."

"Hi, Peter." Her voice betrayed her by shaking. She'd missed him even though she hadn't wanted to.

Peter stood grinning at her until Cynda nudged him. "Oh! These are for you." He offered Thea the bouquet wrapped in lavender paper.

Time stood still. She'd read that in a book a long time ago, but now she knew how it felt. She couldn't move. Why had he brought her flowers? Was it personal or a polite thank-you for her help in his absence?

"Well," Cynda prompted, "aren't you going to take them?"

"Certainly." Her own inadequacy chilling her, Thea claimed them, wishing more than anything she and Peter were alone, so she could ask him why he'd brought her roses. Or did she really want to know? "Thank you, Peter," she said formally.

"What's the occasion?" Cynda asked.

Thea looked up into Peter's dark chocolate-brown eyes and forgot what Cynda had asked.

"They're a thank-you for all your help, Thea. And barring present company, of course—" he grinned at Cynda, then turned back to Thea "—it's also for being the most beautiful resident on Lake Lowell."

"Wow." Cynda looked visibly impressed.

The extravagant compliment made Thea chuckle. After all, she was competing with Mrs. Chiverton and Mrs. Magill.

In spite of this humorous thought, Thea had trouble dealing with Peter's presence. How did he fill up a room, making her feel laughter lurked only a teasing word away?

She forced herself to walk to the cabinet and take down her grandmother's best crystal vase. She wondered if she were radiating the warmth that glowed inside her.

Now don't put more importance on this than you should, her grandmother's voice intruded in her mind. Thea shook her head trying to rid herself of the mocking voice. She would enjoy this moment. *But what do I say next?*

The silence lasted too long. When Thea couldn't come up with anything better, she remarked, "So your camp opens next Monday?"

"Yes. I work here this weekend and next weekend, then the first campers arrive on that Monday. Just eleven days to go!" Peter rubbed his hands together.

"You must be feeling wonderful." Thea wished she could have shared his enthusiasm, but wouldn't the coming of the campers pour fuel on the smoldering opposition? She began individually cutting the stems of the roses and greenery under running lukewarm water and arranging them in the clear vase.

Peter watched the graceful way Thea went about the homey task of dealing with the flowers. She wore white shorts which showed off the most elegant pair of golden-tan legs in northern Wisconsin. The weeks away from his camp had been a trial. As excited as he was about the camp opening, with more and more frequency, Thea's face had begun popping into his mind whenever he pictured returning to Lake Lowell.

But as usual, Thea was impossible to read. How did she keep everything in? Did she like the roses? Was she attracted to him at all?

Despite these questions, he made himself speak confidently, "It does feel great. That spray painting and broken windows kind of shook me. But nothing has stopped my plans. I know this summer is going to be successful. God is providing funds in amazing ways."

Thea glanced at him.

He couldn't read her expression. "What?"

She gave him a bittersweet smile.

Cynda plopped down on the edge of the kitchen table attracting his attention. "She's probably thinking of the county electrical inspector who showed up before lunch today. He livened things up pretty good."

"Electrical inspector?" Peter leaned back against the counter beside Thea and inhaled her perfume. Lily of the Valley. It mingled with the sweet scent of the roses, making him forget about the inspector for a moment. "What did he want?" he asked finally.

Thea glanced at him as though measuring his response. "To see if he could find something wrong, of course."

Peter said, "Everything's up to code. I had that all checked out before I signed at the closing."

Thea added another pink rose to the arrangement. "The inspector's an old friend of Dick—"

"Crandon," Peter finished for her.

He was rewarded with one of Thea's rare dazzling smiles. He continued, "So, what did Mr. Dick Crandon's friend find?"

Cynda spoke up, "Don't know. Said he'd call Monday bright and early to give your dad the good news. Guess what, big sister?"

Peter enjoyed the sight of Thea gracefully tossing her long, golden-brown hair over one shoulder as she turned to face Cynda.

Thea asked, "What?"

"I am now employed."

"Employed? You got a job?"

"Don't sound so surprised." Cynda smirked.

"I knew you would get a job, but how? I thought I was going to take you around again—"

Cynda jumped off the table. "Ask me where I'll be working. I can't wait to tell you."

"Of course, please tell me where you'll be working." Thea put her hands down and gave her stepsister her full attention.

Peter's mother had told him all about the sudden arrival of Thea's stepsister and how in a week's time Thea had already had an obvious calming effect on the teen.

"Next door," Cynda announced with a sassy grin.

"What?" Thea wore an expression of extreme surprise. "At Peter's camp?"

Oh, oh, would this violate Thea's idea of her independence from the camp? Peter pushed away from the kitchen counter. "My parents hired you?"

"Yeah, I'll be working in the camp kitchen with your mom."

Uneasy, Peter turned to Thea. "Do you think it will be all right for your sister to work for me?"

Cynda flared up. "It's not her decision!"

Peter held up his hand. "Cool those jets. There are bigger issues here."

"What issues?" Cynda demanded petulantly.

"Your sister's position in the debate, in this community." Trying to read her, Peter watched Thea for her reaction.

"What?" Cynda looked baffled.

"It's all right." Thea looked up into his eyes, as though letting him know she were serious. Then she glanced toward Cynda. "I think it will be just the place for you."

Peter wanted to move closer to Thea, to let her know that while he still didn't understand her need to maintain her neutrality in the debate over his camp, he thought her wonderful.

"As long as it's all right with Thea." Peter stepped forward, lifted Cynda's hand, and shook it. "Welcome aboard Double L Boys' Camp."

Cynda did a little hop of success. "So, Sis, see I told you I'd get a job. Plus you won't have to drive me to it. And I love Irene. She's such a great listener."

"I must agree." Peter smiled, pleased with Thea's acquiescence.

"Well, are you going to ask her?" Cynda looked expectantly at Peter.

Chapter Eight

"Ask me what?" Thea stared at Peter.

Peter frowned at Cynda. He'd wanted to build up to his invitation carefully. "I'd like some privacy please."

"Okay." Cynda turned to leave. "By the way, Sis, I've got a date tonight, too."

Peter grimaced inwardly. He could do without a kid sister with a big mouth. "Thea, I've made reservations for two over at the Hunt Club Inn. Will you have dinner with me tonight?"

Why did all his experience with women fail him whenever he was around this woman? He wanted so much to know what her feelings for him were. That's what this dinner invitation would decide—with any luck. But the way she looked at him now, he doubted his ability to persuade her to go with him.

"Yes."

Peter felt his heart lift at her reply. Then he wondered—had she agreed out of boredom or pity?

* * *

By his dash clock, two hours had passed. He drove up Thea's drive for the second time and his nervousness, his elation had not abated one iota.

Pale gray clouds raced over the sky. He'd flown up from Milwaukee early enough to miss the weather front coming in after midnight—plenty of time for them to return before the first raindrop.

What is it about this woman, Father? I can't get her out of my mind. I know I never felt this way about Alanna. A shadow flickered through his emotions. Would Thea drop him like Alanna had once she knew all about him?

When he parked by Thea's door and got out, his mood lifted with anticipation. Through her screen door, he saw her walking forward across the kitchen to greet him. She wore a blue, cotton-knit dress gathered at the waist and flowing around her hips. She had secured her long hair above her ears with combs, but had left it hanging loose around her shoulders. Peter couldn't move. Her loveliness overwhelmed him. *I'm so glad she kept her hair down.* For a moment, he feared he'd spoken the words aloud.

"Peter? Come in."

He stepped inside and gave a long, low wolf-whistle.

Startled, Thea looked up, then smiled hesitantly. "I didn't know what to wear. I've never been to the Hunt Club Inn."

"The dress fits you and the Hunt Club Inn to a tee. I chose the Inn because it's a half-hour drive away. I thought we wouldn't have to worry about people seeing us together." *And, yes, I want to impress her. Honestly, Lord, I need all the help I can get here.*

She picked up her purse and walked toward him. "Thank you for understanding."

Maybe tonight he could change her mind about staying

neutral, especially about him. He took her hand as tenderly as a hard-won prize. "For weeks now I've been waiting to take you out on a date."

Warmth coiled through Thea. He'd said "date." A real date, not just a thank-you dinner. Thea's spirits soared even though she tried to hold on to reality.

Peter drove away from the lake, leaving behind all the tensions that separated them. Sitting beside her, close and alone, heightened Peter's awareness of Thea. He noticed her bare slender arms, her graceful hands resting in her lap, her even breathing, the way she sat so serene.

Thea had trouble breathing as though someone had slipped a tight corset around her ribs. Up close, Peter's presence overwhelmed her. He looked so confident in his expensive gray sport jacket and black twill slacks. In her catalog-ordered dress, she felt like Little Miss Country Mouse.

When he turned off the state highway, she asked cautiously, "Did someone give you directions?"

"My real estate agent suggested this scenic route."

"Yes, this road winds around several small lakes." Thea glanced at the ominous clouds as they turned a darker shade of gray and the wind rushed the clouds across the sky.

To break the silence, she cleared her throat. "So, how many campers are you expecting?"

"About twenty. We're starting with a small group to work out any bugs."

"And you said God's been providing for the camp?"

"God's taking care of everything."

Whop! The steering wheel lurched in Peter's hands. He fought to keep the vehicle on the road. *What happened?* The car pulled to the right. He safely guided it to the shoulder and parked. *A flat? Not tonight!* He swallowed an oath, but hit the steering wheel with both palms.

Thea sat very still, uneasy around anger. She'd seen flashes of temper in Peter—like that day at The Café when he'd shouted at Mr. Crandon.

Peter said in a pained voice, "I think I have a flat tire to change." *So much for the perfect evening I'd planned. I asked for help, not a flat!*

His even tone reassured her. He didn't sound pleased, but who would?

Peter opened his door and slid out. Disgruntled, he went to the other side to look at the tire. Definitely flat. No doubt about it. But why?

Thea got out quietly. "Your vehicle and tires look too new to go flat."

"That's just what I was thinking. Maybe there was a blemish in the tire."

The wind kicked up in velocity. Dust and dry grass swirled around their ankles.

"I better get this done as quickly as I can," Peter said.

Looking upward, Thea replied, "Yes, the front looks like it's moving in faster than predicted." Tornadoes had been sighted in Minnesota that morning. Though the weatherman on Rhinelander TV thought the front would veer south. Thea gave the sky a worried glance and murmured, "I hope Cynda is inside somewhere on her date with Thad."

Peter opened the rear door and dug around for his jack and wrench. Looking grim, he brought the parts of the jack near the flat tire.

Thea tried to think of some cheerful topic to take Peter's mind off the chore and make herself forget about the quick-changing weather. ''You were telling me about how God is providing for the camp.''

Peter rewarded her with a full smile. ''I got a donation in the mail yesterday, a check for $562.00.''

''Isn't that an odd amount?''

He chuckled and twisted another part onto the jack. ''That's what I mean! What would you say if I asked you what the repairs on the camp bus cost?''

''Um—$562.00?''

''Give that woman a cigar!''

''Did the donor know about the repairs?'' She mentally gauged the wind. The clouds swept across the sky like the quick strokes of a tar brush.

Obviously unconcerned, Peter shook his head. ''I called her. She said the money was a year's interest from one of her accounts. She'd heard about my camp and had decided she'd send it to us.'' Peter finished assembling the jack.

''I've heard of that type of small miracle happening before.'' Birds in the trees around her began squawking and launching into nervous flight.

''I wish I could just sit down with Mr. Crandon, your grandmother and the others and tell them how God is working to make this camp a reality.''

Thea lowered her chin ruefully. ''I'm afraid their minds are made up.''

He squatted down on the dusty, gritty shoulder and positioned the jack. The shoulder was not the best, but it should support the jack. ''You mean, 'Don't confuse me with the facts.'''

''Regretfully, yes.''

''What does your grandmother think about Cynda spending the summer with you?''

''She isn't happy about it.'' From a nearby lake came

the call of a loon. The sound rushed to her on the wind like a warning. "Peter, you aren't going to be much longer, are you?"

"Don't worry. I'll have this done hours before the first drop of rain." He slid the assembled jack securely under the wheel well and manipulated the jack's lever. The vehicle rose—click by click. "Now, why doesn't your grandmother like Cynda?"

A burst of wind rippled Thea's gathered skirt. She couldn't keep her eyes off the uncertain sky. *Please hurry, Peter.* "Grandmother has never been happy that my father remarried. She says he married beneath us. Just because my great-grandfather made money in lumber and bought most of the land around Lowell Lake, you'd think we were related to royalty or something."

"So your family had money?" He gingerly knelt down on the dusty shoulder in order to get the flat off. Maybe if he was really careful, he'd be able to dust them off without leaving any mark. No dirty knees at the Hunt Club.

Thea's hair flared with the wind. She gathered it into one hand to keep it out of her face. "*Had* is the operative word," she spoke wryly. "My grandfather had a gambling problem. Before my great-grandfather died, he deeded what was left of the lake property to my grandmother so his son wouldn't be able to lose everything."

"Grim. I don't envy your grandmother." He popped off the hubcap and started loosening the lug nuts.

"I think that's why Grandmother is so difficult about 'our position in the community' as she calls it." In spite of Peter's assurance, Thea no longer believed the TV weatherman. Her apprehension mounted, but she continued calmly, "Having a gambling problem in the family must have wounded her pride, twisted it in a way."

"Losing most of a fortune couldn't feel good."

"Peter, are you nearly done?" she asked. The dark currents above had begun tumbling around in eerie tornado-like swirls.

"Yes, almost done." He pulled off the flattened tire, rolled the spare into place. An unpleasant idea came to him. "Do you think Mrs. Chiverton saw us going out?"

"It doesn't matter. My grandmother already thinks of me as spineless. Your camp is just my latest weakness."

"But you've stayed neutral." Mentally he took a deep breath before diving in. "Besides, I was referring to what your grandmother thinks of *me*. If she knew everything about my background, she'd like you dating me even less."

Thea glanced down. Perhaps this was the time to ask. She said carefully, "Irene said you were adopted. All of her children were."

"That's right."

Dust gusted into Thea's eyes, making her blink rapidly.

Peter wiped the dust from his eyes with the back of his and, then slid on the spare. As he pushed it forward, he tried not to touch the black rubber to his pant legs.

The scent of rain came to Thea on a gust of wind. The sun had been cut off by charcoal clouds. "Peter, that's all you do for changing a tire, isn't it?"

He began to lower the jack. *Click. Click.*

A large raindrop plopped onto her nose.

"Yes." He looked down at his knees. Just dusty; no black rubber marks. They'd be late for their reservation, but he'd just have to wash his hands. He tightened the lug nuts, replaced the hub cap, then slid out the jack. Done!

Cold rain poured out of the clouds.

Thea let out a squeak and yanked open her door.

"Get in!" Peter shouted.

She leaped inside and pulled the car door shut. Chilled and dripping, she heard Peter slam the flat tire and jack inside the rear gate.

He opened the driver's side door and jumped in. "*How* did that get here so fast!"

She felt his anger, his agitation. She didn't blame him.

Peter pushed his wet hair off his forehead. He wanted to hit the steering wheel again, but refrained for Thea's sake. He folded his arms over his chest. "Well, we're too wet for the Hunt Club Inn," he muttered at last. "I wanted this to be a great evening for us." Evidently he wasn't going to get any help in dazzling Thea tonight.

"The flat tire and rain aren't your fault." Thea's voice sounded calm and understanding.

But what else could a polite woman say? Of course, Thea wouldn't let her disappointment show. Frustration burned inside him. "I wanted you to enjoy yourself this evening."

She gave him a trace of a smile. "I've enjoyed myself so far."

He looked to her. "You can't mean that! You can't mean you enjoy sudden blowouts! Downpours?"

"Tonight I do."

This woman was an angel in disguise. But it galled him that their first date would end like this and Lake Lowell wasn't rife with trendy spots. Would they be reduced to ordering pizza from the Kwikee Shop? "I guess we better head home."

She pushed damp hair off her face and said uncertainly, "We don't have to go home if you don't want to. There's a little place near here," she suggested tentatively. "Dad used to bring me on Fridays."

"A place where they don't mind wet patrons?" Peter sounded incredulous.

"On a night like this." She motioned to the window. "We'll blend right in with everyone else."

"Really?" Thunder sounded overhead.

"Go on down this road about two more miles."

She meant it. She actually meant what she said. Peter wanted to kiss her. Any other woman would have been upset. But not Thea. She hadn't even complained that her hair or her dress were drenched.

Feeling blessed, he started the motor. Though the wipers fought hard, the rain flowed like a steady river down the windshield. His view remained rainwashed and rippled, but each passing mile lifted his mood.

She said uncertainly, "Will you tell me about being adopted or would you rather not?"

"No, I don't mind." Regret tugged at him. He hadn't told Alanna. In the end, the confession had driven a stake into their wedding plans. "When I talk about my childhood, I sometimes feel like I'm talking about someone else."

She understood. She felt the same way about the years before her mother had died.

Peter steeled himself for Thea's possible reaction. "My mother was ill. She suffered from severe mood swings, manic depression. At the time, there were very few drugs available to help her. Not as many as there are now." He could still hear an echo from the past—Alanna's mother's horrified voice exclaiming, "Mental problems! They can be inherited!"

"How awful for her, for you."

He paused, touched by Thea's quick sympathy for his mother. "Mom took good care of me. When she had to

be institutionalized off and on, she left me with my grandmother. But when my grandmother died, my mother had
no other relatives who would help.''

''How sad.''

''So when I was seven, my mother went into a state
institution. I ended up in foster care.''

''But Irene and Aldo said they adopted you when you
were thirteen.''

''I was in the foster care system in Milwaukee for about
four years. No one wanted a troublesome kid with an attitude.'' He grinned wryly.

But Thea wasn't deceived. He'd been hurt. *A kid with
an attitude.* She said gently, ''I bet you were a cute kid
with an attitude.''

He gave her half a chuckle.

''Here's the turn,'' Thea murmured.

He turned down a narrow, evergreen-lined road. Several
winding turns brought them to a dead end beside a lake
where a small dilapidated café huddled. Its weathered roof
looked like it leaked. He glanced at her. ''Are you sure?''

''Oh, yes, they have the best burgers in the county.''

The many vehicles already parked outside reassured Peter slightly. ''Okay, I'll pull up by the door and let you
out.''

''No, I'm already wet.'' Thea gave him a teasing grin.
''Besides I'm sure I can outrun you.''

A large spontaneous smile took over his face. ''I don't
believe that.'' He parked as close as he could to the entrance, then reached for the door handle.

''Wait!'' Thea strung her purse over her shoulder and
put her hand on the door release. ''Ready, get set, go!''

They threw open their doors and sprinted toward the

bright pink neon sign which glowed, The End of the Road Inn.

Thea screamed with pleasure as she beat Peter by a hair and shoved open the door. He crowded in behind her, pushing her in farther.

"Well!" a contralto voice announced, "another couple of drippy customers."

"Franny, we're drenched!" Thea called back happily.

"Got just what you two need." A tall, bony woman in blue jeans and a frayed sweatshirt tossed them each a large bath towel. "There'll be a towel charge added to dinner tonight. Also a 'you're nuts for coming out on a night like this' charge. Now stand there till you drip-dry some."

In between quick breaths, Thea giggled at this welcome, then turned to Peter, "You see, a little rain is not a problem at The End of the Road." She hung the towel over her shoulder with her purse.

Peter, his pulse still racing from the dash through the rain, only shook his head. Beads of water from his wet hair dripped down his forehead. As he rubbed the towel over his hair and face, he watched Thea bend forward and twist her hair like wringing out laundry. Then she did the same to her skirt, gathering it to one side and wringing it out onto the linoleum. Appearing in public, disheveled and drenched, only made Thea laugh!

Thea smiled to herself. As always only the garish neon beer signs around the bar and candles on each table illuminated the restaurant. She didn't have to feel as though she were on display or that her clinging dress would be immodest. Even so, when she finished wringing all the excess water from her cotton dress and hair, she draped the damp towel around her shoulders modestly like a shawl.

After hanging up his sodden sport jacket to drip-dry, Peter rid himself of rainwater by shaking his legs to fling moisture from his slack hems.

"You do that just like Molly." Thea teased, leaning toward him.

Oh, he wanted to kiss her sweet mouth. *Thea, could you care for me?* Restraining himself, he grinned wryly. "Thanks. Being compared to a dog completes this charming evening."

"But Molly's such a sweet dog." The words came out of her mouth before she could stop them. What did this man possess that loosened her shy tongue?

Leaning close enough to kiss her, Peter asked in a low voice, "Well, I have been known to be a loyal and faithful companion."

"Okay, you two have dried off enough," Franny interrupted. "I got a lake-view booth for you."

"Wonderful!" Thea introduced Franny to Peter.

"Nice to meet you," the woman said gruffly. "Glad to see Thea out for a change."

Thea blushed. Even though it might be true, she didn't appreciate her lack of dates announced to the world.

Peter responded, "The guys around here must be blind in one eye and can't see out of the other."

Franny hooted with laughter. "You said it. But mostly it's that grandmother of yours, Thea. She made sure she scared everyone away so you wouldn't run off and marry someone she didn't approve of."

The older woman's frankness shocked Thea.

Franny tossed down the two menus on the table of a booth along the lake side of the restaurant. "You strong enough to stand up to that old battle-ax, Peter?"

"I have already." Peter let Thea slide in, then he sat across from her.

"Good." Franny marched away.

Peter looked at Thea. "Is she always so outspoken?"

"Franny's always unpredictable, but not usually this outrageous."

"Maybe it's the weather. The negative ions or something." The high-backed wooden booth lit by the flickering candle looked cozy and private to Peter and he began to think better of The End of the Road.

Thea smiled tightly.

"Now, you said the burgers are great here?"

"Yes, and the waffle fries." Fortunately they'd come to a familiar place. She would have been frozen into high politeness at the Hunt Club Inn. Peter's effect on her had grown, leaving her off-kilter.

"Waffle fries! Oh, woman! How did you know they're my favorite!"

As he teased her, Peter's intense gaze never left her face. Heady awareness of him flowed and pooled inside her.

She slid forward against the table. *Peter, come closer.*

Franny stomped back to them. Thea pushed back against the back of the seat.

While Peter gave Franny their orders, he looked across the scarred, worn table at Thea. In spite of her sodden condition, she looked lovely and unruffled. Her hair, pulled back wet and sleek, drew even greater attention to her large eyes, high cheekbones and delicate mouth.

He wanted to tell her that her beauty left him breathless, but he knew she'd only be amazed at the comment. He'd been drawn by her elegance, but her naturalness and lack of coquetry were even more valuable. *Thea, you're one in a million.*

Plumbing the depth of these thoughts, he sat drinking in the sight of Thea, as he sipped his soft drink through a long straw. He listened to the thunder and watched the flashes of lightning outside the windows, feeling the same kind of tumult inside himself.

As Thea listened to the voices of the other diners, the rattle of the windows with each clap of thunder and Franny barking orders to the cook, she and Peter sat together, cozy and content within the high-backed booth.

Peter's wet hair was drying into a jumble of black curls. One fell onto his forehead. How she wanted to reach out and arrange it for him. With his olive skin and high cheekbones, he made her think of a Renaissance painting of an Italian gentleman. Fancifully she imagined him holding out his hand to draw her into a dance. A minuet played in her mind.

Peter relaxed completely. All he needed was to hear Thea's melodic voice to make him totally happy. "What were we talking about when the storm hit?"

She played with the straw in her glass. "You were telling me about your being a foster child. How did Irene and Aldo come to adopt you?"

"I was sent to them as a last resort." As he told her the truth, a frisson of anxiety went through him. Better now than later. "I'd gotten into trouble. I was twelve by then and pretty much unmanageable. You see, I was afraid that my mom's illness would come out in me and I couldn't handle that. And I felt worthless—my dad didn't even stay around long enough to marry my mom." He waited for her response to the fact he was illegitimate.

Thea touched his hand for just a moment.

He breathed a silent sigh of relief. Alanna had been upset he hadn't been honest earlier. And her parents had been terrified of the less-than-perfect genes his mother had given him. "The social worker gave me to the Dellas as a last chance. I tested them to their limits, but they didn't give up on me. Not even when I was picked up for shoplifting and suspended from school repeatedly for getting into fights. None of it mattered to them."

Now Thea understood why high-risk boys were so important to him. Peter had been a high-risk kid. She inched her hand across the wooden table and let it rest next to his. "They seem like those kind of people."

"They taught me about God's love, showed me how to live, how to love myself and others." His hand tingled at the nearness of hers.

Thea pursed her lips, then bent her head. "I wish my grandmother had taught me those lessons." She surprised herself again with her own frankness.

His hand closed over hers. His voiced sounded husky in his own ears. "Someone must have taught you those."

She glanced up, giving him a look of gratitude.

He lifted her hand, intending to kiss it.

Franny brought the basket of hot onion rings and plopped it down in front of them. "Those are fresh from the fryer. Don't burn yourselves."

"Yes, Mom," Peter teased, flashing the woman a smile to distract her while he lowered Thea's hand, but he didn't release it.

Franny punched his arm. "I like this one, Thea. Keep him."

Thea blushed. *Franny, please!*

Alone again, Peter ventured to taste an onion ring, but they were too hot to touch. "I find it hard to believe your grandmother raised you."

Comfort like warmed honey flooded Thea. Peter had

lived the loss of a parent, too. And he held her hand as if she were precious to him. *Could I be special to you, Peter?* Though her mind whirled with ideas and sensations, she made herself chuckle dryly. ''On *that* she would agree with you. But I didn't lose my mother until I was ten.''

Franny plunked down two baskets with huge burgers nestled in the heart of sizzling, golden waffle fries. ''Enjoy.''

Peter let go of her hand. For a few moments, he devoted himself to his juicy burger.

Thea enjoyed his enthusiasm over the viands Franny had delivered. A little juice trickled down the side of Peter's mouth. Boldly she dabbed it away with a paper napkin.

Peter grinned. ''Thanks.''

She ducked her head. To cover her slight embarrassment, she asked, ''I can understand now why you want to help young boys. But why a camp?''

''The summer after I was adopted I went to a church camp. That's where I became a Christian. Knowing Christ changed my life. God finished healing my broken heart. He healed my soul. I began to want the same for other boys like me, ones who didn't have great adoptive parents like I did.''

Thinking of all the conflict over the camp, Thea shook her head.

''Doesn't that make sense to you?'' Peter asked.

''It makes a lot of sense to me,'' she said firmly. ''It's just too bad Mr. Crandon can't hear this.'' She picked up her burger and took a bite.

Peter looked up, startled. ''Does that mean you are changing your mind about staying neutral?''

''You said you wouldn't ask me that.'' She put down her burger.

''Sorry. I thought that's what you meant.''

Thea groped for words to explain her hesitance. ''I want to be thought of as an individual, not just a shadow of my grandmother or someone else.''

''But I wouldn't do that.''

Oh, really? But aloud, she said, ''Not on purpose. But, Peter, you're like a tidal wave!''

He chuckled. ''My mother has called me a tornado in the past.'' He popped a French fry into his mouth and chewed it cheerfully.

She gave him a slight grin. ''Do you understand then?''

''Not really. But that is part of your charm.'' He reached over and took her hand again. His touch persuaded her more than his words.

Much later that night, Peter drove up Thea's road. The evening had taken unexpected turns, but Peter had learned much about Thea while he changed a tire, then teased her in the booth at The End of the Road Inn. *What a name!*

He drove with one hand because Thea held his other. She made him feel as though it were the very first time he'd held hands with any woman. Everything about her drew him—her natural fragrance after the rain had washed away the Lily of the Valley. The softness of her hands. The feeling of rightness—he was meant to be here, to hold her hand, to let her know how special she was.

He'd told Thea the truth about his background and she'd understood and accepted the past for what it was—events which had gone before, separate from the present and the future. A flat tire, a storm and a humble café had set the evening apart, made it memorable.

A formal dinner—all politeness and decorum—would have been an empty, sterile experience in comparison.

He'd asked God for a perfect evening with Thea and his prayer had been answered—though much differently than he had anticipated.

He stopped beside Thea's door and turned to her. Now, the perfect ending to their first evening together—a first kiss. Still holding her hand, he pulled her toward him. He brushed her lips with his. "Thea," he whispered.

Thea pulled away. "Peter, something's wrong. Look!"

Hearing real alarm in her voice, he looked over his shoulder where she pointed to his camp.

"I see the county sheriff's car." Fear came through her voice.

Then Cynda's voice shouting, "Thea! Peter! Come quick!"

Chapter Nine

His heart racing, Peter shouldered open his door. By the time he'd jumped out of his vehicle, Thea had reached the front and halted near him. Even though the high yard lights illuminated the camp, Peter could only see the sheriff's car distinctly. What could have happened?

Panting loudly, Cynda reached them.

"What is it, Cynda?" Thea caught her stepsister by both arms. "Are you hurt?"

Thea voiced Peter's overriding thought.

Cynda swallowed. "I was away with Thad. We got back when the storm calmed down a little. Thad dropped me off because he had to get home. His mom's a real...stickler about getting home—"

"Tell me what happened?" Peter asked impatiently.

"Oh!" Startled, Cynda looked at him. "The sheriff's waiting for you, Peter."

Frustrated by Cynda's wandering style, Peter nudged Thea toward the fence.

Thea took her stepsister's arm gently and drew her along with them. "Tell us while we walk over. We shouldn't keep the sheriff waiting. First of all, was anyone hurt, Cynda?''

Peter held his breath, ready to sprint ahead if harm had come to his parents.

Cynda said, ''No, just some more vandalism.'' Cynda's tone became more lively, ''Hey, Thea, you didn't tell me about the first time there was vandalism before I came. Wow—you must have been scared to death!''

Thea replied in her unruffled voice, ''Yes, I was a bit nervous.''

Peter picked up his pace, running now. First Thea had been terrorized, now his parents. The yard lights around the camp were alight, etching the landscape with ominous-looking shadows. While his parents had gone about their business, what had lurked in those shadows? His mind refused to take it in. He'd never have left tonight if he'd had any inkling of trouble. He reached the sheriff, standing in the doorway of the lodge, first.

''Peter!'' Mom peeked around the sheriff. ''How was your dinner? The storm didn't spoil it, did it?''

Peter blinked his eyes as he walked into the light. Mom and Dad waited inside the lodge's large living room. He noted his mom had made a pot of tea, her answer to all crises. Everyone looked unharmed. ''What's happened?''

''Your vandal or a new one damaged the camp's canoes,'' the sheriff replied.

The news slammed Peter full force. The canoes! It would cost hundreds to replace them! His fists clenched and clenched again. When he surfaced from the haze of his stormy thoughts, his mother was explaining, ''Your father and I went out to the fish fry at the VFW hall. When we got home, we didn't notice anything. It was dark by then, son. Then we heard Thea's dog barking.''

Peter started pacing to release his inner commotion.

Mom offered Thea a cup of tea. Thea accepted it. "And Molly doesn't bark without a good reason."

Peter's dad picked up the story. "I went out. Molly ran back for me and took me right to the canoes stacked against each other by the boathouse."

Peter jammed his hands into his pockets.

Irene said, "Dad yelled up to me to get the sheriff on the line."

The sheriff leaned back against the doorjamb. "It's just the canoes. A quick puncture in the bottom of each one. Wouldn't have taken someone long."

I should have been here. I should have expected something tonight, my first night back.

Thea glanced up at her stepsister. "Did you hear Molly barking?"

"When Thad brought me home, Molly greeted us. Everything was cool. But a while later Molly started barking, then she got quiet and I heard Aldo shouting to Irene about the sheriff. So I started to run over, but the phone rang."

"Who was it?" Thea asked.

"Thad. He wanted to tell me..." Cynda smiled and looked coy. "He had a great time." She giggled.

God, give me patience, Peter shouted inside. Didn't the girl understand the significance of what had happened?

Thea asked, "Had the storm passed by then, Cynda?"

"Yeah, we stayed inside at The Café till the rain was almost over. Then he had to bring me right home so he didn't get his mom mad."

Peter counted silently to keep his temper in check. He didn't want to worry his mom any further.

The sheriff spoke up, "I'll come and look again by daylight, but I doubt I'll find anything."

Thea looked up. "Have you called Mrs. Chiverton?"

Seeing Thea sitting calmly sipping tea as though nothing

had happened didn't surprise Peter. She had that gift of an even temper. But anger at his helplessness churned inside him. He wanted to shout aloud his sense of outrage. *God, why are You letting this happen? We needed those canoes! Why aren't Your angels standing guard over us?*

"I'll call her." The sheriff walked over to the phone on the table beside Thea. He dialed quickly. "Hello, ma'am, this is Sheriff Swenson. Yes, I'm at the boys' camp. Did you hear or see anything unusual before I came?"

Pause.

"Yes, we heard Thea's dog barking."

Pause.

"Canoes were vandalized here."

Slumping in defeat on the couch beside his mom, Peter pressed his fingertips to his pounding temples.

"Well, thank you. I must finish up here and get on with my duties. Goodbye." The sheriff hung up and shook his head indicating no new information.

"What should we do, Sheriff?" Mom asked.

Peter hated the question. It said so plainly he was helpless against this invisible enemy.

"Not much you can do. Things here are stirred up. Crandon and…" The sheriff halted with a pointed glance at Thea.

"Mr. Crandon and *my grandmother,*" Thea interjected sounding grim. "They keep stoking people's fear."

"What are people afraid of?" Cynda asked. "What's the big deal about poor kids coming here?"

A good question, Peter said silently.

A moment of silence passed. Thea spoke up. "They're afraid of new people. Afraid of their hometown changing."

"But I don't get it." Cynda hopped up. "How could a few kids at a camp wreck a town?"

Peter wanted to echo her words. Why couldn't he make the opposition see how wrong they were?

Irene replied, "People here—some people—are afraid. I've heard them say the boys will see how good it is up here and they'll come back when they grow up."

Aldo nodded sadly. "People here read about the crimes and trouble down in Milwaukee and Chicago. They think the distance will protect them."

Cynda looked disgusted. "That's silly. Duluth is farther away than Lake Lowell. Distance doesn't mean anything."

"They're afraid, Cynda," Thea said quietly. "When you're afraid, you don't think clearly."

"So what are you going to do, Peter?" Cynda asked. Everyone looked to him.

Peter's urge to explode had passed. All the work facing him at daylight weighed him down. He gave a labored sigh. "Well, I had planned to patch that last roof, but I guess I'll be patching some canoes."

"Can you do that?" Cynda asked.

"I'll find out. We can't afford new ones." Peter stood up. Sadness filtered through him. "Thank you, Sheriff. I hope you won't have to keep coming out like this."

"Yes, we'd like you to come to dinner sometime, Sheriff." Irene smiled. "I have a new recipe for ziti. I'd like to meet your wife and we don't want you to have a bad opinion of us and our camp."

"No chance of that. My opinion of this camp gets better each time I drop by. Just sorry I keep coming in the line of duty." The sheriff nodded to everyone and left.

Irene threw her arms around Peter. "Honey, are you all right?"

Trying to reassure her, Peter returned her hug. "I'm really fine."

"Not really fine, Pete." His dad put an arm around his shoulder. "You're really mad."

"I was shocked, Dad. Then I was mad. But now I'm just sad."

Irene hugged him tightly. "I know what you mean, dear. Sometimes I just have to cry when I think how mean people can be."

Aldo patted Peter's back and kissed Irene's cheek. "Just remember who you were named for, son. Saint Peter didn't back down from the good fight."

Irene chuckled. "As I remember it, Saint Peter started out just like you did, dear, *too ready* for a fight."

Peter smiled ruefully. "But I didn't plan on having to fight. It's so frustrating."

"Are you going to make me say it?" Irene prompted wryly.

"Anything worth wanting is worth fighting for," Peter said as though reciting a family motto.

"But let's not forget to include God in this fight. This is God's camp. Always has been," his dad said.

Under Thea's surprised gaze, Aldo gathered his son and his wife close to him.

Aldo began, "Father, you know who is doing this vandalism. You know his heart. We ask You to deal with this person, deal with the pain that is causing him to do these destructive things. Open his heart. Heal his heart."

Tears started in Thea's eyes.

Irene spoke, "Father, Peter is the son You gave us. We love him. He is so precious to us. He's worked for nearly twenty years to make his dream, this camp, come true."

Peter joined in, "But it's not just for me, God. You've given me everything I've ever needed or wanted. Your love has been sufficient for me. Let me share Your love with the boys who will soon come. Now let Your love be sufficient for this camp.''

"Amen," Aldo concluded.

Thea brushed away her tears. Out of the corner of her eye, she noticed that Cynda also looked sobered. Putting down her cup and saucer, Thea stood up. "Peter, I think it's time Cynda and I went home. It's been a long evening." She needed time to process the latest event and this unexpected finale.

"I'll walk you home." Peter grinned at her.

She wanted to ask, *How can you smile?* But she knew he could smile because of what she'd just witnessed. He had the love of two warm and supportive parents and a deep belief in God. How she envied him his loving and easygoing parents and their close relationship with God. God always seemed so far from her.

Thea's heart felt as if it would crumble inward at her aloneness. Even after years of burying her own feelings, she had difficulty now holding her emotions in check.

Aldo and Irene hugged Cynda and her and walked them to the door. Thea wished she could linger within the embrace of these loving people. How long had it been since someone had hugged her? In the room full of friends, loneliness nearly choked her.

With Peter on one side and Cynda on the other, Thea walked over the wet, rough camp lawn. Peter held her hand.

Again Peter's confident touch made all her ingrained reserve dissolve. He swung her up into his arms and set her on the top of the low rail-fence. Unable to resist, she put her arms around his neck. For a few seconds, he let his arms encircle her. She wanted to stay within his embrace, but she pulled away. Cynda scooted over the fence without help.

Fleetingly Thea wondered if he would have kissed her good-night if Cynda hadn't been with them. The thought caused her heart to jerk once before beating regularly again. She squeezed his hand, then slid onto her side of the fence. She walked side by side with Cynda to the door.

Peter called over the fence, "Good night, ladies."

Cynda stepped inside the kitchen, then paused to look back. "See you tomorrow, Peter. Tell Irene I'll be over bright and early."

Thea didn't trust her voice yet. Besides, she realized this might be the moment she'd been waiting for in regards to her stepsister.

Her stepsister's words sounded perfectly normal, but Thea still detected a touch of underlying emotion. In spite of Thea's own unsettled feelings, maybe this would be a good time to talk to Cynda about her mother. Thea closed and locked the door behind them.

Cynda yawned. "I guess I'll get to bed. I got to get up early and I'm bushed." Standing in the middle of the kitchen, Cynda stretched like a cat.

"Cynda." Thea sat down at the table. "Let's talk."

"About what?"

"This evening. A lot happened."

"That's for sure." Cynda paused, then gave Thea a pensive look. "Can I ask you something?"

Thea nodded.

Cynda perched on the kitchen counter facing Thea. "Did you ever see anyone pray like that before? I mean, the three of them all hugging?"

"No, I haven't. It was quite moving." Thea felt the memory tug at her again. Peter's family's closeness in prayer had been impressive. In contrast, an image came to her of herself as a child beside her bed. Grandmother stood nearby while Thea had recited, "Now I lay me down to sleep.'' Praying bonded the Dellas to each other and God, but with her grandmother it had been forcing down bitter medicine.

Cynda continued, ''Yeah, it wasn't like an act or anything.''

Thea cleared her throat. ''Irene and Aldo are very open, very sweet people and it's obvious they love God.'' If one wasn't used to such openhearted love, it could be intimidating. Thea could imagine what a shock they had been to Peter when he came to them as a child.

''When I was there today helping Irene in the kitchen, two of their daughters called. Irene spoke so happily to them.''

The note of longing in Cynda's voice touched Thea. ''Yes, but we don't get to choose our parents.''

''Yeah, unfortunately.''

''But they're still our parents,'' Thea said quietly.

Cynda counterattacked, ''You can't tell me you haven't wished you had a different grandmother plenty of times.''

Thea felt convicted, guilty as charged. ''Cynda, I'm not talking about my grandmother right now. You and I share your mother and my father. Together they are *our* parents.''

Cynda perked up. ''Gee, I hadn't thought about that before. We share parents. Cool.''

Thea smiled at Cynda's enthusiasm, but she had something she wanted to make clear to her stepsister. ''I've been thinking about your mother a lot this week.''

As the moment to talk about a topic Thea rarely spoke of came, she grew serious. ''My mother died when I was ten years old. I can't describe to you what that felt like. It was like I kept feeling doors slam inside me. I felt dead, too, but I was still living.''

''Thea.'' Cynda's voice became subdued again. ''You

don't know what it feels like to have a dad just walk out on you.''

"No, but I know what it's like to be ignored by a dad. That's not the point. We could sit here all night trying to decide who's had it worse.''

"What is your point, Sis?'' Cynda eyed her warily.

"It's time you called your mother.''

Cynda erupted, "But—''

Holding up her hands to forestall Cynda, Thea persevered, "How would you feel if something happened to your mother before you could call her?''

"That's low.'' Cynda looked away.

"It's just the truth. Please, Cynda.'' Thea pointed to the phone, which hung beside her. "Call her. Now.''

Looking uncomfortable, Cynda slid off the counter. "What do I say? Can't you do it?''

"I'm not Myra's daughter. *You* ran away. *You* broke faith with your mother. *You* must call her. Cynda, she never ran out on you. Your dad did. Don't take it out on her.''

Hesitating beside Thea, Cynda tucked in her chin. "What if she says I have to come home?''

"I don't think she will. I'll help you convince her that it's all right if you stay.'' As Thea nodded toward the phone again, she prayed Myra had had a change of heart. Cynda followed through this time. Thea listened to the one-sided conversation, pleased to hear Cynda begin to speak more and more easily to her mother.

Finally Cynda turned to Thea. "Mom wants to talk to you.''

Thea took the receiver and reassured her stepmother that she'd be happy to have Cynda stay.

Myra said, "Thea, I appreciate this. After I thought things over, I'm glad she and I will have a time-out.''

"Sure. Myra, when my father comes home, why don't you and he come for a weekend with us?" Cynda had talked to her mother; now Thea needed to talk to her father about Cynda *whenever* he had time.

After hanging up, Thea faced her stepsister. "Do you feel better?"

"Yeah. Thanks." Impulsively Cynda threw her arms around Thea. "I'm so glad I came. Are you?"

"Yes, I am." Thea hugged her back. *Thank you for Cynda, God, and for letting me get to know her. And please keep us and Peter's camp safe.*

"Good morning!" Peter called in Thea's kitchen windows. "Anybody up?"

Thea, wearing her terry-cloth robe over her pajamas, yawned as she opened the door. Seeing Peter unexpectedly made prickles race down her spine. She masked it with a playful grimace. "How can you sound so cheerful so early?"

"Hey, it's almost 7:30 a.m." He walked in and offered Thea a plastic-wrapped plate with a toasted bagel and sliced ripe cantaloupe on it. Thea longed to reach out and take his hand. She'd learned the joy that just touching his strong hand could bring.

"Hi, Peter!" Cynda came out freshly showered and dressed for work in jeans and bright pink T-shirt. "Is Irene baking today?"

Thea set the plate on the kitchen counter and covered her unsettled feelings by getting out coffee, then began running water at the sink.

Peter grinned. "Oh, Mom's got a lot planned for you. First she's got fresh fruit and bagels for breakfast and she's expecting you to come and eat!"

"Great! I can hardly wait to tell her I talked to my mom

last night and she said I can stay for the summer. Thea, I'll be at the camp most of the day. And Thad's taking me water-skiing this evening. Bye!''

Thea pushed away her feeling of disquiet over Thad dating Cynda. *Just because Thad and his mother don't get along has nothing to do with Cynda.*

Waving farewell, Thea watched Cynda go, then turned to Peter. Hiding the buoyant lift just being near Peter brought her, she asked placidly, ''I suppose you've already had your coffee?''

''Yes, I just wanted to see how you were this morning.''

She filled the coffeepot with cold water. ''You mean after last night?''

''It was an evening of surprises.'' His tone was intimate.

She knew he was remembering their closeness as he'd held her hand in The End of the Road Inn booth, then on the way home. Longing for his touch, she concentrated on spooning fragrant coffee into the coffee maker. ''Pleasant or unpleasant ones?'' she asked tentatively.

''Pleasant. I will always remember our waffle fries and burgers and outdoor shower at The End of the Road.''

''Me, too.'' She grinned. Last night's date would be an evening she'd treasure. Then she grew sober as she recalled seeing the sheriff's car outside the lodge for the second time.

Silence. Peter gazed at her.

She wanted to say something supportive to him. But he didn't seem to need any encouragement from her. He plainly didn't have a whipped-dog look. His usual confidence had reasserted itself. How did he do it?

Peter said, ''I'm off to town in a few minutes. Dad's been on the phone and he's already found someone who knows how to patch those old wood canoes.''

"Mr. Willoughby?" She turned on the coffee maker and imagined Peter drawing her into his arms.

"You know him?"

Listening to the coffee begin to drip down, Thea nodded pensively. She wished she had thought of Mr. Willoughby earlier, so she could have suggested him to Peter.

But she spoke up in an imitation of Cynda's pert style. "Peter, I know *everyone* in Lake Lowell! I was going to call you this morning and tell you about him. You Dellas are too fast for me."

Peter caught her eye. "You're okay, then? You looked pretty shaken last night."

She let herself look at him fully. "You did, too."

"Senseless violence always shatters peace. I wish we could find out who is doing this."

"Yes, I keep going over and over in my mind, trying to think of who it might be." She shook her head in dismay. "Because Mr. Crandon is the most obvious person doesn't—"

"I know. Though my mom says grief makes people do strange things sometimes."

"Yes, bitterness only destroys." She'd begun to realize bitterness had been the main motivation in her grandmother's life. All the history she'd shared with Peter pointed toward this. Grandmother Lowell was bitter over the loss of the family fortune, about who Thea's mother had married—if Franny was to be trusted.

Peter reached for her hand.

His warmth came to Thea through their clasped hands. *Oh, Peter.*

He said, "I've got to go and pick up Willoughby, then I'll be busy all day."

"Me, too." A sinking feeling snaked through her as she thought about visiting her grandmother and the organ committee meeting this morning. She held on to Peter's hand for a few seconds longer, drawing strength from his firm honest grip, then let go. She wanted to say, *I support your camp*. But something, maybe fear, held her back.

With a cheerful wave, Peter left her.

Taking a deep breath, Thea sighed. What would it be like to be that confident? She envied Peter his resilience.

From the start, she'd made a point of declaring her neutrality over the camp because no one had ever much cared about her opinions. Certainly Grandmother Lowell had never cared. But now that she had taken the first stand of her adult life, counter to Grandmother, how could she switch to supporting Peter?

If she openly supported the camp, everyone especially her grandmother, would sneer and say she'd just fallen for Peter's good looks. She'd been strong enough to declare neutrality, but was she strong enough to stand against Grandmother?

In school, Thea had learned about a Greek battle where the Greeks had won the battle, but at the cost of their whole army. Thea's experience had taught her that was the only kind of victory anyone ever achieved over Grandmother. What would Thea's openly backing Peter push her grandmother to do? Fear trickled through her like ice water. Could Grandmother have hired someone to spray-paint the sign and puncture the canoes—or perhaps she'd only egged Mr. Crandon on?

Pushing these chilling thoughts out of her mind, she walked to the phone and dialed. "Hello, Mrs. Chiverton, would you like a ride to the organ meeting today? I plan to stop and visit Grandmother on the way. Okay, I'll pick you up in about an hour." *There.* That much she'd accomplished.

She'd made a promise to herself that day she'd intro-

duced Mrs. Chiverton to the Dellas to be kinder to the
elderly woman. Also, she couldn't get past her grandmother's nasty appraisal of her lifelong friend—"Louella
was born a fool."

Thea had begun recalling little kindnesses Mrs. Chiverton had shown her when she'd been a lonely, motherless
child. Little souvenirs brought back from trips. Thea's favorite cookies baked just because she would be visiting
with Grandmother. Thea hoped Mrs. Chiverton would
never find out what her "beloved" Althea said behind her
back.

Carrying a paper bag filled with her grandmother's special linens, Thea walked into the care center beside Mrs.
Chiverton. She felt like she'd entered enemy-controlled
territory.

"It was so sweet of you to stop and pick me up, Thea."

Thea couldn't get over how much offering Mrs. Chiverton a ride had pleased the little woman. It made Thea glad
she'd taken time for the small favor.

In her chirpy voice, Mrs. Chiverton asked, "Dear, do
you think your grandmother will ever move back to the
lake?"

Thea had thought this over at length. She now realized
her grandmother could have remained home after her
stroke. She'd really gone to the care center to hide from
people. Grandmother deemed being partially paralyzed as
a position of weakness, something to be ashamed of. Thea
hadn't realized this fully until she'd heard her grandmother's words the night of the county board meeting. *And
let everyone gloat over me? Never!*

"No, I don't think so," Thea answered simply.

"I guess not." Mrs. Chiverton tsk-tsked.

They walked into Grandmother's room. Startled, Mr.

Crandon looked up from where he sat beside her grandmother.

"Hello, Mr. Crandon," Thea said quietly.

He stood; guilt plain on his face. Obviously Thea had interrupted a plotting session.

Mrs. Chiverton fluttered over to her friend. "Althea, Thea brought me in for the organ committee meeting and we had time to stop here first."

"Louella, Dick and I are in conference," Grandmother snapped.

Thea braced herself. She wanted to see Mr. Crandon's reaction in person to the latest vandalism. "Have you heard what happened last night at the camp?"

"Oh, yes!" Mrs. Chiverton said with genuine dismay. "Someone wrecked canoes at the camp. Isn't that terrible?"

"When is that Della going to give up?" Mr. Crandon asked.

"But, Dick, this is awful!" Mrs. Chiverton surprised Thea by speaking up. "I don't like the idea of the camp changing, but I don't think anyone should go around destroying private property. And I know you don't approve of anything like that."

Thea couldn't have said it better herself. She silently promised to take Mrs. Chiverton to lunch after the organ meeting.

"Of course, I don't approve of destruction of personal property," Mr. Crandon blustered. "But I'm not surprised someone is taking the law into his own hands. Della isn't going to win. My petition to change the camp's zoning to private residential property will put an end to all this."

Thea didn't reply, but walked over to her grandmother. Grandmother preferred sleeping in sheets that held the scent of fresh, summer wind, so Thea always laundered and line-dried her grandmother's bedding in the warm weather. "I brought your linens."

"Set them on the bed." Her grandmother wouldn't look at her.

Thea put the bag on the bed, startled by her grandmother's unusually rude behavior.

"Maybe we should be getting on to the meeting?" Mrs. Chiverton suggested timidly.

Thea nodded with her spirits sinking. If only the final organ meeting would end with an amicable decision. Or in this contentious summer, would it be one more battle royal?

Chapter Ten

Mrs. Chiverton had become less talkative after their visit to the care center, Thea noticed. As they walked into the church for the organ committee meeting the older woman fell uncharacteristically silent. But so many of the givens in Thea's own life had shifted over the past two months, maybe Mrs. Chiverton was experiencing the same kind of unsettled feelings.

Downstairs in the kitchen, Nan Johnson, looking carefree without one of her twins on her lap, sat at the kitchen table. Wearing a denim dress, Vickie was making lemonade. A plate of chocolate chip cookies with large walnut chunks decorated the center of the table.

"Hi, Thea and Mrs. Chiverton," the two young women greeted them in unison, then giggled at doing so.

"Who baked the cookies?" Thea asked, sitting down at the head of the table.

"Tracy did." Nan smiled proudly.

"What a smart little girl!" Mrs. Chiverton sat to Thea's right.

"Who'd like a glass of freshly-squeezed lemonade?" Vickie asked.

Everyone accepted. As Thea took her first tart sip, the ice clinked cheerfully.

Mrs. Magill lumbered in. "Let's get started."

The other ladies smiled at Thea, but put down their glasses. Unruffled, Thea bowed her head. "Father, thank You for this church. Be with us today. Help us to come to the correct recommendation for the church on the organ. Amen."

Calmly Thea looked up at the ladies around the table. Recalling her fears at their first meeting in April made her realize her confidence had grown. Mrs. Chiverton would probably follow Grandmother Lowell's orders to press for the repair of the present organ, a gift from Thea's great-grandfather to the church. Would the committee be able to avoid hurt feelings if the majority backed a new organ? That concerned her now. Thea hadn't been prepared to chair this committee originally, but she was ready today.

Businesslike, Thea looked to Mrs. Magill. "What did you find out about the price of a new pipe organ?"

"One that would fit this church would cost around twenty thousand."

"That much?" Vickie selected the largest cookie on the plate and grinned sheepishly.

"But we might not need a new one," Mrs. Chiverton ventured.

Mrs. Magill harumphed and scowled across at the other senior lady.

Thea intervened, "That was the median price?"

Mrs. Magill nodded.

"Nan, what did you find out about the prices of electronic organs?" The fragrance of butter and chocolate chips proved irresistible. Thea reached for a cookie, too.

"There's quite a range. I spoke to a music shop in Duluth. I described our church and our needs and they suggested one which ran eighteen thousand."

"Is that the only store you checked?" Mrs. Magill demanded.

Vickie spoke up, "I called stores in Milwaukee and Minneapolis, too. Their prices were comparable."

After a sip of lemonade, Nan looked at Thea. "What did you find out about repairs on the existing organ, Thea?"

Thea cleared her throat. "You know that our organ suffers from a 'cipher,' that is, every time I turn it on, one note repeats and repeats. The repairs would be costly and we'd have a long wait for the repairman to get around to us."

Mrs. Magill harumphed again. "So that means a new organ?"

Thea noticed Mrs. Chiverton frowning. Would her grandmother's devoted friend start in now giving Grandmother's ideas? Thea munched her cookie, praying silently for God to calm the spirits of the women around her.

A noticeable silence passed during which Mrs. Chiverton's face became more troubled. Nan asked softly, "Is anything wrong, Mrs. Chiverton?"

"Yes, I want to know why you have to be so gruff, Lilly?" Mrs. Chiverton glanced at Mrs. Magill, then, looked away as though struggling with her distress.

"What does that have to do with anything?" Lilly growled.

Mrs. Chiverton made characteristic fluttery gestures with her hands. "All this trouble over Peter's camp. Molly barking at all hours. Vandalism. Now destroying private property! It's so unnecessary, violent…I'm worried. What if someone gets hurt?"

Thea expected Mrs. Magill to begin arguing with Mrs. Chiverton. She glanced in the large woman's direction. Mrs. Magill looked thoughtful. "I'm worried about Dick," she muttered. "It's like he can't think of anything, but stopping the camp."

"And Althea," Mrs. Chiverton put in, beginning to sound shrill, "she can't find a kind word to say about *anyone* any more. She's gotten more cross every time I've visited her. And I've found Dick there several times with her."

Mrs. Magill snorted. "They've never been able to stand each other."

"That's what's so worrisome." Trembling, Mrs. Chiverton shook her head, making her dangling earrings dance. She opened her purse and pulled out a ruffled lavender hanky.

Looking amazed, Vickie asked, "You don't think they're behind what's been happening at the camp, do you?"

Mrs. Chiverton burst into tears. "I'm so afraid."

That night Thea reclined in her favorite antique wicker chaise on her screened-in porch overlooking the lake. Warm breezes. No commotion at the camp. Thea had watched the sun set in streamers of brilliant gold, pink and violet across the sky, then hadn't bothered to turn on a light. By the glow of the yard lights at the camp, she could make out the silhouettes of the tall pines and maples around her home. The white birches, picking up the light, stood like pale sentinels. On Thea's lap, Tomcat snoozed. Sleepy herself, Thea wished she felt as contented as his purring sounded.

Long after this morning's organ meeting she'd worried about Mrs. Chiverton's bursting into tears. Could the older woman be correct? Were her grandmother and Mr. Crandon using criminal tactics against the camp? But how?

All the excitement last evening, the discovery of more vandalism had ruined her peace. In the past four years, Thea had become used to a quiet, single life. This summer, only two weeks old, had shattered her neatly planned solitude. Before long, Cynda and Thad would return by boat from waterskiing with friends. She'd grown to enjoy having Cynda in the house, but a few hours of quiet... *What a blessing.*

She closed her eyes and napped. The lake breeze brought voices up to her. At first, still half dozing, she didn't focus on whose voices they were. Then she heard Cynda's voice clearly, ''Don't say that, Thad! You can't be one of those dumb people from town!''

Thea roused herself and looked around, disoriented. Then she realized Cynda and Thad must be outside down near the dock.

''You don't know anything about it,'' Thad said sharply. ''You just got here.''

Cynda's disembodied voice replied clearly, ''I know Irene and Aldo are great. And Peter's cool, too. I can't understand what the big deal is.''

Thea felt guilty eavesdropping, but was so drowsy she couldn't rouse herself enough to move yet.

Thad complained, ''The big deal is we don't want some big shot out of Milwaukee telling us how to do things. Peter Della makes me sick.''

Cynda said, ''Peter isn't telling anyone what to do. He just wants to run his camp.''

''He's trying to change everything. And I'm sick of my mom nagging me about me getting a job there. I don't want to be a role model to kids.''

Frowning deeply, Thea thought about Vickie's ill-conceived efforts to push Thad into involvement with the camp. Since his father's leaving his family, Thad needed a role model himself. Why didn't Vickie see how Thad was hurting?

"That's between you and your mom. My mom drives me crazy, too. But I'm working at the camp. Doesn't that bother you?"

"No. You live right next door. What choice do you have without a car?" Thad pointed out.

"I'm worried though. Irene got a poison pen letter in the mail today."

"A poison pen letter? From who?" Thad sounded as shocked as Thea felt.

"People don't usually sign them." Cynda sounded disgusted. "Irene wouldn't let me read it, so it must have been pretty bad."

"Peter Della started this. If he hadn't, nobody would be sending nasty letters to his mom." The rest of Thad's reply was covered up by a rapid knocking at Thea's door.

"Thea!" Peter called in.

Afraid Cynda might see her if she stood up and think she'd been eavesdropping on purpose, Thea rolled off the chaise and crawled through the open French doors into the living room.

"Thea!" Peter repeated.

"I'm here, Peter." Thea stood and hurried breathlessly through the darkened house to open the door for him.

"Hi, I brought dessert," Peter announced. "Mom made strawberry shortcake with real whipped cream." He held out a plastic-covered, glass pie plate, heaped with red strawberries and white puffs of cream.

"In that case, you may come in." Instantly aware of Peter, Thea stepped aside with a gracious gesture. How did he convey his own vitality to her just by coming near?

He walked in and looked around. "Saving on electricity?"

Taking a few steps back, Thea switched on a lamp just inside the living room, to illuminate the kitchen indirectly. "I don't like a lot of lighting on summer evenings. It's too hot, too bright." And dim lighting would conceal her uneasy consciousness of Peter.

"Besides you look lovely in pale light."

Thea wanted to believe his flattering words, but some uncertainty inside her made her draw back. She didn't know what to say, so she made herself busy getting out two gilt-edged china dessert plates, two settings of silver, and two white linen napkins. She motioned for him to take his chair.

"First class tonight?" Peter sat down.

Thea made her voice light, though Cynda's words about poison pen letters pulled at her spirits. "Something tells me your mother's shortcake merits china and silver." She arranged a set in front of Peter and one across from him for herself. Knowing his gaze followed her every motion made her intensely conscious of the smooth coolness of the silver and china, the texture of the starched linen.

She served a generous helping on each plate, then sat across from him. The dessert tempted, but her stomach tightened. Why couldn't all the pressure they were under just stop? Why couldn't she and Peter just enjoy getting to know each other?

Ignoring all these conflicting feelings, she took her first bite. She closed her eyes and savored the flavor of strawberries, rich whipped cream, and flaky shortcake. "Heavenly. If your mother keeps tempting me like this, I won't fit into any of my fall skirts."

"You don't have a thing to worry about, as far as I can

see,'' Peter said appreciatively. He dug his ornate silver fork deep into his whipped cream. ''Mmm.''

To keep the conversation light, she volunteered, ''I should show your mother a large patch of wild strawberries. We could pick some together this week.''

''Sounds like a good way for me to relax next weekend. Just you and me picking strawberries.'' The richness of his deep voice brought sensation cascading through her.

Thea hesitated. ''We'll see. You worked nonstop today.''

He snared her free hand with his. ''If I weren't so busy, I'd be here pursuing you more diligently.''

Accepting his touch, she let her hand memorize the feel of his—its warmth, strength, work-roughened texture. Thea blushed and was glad of the low light. Peter, is this just your natural ebullience or are you really interested in me?

Thea toyed with her fork in the whipped cream, ''I—''

Cynda and Thad barged through the back door. ''Hey! Dessert! Any for us?'' Cynda reached for the refrigerator door. ''I'm starved! Waterskiing gives me an appetite!''

Releasing Thea's hand, Peter rolled his eyes. ''Go next door, Cynda. Mom has plenty.''

''Great!'' Cynda whooped. ''Let's go next door, Thad.''

Thad looked like he'd rather drink sour milk, but all he said was, ''I gotta go home. You know how my mom is. I have to be right on time or I'm grounded.'' Then he turned to leave.

Molly raced in through her hatch and began barking at Thad's feet. Thea leaped up. Pulling on her dog's collar, she scolded, ''Quiet. Molly!'' The dog stopped barking, but looked disgruntled at Thea's interference. ''Sorry, Thad. I guess she doesn't recognize you without your mother and brother along.''

Thad shrugged. "See you tomorrow, Cynda."

Almost immediately the noise of Thad driving away assaulted Thea's ear. Discordant sounds always affected her.

Cynda stopped to grin impishly over her shoulder at Thea. "I'm going over to see Irene, so that means, Peter," she paused as though looking at an invisible wristwatch, "you have about a half hour alone with Thea before I get back."

Letting out a low groan, Thea lowered her head into her hand.

Peter chuckled. "Don't be embarrassed. I know how kids tease. Especially at Cynda's age."

To change the subject, Thea asked, "Did you get the canoes fixed?"

"Mr. Willoughby is working on them." He paused. "But today when I took my tire in to be fixed at Ed's Garage, I did get some bad news." His lingering gaze warmed her in spite of the unromantic conversation.

"Couldn't Ed fix it?" Thea took a bite of strawberry. Its sweet juice rolled over her tongue.

"Ed said the tire had been cut."

"Cut?" She stopped with her fork in midair. "But wouldn't it just go flat then?"

"No, because the cut didn't go all the way through. You see, *that way* the tire would blow on the road."

Thea put her fork down with a clatter. "That's dangerous. But how did it happen?" What next?

"Someone could have done it when I parked my car in town or at the airport."

"Who would *do* something like that?" Thea demanded. Why couldn't this end?

"Who knows? I had the sheriff dust for fingerprints on the tire, but nothing."

Thea remembered the guilty look on Mr. Crandon's face

and her grandmother's when she and Mrs. Chiverton had visited this morning. The two together mixed up a bad combination. Had they taken to writing poison pen letters, too?

Could they have hired someone to continue the pressure on Peter while they pushed the petition to change the camp's zoning? Maybe someone who had decided to do more than just spray paint? Now even Mrs. Chiverton and Mrs. Magill were worried. Thea's own uneasiness ballooned.

"I'm sorry I told you," Peter said. "I didn't mean to upset you. It makes me angry, but I have no doubt we'll find out who is doing this soon. And it's not stopping me." He gave her a pointed look. "I also came to invite you to next Sunday's Open House at the camp."

The idea caught her off guard. "An open house?"

"Yes, I've invited the whole town and several contributors."

"Do you think it's wise?" Stark anxiety surged inside her.

"Wise? Why not?"

"Aren't you afraid the vandal will do something specially destructive for an important occasion?" Her stomach ached with worry.

"I'm not letting my friendly neighborhood vandal stop this camp. 'If God be for us, who can stand against us?'"

Though familiar with the scripture, Thea'd never before heard anyone, who stood in the way of real danger, say it.

He lowered his voice, "Besides I'd like to flush him out before the camp opens. An open house might do that. That's just between the two of us."

Thea shook her head. How like Peter to answer an attack with an attack of his own. She lost what little appetite she had, but for appearance's sake, Thea forced herself to take a bite of shortcake. But apprehension resonated through her mind like a dark, turbulent symphony. *Dear Lord, please bring this controversy to an end. I'm not strong enough to take sides, but you know Peter. He deserves his dream to come true, doesn't he?*

"How did this happen?" Peter murmured into Thea's ear. "I'd planned this to be strawberry-picking for two, not seven." He stroked her cheek with a velvety berry leaf.

Thea smiled distractedly. The unexpected mix of Cynda, Irene, Aldo, Myra and her father blunted her awareness of Peter. Cynda was responsible for the twosome Peter had planned turning into a family affair.

Her father—tall, lean and reticent as ever—caught her attention even more than Peter today. Ever since her step-mother and father had arrived yesterday, Thea had sought an opportunity to confront her father about Cynda.

Like the morning dew evaporating in the sun, the weekend was slipping away. She couldn't let this chance to help Cynda pass. Thea's stomach churned, making her feel queasy in the hot June sunshine.

Nearby Irene was talking to Myra. Slim, blond Myra, dressed in designer jeans and a tailored blue-and-white-striped blouse, was bent over beside Irene. Peter's mother wore one of her bright smocks printed with huge, lively red strawberries which bloused over baggy pants. "Do you like strawberry mousse, Myra? I've got a great recipe for it."

"Is it fat-free?" Myra replied.

Irene chuckled. "Oh, dear, fat-free mousse wouldn't be worth eating, would it?"

Looking startled, Myra straightened up.

Despite her nervousness, Thea turned away to hide a smile. Myra was suffering culture-shock. Thea's stepmother probably had never met anyone like Irene before, a woman unconcerned about fashion and figure.

It wasn't the only change Myra had adjusted to this week. During this first visit, Thea had insisted her parents stay with her and Cynda at the house, not a motel as they normally preferred. She couldn't put the reasons into words, but she wanted them close to Cynda and to her.

Glancing around, Thea found Peter grinning at her. She fought his attraction. She could only deal with so many issues at once. Bending over, she began to pick the small red berries to fill her basket. Thea wondered why this summer everything was fraught with tension.

The ideas she wanted to express to her father were foremost in her mind. How do I start? She felt more queasy. She didn't want her questions to sound like accusations and how could she get a moment alone with her father?

"Is something bothering you?" Peter asked in a low voice.

Startled because she hadn't noticed him slide closer to her, Thea bit her tongue. She winced. Peter's deep brown eyes held such concern for her. Peter always had ideas for himself. Maybe he'd have one for her. "I'm trying to figure out when I can get my father alone. I need to talk to him, but they'll be leaving tomorrow morning and company is coming for supper tonight, an old fishing buddy."

"Why not now?"

"*Here* with everyone listening?"

Peter glanced around. "He's over to one side already. Why don't I kind of draw everyone away? Then you join your father."

Thea surreptitiously surveyed the scene, the meadow of wild grass and strawberry plants around the remains of an old burned cabin. There was that bank of lilac bushes she could lead her father behind. "All right. Thanks."

"Service with a smile."

Bent over and still picking berries, Peter closed in on Myra and Irene and began talking animatedly to them about the berries being bigger over to the other side of the meadow and slowly herded them off to the left, away from her.

When Thea turned around, she saw Cynda gravitate to Aldo, taking him farther into the patch. Her stepsister probably was still trying to avoid her parents. That left her father alone. Thea's heart beat a little faster, but this was a perfect time to talk to him without drawing attention to them. Soon she had "picked" her way over to him.

For a few moments, she just gathered strawberries near him and tried to think how to broach the topic of Cynda to him. "How's it going, Daddy?" Daddy? Where had that come from? She always called him, "Father."

Without lifting his head, he answered, "The berries are really big this year."

At a loss of any other way to begin, Thea said, "Cynda is very unhappy."

He nodded and went on picking.

"Cynda needs you." I needed you. Again she was startled by words which seem to pop up from deep within her.

"Myra understands her better than I do." He gathered more berries.

Thea's instincts wanted her to let it drop, but her concern for Cynda prodded her on. "Cynda needs a father."

He grunted. "Doug shouldn't have put her visit off."

"We can't make her father do what's right. But you could make the difference for Cynda."

"It's too late. She's a teenager now. She won't listen."

"You need to connect with Cynda." Didn't he realize how hard it was for Thea to confront him like this? He didn't even appear to have heard her. Thea felt him withdrawing further from her, just as she did when she didn't feel capable of dealing with something. I am my father's daughter. Neither of them were confronters.

Her father stood up and showed her his long, shallow strawberry basket. "Look at this big one. Here try it." He held the wild strawberry to her lips.

Like a flash, Thea glimpsed a scene from her childhood. In the same field of wild strawberries, her father, years younger, was offering her a berry. She heard herself say, "Daddy, is Mama really going to be all right now?"

Silence.

Then she realized she'd spoken out loud. A silence which vibrated with unexpressed emotion passed between them.

"Thea," her father sounded as dazed as she. "You said that...."

The years which had protected Thea from the anguish of losing her mother had been wrenched away, exposing raw nerves. She trembled with remembrance. "The day Mother died. I'd forgotten we picked strawberries that day."

Her father looked stricken. "I took you away from the house. Your mother wanted you to have an outing. After her emergency surgery, we thought everything was going to be fine."

Taking hold of his arm, Thea drew him with her to the cover of the lilac bushes. "What happened after Mother's death, Daddy? Why did everything change?"

He seemed to pull back, go within himself. He frowned. "Talking won't make the past different." He bent to gather more berries.

The lilac bushes stood between them and the others. The scent enhanced the sensation of déjà vu for Thea. The same bushes had been in bloom the day her mother died. She'd wondered in the past why she always came away subdued from picking berries here. "That's not true, Father. We need to talk about the past."

He didn't meet her glance.

Thea couldn't believe her own persistence, but this week marked the anniversary of her mother's unexpected death from an aneurysm. She'd waited long enough for an explanation. "We have to do this, Father. Talking about the past can change the present and the future." Thea took a deep breath and plunged on, "Daddy, why did you stop loving me the day Mother died?"

He straightened up and faced her.

Though her mouth was dry, Thea went on, "What happened to us? I need to know."

Her father looked shocked, hurt.

Listening vaguely to the voices nearby, Thea searched for words. Old pain, sadness and distress swirled inside her. "You used to tease me. You took me berry picking and fishing. Daddy, what happened to us after Mom died?"

He heaved a labored sigh and mopped his forehead with his pocket handkerchief. "I don't like to speak against your grandmother."

"What happened?" Thea insisted more boldly than she thought possible.

"Losing your mother so young nearly killed me."

His stark words shook her. "Why did you sell our house and move in with Grandmother?"

"I wasn't thinking after we lost your mother. I couldn't. By the time I was thinking again, we were in her house. And I was traveling more and more."

Thea didn't need to ask him who had prompted him to sell and move in. Grandmother, of course. The need to control seemed uppermost in her grandmother's character. Did you ever grieve for your own daughter, Grandmother?

Her father's voice came out stronger. "Your grandmother wanted me out of the picture completely."

This didn't shock Thea. Grandmother wasn't just a difficult elderly woman as she had thought before. Thea'd begun realizing her grandmother's essential selfishness through the last months, but this… "What exactly do you mean?"

"She tried to persuade me I was free to remarry. I could leave you with her. Be unencumbered, she said. You'll be more attractive to single women without a child. I wouldn't do that. I didn't even date for years. I didn't have the heart to."

Thea felt each word—a knife thrust to her heart. Grandmother, how could you?

"If only I'd packed you up after the funeral and left the state. But the longer you were with her, the longer I was afraid of uprooting you again."

Thea searched her father's face. "I understand." Her father, a quiet gentle man, had been no match for his mother-in-law.

"I've always felt guilty about letting that woman take over our lives. Your mother and I together could fight her and win. But after your mother died, I just seemed to lose all my fight."

Thea drew a deep breath and spoke soothingly, "Grandmother is not easy to deal with. Our grief put us at a disadvantage."

He reached out and patted her shoulder clumsily. "Daddy," she whispered, then she hugged him tightly. Tears started in her eyes. Finally she understood. Daddy hadn't abandoned her. He just hadn't been up to challenging Grandmother who would use every weapon at hand to get what she wanted. A woman who would never quit, never admit defeat. Thea understood that all too well.

She wiped away her tears with her fingertips. "Daddy, talk to Cynda. Listen to her. Take her fishing and out to breakfast sometimes like you did with me. She needs you."

Her father nodded solemnly like taking an oath.

From the other side of the bushes, Irene's voice startled Thea. "Teen years are the hardest."

Unseen, Myra replied, "That's what everyone says. I was just glad that Cynda had someone like Thea to turn to. When Thea called me to say Cynda was with her, I was livid. Then I was so relieved I actually felt faint. Anything could have happened to Cynda running away like that."

"One of our daughters ran away repeatedly."

"Really?" Myra's voice sounded surprised.

"Yes, but she was really running away from her natural mother who had run out on her. It's a confused story, but she's fine now."

"Do you think Cynda will run away again?"

"No, I think her summer here will do a lot to resolve her anger. She's upset with her father, but her foundation is strong." Irene's voice began to grow distant. The two women were moving away from Thea.

"I hope so. I hadn't prayed in a long time, but I was praying night and day when I found Cynda gone. I'll never forget the terror I felt when I opened her closet and found her duffel and clothes gone."

Thea strained to hear what Irene would say in response. "Well, I spent nights on my knees praying for my kids. It's the only way I got through it. I realized Aldo and I couldn't make the difference all by ourselves. Our kids had been hurt too badly before they came to us. So we gave them to God and asked Him to make up what we couldn't give them. Giving our children over to God is the most difficult thing we've ever done, but the smartest, too.''

''I wish I had your faith.''

Thea could barely hear Irene's answer. ''It's free for the asking, dear. Just ask God and He'll be right there with you.''

Thea turned to her father and hugged him again.

He ran his fingers through the hair around her face. He said softly, ''Don't worry, Thea. I'll do better with Cynda. I promise.''

She hugged him in response.

''And don't ever think that I haven't always loved you. I made mistakes, but I've always loved you.'' He paused briefly. ''There's one more thing you need to know. Your grandmother called Myra. She wanted Myra to come and take Cynda home.''

After a slight hesitation, Thea kissed his cheek, then bent and began picking strawberries again. Her grandmother's call didn't surprise her at all. Thea had begun by seeking what Cynda needed for healing, but had ended by receiving the healing she didn't even know she was seeking. Confronting her father had been difficult, but it had accomplished much. This gave her new strength.

To Thea, all the challenges and changes in the past few months had made her reevaluate everything she'd taken for granted in her life. The time had come for her to face the past. The time had come to confront Grandmother.

Chapter Eleven

Thea had prayed for several days, prayed for wisdom, for insight. She wanted to let Grandmother know her feelings, but she didn't want to be unkind.

Thea opened the door of the care center and walked down the familiar corridor. The murmur of voices, the odor of disinfectant, the green-and-mauve floral wall paper, a TV playing in the background—everything as usual, but her. Amazingly she felt determined. Ready.

Whether her plan worked or not today, she'd have the satisfaction of stating her case. She walked confidently into her grandmother's private room.

Grandmother Lowell looked up and scowled. "You're late."

Thea smiled. "Hello, to you, too."

The older woman's mouth twisted in a sour grimace. Her grandmother rarely wanted to leave her refuge, but Thea had a plan.

"I've come to take you out for a little sun." Though her grandmother protested, Thea stepped behind the wheel-chair and pushed it out the nearest exit.

Thea strolled behind her grandmother, who complained louder and louder with each step. Though Thea felt badly about ignoring the older woman, she deafened herself to every syllable. She even smiled to bolster her own resolve.

Finally, near the tree-lined bike trail where they would be quite alone and uninterrupted, Thea parked the chair, locked it in place, and sat down on the redwood park bench nearby.

"What has gotten into you?" her grandmother demanded.

As though sublimely unconcerned, Thea stared upward. "What a gorgeous blue sky. This is just what we needed. Some sunshine and fresh air."

"Take me back inside right now!" Her grandmother's slurred voice increased in volume.

Thea's conscience tugged at her, but she resisted it. *I'm sorry, Father, but I have to do this. Please help me.* "You want to walk farther?" Thea glanced around. "But you never know what you really want." How many times had her grandmother used those same words to squash any attempt Thea made to voice an opinion?

Her grandmother started struggling to release the wheelchair with her one good hand, but couldn't quite reach it.

Thea took her grandmother's frail and papery hands and held them. "No, no, that's not good for you." Another technique of Grandmother's. Would the older woman realize this?

"Have you lost your mind!"

"No, I just need to discuss a few matters with you without an audience or interruptions."

Her grandmother wouldn't look at her.

Still unruffled, Thea asked, "You called Myra about my stepsister. You wanted me to be alone again this summer. Why?"

The old woman glared. "It's still my house."

Thea had anticipated this reply. She'd heard it before. "I wasn't trying to sell her the house. I just wanted to help out Cynda. She needed a sister. She needed me."

Grandmother folded her good hand over her weak one. "I don't like strangers in my house."

"Cynda *is* family," Thea countered.

"*I'm* your family."

"But you're not my only family." Thea explained patiently. Of course, the old woman beside her wouldn't cede any ground.

"I'm the only family that matters." Her grandmother began struggling with the catch on her chair again.

Grandmother Lowell's words stung Thea. She recalled her father's version of how Grandmother had intruded between them. But this show of infirmity touched Thea's heart. To be powerless must grate on her grandmother every minute.

"I've been worried about you lately," Thea said softly.

"*You* don't have to worry about me. On the day I die, I'll be sharper than you've ever been."

The often-repeated insult didn't touch Thea; she went on. "You're spending time with Dick Crandon whom you can't stand."

Grandmother glared straight ahead.

Finally Thea brought up what had bothered her ever since the county board meeting. "You're rude to your oldest friend—"

"Louella's a fool—"

"She's a sweet, lonely old woman who loves you very much."

"Humph."

"Peter and his camp are here to stay whether you like

it or not. I hope you haven't done more than talk against him. But that's between you and God, not me.''

Grandmother glowered.

Thea continued, ''I'm sorry you didn't let me bring Cynda on my visits. She's so peppy and cheerful. I've begun to love her and I know I'll miss her when she leaves in the fall.'' The words were all too true.

No reply.

''Myra and Father visited last weekend. I talked to Dad.'' Thea tried to lay a hand on her grandmother's arm. ''He told me—''

The old woman shrugged off Thea's hand. ''He poisoned you against me. That's what this is all about. I warned your mother not to marry him.''

''He's my dad,'' Thea said firmly with a touch of pride.

Her grandmother stared at her. Resentment showed plainly on the old woman's face. ''You're just like him—spineless.''

''I've been spineless, but that's in the past.'' Thea folded her hands in her lap. ''My father is a kind, gentle man who loves me very much and I love him.''

''How sweet for the both of you.'' Her grandmother sneered. ''What would the two of you have done without me after your mother died?''

Thea sighed, recalling the memories the strawberry picking had uncovered—memories of being out in that place with her father once, long ago. ''We probably would have managed somehow. And we probably would have stayed a lot closer to each other. I always wondered why my father loved me less after Mama died. Now I know his love hadn't changed. It was you working to separate us.'' All those years wasted in misunderstanding.

Her grandmother looked away briefly, then turned back with a malicious expression on her face. ''You've lost your head over that Della. That's what this is all about. You think I don't know what you've been up to, but I hear all I need to know. You're a fool, Thea. That man's just making up to you because of the camp.''

Instead of angering Thea as intended, thinking of Peter ignited joy inside Thea, a cozy spark. ''Maybe I have fallen for Peter. There's no law against it.'' These were brave words, but Peter had been open about wanting to get to know her. This alone made her happy.

Grandmother pursed her lips. All the deep wrinkles around her mouth made it look like the tightened opening of an old-fashioned drawstring purse.

Thea didn't feel intimidated by her grandmother's displeasure. Their connection had been weakened by the truth.

Silence fell. Thea studied her grandmother's profile, hoping for some sign of softening or recognition of what had been said to her. There was nothing but indignant wrath.

Thea sighed. ''I'll take you back in now.''

The old woman scowled. ''What has gotten into you today?''

Thea stood up. ''I just wanted to play turnabout this once.''

''Turnabout?'' The elderly woman snapped.

''Yes, how did you like my acting like you and your portraying my role?''

''Take me in.'' The old woman's words vibrated with anger.

''Very well. I'll go back to being me now.'' Thea released the lock and pushed her grandmother back to the care center. A red cardinal flew overhead calling to his mate. Grandmother's displeasure now held no fear for

Thea. She hadn't expected reconciliation, just sweet release.

When she reached her grandmother's room, Thea situated the chair exactly as it had been when she had arrived.

Grandmother Lowell glared up at her. "Don't ever come here again."

"No, sorry. *You,* Grandmother, would never come. But I'm Thea. I'll be back. I love you." Though the old woman turned her face away, Thea kissed her grandmother's dry cheek, then walked out. "Love your enemies" came to mind. *I will, Lord.* Confronting her bitter, controlling grandmother had hurt, but there was always hope Grandmother might change. Most importantly, now Thea was free to show support for Peter. What would be the best way?

On Saturday afternoon, knowing Peter liked her hair down, she'd left it unbound. Leaning close to the three-way vanity mirror, she studied her reflection. Cynda had told her a little eye makeup would help, but Thea told the mirror, "Everything else in my life has changed. I'd better leave my face the same." She slipped on her blue-and-green plaid sundress and walked into the kitchen.

With a pitiful expression, Molly lay on the kitchen floor. Sitting beside Molly, Tomcat looked up grumpily, too.

"Sorry, dear friends, but I don't want you two next door at the open house. People only."

Tomcat turned around, tail held high, and exited clearly in a miff. Molly moaned touchingly. Thea patted her dog's head, then walked out the door shutting it firmly behind her.

On the other side of the fence, the open house was in full swing. The parking lot was filled with vehicles—many luxury sedans and expensive-looking sports cars—definitely from out of town. As Thea eased over the fence and strolled toward the camp cafeteria on the perfect June Saturday, the chatter of voices floated over the lawn.

Thea hadn't seen Peter yet this weekend and felt disappointed. An inner voice taunted her, *Did you think he'd stop by with roses every Friday night?* Thea booted the unfriendly voice out of her mind.

Cynda had reported Peter had gotten in late last night and had been busy since dawn helping get everything in shape for this afternoon. Of course, he hadn't had time to drop by. Besides he knew she would attend the open house. Thea wondered what he would say to the proposal she'd come up with for the camp. A trace of a smile touched her lips.

Inside the cafeteria, people milled around the long trestle tables. The noise of so many voices irritated Thea, but her feeling of well-being helped her overcome this.

She scanned the crowd looking for Peter. But she heard his low, hearty laughter first. She smiled and turned to locate him. Wearing a navy blue linen sport jacket and chinos, and looking more handsome than any man should, he stood in the midst of a group of well-dressed strangers—men wearing suits and ladies in expensive-looking summer dresses.

She took one step, then paused. Perhaps he was with potential donors and would not want to be interrupted.

"Thea." Pastor Carlson touched her elbow. "How nice to see you."

Thea repeated the polite phrase back to him.

"I'd like you to meet Bishop Powell. This is our organist, Thea Glenheim."

As Thea shook hands with the bishop, she detected Peter moving away from his group. He seemed to be heading for her.

"I heard your committee recommended a newer electronic organ for the church. How did you manage that, Thea?" the pastor asked.

Though her eyes wanted to continue tracking Peter's progress toward her, Thea glanced to the pastor politely. "I was surprised how easy the decision was. It was just a matter of being practical."

The bishop spoke up, "It's too bad, really. I've seen your organ. A real period piece."

"Its period is over." Mrs. Magill loomed up on Thea's other side.

Pastor Carlson and the bishop chuckled.

"Thea ran a good meeting," Mrs. Magill said. "She didn't waste time with a lot of blabbing. Just straight to the point."

Peter neared Thea. She smiled in anticipation. Then a couple stopped him. The woman wore a white straw picture hat. Thea had never seen anything like it outside the covers of a fashion magazine.

Thea brought her mind back to the subject at hand. "I had trouble trying to find someone to do repairs," Thea explained. "In the end that was what made our decision."

"Two meetings were enough." Mrs. Magill made a hand gesture like an umpire motioning, Safe.

Peter detached himself from the couple and headed right for Thea's group. Pastor Carlson turned and intercepted Peter and introduced him to the bishop.

Thea thought she noted Peter looked sideways at her, but couldn't be sure.

Cynda walked up, blocking Thea's view. "Hey, Thea, did you try the punch? I made it."

Thea shook her head and peered around Cynda, trying to gauge when it would be appropriate to join Peter and the clergymen. Under Thea's dismayed gaze, Peter led the pastor and bishop over to another group of people.

"Punch? Thea?" Cynda waved her hand in front of Thea's face.

"Yes," Thea said automatically, "I'd like some punch." As the host, Peter couldn't spend the afternoon hovering around her. Still, she felt keen disappointment.

Cynda led her to the buffet table near the kitchen.

"Hello, Miss Glenheim." Tom manned the punch bowl, filled with seafoam-green punch.

She smiled and asked for a cup. Under Cynda's rapt gaze, Thea took a sip. "Mmm. Just right. What's in it?"

Cynda said eagerly, "Ginger ale, lemonade and lime sherbet."

From just a couple of feet away, Peter laughed again. Thea quivered with awareness of him despite the people separating them. She glanced toward him and found his gaze on her. He drew her like sunshine drew sunflowers. She took a step toward him.

Immediately, an older man moved between them blotting out her view of Peter. Cynda excused herself and went to help Irene in the kitchen.

Thea swallowed frustration. *It isn't his fault Peter hasn't come to me. He has to act as the host. The camp comes first.* This piece of logic didn't prevent her mood from drooping another notch.

"Thea, dear." Mrs. Chiverton joined her at the buffet table. "Did you see? I made your favorite almond cookies."

"No, I didn't." Thea picked up one and tasted it. In spite of its buttery flavor, the cookie tasted like dust in her mouth. Being separated from Peter drained away her enjoyment. Would she ever get to speak to Peter and tell him her idea? "Mmm. As delicious as ever. I didn't know you were helping—"

"Oh, yes." Irene wearing a bright purple shirtwaist dress bustled out of the large camp kitchen. "Louella dropped by yesterday afternoon and offered to contribute these delectable cookies."

Mrs. Chiverton beamed. "I hadn't baked so many cookies in such a long time."

"You should have called me," Thea said still tracking Peter. "I would have helped you."

"Irene," Mrs. Chiverton said with a smile which lifted her face and showed how attractive she had once been. "Thea always used to bake cookies with me every Christmas. Then we'd wrap them up and take them to shut-ins."

"Sounds like something the three of us should do this winter." Irene swiftly straightened the white buffet tablecloth and dusted off cookie crumbs. "My children will all be arriving during the holidays, so I'm going to start baking the week before Thanksgiving."

"Oh, how wonderful." Mrs. Chiverton clapped her hands. "I'd love to help. You have grandchildren, don't you, Irene?"

Irene nodded, then at Tom's request hurried back into the kitchen for more punch.

"Thea." Mrs. Chiverton crept closer. "I visited…I *tried* to visit your grandmother this morning. But she wouldn't speak to me."

"She probably heard about the organ decision or maybe it's my fault." Thea sighed. "I tried to let her know I had to make my own decisions about Peter…." Thea blushed at her slip. "I mean, the camp. I'm afraid Grandmother didn't take it very well."

Mrs. Chiverton laid a hand on Thea's arm sympathetically. The older woman shook her head. "Do you think Dick might come today?"

Thea felt shock. "He wouldn't show up here, would he?"

Mrs. Chiverton frowned. "I don't know, but he was coming in to see your grandmother just as I was leaving. And he said, 'See you later.' But, Thea, I'm not going anywhere else today."

"How would he know you'd be coming here?"

"*Everyone's* here! Look around."

Thea turned. She'd been so busy trying to get Peter's attention, she'd not realized most of Lake Lowell was in evidence—Vickie, Nan and her whole tribe, and most of their church. If Mr. Crandon did come, he wouldn't be pleased. Popular opinion appeared to have shifted to Peter.

"Well, look at that." Mrs. Magill startled Thea from behind. "Dick just walked in."

"Oh, dear," Mrs. Chiverton shrilled.

Thea glanced around in time to see Sheriff Swenson and his brother, the county board chairman, converge on Dick just inside the door. After a moment's conversation, Dick strutted away from them.

Undeterred, the sheriff trailed behind Crandon, not close enough to be provocative, Thea thought, but near enough to be a deterrent. Thea's thoughts careened back and forth in her mind. Had Mr. Crandon come to cause a scene?

"Mountain out of a molehill," Mrs. Magill muttered.

Mrs. Chiverton frowned. "I know Dick is hurting over losing his son, but how do we stop him—"

"From making a fool out of himself?" Mrs. Magill finished.

Or worse, Thea thought.

Had Peter seen Mr. Crandon come in? Would the older

man make a scene? Thea scanned the gathering for Peter. *There he is.*

"Pardon me, ladies," Thea murmured and walked toward Peter, ignoring the fact he wasn't alone. Her confidence waned when she studied the middle-aged man and young woman Peter spoke with. The woman's mint-green linen dress made Thea's simple sundress look bargain basement. Thea stopped a few feet from Peter, hoping to attract his attention, but unwilling to force him to notice her.

Peter was discussing commodity shares with the man. As she listened vaguely, she kept track of Mr. Crandon's movements about the room. The portly Mr. Crandon greeted everyone as though this were his open house. But Thea noted he didn't linger long with anyone and his smile became more and more artificial. She noticed that while the sheriff stuck to Mr. Crandon, the county board chairman gravitated toward Peter. Qualms trembled through her. *Should I call Peter's attention to his enemy or just let Peter handle matters?*

"Well, Della," Mr. Crandon said in a bluff, cheerful voice. "You've attracted quite a crowd today. Free cookies and punch are quite a draw."

Peter paused in his conversation and smiled. "Glad to see you came."

"I came to talk to people about signing my petition."

"Petition?" the man Peter had been talking to asked.

Peter said, "Mr. Crandon, have you met Judge George Hansen of the Circuit Court and his daughter?"

"No, I haven't." Mr. Crandon shook hands with the judge and his daughter. "But he can tell you if my petition succeeds, you'll be selling this land and moving on."

The county board chairman spoke up quietly, "Why

don't you admit Althea Lowell is the only one left on your side now?''

Crandon scowled. "I'll win in the end."

Peter smiled. "That's in God's hands, don't you think?"

"Humph. That's what I'd expect you to say, Della, but I'm not giving up." The older man stalked away.

Peter turned and touched her hand. "I'm glad you came."

Thea longed to talk to Peter, but now worry trapped her words. She wanted to tell him about her grandmother, Mr. Crandon's mental state, but instead she squeezed his hand. The sheriff tapped Peter's shoulder. As Peter turned away from her once more, her spirits hit bottom with a hollow thud.

Beside her, Aldo asked, "Thea, would you be sure to let Molly loose tomorrow night? Because of a last-minute mix-up, I have to go with Peter to bring the kids up Monday. The sheriff will patrol more often. But I'd like to have a good watchdog around the camp, too. And please don't mention anything about this to anyone."

"Of course not."

Aldo smiled wryly and patted her arm. "I know we can trust you. I just don't want to send out an invitation for our friendly neighborhood vandal to stop by tomorrow night."

Thea watched Peter across the tables which separated them. So near, yet far.

Chapter Twelve

Dejected, Thea walked out of the camp cafeteria. Afternoon shadows cast from the trees stretched across the lawn. The last hour of the open house had been agony. Peter had come close to her again several times, lifting her spirits each time, only to plummet when he was halted, turned or pulled away.

She tried to rationalize that Peter was the host and had many contributors to entertain. It didn't help, though, that so many of them were young, good-looking, very chic women. Feeling frumpy and outclassed, Thea headed toward home. Her plan to help the camp probably wasn't any great brainstorm. Staying any longer, just to be disappointed, would destroy the last scraps of her self-confidence.

As she approached the low rail-fence, Thea thought of her grandmother's unkind words about Peter and herself. She brushed them aside. *Peter isn't conning me.*

But the open house made her realize Peter belonged to a world that she knew nothing about and into which she would never fit. A world of designer hats and dresses, judges, BMWs and Mercedes. Not her world at all.

"Thea! Thea! Wake up! It's Molly!"

Morning sunshine seeping into her closed eyes, Thea felt herself being shaken and heard Cynda's choked voice. At the mention of Molly, Thea's eyes opened and she sat up.

"It's Molly. I found her outside!" Cynda said tearfully.

Without replying, Thea jumped out of bed, then pulled on a pair of worn sweats over her short pajamas. "Where is she?"

Cynda started toward the kitchen and Thea kept pace with her. "I was on my way to the camp to help Irene get lunch ready for the campers arriving today. I jumped over the fence. Then I saw Molly."

They were outside now hurrying toward the fence. Thea heard a low canine moan. The sound made Thea shiver with fear.

"Oh! She's alive!" Cynda shouted and took the fence like a hurdle.

Thea followed suit and ran straight to her golden retriever who struggled to get up off the ground. "Molly!" Thea dropped to her knees and began deftly examining the dog's body. "Where does it hurt, Molly?"

"She was out completely!" Cynda nearly sobbed with relief. "I thought she was dead!"

Fear swirled inside Thea. *Molly, oh, dear Lord. What's happened?*

Cynda exclaimed, "Do you think she had a fit or something? We had a neighbor once whose dog had epilepsy."

Molly finally succeeded in getting to her feet. Thea tried to restrain her and continued probing the silken gold fur in vain. Molly staggered, then collapsed again. *What's wrong!* Tension knotting inside her throat made it impossible for Thea to speak.

"She looks like somebody drugged her!" Cynda said.

Confused, Thea stood up, watching Molly struggle back onto her feet. "I can't see what the problem is—"

A scream.

"That's Irene!" Cynda yelled.

Chilled by the sound, Thea broke into a run beside Cynda, heading for the camp.

Cynda sprinted ahead and reached Irene first. The older woman huddled on the broad wooden steps to the cafeteria. With her head in her hands, she moaned.

With Molly straggling behind her, Thea knelt beside the older woman and spoke as calmly as she could, "What is it, Irene? Are you hurt?"

Irene pointed to the door behind her.

Cynda moved toward it.

"Cynda, wait!" Fearful of what Cynda might see, Thea leaped up and grabbed Cynda's arm to stop her, but she was too late.

Cynda shrieked.

Abandoning Irene, Thea raced up the few steps. She looked inside and gasped. She felt weak in the knees at what she confronted.

"Who could do something like that?" Irene moaned.

At first, Thea couldn't make sense of the disaster before her eyes. But the odor of spoiling eggs and raw hamburger assaulted her nose, making her sick to her stomach.

The cafeteria was a wreck. Someone had smashed dozens and dozens of eggs on the tables, on the walls, floor, benches—even the ceiling had been pelted. The smashed eggs' shells and yolks and stringy whites had been swirled with ketchup, mustard and pickle relish. Over all, the scent of maple syrup hung in the ungodly hodgepodge of sickening smells.

The sheer wanton nastiness of it appalled Thea. She felt a cry start deep inside her but clamped her lips shut against it.

Irene stumbled up to Thea. "Someone must have emptied the refrigerator and some of the cabinets. How *could* they?"

Cynda looked nauseated. "This is sick, really sick."

Large tears rolled down Irene's full cheeks. "Peter's coming back with the campers by noon. Cynda and I are supposed to have sloppy joes ready." She wiped her eyes with the hem of her neon orange smock. "He's bringing possible contributors, too. We'll never be ready now!"

Thea listened to Cynda and Irene only vaguely. Her fear for Peter nearly overwhelmed her. A busload of kids and possible donors on the way—this could make those boys feel unwelcome and stop the money Peter needed so badly!

Righteous anger flamed through her and iron determination followed it. "Whoever did this is not going to win! Cynda?" Thea shook her stepsister by the shoulder. "Run home to our garage. Bring back the two snow shovels and the box of leaf bags." When Cynda continued to stare without moving, Thea physically spun her around and pushed her toward the steps. "Run!" Then Thea turned to Irene. "Have you got some rubber gloves?"

The woman looked up at her with obvious bewilderment. "Yes, but Thea there's no way the three of us can have all this cleaned up in time."

"Oh, yes, we can. We will." Thea's voice vibrated with defiance. "You go get out all the gloves you have and I'll get help." Thea charged down the steps and ran straight for the lodge and its nearest phone.

She dialed. "Sheriff, this is Thea. I don't have time to

explain. Get right over to Peter's camp and bring your camera.''

''What—''

Thea cut him off and punched in another number. ''Pastor Carlson, I don't have time to explain, but we've got a terrible mess at the camp. Please bring shovels, mops, garbage bags and bring anyone along that can help.''

''Thea, what—''

''Sorry.'' She cut him off.

She took a breath to think. *Who else can I call, Lord? Who else?* A name came to her. She rapidly dialed Mrs. Chiverton. ''Louella, I don't have time to explain. We need your help at the camp.''

''Oh, no, what—''

''I know you keep a lot of paper towels and cleaning supplies on hand. Bag up some and come right over.''

''I will and I'll call Lilly.'' Mrs. Chiverton hung up on her.

Thea turned around and came face-to-face with Irene.

Irene held a handful of rubber glove packages. ''Thank you, Thea. I don't know people around here well enough to ask them to pitch in like that.''

Moved by Irene's approval, Thea patted the dear woman's shoulder.

''Thea, I'm back!'' Cynda shouted from outside. ''And guess what. Molly looks fine again. Guess the drug or whatever it was is wearing off.''

Molly! Poor, dear. Thea had forgotten about her. She'd check on her soon and take her to the vet later just to be sure she was all right.

''Okay. Let's get busy!'' Thea ordered.

Within minutes, the three of them had donned bright yellow rubber gloves. Thea took one of the snow shovels and handed Irene the box of brown plastic leaf bags.

"Now, Irene, Cynda and I are going to start shoveling. You get a bag out and hold it while we fill it. Okay?"

She and Cynda dug their shovels into the disgusting mixture. Irene slapped open the first large bag.

Thea tried not to dwell on the disgusting garbage she was moving with the shovel. The odors had already strengthened as the morning began to warm. The women stopped to cover their mouths with bandanas, to minimize the effect. They had shoveled their way to the first row of tables when Thea heard the whine of the police siren approaching. The car sped through the entrance and parked with a jerk at the nearest edge of the lot.

The sheriff came at a run; his camera strung around his neck bouncing wildly. "What happened? I patrolled here every half hour and walked the grounds three times last night! Good grief!"

Thea glanced up and saw that the sheriff did look tired with dark shadows under his puffy eyes. And his look of revulsion reassured her that she hadn't imagined everything. "Start taking pictures because we're cleaning this up before it gets any warmer. The stench will be unbelievable before long. Don't tell me you have to look for evidence. Just start taking pictures while you can." Thea thought to herself, *I sound just like Lilly Magill.* But she went on as she lifted another gooey shovelful, "And don't tell us you need time because this cafeteria is going to be ready by the time Peter arrives with the boys." Her commanding voice sounded unusual to her own ears.

"Yes, ma'am." Sheriff Swenson grinned, saluted, then began snapping pictures.

Mrs. Chiverton arrived just as Pastor Carlson pulled up. "More help is coming," the pastor said. "I stuck my head into The Café on the way." Pastor began shoveling beside Cynda.

"Thank you, Pastor. Mrs. Chiverton—"

The old woman had come out in such a hurry she'd forgotten to put on her wig. Her thin gray hair was pulled into a bun at her crown and she wore a faded blue print housedress. "Call me Louella, dear. I liked it when you called me that this morning." She began lining up the cleaning supplies she'd brought on the highest step to the cafeteria. "You're all grown-up. I never did like the way Althea wouldn't let you call me Aunt Louella when you were a child. She always insisted you speak so formally."

"I'll be happy to call you Aunt Louella." Filled with gratitude and a bit surprised, Thea grinned and felt the grin go all the way through her, making her glow with pleasure in spite of the chaos around her.

"You could just call me Louella."

"If you don't mind, I'll include the Aunt because I don't have any other aunts." *Thank you, Lord, for letting me finally see the truth about this dear woman.*

"Wonderful, dear." Louella donned rubber gloves. "What do you want me to do?"

"Follow me to the kitchen. The stove needs intensive care." Thea shoveled a path for Mrs. Chiverton to the kitchen. There the older woman began the detailed work of cleaning the "slimed" and encrusted stove.

Thea shook her head over the condition of the kitchen. Flour and sugar "snowed" every surface. Salt gritted under her shoes.

Mrs. Magill arrived wearing overalls cut off at her knees and her fishing hat. Thea showed her how to hold the bags and Thea began shoveling.

It took them over an hour just to shovel out the disgusting mixture into nearly fifteen bags. Nan and Tracy arrived just in time to begin the scrubbing. With rubber gloves on, Little Tracy began washing a bench with a stiff brush while her mother started spraying cleaner, then swabbing down tables.

"Where are the twins?" Thea asked.

"I left them with Vickie at her beauty shop. She said she'd call Tom to come help her with them, so she could still carry on business! She told me she's sorry she couldn't come. She'd try to send Thad over."

Cynda piped up, "He won't come. He sleeps till noon every day, then works all afternoon and some evenings."

Pastor Carlson found a ladder and climbed it to attack the egg smears on the ceiling. Finished taking evidence photos, the sheriff put his camera in his car and came back barefoot.

This sight startled Thea. "What are you doing, Sheriff?" She paused while scrubbing a windowsill.

"There's an easier way to loosen this scum." He rolled up his sleeves and pant legs, then stepped outside again.

In a few moments, he aimed the hose in and began spraying the ceiling. "Hey, Pastor, get down from that ladder before I spray you off!"

The high spray sent sprinkles of welcome water over them all. The sun was climbing and bringing a hot sunny day with it. Thea felt sweat trickle down her back, an unusual sensation for her.

The pastor scrambled down and folded up his ladder. "Great idea! I'll get the push broom and sweep the water outside!"

Soon the men took turns spraying the ceiling, log walls, plank floors and the old scarred tables and benches, or sweeping the water out the door with the large push broom. Of course, the sheriff couldn't resist "accidentally" splashing the women with cold water.

After some indignant squealing, the women moved out of range, gathering in the kitchen behind its door to do the detailed cleaning of the appliances and cabinets. When Thea took a good look, she saw the vandal had splashed raw egg and maple syrup over the flour and sugar in the kitchen, too.

The women shoveled out the mess into bags, then called the men to spray the floor. Afterward, they began disassembling the refrigerator shelves and stove parts for a thorough scrubbing. Over two hours later, everyone drenched by sweat, soaked with water, and smelling of lemon-scented cleaner collapsed onto damp benches. Thea felt exhausted by emotion as well as the exertion.

"I can't believe we did it," Nan exclaimed, with a beaming Tracy at her side.

"We sure did!" the little girl agreed.

"We can never thank you all enough." Irene mopped her forehead with the hem of her orange smock. "The lunch menu has changed. Pastor, could you drive into town and buy us about six dozen hot dogs and buns, about ten bags of potato chips, and the fixings for today's lunch?"

"Glad to." Standing, the pastor began rolling up the hose around his right arm to take it back outside. He paused. "Thanks for calling me, Thea. I really feel like we did God's work today."

Thea nodded.

Irene looked to Cynda. "Now, dear, you run home quick and change clothes, then come back and start lunch while I change."

"Okay!" Cynda took a paper towel from a depleted roll at her elbow and wiped her face with it. "I really worked up a sweat."

"My dear," Louella said with a twinkle in her eye, "a lady never sweats. She perspires."

Cynda looked surprised. "What?"

Lilly Magill laughed and slapped her bare, very pudgy knee. "Louella, you crack me up."

Louella stood up slowly. "Oh, I ache all over."

"Stop bragging," Lilly barked, then roared with laughter at her own joke.

Louella giggled. "Oh, we're slaphappy. This was dreadful, but I haven't felt this tired or this alive in a long, long time."

Irene smiled and patted the older woman's thin arm. "You were great. Both of you. I could hardly clean fast enough to keep up with you two."

Cynda approached Thea and pulled her up from the bench with both hands. "Come on, Sis. You're a mess."

Feeling much in tune with Aunt Louella's aches, Thea moaned, but allowed herself to be pulled up. "The same to you, my dear."

Cynda linked elbows with Thea and they walked arm in arm out of the cafeteria. The dampness of Thea's clothing lessened the warmth of the nearly noon-high sun. With her free hand, Thea waved behind them to the ladies. Thea followed her sister's lead and they walked still linked toward the fence. Molly bounded over to join them.

"You know, Thea, you were really great this morning. I didn't think you could take charge like that."

Pleased, Thea pondered what Cynda had said. "I kind of surprised myself, but I just couldn't let whoever did this win. He wanted to spoil things for the boys coming in today."

"Thanks to you, he didn't win." Cynda fell silent for a few moments. "You know, Thea, I always wanted a sister and I feel like I finally got one this summer."

Thea felt a lump in her throat. "I feel the same way."

Cynda slipped her arm out of Thea's and put it around

Thea's waist for a side hug. Thea returned the pressure. Deeply touched, she fought the tug of tears.

Then Cynda lifted a clump of Thea's unbound, golden brown hair and looked at it quizzically. "Thea, I've heard of people with egg on their faces, but I've never seen anyone with egg in their hair. Yuck!"

Giddy joy bubbled up inside Thea. "You've got mustard on your nose!"

"Yuck!" Cynda broke away and started running. "I get the shower first!"

"Oh, no, you don't!" Giggling, Thea chased after her.

Cynda taunted, "The last one over the fence is a rotten egg!"

"Don't you dare mention eggs to me ever again!" With Molly at her heels, Thea sped up running full tilt toward the fence.

With a shout of triumph, Cynda leaped over it.

As Cynda did a victory jig, Thea cleared the fence, jogged around her stepsister and charged through the kitchen door, heading for the shower.

Cynda pelted in after her shouting, "No fair! No fair!"

Smiling broadly, Thea sat down and waved her sister toward the bathroom. "Irene is waiting for you. Go on."

Thea knew she, too, would have some tight muscles tomorrow morning, but her sense of satisfaction grew. The only dark spot was that the vandal had struck a third time and probably would again. Thea sent a plea heavenward for wisdom and justice.

Finally a scrubbed and freshly dressed Cynda left for the camp for the second time that morning. Thea took a shower, then soaked in a warm sudsy bath as well. The disgusting mess she had helped clean up left her feeling extra dirty, but also she needed time to recharge her batteries. Drained of energy and emotion, Thea'd never lived a morning like this one before.

At last, she finished bathing, dressing and combing out her damp hair. She stepped outside her kitchen door. The sunshine dazzled her eyes and heat radiated from the asphalt drive.

Molly greeted her with a cheerful dance of wiggling and barking. Thea sat down on the bench by her door and examined Molly once more, trying to see if the retriever had received any injury. Molly appeared unhurt, but Thea still couldn't be easy in her mind. What had been done to her faithful dog?

She must have been drugged. Unwilling to believe this dreadful thought, Thea went over in her mind all the possible suspects, but only came up with Mr. Crandon and her grandmother. Still, she couldn't picture either of them drugging her dog. Ridiculous! "Molly, you're going to see the vet today."

Molly barked her approval.

Thea stood up and headed toward the camp. For her own satisfaction, she wanted to see the first round of boys eating hot dogs and chips while they sat on damp benches where disgusting chaos had reigned hours before.

The noise level inside the cafeteria was too high for Thea's comfort. How could twenty boys make such a racket? She grimaced, but walked by the campers toward the kitchen. Stepping into it, she came face-to-face with Peter.

"Thea, I hoped you'd come earlier! I'm on the run now!"

"Of course, this is your big day." Her smile froze into place. Peter would be too busy for her again.

For a millisecond, he pulled her close, then dashed off.

Cynda shouted for Thea to come to the kitchen for lunch, but Thea's stomach tightened with disappointment. *Peter.*

Peter switched off the light in the last dorm. "Good night, boys!"

"Good night, Mr. Della!" This phrase came to him in various boyish voices from the boys bedded down on cots in the dorm.

"Good night, Pete!" the young counselor, his nephew, Tony, called back with a teasing tone.

"Good *night.*" Peter shook his head as he walked away. The opening day of the camp had been exhilarating, exhausting.

He strolled through the darkness lighted by the camp yard lights. As he passed it, he stared at the cafeteria, now empty and closed up for the night. He tried to imagine how someone had slipped into the cafeteria and trashed it while the sheriff patrolled the grounds. Evidently the perpetrator had slithered in unseen and lain low whenever the sheriff had come through. He didn't want to think how much money in food they'd lost due to the unknown vandal.

As he approached the lodge, his mom, wearing her favorite tropical print robe in hot pink and electric blue, opened the back door. "Son, time for you to come in now."

He smiled. "When I was a little younger, I remember you telling me that a lot." He walked up to her.

"Dear, you look really down."

The sympathy in her voice touched him. He gathered her into his arms. "I love you, Mom."

"I know, dear. I love you, too."

They stood together for a few minutes. Then his mom

pulled him inside. "Thank God for Thea."

"Why do say that? I mean I agree, but—"

"Didn't the sheriff tell you she's the one who saved the day for us?"

"Thea? How?"

"Well, I'll tell you. She ran over, sweats over her pajamas, with Cynda to help me. After I saw the mess, I couldn't function at first. Thea got me going and called everyone to come and help clean."

Peter hit his forehead. "No one *told* me! I just thought Thea helped with everyone else."

"Oh, dear I thought you knew. But how could you? We were all so busy all day. But, Peter, if it hadn't been for Thea, Cynda and I could never have gotten everything ready for you in time! She organized everyone! What must she think of you for not even thanking her? I wondered why she looked a little down when she came over for lunch."

"I'm going." Peter walked back outside, irritated with himself. *I should have asked about Thea's part. But how could I have guessed that quiet, reserved Thea would break out of her shell like that? Thea called and organized everyone? And I didn't even thank her!*

In front of Thea's door, Peter paused, then knocked lightly.

Cynda came to the door and looked at him through the screen. "Jerk!"

Peter drew in a deep breath. "Evidently I am one. Will Thea see me?"

"Probably. And *probably* she'll be too polite to say 'you, jerk'—"

"You're *probably* right, but since you have and I have, please may I come in and thank her properly?"

"All right, but it better be good." Cynda walked away,

motioning him to follow her through the living room out onto the screened-in porch. "The jerk finally came over."

"Cynda! That's not a polite way to talk," Thea objected. She sat on a wicker love seat on the unlit porch.

The sight of her moved Peter. He cleared his throat. "It may not be polite, but it does accurately describe how I feel. I'm deeply in your debt and I didn't even thank you."

Cynda cocked her head toward Thea. "Do you accept his apology?"

"Of course, I do."

Thea's warm, calm voice made Peter feel even more guilty.

"Then I'm off to bed. I'm expected early at the camp to do breakfast." Cynda walked through the open French doors back into the living room. She paused. "Oh, Peter, is your nephew Tony dating anyone?"

"Ask my mom. She'll know."

"Cynda, what about Thad?" Thea asked sounding curious.

"We're just friends, sister dear. Good night."

Finally alone, Peter stood looking at Thea and beyond her at the thin moonlight ripples on the lake. Just being near Thea filled him with a sense of keen anticipation. His feeling for her grew each time they were together. "I really feel bad, Thea."

"Don't. Please sit down, Peter."

At her invitation, he sat down beside her, but he angled his back against the rolled arm so he could face her. Her white cotton shirt shone in the dim light and reflected a glow onto her face. One of her long legs stretched out before her. Her cool elegance came from deep within her and didn't depend on any art she employed.

Thea smoothed her gold-tinged hair back. "You're not in trouble."

''I wish you'd just slugged me or something to get my attention.''

Thea chuckled lightly and leaned her elbow against the back of the love seat, making the crunching noise wicker made at any movement. ''I don't make a habit of slugging my neighbors.''

''Even when they deserve it?''

''You've got a lot on your mind. And after spending my morning at your kitchen—''

''My mom said you were wonderful, that you called up everyone and organized the whole operation.''

''She's exaggerating. I just called the sheriff, Pastor Carlson and Aunt Louella to help. Lilly and Nan with Tracy came, too.''

''Aunt Louella and Lilly?'' He longed to stroke Thea's hair, to feel it flow silken through his fingers.

''Yes, isn't it sweet? Mrs. Chiverton wants me to call her Aunt Louella and Mrs. Magill wants me to call her Lilly.''

''I would have guessed Lil would be more appropriate,'' he teased, realizing his own voice had become husky.

''She doesn't like Lil. She says it makes her sound like a dance-hall girl in an old Western.'' Thea gurgled with laughter.

Her laughter filled him with joy. In wonder at her gentle spirit, he shook his head. Thea had remained calm like this when they had been caught in that rainstorm. He felt humbled by her sweetness. Contrasting her to Alanna, he now knew he'd loved what he thought Alanna was, not what she really had been. Completely without artifice, Thea radiated honesty and love.

He let himself enjoy the moment. He listened to the bullfrogs on the nearby wetland, watched the small boat lights pass by, hearing the chugging motors of the boats.

Over all, crickets chanted. "Is Molly all right?" he asked at last.

"Yes, she was fine after she woke up. It really scared Cynda, though. She thought Molly was dead at first. This afternoon I called the vet and took Molly over, just to be sure. He said she was just fine."

"I don't like it. Whoever did it might have given her too much and..." Feeling protective of Thea, he didn't want to say it might have killed Molly.

Thea said softly, "I'm going to keep her in at night. I'm sorry, but—"

"That's fine. I don't want to put Molly in danger. I never thought of someone doing anything to her."

"Neither did I." She paused. "When is this going to end?"

"I honestly don't know. For some unknown reason, God is allowing this. All I can think is that someone is hurting badly. I don't believe this vandalism really has anything to do with my camp. Someone is shouting for help, but who?"

"I keep thinking about Mr. Crandon losing his son this year. Do you think that he might have become unbalanced?" Her voice quavered uncertainly on the last word. "I've been worried that he and my grandmother..."

He gazed into her golden eyes whose clear luster shimmered in the near darkness. "Has she said anything—"

"No." She took a deep breath. "But I discussed other matters from the past with her."

Thea had questioned that old dragon? He chose his words carefully. "You mean like you did with your father the day we went berry picking?"

"Yes."

Trying to read her, he asked, "How did she react?"

Thea smiled sadly. "She told me never to come again."

He couldn't imagine his mom saying anything so cruel. "That's awful."

"It's exactly what I expected. I told her I'd come when I wanted to. I'm through with her telling me what to do—manipulating me."

His sympathy aroused, he reached for her hand. "I wish I weren't so busy. I haven't had the time to be here for you. I'm sorry."

"Don't be. You don't have to nursemaid me. I'm a big girl."

"You're a beautiful woman." He drew her slim, delicate hand to his lips and kissed it. "Thea, I've fallen in love with you."

Chapter Thirteen

She stared at Peter in the moonlight. Had he said the words she'd longed to hear?

"I love you, Thea. I don't believe in love at first sight. All I know is every time I've seen you, been with you, you've become more and more dear to me."

She looked down in confusion.

"I know it's probably too soon. I should have waited." He paused. "But I can't hide my feelings for you."

A moment passed. She looked up. "You love me?"

"I love you. Do you have any feelings for me? You're so special." He leaned forward.

He's going to kiss me. She wanted his kiss, but she stopped him by pressing her fingers to his lips. "I'm not special...."

"Yes, you are." He drew her hand to his lips and kissed it, then he turned it over to kiss her palm. His lips touched the inside of her wrist.

Exquisite awareness of him rippled through her. She sighed.

He pulled her to him, but just before she reached him,

he turned her and tucked her spine next to his chest. When he wrapped his arms snugly around her waist, she shivered.

"Cold?"

"No," she said honestly, "it's being close to you." *Is this really me in Peter's arms? It's too good to be true.*

"I've wanted to hold you for weeks." He buried his face into her hair and breathed in deeply. "Lily of the Valley will always mean Thea to me. Sweet Thea."

With her cheek next to his, she moved against him, reveling in the support his broad chest provided her.

"Don't try to get away," he teased. "I've got you and I'm not letting you go."

In spite of her uncertainty, she rested her head back against his shoulder. She trailed her fingertips along his bare arms, feeling his abundant, springy hair. "How can you be so sure you love me?" Her voice trembled.

He nuzzled the side of her neck. "You're a gift from God. I've prayed so long for a woman like you. I love you. Tell me you love me, too."

His tender touch glided through her like a violin solo—soulful, thrilling. *He loves me. I didn't dare to dream of this moment.* Elation lifted her heart—for only a moment. Dark clouds floated over the nearly full moon making ghostly patterns of light and shade. "I'm frightened."

"Of me? Of falling in love?" Brushing a gentle kiss against her ear, he tugged her closer to him.

"I don't know." *If only it was just the two of us—with no one else looking at me, telling me I'm inadequate.*

"You know." His deep rich voice rumbled through her.

I want to be with you, but... She wanted to forget talking and just let herself float on the lush sensation created from being near Peter. She turned in his arms, came nose to nose with him. Intense awareness flowed between them like captured sunshine. She studied his lean, classically handsome face and became breathless.

He tilted his head, stroked her cheek with his silky eyelashes. He whispered, "Butterfly kisses."

She shyly buried her face against his throat where it fit perfectly. Her thoughts fled and her heart spun a symphony from every soft emotion within her. The lyric sang, "Peter, Peter."

Suddenly the call of a loon on the lake broke through to her like a cold splash of reality. She spun in his arms; once again she sat with her back flush against his chest. Her heart beat as though she'd run a race. She'd let him sway her, but her fears couldn't be ignored.

"What's wrong?" he whispered against her ear.

Could she put her hesitance into words? *Dear God, we're so different. How can we ever belong together?* She went back to the verse that always soothed her. *Lead me beside the still waters, Lord. Restore my soul. Give me Your answers.*

Though feeling lost and afraid, she had to take them back to reality. She searched for a topic, then blurted out the first thing that came to mind, "I wanted to tell you about an idea I had for your camp."

"Camp?" He sounded stunned. "You want to talk about the camp—now?"

Fighting her attraction to him, she said, "I was wondering if you'd thought of adding music to your camp activities?"

"Music?" His bewilderment was obvious.

She plunged ahead, "I have a few used guitars someone gave me—"

"Oh." He paused. "Are you offering to break your neutrality?" He wrapped his arms more tightly around her and pressed his face into the curve of her neck. "You'll support my camp now?"

His breath fanned her right ear and his rough chin rasped her cheek. She tingled wherever his warm flesh touched hers. "Yes."

Peter spoke in the stillness. "I've waited for this moment."

She pulled away trying to elude his overwhelming effect.

He tugged her back to him. "Now I can ask you. I was hoping to persuade you to go with me to a silent auction, a fund-raiser for the camp."

"Why?" she asked, feeling warning prickles along her spine.

"I want to walk into the auction with you by my side."

"But—"

"I need you." His soothing voice tempted her. "It's at a county club near Madison. It will be a special evening— if you'll come."

"But—" After her experience at the open house, this was just the type of function she dreaded. *You don't need me, Peter. You don't see how shy, how inadequate I'd be in that setting.*

"Please say you'll go." Abruptly he turned her in his arms. His lips played over hers, giving her everything and drawing every objection from her. A dreamy intimacy knit her to him. How she'd longed for his kiss, imagined his kiss, but more importantly—Peter needed her. She sighed, feeling weightless.

"Go with me," he whispered against the corner of her mouth.

His persuasion overwhelmed her. "I'll go."

* * *

"How's that?" Vickie handed Thea a mirror off Thea's kitchen table. Vickie had come to do her hair for the silent auction.

Aunt Louella chirped, "I'm so glad I asked Irene how formal this auction was. Otherwise we wouldn't have turned you out in style."

Thea peered uncertainly into the mirror. She'd never had her hair done before. Vickie had swept her hair up on both sides into high combs, then had braided Thea's long hair into several braids and had fastened them to her head in elegant loops at the back. Very chic, sophisticated. She didn't look like herself at all. "Oh, my."

Louella clapped her hands. "You look lovely, my dear."

"Absolutely," Nan agreed.

"Not bad," Lilly said.

Tracy jumped up from Nan's lap. "You're prettier than ever!"

Thea smiled self-consciously and put down the mirror. Her anxiety over this evening had escalated each day since Peter's invitation. She and Peter were opposites. His life away from Lake Lowell must be completely different from her modest life-style.

"This hairdo won first place for long hair design at the Chicago Hair Trends Conference last month." Vickie sprayed the upswept sides one last time, engulfing Thea in heavy perfume. "Done."

"Time for your dress," Cynda ordered.

The women followed Thea into the bedroom. Garbed in her long white robe, she felt like a queen accompanied by her ladies-in-waiting. Tracy hopped onto Thea's bed and folded her legs under her, Indian-style. The dress hung on the back of the closet door. Thea reached for it.

Cynda beat her to it. "Allow me, dear sister."

Thea slipped off her robe.

Tracy oohed. "I like your underwear." The women chuckled.

Thea agreed with Tracy. Her white cotton underwear had been banished for the evening. Everything she wore was brand-new from the skin out. *Maybe I will be a new me tonight. Maybe I'll fit in with Peter's friends.* Then she recalled the fashionable people who had attended the open house and her hopes dimmed.

In the silent room, Cynda unzipped the dress and slipped it over Thea's head, careful not to disturb her hairstyle. The teal green dress, a silky sheath, fit Thea snugly—flowing over her like a tropical sea swirling in waves at midcalf. Short cap sleeves and a boat neck topped the dress. The ladies had all agreed, while shepherding Thea around the stores in Wausau, that a simple classic style would suit her best. Thea felt a growing tension in the room as though the women were awaiting the grand finale.

Cynda zipped up the dress. "Tracy, get Mrs. Magill's necklace and earrings please."

The little girl hopped over to Thea's vanity and picked up the black suede jewelry box. She carried it like a crown for a coronation. Cynda received the box. Nan jumped up and lifted out the glinting, rhinestone necklace, a simple wreath of bright gems with a classic arrangement of oblong and diamond-shaped rhinestones at its center.

As Nan hooked the clasp from behind, Thea shivered at its cool touch, then she slipped a matching earring into each ear. She turned to let them view the finished art. Her heart beat erratically. "The necklace and earrings are lovely."

"The jeweler who cleaned them told me they're worth plenty now—called them vintage. My husband gave them to me as my wedding gift." Mrs. Magill's voice became gruffer. "He liked that sort of thing."

"Here, dear." Reaching for a box on the dresser, Louella opened it and folded back white tissue paper. She handed Thea a beaded purse. "This was Mother's. My father brought it home from Paris after World War I."

"Oh, Aunt Louella, it's beautiful!" Thea stroked the beaded fringe along the small snap purse's bottom, feeling the translucent blue, red, green beads dance at her touch. She hoped her friends didn't notice her hands trembled.

"I know you are a little nervous about your first formal event. But with Lilly's jewelry and my mother's purse you will be the most elegant young woman there tonight."

Thea was grateful to these women who'd become so dear, but something close to panic crept into her veins. *They've done the best they could for me, but fancy clothes won't hide the fact I don't belong at a country club.*

A knock came at the door and Peter's voice called her. Followed by her entourage, she walked to meet him. He stared at her—openmouthed. *Oh, dear, he must think I'm not dressed appropriately!*

"Wow!" He gave her a wide grin. "You look incredible."

She blushed at his words and the ladies around her chuckled. *But, Peter, what if I fail you?*

"That was quick, wasn't it?" Peter shut down the single engine plane. "This is going to be fun."

Thea let herself breath again. She hadn't told Peter she'd never flown before and that small planes terrified her. When he'd driven her to the local airport, she'd been too stunned to protest. *Thank you, God. We didn't die.*

"I can't wait to fly you over the lakes this winter after a few good snows. It's an incredible sight."

Feeling woozy, Thea closed her eyes and ignored Peter's words completely. After a blur of night driving through a strange town, Peter stopped the rented car under a canopy. He helped Thea out and gave his keys to a valet. As he led her up the blue-carpeted ramp to the country club, he whispered to her, "I've told my friends I'd be bringing a special lady with me."

Only her feelings for Peter had given her the courage to come this far. He needed a woman who could help him in his work. *If only I could be that woman.* Inside, he led her through an elegant ivory ballroom to a distinguished gentleman. "This is Bob Smith, our host tonight."

She greeted him. He led them to the donated items. Among them were an antique bowl and ewer in white, painted with pink rosebuds; an original watercolor of a lake scene; and a new set of golf clubs. All had been donated for the silent auction.

Bob explained, "We've set up the auction a little more loosely than usual. We'll let people write down a bid, then come back and raise it if they choose. We figured it would push the bids higher and make more money for the camp."

"Great!" Peter put his arm around Thea. "Are the people who donated these items here tonight?"

Bob nodded. "I'll introduce you to them."

As they walked around the hall, the room began to fill up. Thea eyed the women discreetly. They glittered with diamonds and emeralds over linen suits, silk dresses. Would her simple sheath, vintage rhinestones and purse pass muster? The high pitch of their voices floated and danced above the low tones of the men. And every woman's eyes located Peter's attractive figure and lingered there. She couldn't blame them, but with each appraising look, she felt her self-confidence dwindle.

Soon people lined up in front of the tables with the auction items on them and began writing bids. Thea concentrated on smiling and repeating names correctly while

Peter told jokes, complimented ladies and talked sports with everyone. Peter's animation and enjoyment grew with each person he met. *How does he do that?*

She, in contrast, seemed to lose a bit of herself, of her presence with each introduction to another stranger. Moment by moment, she felt herself shrinking.

"Thea, is that you?"

Hearing her name, she turned to see an older man, one of the fishermen who'd stayed at her family's fishing cabins as long as she could remember. "Mr. Schyler."

"What are you doing here?" He shook hands firmly with her.

Thea motioned toward Peter who was in the middle of telling a joke to another couple.

"You came with Peter Della?" the man asked in a surprised tone.

"Yes, his camp is the Double L, you know, the one right next door to our property."

"And he brought you with him?" The older gentleman looked puzzled.

"Yes." It was obvious that the man couldn't understood why Peter would bring her here. Was it so obvious she didn't belong in this exclusive setting?

Peter pulled her close to him. "An old friend?"

She introduced them. Peter greeted Schyler cordially. The two of them chatted about fishing. But the disbelieving look in the old fisherman's eye crushed her. Another measure of her self-assurance dwindled.

Thea's smile froze in place. She couldn't concentrate on the words being said. The voices in the room blended into a raucous sea of sound. She felt queasy after a while from the sheer volume. She finally pulled away from Peter, whispering she needed the powder room.

Inside the sheltered confines of the luxurious ladies

room, Thea sank gratefully onto the tapestry-covered sofa. A young auburn-haired woman came in. After a few moments at the mirror, she glanced at Thea, then away, then back. Thea became wary.

The redhead sat down beside her on the sofa. "Hi, I'm Brooke Martin. And you're the mystery woman who arrived with Peter."

Thea smiled politely. *Why are you talking to me?*

"I haven't seen Peter look so happy in, well, in three years now. I hear you live right next to Peter's camp."

Thea nodded.

"I'm so glad Peter's taking another chance on love. After Alanna jilted him just a month before their wedding… *Well!*" Brooke threw out her hands in a broad gesture. "I'm so glad he's put it into perspective at last. Alanna just wasn't meant to be with Peter, don't you agree?"

"I never met her." Thea's heart lurched and beat in a wild irregular rhythm.

Brooke squeezed Thea's hand. "We'll talk later. I have to get back out and see if I need to raise my bid on that watercolor!" Before she left, she turned back. "You're just right for Peter. He needed someone more down to earth. Bye!"

Down to earth? What did that mean? Thea didn't know, but obviously Alanna had not been. Why hadn't Peter ever mentioned that he'd been engaged? Why hadn't she realized that a man like Peter would have had serious relationships before? Wouldn't a man tell the woman he loved about a previous engagement? Nothing in her solitary past had prepared her for falling in love—especially with someone like Peter. *Why didn't you tell me?*

Finally Thea made herself get up and go back outside. Though she heard Peter's voice, she didn't go to him. Instead, she found a chair near the auction items. Hopefully with all the activity around her, she would go unnoticed.

She folded her hands in her lap and watched the bidding, trying to distract herself. Everyone seemed to be having a wonderful time, laughing and teasing. The sounds of hilarity made her own solemnity feel more pronounced. *If I'm in love, why do I feel so isolated, unsure?*

Peter knew what being in love felt like. He had been engaged to a woman named Alanna. And Mr. Schyler's puzzled expression had spoken volumes. Obviously Thea was too plain, too small-town for someone like Peter. Maybe she hadn't worn the price tag on her dress, but she hadn't fooled anyone. *Was that what Brooke had meant by "down to earth"?* Thea's sensation of being a trumpeter trying to play with a stringed quartet grew with each troubling thought.

A sob swelled inside her. But years of living with Grandmother Lowell had schooled Thea in hiding her emotions. She squeezed the clasp of the beaded purse with tight fingers, but kept her outward serenity.

"Are you all right?" Peter bent over her.

She jumped. She'd been so lost in thought she hadn't noticed Peter approaching. "I'm just a little tired."

"Sure?" He traced his finger down her cheek.

She quivered with the agony of craving his touch, but feeling unworthy of it.

"Having fun?"

"Of course," she lied.

"You don't want to just sit here, do you?"

"I'm enjoying the bidding." A burst of laughter around the auction table interrupted them.

"Well, I'll sit with you—"

"No!" She pushed him away. "You need to make contacts. That's why we came."

"Contacts aren't as important to me as you are. If you're going to sit, I'm going to sit, too." He reached for a nearby chair.

Thea didn't doubt him. She stood up. "I'll come along. You came to make contacts."

He tucked her close to his side and took her away with him. "I love having you with me. You do me proud."

Each word he said seared like a hot iron to her heart. For almost three hours, Thea smiled a frozen smile, repeated names she would never remember, laughed at jokes she didn't follow. She gagged down caviar. Her feet ached. Her head echoed with loud voices. She pulled deeper and deeper within herself until she thought she might vanish from sight. Finally the agony ended.

In the car on the way to the airport, Peter's enthusiasm bubbled over. "What a night! Almost six thousand dollars in cash from the silent auction and pledges for another three thousand. You were great! Did you have a good time?"

She nodded. *Peter, I failed you! Why can't you see that?*

Finally he drove through the entrance of the small airport. "You're so quiet."

Even her fear of flying had waned. The plane was the quickest way home. She couldn't wait to get onboard. She had begun to feel like a shell of a person, a hollow fake. "It's been a long day."

"Yes, it has been. When we get into the plane, you just rest your head. I'll be quiet and fly us home."

The flight home took forever because she relived her failure this evening. *I thought I loved this man. But what do I know about being in love? Surely I should feel in harmony with him, not so inadequate, so distant.*

Past comments from Grandmother filtered into Thea's

weary mind. *You didn't want to go to the prom anyway. You're not the flashy type. Some women just aren't meant to gadabout.* Had Alanna been the "flashy" type?

Tonight in spite of Peter's words, Thea had been no help at all to him. He needed a wife who could connect names and faces and remember them, who enjoyed being in crowds of people, who could think of charming or funny things to say to strangers. As she feigned sleep, a tear trickled down her cheek. Grandmother Lowell's voice taunted her, *He didn't ask you to marry him, did he?*

Finally Peter drove them home over the quiet forested roads. "Thea, you're not just tired. You're upset."

"Why didn't you tell me about Alanna?" She couldn't have stopped these words from coming out any more than she could have stopped the moon rising over them.

"Was it Brooke who told you about Alanna?" He sounded perturbed.

"Why didn't *you* tell me about her?" Thea hated the tremor in her voice.

"That was three years ago."

"Alanna was very different from me, wasn't she?"

"You're nothing like her!"

The words flayed her like a whip. She could imagine the sophisticated, educated, beautiful Alanna as if she'd seen her. Thea looked over at him in the dim light. Pain from her failure cut her to shreds inside. "I don't think you understand that I'm *not* what you think I am."

"What do you mean?"

"This evening was an absolute agony for me. I don't belong in your world."

"I don't understand what you mean. You were wonderful tonight. More importantly, you're the woman I've waited for, the woman I want to spend the rest of my life with.''

Thea became an ice sculpture.

Peter talked on, argued on, but the words flowed over her, adding layer upon layer to the ice she felt inside and out. At long last, he drove up to her door. He gripped the steering wheel, his knuckles turning white. "Why won't you *listen* to me!"

Emotionally drained, Thea turned to him. "I'm sorry. You need someone I can never be."

"I don't need anything but your love!"

"I'm sorry." Thea got out of the car and walked to her door. Her sorrow flowed through her like someone singing a dirge, soft and true.

As Peter watched her walk away, he felt an ache inside him. He recognized it—rejection. The crushing pain of it snuffed out his anger. How could she just walk away? Holding in the torment, he cried out silently to God, *Is this how it's always going to be! Am I always going to be the one left behind?*

Chapter Fourteen

Thunder rattled the kitchen windows. Fearfully Thea looked out. Lightning crisscrossed the black sky. Raindrops splashed the windows. Molly whined at Thea's feet. Thea felt like whining, too.

"Don't worry, Molly. We'll just stay in tonight. I just wish Cynda was home from the lodge." *So I wouldn't be here alone and miserable in a thunderstorm.*

Molly gave her another whine. The phone rang. With a sigh, Thea lifted the receiver.

Cynda's voice came clearly, "Thea, I'm going to spend the night over here at the lodge."

"That's probably a good idea." What she said was the truth, but she wanted Cynda home to take her mind off failing Peter. "This is just the beginning of what's supposed to be a bad night. When this front is done with us, another one is on the way."

"Yeah, the sheriff called and said the storm was good for the camp. He said the vandal won't come out tonight."

"That's true." Thea hadn't thought much about the vandal. Her misery had been too deep.

"Irene says I should get off the phone. It's dangerous with this storm."

"She's right."

"Thea, wait! You'll come over tomorrow for lunch, won't you? There'll be thirty campers this week and Peter's bringing a whole bunch of people, you know, donors."

"I'll try." Thea hung up. More campers tomorrow. Peter wouldn't stop his plans. He would go on. *But what about me?* Thunder pounded overhead. Thea sat down. Alone. Glum. Cynda's cheery voice played in her mind, making her more dejected by contrast.

Peter.

Thea pressed her fist to her mouth to hold back tears. She'd spent the week hiding tears from Cynda, her piano students, Aunt Louella. Hot tears beaded in her eyes.

"Well, I'm alone now." A sob shook her. Leaning her head on her hand, she wept in huge swells like the waves of rain drenching the kitchen windows. "Why did you make me the way I am, Lord? Why couldn't I be the kind of woman Peter needs? I love him so."

The phone rang. As though swimming upward from deep water, Thea swallowed her tears and lifted the receiver. "Hello."

"That Della just doesn't get it." The voice was harsh and muffled.

Thea stood up.

"He won't stop till I hurt him."

Shock echoed through her. *It can't be!*

"Tell him not to come back tomorrow or he'll get a nasty surprise." Click.

Thea hung up and stood staring at the phone. Then her knees weakened and she sank onto the chair. *Oh, no, dear*

God. What she had just discovered shocked her to her core. It couldn't be, could it?

Yesterday Thea had received a poison pen letter from the vandal. She hadn't recognized the scrawl. But tonight she recognized the voice.

He'd tried to disguise it, but she knew…she knew the vandal's identity. *I have to tell the sheriff!* But her mind rebelled.

Crash! Thunder exploded over the lake. The lights went out. *A power outage.* Thea lifted the receiver off the hook. No dial tone.

"I'll have to drive to the sheriff's office," Thea muttered in the darkness, quaking inside with disbelief and dread. Her distress demanded expression. Over the thunder, she began shouting, "Lord, can't someone else do this? I don't want to be the one to turn him in. This is an awful storm. I should stay home! Lord, I don't want to be the one!"

Even as she argued with God, she pulled on her khaki slicker, grabbed her yellow lantern flashlight and went through the breezeway to the garage. She didn't have a choice and she knew it. "I know. I have to do it!"

Thea started the car and backed it out of the garage into the lashing wind. She hunched over the steering wheel trying to see well enough to drive. Lightning flashed like a child flicking a light switch for fun. The deluge coursing down her windshield nearly blinded her. Her knuckles on the wheel turned white from her intense grip.

Thea raised her voice over the wind and rain. "I'm scared, Lord! Why do I have to drive through this killer storm to turn in the vandal? I'm frightened. What if the sheriff doesn't believe me?" Another thought upset her more. "What did he mean about a 'nasty surprise'?"

She drove over a narrow bridge. As she went through a

low spot, sheets of water flew up from under her wheels like unfurled wings. The thunder accelerated—pounding, exploding like the finale of the "1812 Overture" conducted by a madman.

Thea swerved on a slippery slope and felt a momentary loss of control as she skidded. She shouted, "Help! I'm frightened, Lord! No one else knows who he is! Something could happen to Peter! But I'm scared! Help me!"

For God has not given us a spirit of fear. The words came from the recesses of her memory. The phrase repeated, then Thea, remembering the rest, finished the verse aloud, "But of power and love and discipline. Second Timothy 1:7."

Trembling, Thea pulled over and parked. She felt weak with fear. She turned on her four-way flashers. Leaning her forehead onto her steering wheel, she prayed, "Father, being afraid isn't anything new for me. I've been afraid as long as I can remember—ever since Mama became ill. But I don't want to be afraid, Lord. I know this fear isn't from You. You're not the one who has used my fear to control me."

For God has not given us a spirit of fear....

"I know, Lord. I love Peter. But I've been so scared. I've been so frightened that I may have lost him. But I don't want a life without him. Keep him safe. Give me courage. Make the sheriff believe me!"

The thunder became more distant. Thea felt tension leave her. Her heart began to beat normally again. She released her four-way flashers and eased back onto the road. She drove on, but the lessening thunder and lightning no longer seemed a nightmare. She grew calm. She felt the gloom she'd carried ever since the disastrous auction lift. She repeated to herself, "'For God has not given me a spirit of fear.'"

She pulled into the parking lot of the sheriff's office, then ran through the quiet rain inside. The sheriff sat at his desk, alone in the office. "What brings you out on a night like..." He interrupted himself by surging to his feet. "Has something happened at the camp!" He reached for his hat.

"Not yet." Now that she was here she didn't know the words to say.

He froze. "What's that mean?"

"I got a call. The vandal called me," she explained.

"He called you? He told you who he was?"

She nodded. "Sort of. You know I brought that hate mail in yesterday." *What if I'm wrong?*

He nodded.

"Well, maybe a handwriting expert could figure out whose writing it was—"

"What's your point?"

"I'm a sound expert." She groped for words. "I mean, I'm an auditory person. The vandal called tonight and I recognized his voice. He tried to muffle his voice. But I know whose voice—"

"Who?"

She took a deep breath. "Thad Earnest."

"Thad! Why I never... He's just a kid."

"A very unhappy kid." Thea stared at the sheriff.

"You mean with his dad running out on his family?"

Thea pressed on. "And his mother trying to push him into helping at the camp—"

"She kind of made it a target?"

"I'm afraid so."

He crossed his arms. "That's pretty slim evidence. I mean, I think it makes sense but—"

"It's worse. Thad said, the caller said, 'Della won't stop till I hurt him.' Then he said to tell Peter to stay away tomorrow or he'd get a nasty surprise.'' Thea's pulse raced with each word.

The sheriff looked thoughtful. ''Well, that changes things. If there is any chance Thad may have done something which might harm someone, I have to bring him in. Even if it doesn't pan out. You wait here. The phones are down, but the radio is still working. My deputies are both out already. Here, I'll show you how to answer and send.''

Thea nodded and took a seat by the radio. The first storm stilled. Outside, just pattering of raindrops kept the storm alive. Thea began to pray for Peter, Thad, for his mother. She felt like a traitor.

''I still can't believe you brought Thad in to question him.'' Vickie's voice rose shrilly as she led the way into the office followed by her son and finally the sheriff.

''Mrs. Earnest,'' the sheriff replied, ''if Thea has evidence, it was her duty to bring it to my attention.''

''What evidence? Why won't you tell me?''

''I'm following proper police procedure.''

Vickie caught sight of Thea and hurried toward her. ''How could you tell the sheriff my son had anything to with the vandalism at the camp? I thought you were my friend!''

Thea stood up. Her heart broke for Vickie. She couldn't think of anything to say. The charge she'd made against Thad was too dreadful. Her stomach clenched painfully.

''Thea, don't say anything.'' The sheriff pushed Thad farther into the room. ''I have to question Thad privately.''

''No, you won't!'' Vickie shouted. ''This is completely uncalled for.''

''Ma'am, shouting won't help. I'm bound by law and my oath—''

"I refuse to let you question him without my being present!" Vickie began to sound hysterical.

"It's not within your power to stop me. I have the right to question—"

"I demand to have a lawyer present—"

"Shut up!" Thad shouted. *"Shut up!"*

Stunned silence followed.

Vickie started, "Thad, I know—"

"I don't need your help!"

"But you're innocent!" Vickie appeared desperate. "They can't treat you—"

"I'm *not* innocent! I am the vandal!" He waved a clenched fist. "Do you hear me? I'm the vandal!"

Vickie looked as though someone had hit her with a ball bat. White-faced, she looked as though she might faint.

Thea took a step toward her.

Vickie stepped out of Thea's reach. She looked at the floor and rubbed her forehead as though it pained her. "Thad, you're just trying to upset me. That's why. You just—"

"It's the truth," her son said angrily. "This *isn't* about you." He stabbed his thumb at his chest emphasizing each word. "It's about me!"

Vickie collapsed into the nearest chair, her gaze still on the floor. The storm outside surged back to life. The radio crackled with storm static. Lightning flashed outside the windows.

The sheriff cleared his throat. "I don't believe you. How did you manage to mess up that cafeteria? I'd have seen your car—"

"I parked on the other side of the lake, then I'd walk through Old Lady Magill's woods, then swim across to the Double L pier," Thad bragged. "I never left a trace, did I?"

"You drugged Molly," Thea accused.

Thad glared at her. "I didn't hurt her. I just took one of Mom's sleeping pills. I was at your place with Cynda. I just slipped a part of the pill to her along with a doggie treat."

Grimly the sheriff shook his head. "Son, you have the right to remain silent…" He droned through the Miranda. With his arms crossed, Thad stared at the ceiling.

Thea felt tears clogging her throat. She sat down and struggled to hold herself in check, but the sob broke through her reserve. Distant thunder echoed, sounding louder in the stillness around Thea.

The sheriff tapped Thad's shoulder. "Young man, do you understand what I have just told you?"

Thad nodded.

"Okay. Sit down here." The lawman pulled out a chair beside his desk. "I'm going to ask you some questions. You can answer them or not." The sheriff stared into the teen's face. "But I warn you if you've planned something to hurt Peter Della or anybody else, it would be better to tell me now—before anything worse than vandalism happens. I'll be taping this."

Guilt weighed Thea down. She wished she could just vanish from the room.

The sheriff sat down at his desk and clicked on the Record button on a large tape recorder. "Now, Thad Earnest, you just admitted that you are responsible for the vandalism out at the Double L?"

"Yeah."

"No, no," Vickie moaned, shaking her head at her son. *"Yes, I did."*

"Mrs. Earnest, you're only making things more difficult," the sheriff said kindly. "Would you rather wait in another room?"

Vickie shook her head and wiped a stray tear away.

The thunder outside boomed louder, making Thea glance out the window. Hard rain dashed against the panes again.

The sheriff took a deep breath. "Thad, you spray-painted the camp sign? Broke windows? Punctured canoes? Trashed the cafeteria?"

After each question, Thad replied sullenly, "Yeah."

"Why? Why?" Vickie spoke through tears.

"I don't know." Her son wouldn't look at her.

"It's because your father left us," Vickie sobbed, sounding as though near her breaking point.

"No! I was glad Dad left! He was always getting on my case! Old Crandon's right! No big shot is going to tell me what to do! Della thinks he knows so much about kids. The camp's just a power trip for Della. Those kids don't need him. He's nobody's father!"

The sheriff cut in. "Is that why you planned something to hurt Della?"

The thought of anyone hurting Peter—so vibrant and strong—chilled Thea.

"Yeah." Thad's tone lost its belligerent edge.

"What have you done?"

"I'm not telling."

Thea pleaded silently, *Thad, just get this over with please. Tell the truth—please! God, help him tell us.*

"It'll go better on you if you do. Right now I've only got criminal mischief against you and you're a minor. You'll just get something like probation and community service. But if someone gets seriously hurt, you could be tried as an adult."

Thea held her tears rigidly in check. *Lord, please soften Thad's heart before it's too late for Peter.*

Thad stared at a point just above the sheriff's head.

Thea cleared her throat. She spoke softly, "Thad, I'm in love with Peter. Please tell us what you've done. I couldn't stand it if anything happened to him." Her voice broke on the last word. New tears sprang to her eyes.

Thad glanced her way.

Gazing at Thad, Thea willed him to believe her. "Please. I know you're angry, but you're not the kind of person who can hurt someone without it crushing you, too. I know you're not. Cynda wouldn't have become your friend if you were like that."

Thad stared down at his hands.

"Please," Thea whispered. The thunder was steady now and drawing nearer.

"All right," Thad muttered disgustedly. "I saw some stuff about bombs—booby traps—on the Internet."

The sheriff nodded to Thea, silently giving her permission to proceed.

Crushed-looking, Vickie glanced sideways at her son, tears pouring from her eyes.

"Please," Thea coaxed gently.

"I rigged something up at the back gate of his truck. It shouldn't kill him. I mean, at least, I don't think so. I didn't want to hurt anyone bad."

Thea swallowed a sob and squeezed Thad's arm. "Thank you. I know you didn't." Her heart wrung with pity.

The sheriff stood up and snapped off the recorder. "Son, I'm going to have to put you back in the holding cell." He pulled a large key ring out of his drawer.

Thea pulled herself together. *Thank you, Lord. Protect us all.*

He walked over to Thad, who stood up and moved in front of the sheriff. Within a few moments, the sheriff returned. "Mrs. Earnest, my deputy is out on a call already. The dispatcher's home sick. Could you watch things here? I can't waste anytime getting out there. I'll radio the state police from my car for help in defusing an explosive. Maybe they'll have a car nearby.''

Still looking as though she couldn't grasp what had happened, Vickie stood up. ''But Peter won't be here for hours.''

''Yes, but what if Aldo decides to go out and get something out of Peter's vehicle?''

''In this storm?'' Vickie objected.

Thea looked around and found her keys and stood up. *Vickie, please we've got to go!*

''What if the explosive triggers by itself? An inexpert device can go off by itself. I mean, we don't even know where the vehicle is parked. It could go off and start a building on fire.'' The sheriff headed for the door.

''I'm coming, too!'' Thea gave Vickie a quick reassuring hug and started after him. She wished she could just fly over the miles that separated her from the camp.

''I don't need your help!'' the sheriff objected.

''Well, the car's next door to my home and Cynda's at the lodge tonight!''

''Suit yourself. I don't have time to argue.''

Thea hurried after him, then ran through the pouring rain. The storm raged stronger than ever. Wet wind lashed her face.

The sheriff's car sped away and Thea took off right after it. Following the sheriff's red taillights made the drive to the camp easier than the drive to town had been. The second storm front had hit them even harder than the first. Lightning zigzagged around the car. The winds fought her for control of her car and thunder raged growing louder, stronger.

Thea nearly wept with relief when they finally drove up

to the lodge. The sheriff parked and got out of the car. He bounded up the steps of the lodge and pounded on the door.

Thea parked right behind him. They stood together under the dripping overhang waiting for the Dellas to answer the door.

Aldo, in sweats and a robe, opened the door. "What is it, sheriff? More trouble?"

"Where's Peter's vehicle?" the sheriff asked brusquely.

Aldo motioned to the east toward Thea's place. "We parked it near the lodge. What is it?"

Thea could hardly hold in her impatience.

"We have reason to believe someone may have tampered with it. Maybe rigged up an explosive."

"What!"

The whine of another police car competed with the violent sounds of the storm. Fighting the gusts of wind and torrent of rain, Thea charged around the side of the lodge.

The sheriff shouted after her, "Where are you going? Don't touch that car!"

"I just want to see how close the truck is to my house!" Thea ran around to the side of the lodge. As soon as she made sure the Dellas and Cynda were safe, she could relax. Peter's red vehicle sat parked beside the garage.

White, brilliant lightning streaked overhead, followed instantly by an explosion of thunder. *Boom!*

Thea felt vibrations of the strike go through her. Cracking. She heard the loud sound of wood splitting apart.

She looked up in horror. An ancient pine had been hit by lightning and was breaking in half. Thea screamed. The top half plunged to the ground between Peter's vehicle and her. On impact it bounced with deadly force.

Boom! Impact! Thea screamed again and staggered. White flames shot up from the truck. From the shattered tree trunk. Rain sizzled as it contacted flame. Searing pain. Heat and blackness smothered her. ''Peter!''

Chapter Fifteen

"Thea?"

A deep voice penetrated her fuzzy mind.

"Thea, it's time you woke up."

She tried to open her eyes, but her lids felt heavy.

"Wake up, sleepy head."

The deep bass voice finally registered. Her eyes fluttered open. "Peter?" She moved her sluggish-feeling lips into a smile.

"Oh, thank God." He was sitting beside the bed. "You've had me worried." He gently ran his fingers through her hair, bringing her wide awake.

Looking around at the hospital surroundings, she frowned. "What time is it? Where am I?"

"At the county clinic." Peter took her hand. "Don't you remember?"

"Was I hurt?" She watched him kiss both her hands, then turn them over and kiss her palms. His irresistible touch made it hard for her to breathe.

"Do you remember the explosion?"

She shook her head. She squeezed his hands tightly

while she gathered the facts she needed to know. "I remember the tree being hit by lightning. Did it hit me?"

"No, the sheriff thinks the vibrations of the tree falling set off the primitive explosive in my truck. It was the impact of the explosion that threw you to the ground." He drew her hand to his lips again as though he couldn't stop himself.

"Explosion?" she asked weakly, unable to imagine she'd been near an explosion, unable to control her reactions to his gentle touch.

"You lost consciousness. Your head must have struck a rock or maybe a chunk of debris hit you. You've quite a knot on the side of your head, but no other injury. You just scared us by sleeping this long."

As he said this, she drew her hand away from Peter and touched her scalp and found the tender spot he had mentioned. Wincing, she tried to think, but her memory failed her.

"They were afraid you might have a concussion."

"Do I?" She searched his eyes, reading there his deep concern for her.

"We'll call the nurse and see what the doctor says now that you're awake." He reached for the nurse's call button.

Thea tried to remember what she had done the night before, attempting to put events in order. "I went to the sheriff. Thad— "

"Yes, I never suspected him. Well, frankly I didn't have a clue who the vandal was."

She let her gaze drink in Peter's deep brown eyes, dark skin, classic features. "Peter, I love you."

He looked startled, then a smile spread across his face. Standing, he bent and kissed her. The tender touch of his lips sent warmth through her.

She ran her fingers through his rich hair as his lips

teased and delighted her. When he pulled away, she sighed with pleasure. "It's not too late for us then?" she whispered.

"Of course not, I need a heroine like you coming to my rescue." He kissed her nose.

"Really?"

He chuckled, then sobered. "No, don't you ever do anything like that again! When I arrived this morning and Mom told me, I couldn't get here fast enough!"

Thea became thoughtful. "I had quite an experience before the explosion."

"What?"

"After I got the phone call warning me you were going to be hurt, I started driving to the sheriff.... The storm scared me, but more than that, I was afraid the sheriff wouldn't believe me. My car skidded. Then..." She looked at Peter solemnly. "A Bible verse I must have memorized as a child came to mind."

"What verse?" He sat down again.

"Second Timothy 1:7."

"Refresh my memory," Peter said enfolding both her hands within his.

"For God has not given us a spirit of fear, but of love and power and discipline."

"Wow," he said quietly.

"Yes, it was exactly what I needed. I've been filled with fear most of my life and I suddenly realized that God didn't want me to be afraid. I told you I couldn't love you because we were different. But in reality, it was my fear that was separating us."

"Thea, there's good fear and bad. Mom told me you tell the good from the bad by how they affect your life. Bad fear brings sorrow and loss. Good fear protects you."

"I know!" Her excitement bubbled up. "God doesn't

want me to be afraid of loving you. You're so good for me, Peter. My life has changed because of you, because God brought you into my life.''

She laid one hand on each side of his face. ''But I don't need to tell you that. You live His power and love.''

He chuckled dryly. ''Maybe. But I think I could use the discipline part. You've seen how I lose my temper.''

''Oh, that doesn't bother me.''

He placed his hands over hers. ''It bothers me. You deserve the best of me, Thea. With God's help, you'll get it.''

She leaned forward to kiss him, but paused to speak just a fraction of an inch from his lips. ''I love you.''

''I love you.''

She couldn't take her eyes from his face. She claimed his lips boldly.

Peter pulled back a half inch. ''Oh, Thea,'' he breathed into her mouth, then his lips closed over hers.

''Well! You seem to be feeling better!'' the nurse exclaimed cheerfully upon entering the room.

That sunny afternoon, Peter drove them to the lodge and parked. He walked around and opened Thea's door and helped her out. On Peter's arm, she had barely taken two steps when Molly galloped to her, barking excitedly.

She bent to pet her retriever. ''Did you miss me, girl?'' Leaping up, Molly licked her face like a puppy. Thea giggled. ''I missed you, too, Molly.''

''Thea!'' Cynda, Irene, Aldo and Aunt Louella ran down the steps to greet her with hugs, kisses and questions.

Peter hung back a few steps as though enjoying the sight. A car drove up and parked behind Peter's vehicle and Peter glanced around.

Catching sight of the new arrival, too, Louella exclaimed, "Dick!"

Grim-faced, Mr. Crandon walked over and planted his feet squarely on the ground in front of Peter. Without preamble, he said, "Della, I've given you a hard time about this camp." He paused and averted his eyes. "I think I might have set a poor example for Thad."

Looking back to Peter, he continued, "I got excited over nothing. Everyone but Althea Lowell has been arguing with me for weeks. But I wouldn't listen."

"Stubborn. That's what we told you," Louella muttered.

Mr. Crandon frowned. "Anyway, I feel responsible to some extent for Thad's actions. I was wondering if I offered to make things right by writing you a check for your camp, would you consider not pressing charges against Thad?"

Peter folded his arms and said calmly, "I don't need any more money for expenses this year. The prospective donors who came with me were so upset about this latest event that they pledged enough to fund the camp for the rest of this year."

"You won't consider it then?" Mr. Crandon rumbled.

Thea stepped closer to Peter.

Peter put his arm around Thea. "I've already made a deal with Thad. He's agreed to work around here for the next twelve months and I've agreed to drop the charges against him. I figured a year with my dad would do him more good than anything else."

Strong emotion played over the older man's face. "That's decent of you. I'd like to bury the hatchet—"

"So would I." Peter stuck out his hand. The two men shook hands.

Thea had to bat her eyes to ward off tears. Pride in Peter's kindness filled her with joy.

"Anything else I can do for you?" Mr. Crandon asked gruffly.

Peter grinned. "Yes, I've heard you carve decoys for a hobby. Would you give a demonstration to my campers?"

Mr. Crandon smiled and shook his head. "You're something, Della. Anything else?"

"As a matter of fact, yes." Peter tucked Thea close beside him. "Thea and I are planning a fall wedding here at the camp. Would you mind spreading the news for us? Everyone in Lake Lowell is invited."

"Peter!" Thea shrieked in shock. "When did you propose to me—when I was unconscious!"

"Well, no, I did it right now, I guess." He hung his head.

Thea caught his chin in her hand. "Peter—"

Irene spoke up, "Oh, Thea, you know Peter. He always has a big new idea. You might as well get used to it."

Thea chuckled. "I might as well. It will be for life."

Peter beamed at her and pulled her to him.

"Thea! Cool!" Cynda shrieked. Molly began barking.

Peter and Thea were cheerfully mobbed on all sides. Peter, ignoring the hubbub, wrapped his arms around Thea and kissed her.

Letting her lips communicate her gladness, Thea kissed him in return, unmindful of the happy crowd around them.

"I'm so happy I could cry." Aunt Louella dabbed her eyes.

"A wedding at the camp!" Irene clapped her hands together. "We're going to have a great time planning this! I'll make a tiered cake decorated with fresh flowers!"

"I'm going to be maid of honor!" Cynda gave a cheerleader jump.

Peter looked into Thea's eyes. "Well, Thea, so much for your quiet life."

Laughter bubbling up inside her, Thea threw her arms around his neck. "Thank heaven!"

* * * * *

Dear Reader,

Often we form opinions too quickly and learn later that we're wrong. How irritating! How humbling!

God never makes mistakes. When He looks at us, His eyes examine our hearts. He's never fooled.

Thea learned this when she began to look more deeply into the hearts of people she'd known and taken for granted for years and years. Peter Della, the new man in town, caused a transformation in Thea's thinking and her community.

God often uses the unexpected to force us to stop and reexamine our lives. While this process is taking place, we are often uncomfortable or unhappy.

But at the end when we look back, we see that God's plan was best. And we can only be glad that God shook us out of our comfortable ruts.

Lyn Cote

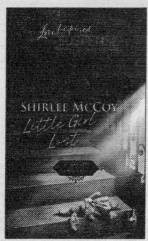

REQUEST YOUR FREE BOOKS!

2 FREE INSPIRATIONAL NOVELS
PLUS 2
FREE
MYSTERY GIFTS

Love Inspired®

YES! Please send me 2 FREE Love Inspired® novels and my 2 FREE mystery gifts. After receiving them, if I don't wish to receive any more books, I can return the shipping statement marked "cancel." If I don't cancel, I will receive 4 brand-new novels every month and be billed just $3.99 per book in the U.S., or $4.74 per book in Canada, plus 25¢ shipping and handling per book and applicable taxes, if any*. That's a savings of 20% off the cover price! I understand that accepting the 2 free books and gifts places me under no obligation to buy anything. I can always return a shipment and cancel at any time. Even if I never buy another book from Steeple Hill, the two free books and gifts are mine to keep forever.

113 IDN EF26 313 IDN EF27

Name	(PLEASE PRINT)	
Address		Apt. #
City	State/Prov.	Zip/Postal Code

Signature (if under 18, a parent or guardian must sign)

Order online at www.LoveInspiredBooks.com

Or mail to Steeple Hill Reader Service™:

IN U.S.A.: P.O. Box 1867, Buffalo, NY 14240-1867
IN CANADA: P.O. Box 609, Fort Erie, Ontario L2A 5X3

Not valid to current Love Inspired subscribers.

Want to try two free books from another series?
Call 1-800-873-8635 or visit www.morefreebooks.com

* Terms and prices subject to change without notice. NY residents add applicable sales tax. Canadian residents will be charged applicable provincial taxes and GST. This offer is limited to one order per household. All orders subject to approval. Credit or debit balances in a customer's account(s) may be offset by any other outstanding balance owed by or to the customer. Please allow 4 to 6 weeks for delivery.

Your Privacy: Steeple Hill is committed to protecting your privacy. Our Privacy Policy is available online at www.eHarlequin.com or upon request from the Reader Service. From time to time we make our lists of customers available to reputable firms who may have a product or service of interest to you. If you would prefer we not share your name and address, please check here. ☐

LIREG07